2084: AMERICAN APOCALYPSE

BOOK ONE OF THE PATHLESS LAND TRILOGY

JAMES KEENA

ILLUMIFY MEDIA GLOBAL
Littleton, Colorado

Copyright © 2020 by James R. Keena

All rights reserved. No part of this book may be reproduced in any form or by any means—whether electronic, digital, mechanical, or otherwise—without permission in writing from the publisher, except by a reviewer, who may quote brief passages in a review.

The views and opinions expressed in this book are those of the author and do not necessarily reflect the official policy or position of Illumify Media Global.

Published by Illumify Media Global
www.IllumifyMedia.com
"Write. Publish. Market. *SELL!*"

Library of Congress Control Number: 2020902659

Paperback ISBN: 978-1-949021-86-8
eBook ISBN: 978-1-949021-87-5

Cover design by King's Custom Covers: www.kingscustomcovers.com

Printed in the United States of America

To Audrey: My love, my muse, my best friend, and my eternal partner.

ONE
DANGER

> I do not know what I may appear to the world, but to myself I seem to have only been like a boy playing on the seashore finding a smoother pebble or a prettier shell than ordinary, whilst the great ocean of truth lay all undiscovered before me.
>
> — Sir Isaac Newton

"They're going to kill us."

"You're such a momma's boy," Cammy replied to her brother Curious. "You're ten now. Man up."

Curious sneered at his older sister. "Every time I go along with one of your plans, something bad happens. And then I get blamed for it."

The two strolled through a meadow on a glorious September morning. The wildflowers were in majestic bloom, the air was pristine, the sky was a deep blue, and they could see for miles. On such a day, when nature tempted like a Siren of Greek lore, the urge to abandon their responsibilities was overwhelming, especially since it might be the last perfect day of the year.

"Dad's going to be mad," said Curious.

"He can go a day without schooling us," Cammy snapped. "I'm so bored with his lectures. Today is our history lesson," she said in a deep voice parroting her father. "Blah blah blah. The American Revolution started in 1775. The first Constitution was ratified in 1788. The first Civil War started in 1861. The second Constitution was ratified in 2041. The second Civil War started in 2053. We played hooky in 2084. Blah blah blah. Who cares?"

"Dad."

"I've got all day to think up a cover story," said Cammy. "And it'll explain that this was your idea."

"Why isn't there a real school we can go to, like kids used to do?"

"Why isn't there anything like there used to be?" replied Cammy. "Dad says it's because of the civil war."

"When I grow up, I want to study how to take care of sick animals for people."

"There aren't any people around here. And you can't even take care of yourself. When I grow up, I'm going to be stuck taking care of you."

Curious mused that Cammy didn't need to take care of him, she just liked to boss him around. Her constant bullying annoyed him, but when he retaliated it always ended badly. Turning the other cheek was a more peaceful approach. Besides, he was pretty sure that deep down she really did like him, if only because there were no other playmates for miles around. Secure in this knowledge, he reached up and yanked Cammy's long platinum hair, and then tore off through the amber meadow toward the woods.

Cammy took up the chase, but despite her two-year age advantage over her brother, she couldn't close the gap. She could never beat him in a foot race, which was the only way in which he excelled over her. She wasn't concerned about catching him, though, because she knew he would stop soon.

When Curious neared the edge of the woods, which was shrouded in darkness under a dense canopy of brilliantly colored leaves, he stopped running. He didn't like the dark. Or the woods. Feral cats and dogs lurked there, abandoned long ago when their owners fled the ravages of the war. He and his sister had once found the skeleton of a dead soldier in there. Half of the body was missing.

Cammy caught up to him and pulled on his tangled blond hair with the full vengeance of a spiteful sibling.

"I...knew...you'd...stop!" she chided, her thin frame heaving as she caught her breath. Her blue eyes were afire with the joy of revenge. She slugged him in the arm.

"Ow!" he yelped, grabbing his arm and stepping away from her.

"You're a scaredy-cat!"

"I am not!" he protested. "I stopped because . . . because something's wrong."

"Oooohhh. Is there a monster in the woods? A big bad wolf Another dead body?"

"Stop it!" Curious said, hoping she wouldn't spot the tears of humiliation forming in his large brown eyes. "There's something really wrong!"

Cammy sensed a fear in her brother that went beyond his usual reluctance to go into the woods. "What is it?"

"Didn't you notice while we were running?"

"Notice what?"

"No birds flew up out of the grass? No critters ran away?"

Cammy scanned the horizon. The prairie was indeed eerily still. She was used to the absence of other people, but there were always plenty of squirrels, rabbits, and deer. Huge flocks of birds usually gathered this time of year to head south. But now every creature seemed to have gone into hiding. She caught some of Curious' anxiety by contagion, but that didn't deter her. "Let's go into the woods and check it out," she said impishly.

Curious gaped at her in horror. He knew from reading the scary books left behind by their grandfather that heading toward the source of danger was always the wrong choice. "Don't do it!" he said, much too loudly for the otherwise silent meadow.

Cammy scanned the horizon once again. There was still nothing stirring on a prairie that was usually alive with activity, which heightened her anxiety. She reached for the back pocket of her jeans and pulled out a slingshot, a gift fabricated by their father from scrap materials around the farm. From her side pocket she pulled out a stone. She was a talented sharpshooter with the crude device.

"Why do you need that?" Curious asked nervously.

"We're not going into the woods, but this stone will." She loaded the slingshot, drew it back with uncommon strength for her age, and launched the projectile toward the canopy of trees. It shredded through foliage and rattled against branches before disappearing into the dark netherworld. It made enough noise to startle any creature within earshot. But there was no reaction to the disturbance. No birds flew up. No critters bounded to safety. Everything remained eerily still.

Cammy shrugged her shoulders and pulled another stone out of her pocket. She launched it into the canopy of trees, creating the same disturbance and yielding the same quiet pall afterward. She grabbed another stone and fired it into the great mass of trees.

This time something was startled.

There was frantic thrashing in the treetops nearest them. Suddenly, a large black crow flapped out awkwardly. It was the biggest crow they had ever seen. It moved so unnaturally that Cammy wondered if she had miraculously wounded it with her wild shot.

They were mesmerized as the strange crow banked into a looping pattern high above their heads, rising and falling silently in the gentle breeze. It did this aerial ballet for several minutes as it hovered above them.

"It's watching us," Curious said.

"Maybe it's planning to attack," replied Cammy, half in jest.

"Let's go home," said Curious.

Cammy hesitated. She hated to show fear or weakness in front of her brother because the appearance of strength served her well in her ongoing effort to dominate him. But then the crow dipped much lower. Its large, menacing shadow passed directly through where they were standing. In the brief chill of its shade, Cammy decided homeschooling was a better option than what the swooping black predator might have in mind.

"Run!" she shouted.

They tore off through the meadow toward their one-story ranch, which was surrounded by a few acres of tilled farmland and endless miles of prairie. Curious set the pace, but Cammy was close on his heels. They sprinted for several minutes to separate themselves from the stalking crow. When they stopped for breath, they looked up, hoping to see an empty blue sky. But the crow had settled once again into a looping pattern above them as the kids gawked. Cammy pursed her lips. "I'll teach that pest a lesson." She reached for her slingshot again, loaded it, and aimed.

"No!" Curious shouted. He had spent much of his young life rescuing and healing wounded animals. He had no stomach for the intentional maiming of innocent creatures and could never understand why anyone would even want to cage one. "It hasn't done anything to hurt us . . . yet."

Cammy ignored him and released her shot. The stone missed as the bird changed course ever so slightly. They looked at each other in amazement, wondering how the bird could see the onrushing projectile and evade it in the blink of an eye. It continued to loop above them.

Cammy reloaded and fired, this time at the lowest point of the bird's looping pattern so that it would have less time to react. She scored a hit. The result was startling.

Instead of a dull thud emanating from the impact of stone against flesh, a metallic clank rang out. The crow ceased looping and began a slow, erratic descent. It zigged and zagged as it glided toward the ground. Their eyes followed its path with great interest, until they saw where it was likely to crash.

It was spiraling directly toward the well-manicured patch of white flowers that their father meticulously tended. The blossoms were among his few prized possessions, second in value only to the collection of books left behind by his father. The wounded crow plowed into the very center of the patch, thrashing madly in its death throes. It left behind a jagged trail of broken stems and shredded petals.

Cammy ran toward the flower patch, driven by an instinct to retrieve the crow and dispose of it. That way there would be no evidence that she had shot a bird or had somehow caused the damage to the plants. Perhaps Dad would assume a wild animal had rampaged through them.

Curious followed behind, although at a safe distance. When they got to the flowers, they stepped gingerly between the bushes, carefully moving stems aside to avoid the wrath of the thorns. They came upon the dead crow. They squatted and turned it over.

To their surprise, it wasn't a crow. Cammy's stone had torn open the shell of the thing. Its innards were an assortment of wires, blinking lights, and mechanical devices that were far beyond their comprehension. It had an oily smell.

They stood up and looked around. The prairie was still silent. Something was indeed not right.

They followed the age-old instinct of all youths—when in doubt, run for the protection of your parents. Cammy grabbed the mechanical crow and trotted toward the farm's dump. She heaved the contraption atop the heap. As they loped toward the ranch, they breathlessly discussed their strategy. Whatever story they came up with for their parents would have to exclude any mention of shooting at birds, ruining the flowers, or finding a bizarre mechanical crow.

By the time they reached the house, they had settled on a tale about a strange animal they spotted in the meadow. They decided to investigate, which is why they were late for their morning studies. In their story, they would say they tracked the animal to the woods but never caught up with it. And when Dad discovered the mangled flowers, they would suggest it was the handiwork of the mysterious beast.

They would say it was Curious' idea to track the animal, because even though he always got the blame, he never got punished. Mother always softened when he flashed his large brown eyes and impish smile.

Cammy resented her mother's protectiveness of Curious, even though Cammy was the one he usually needed protection from.

Their cover story was solid. But in their haste to rush home while crafting a compelling tale, they were oblivious to a second large black crow hovering over their house.

It had been hovering there for two days.

TWO
DARKNESS

> It came like a thief in the night,
> The evil that devours all light.
> Born of intentions thought well,
> Spawning nothing but living hell.
>
> *— The Poems of Dark Sun*

Something was wrong.

Dark Moon tried to locate the source of the unnatural sound she had just heard. She peeked out the cracked windowpane in Curious' musky bedroom. She knew that peering into the darkness was pointless because it was a cloudy night on the prairie. But she had to check.

Her ears were finely tuned to the usual nighttime sounds on their secluded farm—wind swishing through the tall grass, tree branches creaking, goats bleating, and the chatter of owls and whip-poor-wills. But the noise she had heard had a mechanical edge. She considered it might be a complaint from the old windmill out back, but the night's gentle Autumn breeze couldn't possibly budge the stubborn vanes.

Dark Moon listened intently, but the sound had stopped. Perhaps she had imagined it. It was easy to get spooked living in such isolation. Or maybe she was still unnerved by the strange behavior of the kids when they returned from their morning escapade, ashen-faced and babbling about a strange animal.

She glanced down at Curious. He was snuggled in his patchwork quilt on this chilly September night. She adored her son. She gently tousled his sandy-blond hair. He had boundless energy and an intoxicating personality that frothed with life. He was compliant and trusting, so much so that Dark Moon worried others might forever take advantage of him. His older sister rarely missed an opportunity.

Dark Moon loved being a mother, despite the difficulty of their austere lives. She had never wanted to be anything else, especially after losing her own mother. Mothering for her was an act of unconditional love and selfless generosity. It was an act of creation, not only of life itself but also of personality and purpose. She felt every emotion that poured forth from her children more powerfully than she felt her own joy and suffering. Her two kids gave meaning to the drudgery of splitting wood, washing clothes by hand, and making stews and soups from wild game and homegrown veggies. Her torn jeans, shabby barn coat, and soiled work boots were badges of honor.

She shared a tenacious resolve to carve out a sparse living with her husband on a farm in what used to be Kansas. Growing food wasn't much of a problem because they were decent farmers. But crafting everything else they needed to survive in isolation was challenging. They led an Amish-like lifestyle, not for distaste of modern technology but because modern technology had disappeared. Each day ended in exhaustion.

She sighed heavily, pushing aside her anxiety about the strange noise. She kissed Curious on his dirty forehead. He was asleep in that innocent holiness that rarely survives childhood. He was probably dreaming of hiking in the meadow or tending his farm critters, which were among his many outdoor passions. She kissed him again, this time on the cheek. She caressed his thin hand and silently wished him happiness. A familiar joy welled in her heart as she performed this nightly ritual.

Dark Moon blew out the homemade candle that flickered shadows across their faces. Darkness enveloped them. She reminisced about the electric lights that used to brighten her childhood home. Such luxuries were distant memories now. Social order had collapsed after the civil war started in 2053. That's when the Darkness descended upon the warring factions. Their irreconcilable differences proved that society was a fragile balance of complexity that could come unhinged quickly, violently, and with intense acrimony. There was no end in sight to the conflict.

The worst aspect of the Darkness was the loss of identity. Dark Moon rarely evoked the memory of her real name. The person formerly identified by that name had gone into hiding. Nearly everyone west of the Appalachians had adopted aliases. Their birth names were poisoned artifacts in the massive databases of the Elites. They were Orwellian collars used for extracting taxes and monitoring social compliance.

Her alias, Dark Moon, reflected her desire to go off the grid and hide from the computers and scanners of the Elites. It also reflected her reluctance to abandon the burning light of life within her. She pictured her essential inner self as a glorious full moon, glowing harvest yellow on an autumn night in defiance of the blackness all around. She considered the yin and yang of "Dark" and "Moon" to be a perfect metaphor for her spirit.

She hoped to someday shed her self-imposed camouflage. It didn't seem possible that life could be synonymous with darkness for the rest of time. To her, life was the *opposite* of darkness. Life animated the inanimate. It was the spirit in the spiritless. It was the temporal flame of passion in the cold void of infinity. It was a burning ember that somehow radiated heat no matter how hard the rain, how dark the night, or how cold the winter. At least that's what she hoped.

It was because life was so precious that Dark Moon and her husband Dark Sun chose to conceive Curious. It was a decision rich in joy and fraught with dire risk. Very few parents had more than one child. It was challenging enough to raise just one. And having more than one was against the law.

Decades ago, gut-wrenching austerity from a worldwide depression triggered riots and civil unrest around the globe. In America, the One Child dictate was a draconian attempt by the Elites to ration dwindling resources. The Elites had long ago taken on the responsibility to feed every child, but when food became scarce, their solution was to permit fewer children.

Dark Moon and Dark Sun didn't care that conceiving Curious was against the law. For them, the concept of law had lost its meaning. It had devolved into a pretext for the Elites in Washington to wield a capricious power that was more bureaucratic terrorism than governance. But even if laws still had meaning, the ultimate source of meaning was life because laws were created by living people. Life was the most precious thing in the universe because preciousness had no meaning without life. And the most precious act was to create another life.

They named their son Curious because one of the great joys of life is to explore its secrets, pleasures, temptations, and challenges. Like his sister Cammy, Curious wasn't passed a surname by his parents, who had abandoned their own. He wasn't assigned a Social Identification Number because he didn't officially exist. He also didn't have a SIN tracking chip implanted in his ribs. He was born after the Darkness had set in and into a world where the remnants of the Elites were pre-occupied fighting the civil war.

Dark Moon pivoted in the darkness and bumped into Dark Sun, who had just tucked Cammy in for the night. They hugged instinctively. Their affection was a vital counterpoint to the isolation of their ranch. "I love you, Moonbeam," he murmured in his deep, soothing voice. "I love you too, Sunshine," she echoed.

Dark Moon enjoyed the reassuring feel of her husband's tall, sturdy body, which had been hardened by years of work on their farm. She ran her fingers across the stubble of his salt-and-pepper beard. She toyed with his tangled shoulder-length hair. In the light of day, there would have been a tinge of red in his brown hair, hinting at his Celtic ancestry. There also would have been streaks of gray, marking the years that were slipping past him.

They were everything to each other, because they had to be. They were lovers, best friends, farmers, cooks, mechanics, menders, builders, hunters, doctors, and every other role necessary to sustain their family.

Their only help was from two stray German shepherds that they had taken in many years ago. Brutus and Spartacus helped keep their livestock in check and predators and intruders away. Sometimes feral animals stalked the farm. If the two dogs didn't deter them, the family fought them off with makeshift weapons. Sometimes vagabonds tried to pilfer grain from their silo. Dark Sun and Dark Moon usually chased them away with hatchets and knives.

"Sunshine, I heard a strange noise outside," said Dark Moon.

"Was it the mysterious animal the kids invented this morning?"

Dark Moon chuckled. "No, it was mechanical."

"The windmill?"

"There's not much wind tonight, and the sound came from out front."

"I'll go check," Dark Sun volunteered. He hadn't heard anything, but her hearing was better than his, and she wasn't easily spooked. He whistled for Spartacus and Brutus and then headed out the door. When he saw how dark it was under the cloud cover, he silently wished for the impossible luxury of a flashlight.

His eyes adjusted, but it made little difference. He circled the house with the two dogs, listening intently for any sound beyond the padding of their paws on the ground. The dogs meandered and sniffed but did not seem alarmed.

When they returned to the front of the house, he scanned the horizon one last pointless time. Nothing but darkness. Spartacus, however, stiffened as he faced the old road leading to the property. He growled, low and guttural. Dark Sun squatted and gave him the "follow target" signal. He trailed Spartacus for a hundred yards toward the road, but then the animal lost interest in his quarry and turned back for the house.

Dark Sun shrugged, guessing that a raccoon had caught the dog's attention. They headed to the front door. When he got back inside, Dark Moon was standing there with her hunting knife pulled from its belt sheath. "Well?"

"You can put that away," Dark Sun said. "There's nothing unusual out there. Maybe you heard a raccoon."

She flashed him a skeptical look. "Raccoons don't make mechanical sounds."

She sighed and wrapped her arms around him, partly as a gesture of thanks for his search and partly to calm her jangled nerves. There was no one to help them if something bad happened. She slid her hand inside his shirt and stroked his muscular chest. She gently massaged the scar where she had sliced open his abdomen with a razor blade and extracted his SIN chip. She had an identical scar on her torso, as did millions of others.

Carving out the SIN chips was necessary to avoid the constant surveillance by the Elites. Decades ago, chips were implanted in every newborn child. The devices emitted information to countless sensors around the country. The technology was originally intended to track lost or abducted kids. Over time, it morphed into a national identification system linked to powerful computers that compiled electronic dossiers on everyone.

When society splintered, there was no other purpose for the SIN chips and the dossiers than for the Elites to hunt suspected enemies of their regime. There wasn't enough government left to form a cohesive nation, but there was enough to harass antagonists, settle political differences, and wage civil war.

Dark Sun stroked Dark Moon's toned arms and back. She was a tall Slavic tomboy hardened and burnished by the rigors of farm life. Her calloused hands and sinewy muscles contrasted with the feminine aura cast by her shoulder-length platinum hair and stunning blue eyes.

She kissed Dark Sun with her sun-chapped lips and then slid past him into Cammy's room. She leaned over to caress her sleeping daughter's tanned forehead. The young girl's long, silvery hair shimmered faintly in the dim light of a candle by her bed.

Cammy's full name was Chameleon. Her parents had chosen it because of the social chaos into which she was born. As the civil war raged, many people avoided joining a faction. Instead, they drifted along in the maelstrom, believing that joining a faction was either a step toward surrendering their freedom or a step toward joining a war against people with whom they had no quarrel.

Sometimes, however, these drifters pretended fleeting allegiance to one faction or another to ease the risk of conflict. This strategy of changing political colors whenever necessary was the path that Dark Sun and Dark Moon had chosen during their drifting days. When their daughter was born, the name Chameleon leapt to mind as a reflection of their survival strategy.

The name fit her moody personality well. She could be ruthlessly domineering one day, then affectionately compliant the next. She could stomp her feet one moment, then dazzle with a playful dance the next. She hid from chores, then cried out for attention when she was ignored.

Dark Moon and Dark Sun couldn't offer a firm foundation for her erratic personality to rally around. There was no civil structure in the Darkness. They had no relatives or friends nearby. They had no connection to a past with any meaning. They had no future with any certainty.

They could, however, provide their kids a sense of family, even though the two of them weren't married. The sanction of church or state on their relationship was impractical in their isolation, but their commitment to each other transcended the blessing of a priest or the license of a state. They also provided their kids a sense of place, despite the collapse of society. Certainly, their country no longer existed. The region in which they lived used to be called Kansas. It was a borderless, ungoverned territory now. The nearest town, a small hamlet along the Verdigris River called Independence, was deserted.

However, Dark Sun and Dark Moon owned property, and it had meaning for them. Their house and farmland once belonged to Dark Sun's parents. They returned to the abandoned site after drifting during the years before Cammy was born. Their house was a typical prairie ranch in need of repair, most of which would never happen. But it offered the solace of a connection to the past, and the surrounding land enabled them to craft a sparse living.

Dark Moon's hand froze on Cammy's forehead in mid-caress. She heard that eerily unnatural sound again. This time it was much closer. Brutus barked in another room and then so did Spartacus. "Did you hear it that time?" she whispered to Dark Sun. She moved to the window in Cammy's room.

"Hear what?" he whispered back. Her nervous agitation and the reaction of the dogs put him on edge. Brutus and Spartacus scratched at the front door. His muscles stiffened. The hair on the back of his neck prickled.

"It sounds like—"

BAM! Shards of glass and splinters of wood exploded around them. Dark Moon screamed and threw her body over Cammy. Shadowy, helmeted figures with night-vision goggles poured like giant black beetles through the demolished front door and shattered windows.

Men shouted commands that were unintelligible in the chaos. Two of them grabbed Dark Moon, ripping her away from Cammy's bedside. Despite her athleticism, she was overwhelmed by the intruders, who had the advantage of surprise, numbers, and night vision.

One of the intruders clubbed Dark Sun in the head. He crumpled to the floor, stunned by searing pain. Amid the mad scramble of bodies, he groped for the hatchet that they kept under every bed as part of their meager defenses against a dangerous world. His fingers found it.

He jumped up and swung it wildly at one of the black-clad figures who was assailing Dark Moon. The hatchet found its mark, sinking with gruesome finality into the screaming attacker's back. He quickly wrenched the hatchet from the carcass. He swung it at a man dragging Cammy from her bed. He clipped the attacker's shoulder and heard a confirming yelp of pain. Two men tackled Dark Sun from behind before he could swing his hatchet again.

Brutus and Spartacus charged into the melee, barking fiercely, hellbent on protecting their family. They leapt onto the men who had pinned Dark Sun and tore at their flesh with fangs and claws. Brutus locked his jaws onto the throat of one. Blood spurted from a severed artery.

Dark Moon disentangled from the attacker that Dark Sun had killed. She pulled the hunting knife from her belt. She lunged for the wounded assailant who was dragging Cammy by the ankles across the bedroom floor. Her knife missed its mark. She was tackled by another clandestine attacker. Cammy screamed incoherently.

Dark Moon flailed and kicked and stabbed wildly, forcing her attacker to slacken his grip. She twisted free and stumbled toward the sound of Cammy's shrieks, which were now coming from the front doorway. Curious was screaming outside their home. His screams were borne of agony rather than fear.

Dark Moon rushed through the front door. She leapt down from the porch and sprinted after the four men who were dragging Curious and Cammy toward the dark silhouette of an imposing vehicle. She plunged her knife with anguished ferocity into the first attacker she caught up with. She was maddened with the primitive savagery of a mama bear defending her cubs.

The other man dragging Cammy let go of her and swung his gun at Dark Moon's head. She ducked and then stabbed him in the stomach. The wounded brute swung his gun at her head again. This time it connected with a sickening thud. She collapsed.

Inside the house, Dark Sun raged against the remaining two men who grappled with him despite the savage assaults by the dogs. He kicked one man in the face with the heel of his boot; he heard teeth and bone crack from the force of the horrific blow. He clawed at the eyes of the other assailant, gaining a momentary advantage that allowed him to break free. He spun around behind the man, caught him in a headlock, and twisted so violently he snapped the man's neck. The attacker dropped to the floor.

Dark Sun dashed out the door and catapulted over the porch railing, with Brutus and Spartacus on his heels. He saw a terrifying scene panned by the headlights of a large vehicle. Dark Moon lay motionless on the ground next to an inert assailant. Curious and Cammy were both screaming as two attackers tossed them like potato sacks into the back of the vehicle. The boy's left leg dangled at a grotesque angle as he was heaved aboard. A third attacker was doubled over in pain. Blood oozed from his stomach. Spartacus tore into him with mortal vigor.

The two uninjured men ran toward Dark Sun. He squatted and prepared to fight. The first to reach him grappled his legs, but Dark Sun wrapped his arm around the man's neck and yanked hard as they both fell to the ground.

Brutus raced toward the second runner. The man stopped abruptly and fired his gun. The German shepherd howled and then tumbled into a quivering heap. The runner gaped at his companion who lay dead at Dark Sun's feet. Then he noticed Spartacus, who had bloody bits of flesh dangling from his jowls. Wild-eyed, he hurled a grenade high over Dark Sun's head. Then he spun around and sprinted toward the vehicle. Dark Sun scrambled to his feet, pulled out his hunting knife, and threw it at him. It buried to the hilt in the back of the fleeing attacker's thigh. Spartacus chased after the limping man.

When the grenade hit the house and detonated, a concussive shock wave pummeled Dark Sun. He was tossed like a rag doll and lost consciousness.

The two surviving attackers fired wildly at Spartacus to keep him at bay. Injured and bleeding, they collected the weapons of their fallen comrades and then hobbled to their vehicle. They sped off with Curious and Cammy as captives.

Hours later, when the flames incinerating their house died down, the prairie was darker than ever before.

THREE
JOURNAL

> Forgive me, my dear innocent child
> For bringing you into a world gone wild
> I did nothing to stem the tide
> Of a terror no human can abide
>
> *— The Poems of Dark Sun*

The cold water on Dark Sun's forehead brought him to his senses. He slowly opened his eyes, then recoiled from a sledgehammer of pain. He smelled acrid smoke. He tasted the coppery tang of blood.

Dark Moon was wrapping a compress around his forehead as he lay in the darkness on the singed prairie grass. She brushed his sodden hair away from his face. "At first I thought you were dead," she said, gently wiping blood from his beard. Spartacus sat on his haunches nearby, whimpering.

Dark Sun sat up with a jolt and winced at the pain. "Where are

Curious and Cammy?" The dulled memories of the vicious attack on his family were slow in coming back to him.

Dark Moon didn't answer. She began weeping into her bloodied hands. Her body shook uncontrollably as she fathomed that dark and desolate inner chasm that only the victims of unimaginable tragedy come to know. Spartacus eyed them both with grave concern. He gently pawed Dark Moon's leg and nudged her with his snout.

"They took them!" she finally choked out through bitter sobs.

The caustic memory of his two children being thrown into the mysterious vehicle snapped back at the sound of her agony. "Where?!"

"I don't know!" Dark Moon's lips trembled. "I fought them . . . but . . ." She sobbed uncontrollably again.

Dark Sun knelt helplessly by her side. He didn't know how long he had been unconscious. It was still night, but the clouds had cleared. By the position of the moon and stars, he estimated it was 1:00 AM. The kidnappers had a vehicle, which meant they were likely far away by now. Away to where? It was a terrible, unanswerable question.

He kissed Dark Moon's cheek, but she had fallen into that dark cavern of spiritual anguish from which little emotion could escape. He laid her down and wrapped his arms around her to ward off the autumn chill. Spartacus curled up next to his back.

They laid on the grass for some time. Dark Moon sobbed and spasmed periodically. Dark Sun's mind raced as he embraced her. His instinct was to get up and begin searching for their children, but he knew it would be futile. It was dark, the attackers had a motorized vehicle, and he had no idea in which direction to head.

With nothing purposeful to do until sunrise, he ruefully considered their plight under the canopy of stars. It was a gruesome exercise. He was so overwhelmed by gut-wrenching fear about Cammy and Curious that he became nauseous. The tragedy of their situation crashed down upon him. Their kids were gone. Their house was destroyed. Their lives were ruined. They had nothing left. They had no one to go to for help. And it all happened so fast.

In the darkness of the night and the darkness of his soul, he felt his will to go on living ebb away. He decided to shut his mind down, at least until morning.

Dark Sun woke with a start. The sun peeked above the horizon. He struggled to his feet with wobbly legs and surveyed the surrounding devastation. Their home was a heap of charred wood and broken masonry. Smoke rose lazily from the ruins. It wafted away on a feathery prairie breeze, evaporating what little was left of their life's work into the ether of eternity.

He scanned the endless amber prairie. He could see for miles in the clear autumn air. Nothing moved, other than rustling grass and a few scudding clouds that cast drifting shadows. His head throbbed. He fingered the gruesome knot where he had been clubbed by the attackers. He looked down at his bloodied and torn clothes. The shrapnel from the grenade had made a mess of him, but the lacerations seemed to be superficial. His gaze wandered to Dark Moon, who was still in repose. There was blood caked in her blond hair, likely from a blow during the melee. She appeared otherwise uninjured. He gently woke her. It was time to devise a plan.

She groaned as she stirred. She sat up and blinked her eyes a few times, then stared at their devastated home. "It looks worse in the daylight," she observed wryly. "What do we do?"

Dark Sun was relieved that sleep had eased her state of shock. "There's no point staying here," he said. "But I don't know where to go."

She scanned the endless prairie and then sighed. "We need to get help."

"That's true," he replied. "But from who? From where?"

Dark Moon's shoulders slumped. They had always considered their isolation from society a great advantage. Now, it was devastating. There was nobody to rescue them. They were separated from everyone they had ever known.

"Let's head to Independence," she suggested.

"Why? Nobody lives there anymore."

"I know. But the tracks from the vehicle head in that direction. And Independence is on a main road. We're more likely to encounter some wanderers there. Maybe somebody saw something."

Dark Sun considered her proposal. The town was ten miles away, a distance they could walk in less than half a day. But even if by miraculous coincidence they headed in the same direction as the kidnappers, the villains were driving much faster than they could walk. At least the stroll would give them time to strategize, and the physical activity would feel like progress.

"Okay," he said. "But before we leave, let's search the rubble of our house for anything useful."

She nodded and arose, letting out a yelp of pain. They walked to the house hand in hand, eyeing with overwhelming sadness the remnants of a life that no longer existed. Spartacus loped behind them, sniffing the ground and looking forlornly from side to side for the children and Brutus.

They spotted the bloodied hunting knife that Dark Moon had wielded during the attack. She picked it up, wiped it on her jeans, and returned it to her sheath. They searched the bodies of the two dead attackers sprawled on the ground. They had no identification or weapons.

They rummaged through the smoldering devastation that used to be their home, occasionally inspecting pieces of debris, then discarding them as useless or ruined. Scorched books were strewn among the rubble. Dark Sun picked up a few and thumbed through them with calloused fingers. He loved his father's old books, but it would be foolish to lug them around now. He tossed them back onto the heap with a pang of regret.

In the basement, they found some clothing that wasn't ruined, which they bundled into a makeshift satchel. They searched a while longer but didn't find anything else of use. Dark Sun noted to himself that forty-four years of living should have yielded more bounty than their humble bindle.

As they stumbled out of the wreckage, his boot clanged against a metallic object that was partially embedded in a jumble of broken masonry. He vaguely recognized it. With help from Dark Moon, he extricated it from the wedged cinder blocks. It was a metal chest about the size of a large briefcase. He recalled that his father had discretely used it for something before he disappeared decades ago. The explosion must have unearthed the chest from a clever hiding place. It was dented and covered with dust. He unclasped the lid and opened it.

The pistol caught his attention first. It was loaded. The lethal device made him feel nervous and secure at the same time. He slipped it into the waistband of his jeans.

Underneath the gun was a desiccated white rose laminated between clear sheets of plastic. It was about the size of a post card. He puzzled over its significance. His father used to obsess over a patch of white roses, for reasons he never shared. Dark Sun maintained the rose patch over the years in remembrance of his dad. He was about to discard the laminated rose, but then thought it might have been a symbol of affection between his parents, so he kept it as a memento.

He rummaged deeper into the chest and extracted a black pouch. He peeked inside and was astonished to find seven small gold bars. Near the bottom of the chest was a brown cigar box containing ammunition. Underneath the cigar box was a book. He pulled it out and inspected it. It was bound in black leather with no identification. He opened it.

The first page simply read: "Journal—May 2054 through _____." His hands immediately began shaking and his skin crawled.

The distinctive handwriting was that of his father, who had supported the rebellion against the Elites and was captured in November 2057. Dark Sun held in his hands an intimate time capsule.

Dark Moon noticed the impact the find had on him. "What is it?"

"My Dad's last thoughts," he replied as tears formed in his eyes.

Dark Moon rubbed his arm in sympathy. "Why do you suppose he hid those things down here in the basement?"

"Back then, the Elites were always snooping for illegal items. This collection does seem odd, though. I don't think it was illegal to have a white rose. Or a journal."

He shrugged his shoulders and stashed the rose, the gold, and his father's journal into their bindle. When the time was right, he would savor every word written by the father he had lost twenty-seven years ago. He hefted the cigar box of bullets. Dark Moon picked up the satchel. They climbed the basement steps and clambered over fractured and charred lumber to begin their journey to Independence.

After they had taken a few strides toward the road, Dark Moon stopped in her tracks. She pointed toward the distant horizon.

"Someone's coming."

FOUR
SYNDICATE

> Violence cannot conceal itself behind anything except lies, and lies have nothing to maintain them save violence. Anyone who has once proclaimed violence as his method must inexorably choose the lie as his principle.
>
> — Aleksandr Solzhenitsyn

President Regis glared at Cosimo.

His unwelcome visitor was seated on the other side of the Resolute desk, which was gifted from Queen Victoria in the nineteenth century. "Put your cigarette out," Regis implored. "This is the Oval Office. Show some respect for it . . . and for me."

Cosimo took a deep drag from his cigarette and calmly blew a smoke ring that drifted over Regis' head toward the three tall windows behind him. "You make the rules for many people," he said in a gruff voice, leaning back in his chair and putting his feet on the president's desk. "But not for me."

Regis eyed the scuffed leather soles that now obscured his view of Cosimo's inscrutable face and dark brooding eyes. Regis sullenly mused that he was being put in his place by the finely crafted Italian footwear and odious rings of smoke of a shadowy man who was loyal only to nebulous confederates.

The grandfather clock chimed twelve times. "Why are you here?" Regis asked.

Cosimo flicked ashes onto the circular carpet bearing the seal of the president, taking care not to sully his impeccable suit. "You're failing. My visit shouldn't surprise you."

Despite the trappings and power of his office, Regis suddenly felt insecure in the presence of the Syndicate's dapper consigliere. Even though Regis had the general appearance of an aristocratic politician, deeper examination revealed less substance. His frail body was dwarfed by the tall, trim physique of his ruggedly handsome visitor, who was in his seventies but carried it with elegance. In comparison, Regis felt ashamed of his balding head, his narrow gray face, his much-to-prominent nose, and his dark eyes buried deep in hollow sockets. He felt emasculated and exposed, much like the Wizard of Oz when Toto pulled the curtain aside to reveal a withered sideshow con man. His liver-spotted hands trembled.

"I've done everything the Syndicate asked of me," Regis said. "For decades."

"Perhaps. But the civil war has dragged on too long," said Cosimo through a haze of smoke. "And now it's taken a turn for the worse. Your empire has dwindled to east of the Appalachians. It's hard to tell whether you're a national dictator or a feudal baron now. Not that I care what happens to you, but I care which faction might replace your regime if you lose this war."

"Your concerns are unwarranted. We Elites will rule for a thousand years."

"You Elites rule nothing. The Syndicate has ruled for centuries, and it will always rule."

"The Syndicate encouraged this war," Regis reminded gently.

"Of course we did," replied Cosimo. "If wars are played well, there's money to be made, power to be grabbed, and great opportunity to keep the surviving proles in their place. Especially if you're clever enough to play both sides. However, we didn't expect your disastrous performance. The Outcasts are conquering the South. The Caliphate is gobbling up territory in the Midwest. The Jackals are swarming up from Mexico. Millions of your proles are fleeing to the Blessed monasteries. The Syndicate has a long history of deciding who wins elections and wars. You're disappointing us. Tragically."

"I won't fail."

Cosimo patted his head to make sure his receding salt-and-pepper hair was still well-coiffed. Regis caught a glimpse of the familiar ring on his right hand, which was made in the shape of a jeweled snake encircling the globe.

"Bold words," said Cosimo. "Especially when the Outcasts are invading the Carolinas as we speak. What's your plan?"

"I've launched a clever scheme that even you would appreciate."

Cosimo sneered. "I hope it's better than your ridiculous One Child dictate."

"I've discovered a vital secret. It will change the tide of the war."

"I doubt that you've discovered anything. You're just a politician. An eloquent ornament."

"I have tremendous power!" Regis' hands still trembled.

Cosimo looked pointedly at Regis's shaking hands. "Let's talk about power, shall we?"

Regis looked toward the three doors that ringed the Oval Office. He was momentarily reassured knowing that his black-shirted Secret Service agents were just the push of a button away. But he knew that pushing the button would result in mortal retribution from the Syndicate. "Who am I to say no, your Eminence?" he asked acerbically.

"Exactly, Mr. President. Who are you to say no? Lucky for you, you've always followed our orders well, and you spin our myths like a maestro directing a philharmonic. Complicated lies often overwhelm simple truths, if they are repeated often enough. The Syndicate appreciates your skill as an artful politician who has conned untold millions, all to our advantage. But surely you realize your place in our grand scheme."

"You've never shared any details—"

"I'll share this," Cosimo interrupted. "The Syndicate is achieving complete financial, intellectual, military, and ecclesiastical dominion over the entire world. Our shadow looms over every government. Those are all the details you need to know."

"I've been loyal to you for a long time. When do I get a peek inside the Syndicate?"

"Never. You knew that from the beginning. We kept our end of the bargain. We funded your political campaigns, we aligned the media behind you, we pushed your agenda in the schools, we instigated the cultural fawning over you, and we even crafted the sermons from the pulpits. In return, you sold the Grand Illusion to the witless proles while enjoying the bountiful perks of your office. Unfortunately for you, the civil war isn't going as planned."

"I'm starting to wonder whose side you're on."

Cosimo laughed. "Are you really that naïve? There are no sides. There never were."

Confusion washed over Regis' face. "Sometimes the Syndicate seemed to support the Left. Other times the Right. Now I can't tell anymore."

"Right, Left, up, down, it was always an illusion. The proles madly aligned themselves with one political faction or another, chanting their vapid slogans, carrying their insipid signs, waving their puny fists, genuflecting to their inane dogmas, and casting their worthless votes for the Manchurian candidates we chose. But each side was just a different face of the same coin—a coin that the Syndicate holds in its own pocket."

Regis paled. "It wasn't an illusion to me. I believed in what I preached to my people about hope, equality, and social justice. And they believed in me.

"You have indeed been a useful idiot." Cosimo flicked more ashes onto the presidential seal on the floor. "The proles have hope, but only if they follow our dictates. Equality is a virtue, but it's applicable to them not us. Justice is wonderful, as long as it benefits the Syndicate. But you're not really an idiot because you figured out how to take glorious advantage of the perks of your office. You followed the money like all politicians."

"Of course I enjoy my lifestyle, and I enjoy the power at my disposal. But I used it faithfully to implement my vision to make the world a more compassionate place for the underclass and the victims."

Cosimo's face hardened. "There's only one vision for the Syndicate—that all of its members live like gods. The rest is all bullshit. You don't really believe you were helping the common man, do you? Look at the devastated nation that you lead. It's at war with itself. Your government is bankrupt. Your bureaucracy is a useless monstrosity run by small-minded apparatchiks. The economy has collapsed. Many of your citizens are dying from famine, and the rest are living in poverty. Your armies are being overrun by barbarians. It was all a sham, and you were the leader of it. At least that's what future history books will say when we write them."

Regis' shoulders sagged. "Then why did you abet my career for decades?"

Cosimo took his feet off the Resolute desk and leaned forward in his chair. "Think of it like a chess match. Every piece has a role to play. The pawns labor for us in their otherwise meaningless lives until they die. The knights bravely fight our wars until they die. The bishops keep the pawns and knights in line with our magnificent illusions, but they too are sacrificed in the end."

"Am I the rook, existing solely to protect you the king?"

"What sane person wants to be king?" exclaimed Cosimo. "His head is heavy from the burden of wearing the crown. He sleeps with one eye open and can't eat a meal until his taster survives the daily sampling. Every sound in the hallway is the approach of an assassin. Every shout from the rabble outside the castle is the opening volley of a revolution. No, *you're* the king. Thank you for your loyal service."

Regis shot him a malicious leer. "So then what's your role in this grand chess match of humanity?"

Cosimo puckered his lips and blew a puff of smoke directly into Regis's face. "I'm one of those *moving* all of the pieces."

Regis waved the pungent smoke away, resisting the urge to let a stray swipe of his hand smash the smug grin off Cosimo's face. "Toward what end are you moving the pieces?"

"The end that the Syndicate desires."

"Will I be sacrificed too? The king is supposed to be protected in chess."

Cosimo stood up and reached for his overcoat. "Even the rules of this game are an illusion. You've been very useful for many decades. The Syndicate values loyalty. But if you lose this war, you'll be killed. If the Outcasts win, not even I will be able to save you from the apocalypse that will follow. The only survivors will be the proles and the animals, which would be a tremendous waste of five thousand years of civilization. Win the war!"

Regis nodded submissively. He had no other choice.

FIVE
SUSPICION

> Hope like a gypsy princess dances
> With dazzling allure she prances
> Offering opportunity without measure
> And sometimes priceless treasure
>
> — *The Poems of Dark Sun*

Dark Moon pulled her hunting knife out of its sheath as the lone horseback rider approached.

Dark Sun pulled his father's gun out of his waistband.

When the horse trotted to within fifty feet, Dark Sun aimed the pistol at the intruder and yelled "Halt!" The hooded rider pulled on the reins and dismounted with catlike agility, ignoring the militant posturing of the two injured people standing amid the rubble of a destroyed home.

"Who are you?" Dark Sun challenged with as much bravado as he could muster.

The rider pulled back the hood, revealing a young woman with unkempt curly black hair held somewhat at bay by a colorful headband. Her unblemished brown face framed large dark eyes that were fearless and mesmerizing. She was beautiful, in an unadorned, angelic way. She wore a vibrant green cloak draped over a cream-colored tunic decorated with intricate Celtic patterns. Her denim jeans were a size too big for her wispy frame. Her leather hiking boots were scuffed and worn by untold miles. Her manner was gentle and non-threatening.

"I'm Fatima. My tribemates call me Teema. Who are you?"

Dark Sun and Dark Moon fell silent for a few heartbeats, trying to sort out the implications of Fatima's arrival. The lone, angelic stranger seemed ethereally disconnected from their present circumstance. They lowered their weapons.

"I'm Dark Sun. This is my wife, Dark Moon."

Fatima nodded politely. "Pleased to meet you. What happened here?"

Like a dam bursting, Dark Moon poured out the woeful tale of the attack on the home and the abduction of their kids, sobbing as she spit out the words. Fatima listened with somber earnest. By the end of Dark Moon's wrenching explanation, Fatima's eyes were reddened and moist.

"I'm so sorry," she said. "No one should have to endure such suffering."

Despite Fatima's apparent sympathy, Dark Sun felt of wave of suspicion. This strange woman had magically appeared out of thin air. "What are you doing here?" he asked.

"We heard an explosion from town last night. We saw flames on the horizon. When the sun rose, I came to see what happened."

Dark Sun frowned. "No one lives in Independence anymore," he said. The wispy girl seemed harmless, but he began to suspect that she and her cohorts were involved in the abduction. She was the first person they had seen in months, other than the attackers.

Fatima noted his suspicion. Her placid dark eyes held his hostile glare. "We were passing through the area. We stopped in Independence for the night, hoping to trade for supplies, but it is indeed a ghost town."

Dark Sun pondered her story. Perhaps she was involved with the drug-dealing and child-trafficking gangsters who were migrating northward from what used to be Mexico. "What faction are you with?"

Fatima smiled serenely. "None. I'm a gypsy. We're peaceful traders."

Dark Sun scowled. Popular lore suggested otherwise. It was well known that the various bands of gypsies roaming the wastelands of America trafficked contraband like guns and drugs. They were modern nomads, scratching out an existence by grifting in the towns they passed through. "Independence is pretty far off the beaten path. Where did you come from? Where are you headed?"

Fatima shrugged her shoulders. "Anywhere. Nowhere. Does it matter?"

Dark Sun had no answer. He was still uncertain of her motives, but she didn't seem to be a threat. "We don't know where we're going either," he sighed.

"Then come join us," Fatima invited, pitying the despair of the bloodied couple.

"What good will that do?" asked Dark Moon. "Unless you're with the kidnappers."

"We would never do such a thing!" Fatima asserted. "But we have horses and guns. We know our way around. We can go almost anywhere, because we barter with things that most people want. Joining us would be better than searching for your kids on foot."

Her offer struck Dark Sun as just a way to go nowhere faster. They needed to find their children, not roam the country aimlessly.

Fatima sensed his palpable doubt. "There's one more reason you should come with us."

Dark Sun looked up. He stared into her face, which was suddenly world-weary. She looked as if a darker being had magically replaced the sympathetic angel who found them.

"I can help you find your children," she continued. "I'm one of them."

"What do you mean?" His suspicion was redoubled.

"I know who took your kids. I know why."

Dark Sun's eyes widened. Her answer seemed to confirm she was somehow involved in the disappearance of their children. He took a step closer, towering over her. His hand tightened on the grip of his pistol. "How do you know?"

"It's obvious," she replied, seemingly oblivious to his glare and aggressive posture. "You have two children, which is illegal. Someone ratted on you. Your kids were taken hostage by the Elites. That's their usual punishment."

"How can you possibly know that?" Dark Sun conjectured the real story was that the gypsies had kidnapped his children. This deceptive waif was sent here to make sure that he and Dark Moon survived long enough to pay a ransom. That would be ironic, because they had almost nothing left.

Fatima sighed as a wave of sadness washed over her face. "My brother and I were kidnapped years ago for the same crime—my mother had two children."

Dark Sun's mouth fell open. This was either a remarkable coincidence or a devious con. "Say more."

"The Elites found out about my family, like they find out about everything. They snatched my brother and me and sold us as slaves. I never saw my mother or my brother again. A few years later, I escaped. I wandered aimlessly until a gypsy caravan found me and welcomed me into their tribe."

Icy fear gripped Dark Sun's heart. "Who did the Elites sell you to?"

"I was lucky. I was sold to the Mexican drug lords. You may know them as the Jackals."

"That was lucky?"

"It could have been worse," she said gently. "Even though the Jackals are a heartless mafia that uses kids to run drugs, they didn't hurt us much, as long as we made the deliveries and returned with the gold. I wasn't raped until I was thirteen. That's when I ran away."

Dark Moon shuddered. Cammy was twelve. "What could be worse than that?"

"Being sold to the Caliphate. They make their girl slaves concubines, and they indoctrinate the boys into their cult of terror. They crucify those who refuse. I'm certain they would have killed me, if I had returned to them."

Dark Moon's heart constricted. The blood drained from her face. When she and Dark Sun were drifters, they heard gruesome tales about the Caliphate. It was a violent Islamic faction that spread around the world from its base in the Middle East. It took root in America when Arabic immigrants poured into enclaves like Dearborn and Hamtramck. They publicly espoused peace but many of them privately prepared for the jihad prescribed in their holy book. Once their population reached critical mass, they took control of the local police and governments. The fanatics among them dragged their less-militant religious brethren along in their wake. Non-Muslims fled these "no-go" zones. After annexing Michigan into their international Islamic State in 2056, they spread their Sharia law into surrounding states. Led by the Caliph Timur, they accomplished this without interference by the federal government, because the Elites were embroiled in the civil war that was escalating all across America.

"Is there anything worse than being sold to the Caliphate?" Dark Moon asked in a hoarse whisper.

"For me, no. It would have meant torture and then death. I'm Arabic. My mother, Ayaan, was an apostate who fled with my brother and me from the Caliphate long ago, as a matter of conscience. But for other hostages, it would be worse if the Elites harvested their organs so that older Party members could use them."

Dark Sun swallowed hard. His throat was as dry as a desert. His head was a terrible muddle of conflicting fears and suspicions. Which faction was this strange Arabic girl really involved with? Why did she magically appear here at this very moment? Where were her cohorts?

"Why should we believe it was the Elites who kidnapped our kids?" he challenged.

"You broke the One Child law." Fatima gestured toward a horizon unbroken by any hint of civilization. "What else could explain what happened here?"

"Bullshit!" exclaimed Dark Sun. "Why would the Elites bother with us? Laws mean nothing out here." In his view, the Midwest was as lawless now as it was when the first waves of settlers arrived centuries ago. "There must be some other reason why the attackers blew up our house and left Dark Moon and I for dead."

"Some laws exist only to maintain the power and privilege of a few. Enforcing the One Child law is an excuse for the Elites to profit by selling your kids. There's a lot of money in human trafficking."

Dark Sun shook his head violently in confusion. "Why should I believe anything you say?"

"You're right to challenge me," Fatima said calmly. "Doubt is the mother of truth. The Elites lie. The Caliphate lies. The Jackals lie. And they all claim we gypsies lie. Every tribe fabricates its own reality. It's been that way forever."

"Is everything a lie then?"

"There are some truths," replied Fatima. "We come into this world alone, and we leave this world alone. From the moment we're born, we all live under death sentences. In the meantime, we band together in families and tribes for love and protection. We're all humans, despite our different colors and creeds."

"Did you learn that from the Jackals, the Caliphate, or the Elites?" asked Dark Moon sarcastically.

Fatima glared at her with an unexpected ferocity. "They only taught me to hate! My mother and Osiris taught me everything else."

"Who's Osiris?"

"The leader of our gypsy tribe," she said with pride and a hint of something else. "Come with me to meet him. I know you don't trust me, but I promise I want to help you."

Dark Sun was still suspicious. He wondered how Fatima's tribemates could send such a slight woman alone to investigate an obviously violent event. Perhaps she was just a decoy and her cohorts were lurking in the tall grass nearby. He scanned the prairie around the farm. "Weren't you afraid to come out here by yourself?" he asked warily.

Her demeanor suddenly changed again. Her face hardened, as if yet another personality lurking inside took the helm. She pulled back her cloak to reveal a hefty hunting knife strapped to her waist. Then she reached inside her tunic and pulled out a pistol, admiring it like a work of art as she balanced it effortlessly in her hand. "No one will ever abuse me again without the bloodiest fight of their life."

Dark Sun studied Fatima, wondering which of her personalities was truly in charge. Was she a Good Samaritan coming to the aid of two stricken strangers? Was she a sympathetic victim of the same plight that had befallen his two children? Was she a hardened fighter turned ruthless by the abuse of the Jackals or by the cult of the Caliphate? Was she part of a heinous scam targeting his family? Or was she a combination of all of these?

He shook his head. Regardless, they had no other option. Life wasn't a choice between wishes, it was a choice between available alternatives.

"Sunshine?" Dark Moon whispered.

Dark Sun looked at Dark Moon, whose mood seemed less grim than just a few moments ago. "Yes?"

"I can tell you don't trust Teema, and I don't either." Dark Moon glanced at Fatima sheepishly, knowing how blunt her assessment was. "But we can't just stand here fretting about the horror that Cammy and Curious must be going through. Teema's offering us hope, which is something we didn't have a few minutes ago. Let's go with her."

Dark Sun nodded. He recalled something he had read long ago. The world often trembles under the march of jackboots and the rumble of war machines, but nothing is more powerful than a wisp of hope in the heart of a hopeless man.

SIX
FEAR

We can easily forgive a child who is afraid of the dark; the real tragedy of life is when men are afraid of the light.

— Plato

Curious screamed again.
He cried out whenever the military vehicle lurched over the washboard road. Cammy squeezed his clammy hand and patted his perspiring forehead. There was nothing she could do for his injured leg. She could see from the unnatural alignment of his thigh and shin that serious damage had been done by their attackers. She wedged some army blankets around it to stabilize him, but the ride was very rough. Whenever her brother moaned, she felt a wave of regret for every time she had tormented him over the years.

They were trapped in a dark, windowless compartment in the back of the vehicle. It smelled like urine and feces because Curious had peed and defecated in his pants. There was nothing she could do about that either because any attempt to move him caused horrific agony. He would have to lie in his own excrement until . . . she had no idea when.

Two men occupied the cab of the vehicle. They were dressed in dark clothes that had no insignia. They had opened the rear compartment twice, once to toss in two bottles of water, and once to yell at Curious because of his unrelenting screaming. The two men seemed angry at them, which was incomprehensible. Sure, they had blood stains on their clothing, and they grimaced when they moved. But their injuries weren't her fault. She couldn't conceive of any reason for what was happening. She just knew there was hatred involved.

Cammy had lost all track of time, but she hadn't slept or eaten since their capture. Even if food had been available, she would have been too nauseated by the stench in their confined quarters to eat. She wretched a couple of times, but the convulsions yielded nothing more than dry heaves. Her stomach was in knots.

She feared for Curious and her parents to the point where she didn't have any emotional energy left to fear for herself. The assault on their home was quick, violent, and confusing. It was a tumult of shouting and fighting. She didn't know if her parents were still alive. There had been a dreadful explosion as their vehicle drove away from the farm, but other than the noise and the shock wave, she was oblivious to the consequences.

Cammy also had no idea where the kidnappers were taking them. When the men opened the door to toss water bottles into the back, she overheard one of them expressing concern about getting back across the river, but there were rivers everywhere. Since she couldn't see outside, she was unable to get her bearings from the orientation of the sun or the stars. Cammy had a deep passion for nature and the open range. Now, her environment was limited to a loathsome dark box.

Two awful things dawned on her as she pondered their predicament in the noxious darkness. It was possible that she was now the adult in her family and that years of maturation had been compressed into mere hours. It was also possible that none of it was going to matter for much longer.

SEVEN
ENTROPY

From star dust to bone dust
Darkness before and after
Make things better we must
Else all order will scatter

— *The Poems of Dark Sun*

Dark Moon rested on Fatima's horse while Fatima led it cautiously down the overgrown road. Dark Sun hobbled beside them. Spartacus loped easily alongside the group.

Dark Sun was tormented by the fear that his children were speeding even farther away in the kidnappers' vehicle. He felt like the tortoise chasing the hare, except he had no idea where the hare was headed or where the finish line was.

They paused to rest when they were halfway to Independence. Fatima fashioned a crude bandage for Dark Moon's head. Dark Sun fished his father's black leather journal out of the saddlebag. During their walk, he had become quite curious about its contents. He sat down under a tree and opened the journal to the first entry. His fingertips caressed the faded, musky pages once touched by his dad. A wave of intense anticipation washed over him.

Nearly three decades had elapsed since he last saw his dad. He had no pictures or videos of him, just blurred images flitting in his memory. His father had been his rock, his teacher, and his last tether to a secure world that no longer existed.

Dark Sun had been seventeen when his father was captured by the Elites in 2057. On that dreadful day, he became a man, unprepared though he was. Tears welled in his eyes as he began reading:

May 1, 2054

I became a killer today.

I had no choice. The dreaded agents of the Elites came to take my mother away. Their warrant decreed she had been assigned to a distant nursing home. Everyone who turns 70 is served one.

Years ago, the elderly submitted to the warrants. Submission was the natural order of things back then. But after too many of them were "lost in the system," families began to resist.

We suspected there weren't really any nursing homes. Wild rumors flew that the elderly were actually routed to rendering centers because the Elites had run out of money for their pensions and medical care. The rendering centers stole their valuables and cremated their bodies. It's hard to imagine such rumors are true, but I suppose that European Jews never expected a horror such as Dachau to exist.

Any horror seems possible these days. The Elites had no right to abduct my mother, regardless of what they intended to do with her. I decided not to take any chances.

When the agents presented their damn warrant, I told them I was going to fetch Mom. I returned with a shotgun instead. I had the advantage of surprise, so it was over quickly. I took their guns and burned their bodies in the old smith behind the barn. I suppose that counts as irony.

We're sending Mom to stay with relatives who have already fled to Montana. The Elites avoid that survivalist bastion, so she'll be safe, at least for a while. It's awful that the world has come to this.

Dark Sun was stunned. He dropped the journal into his lap. His father shot two men? His grandmother was hidden away? His parents said Grandma was sent to a nursing home just like other grandmothers. He wondered what else his parents hadn't told him. He resumed reading:

Nobody trusts the Elites anymore. I've been helping the underground resistance by handing out pamphlets and smuggling supplies. Until today, I wasn't a combatant.

The visit by their agents changed that. The Elites have led us down an obscene path. Our social insurance programs are bankrupt. People are starving. It's no longer about "shared sacrifice," "social justice," or any other empty platitude worth nothing more than the price of our submission. Now it's about survival, and it's clear that the Elites are interested in theirs not ours.

All hell is breaking loose. Martial law has been declared in response to the rioting and looting. They're jailing people without trial, and they're banishing malcontents to an awful place called Outcast Island.

The unfolding civil war might go on forever. The fault lines in society have rived into unbridgeable chasms. People with deep-rooted enmity are dividing up by religion, race, class, and ideology. Each faction is hell-bent on provoking, condemning, and defeating the others. The vitriol, which has been fermenting for decades, has boiled over into widespread violence. America has become a terrifying morass of mass migrations, resource conflicts, and unforgivable atrocities. Georgia, Alabama, and South Carolina voted to secede from the union in the past few months. Other southern states will be voting on it soon. Decades of cold civil war are turning into a hot civil war.

In retrospect, it's hard to imagine that our diverse factions ever coex-

isted peacefully. Maybe they never really did. Like in the first Civil War, the conflict will be settled by guns.

Lincoln famously declared that all the armies of Europe and Asia could never take a drink from the Ohio River or blaze a trail on the Blue Ridge Mountains. The only enemy that could defeat us was ourselves. Our nation would live forever, if it didn't die by suicide.

He was right. We've lost the magic elixir that was our bond. We're no longer the "United" States. We're estranged tribes killing each other. We're a nation cutting its own throat.

Long ago, experts speculated that the apocalypse would be the result of a cataclysmic event, like a nuclear holocaust, a runaway disease, cyberattacks on the grid, rogue artificial intelligence, or a climate catastrophe. Instead, it was the result of termites that devoured our civic foundation.

Now that I've become a warrior in this conflict, I suppose my fate will be that of many rebels. Eventually I'll be killed, or I'll be captured and sent to Outcast Island.

In the meantime, I'm going to record my thoughts in this journal. I'm not sure why. Perhaps it's a way for me to maintain my sanity in the chaos to come. Or maybe it's because if I don't leave behind some tangible evidence of my existence, my life will have meant nothing.

It probably means nothing anyway. Entropy always wins in the end.

The journal entry ended on that dour note. Dark Sun pondered the cold fatalism of the closing words. He vaguely recalled the implications of entropy from his father's science books. Everything in the universe is heading toward disintegration. Things break and don't fix themselves. We grow older not younger. Existence will ultimately become frigid, dark, and disordered.

The picture of his father revealed by this journal entry was far different than the father he remembered all these years. He remembered his father as a hard-working farmer and a teacher not as a killer burdened with such grim thoughts. He sighed heavily.

They resumed their slow march toward Independence as colorful leaves fluttered to the ground. It had been years since they had ventured this far from their ranch. He wondered why. Fear? Routine? It struck him how mechanical their lives had become. And now it was completely ruined. Their isolation had been a blinding illusion of normalcy.

Dark Sun was forty-four years old, the same as Dark Moon. Until yesterday, he was proud of his ability to sustain his family in difficult circumstances. He had tended their meager livestock, grew stilted crops in depleted soil and kept their deteriorating home in marginal repair.

His life had been filled with manual labor, mechanical breakdowns, and an unending string of challenges. They had no indoor plumbing, so he had to fetch water from a well. When nature called, it was off to the outhouse. Heat for cooking and comfort came from a meticulous stack of wood he had cut and split. There was little time left for anything else.

Over the years, the mundanity of their lives seeded a frustrated wanderlust in him. He harbored a simmering yearning to experience adventures beyond the limited horizon of their hermitage.

But he always knew that leaving their farm was impossible. He reluctantly buried those desires deep in his soul. His grand quests were forever limited to repairing broken fence rails and fixing the hand pump. He resigned himself to standing at the foot of a mountain of dreams that he would never climb.

In every hero lurks a coward, in every coward lurks a hero, and in every person lurks the dilemma "which shall I be?" Dark Sun had ignored that dilemma for a long time, but the kidnapping of their children punched him squarely in the face. Heroism was required now, but it seemed improbable for him. He wasn't a warrior. He was a quiet man who pondered deep thoughts while laboring on the farm.

He yearned to be a writer or a poet. He fantasized about an impossible future where his words would capture the attention of the world. But he never had time for such self-indulgence. Besides, he had no paper or utensils with which to write, and his intense contemplations were usually muddled. So his ambition to write remained unfulfilled, crowded out by the burdens of their rudimentary lifestyle. Like so many people who wrestled with the choice of pursuing dreams or succumbing to banality, Dark Sun had surrendered long ago. The contrast of his dull life against the inner fire of his suppressed ambitions had inspired his alias when they shed their birth names.

His one guilty pleasure was reading. His father had left behind a treasure trove of books in a compartment under the cellar floor. Most of the books were banned by the Elites, but there was little likelihood that they would discover his illicit collection, given the isolation of their farm.

As he devoured the books, he remembered his father, who had labored for years to educate him. The books were tantalizing surrogates for his frustrated wanderlust. Through them he explored distant horizons, learning much about science, literature, and philosophy. He was mesmerized by the stories of ancient heroes, even though their exploits amplified the staleness of his own feckless life.

He snapped out of his reverie as they crossed the arched bridge over the Verdigris River. They were headed down Main Street toward the center of Independence. It was deserted, giving it the feel of an Old West ghost town—dusty streets, ramshackle buildings, and drifting tumbleweeds.

When they passed the gothic Montgomery County Court House and the historic Booth Hotel, they came upon a parking lot of a crumbling store called Walgreens. There he saw an extraordinary sight that blew away his despondent musings about entropy and his vacuous life. He felt like Dorothy stepping out from her tornado-tossed, drab Kansas house into the vibrant extravaganza of Oz.

EIGHT
BLESSED

> Authority of any kind is blinding; it breeds thoughtlessness and engenders power. Power always becomes centralized and corrupting; it corrupts not only the wielder but also the follower.
>
> — Jiddu Krishnamurti

The hotline rang in the White House Situation Room.

Regis glanced nervously at the phone. He felt the stares of his assembled team, which included his national security advisor, homeland security advisor, White House chief of staff, and the chairman of the Joint Chiefs of Staff. They had gathered to strategize in the face of continuing battlefield losses in the civil war. The on-duty Watch Team of senior intelligence agents skulked in the background, monitoring curved banks of displays. The Watch Team assessed endless streams of classified data, including real-time access to the SIN locations and dossiers of individuals.

The phone rang again. Regis picked up the receiver. "This is the president," he announced.

"For now," said Cosimo, who was on the other end of the line. "An Outcast army has crossed into Virginia. They're setting up camp in Danville."

Regis' aching back stiffened. "I'm aware. What can I do for you, your Eminence?"

Cosimo grunted over the encrypted line. "Win the war! But since it's a steaming pile of shit, the important question is how can I help you?"

Beads of sweat broke out on Regis' wrinkled brow. When the Syndicate offered help, it wasn't in the ordinary sense. Help from them was a one-way street to self-enrichment. It didn't matter who they harmed along the way.

"Are you still there?" asked Cosimo.

"I'm here," Regis muttered. "Some tanks and airplanes would help."

There was a brief silence. "You know we don't have our own military. We use yours and many others to suit our purposes. However, I do have some capable leaders on standby . . . in case something should happen to you," Cosimo said ominously.

"I have the situation well in hand." Regis replied.

"You would say that even if the Outcasts were battering down the front door of the White House. Is that why your staff is hunkered down in the West Wing basement?"

"The Outcasts will never make it to Washington," Regis replied. "As I said before, my plan is underway."

"And how long will it take for your plan to play out?"

Regis flinched. "A few weeks, perhaps. We've hit a bit of a snag."

"Of course." A daunting silence ensued.

Regis heard Cosimo take a long drag on his cigarette. He nervously fingered the State Department's *Morning Summary* that was splayed on the table in front of him. He interrupted the nerve-wracking silence. "I could use your advice."

More silence.

"Are you still there?" Regis asked.

"Of course. The Syndicate is the only permanent institution in the world." There was a heavy sigh on Cosimo's end of the line. "What advice do you need?"

"How to deal with the Blessed."

Another heavy sigh. "What about them?"

"Many of my people have fled across the Appalachians to the Blessed monasteries along the Mississippi. I'm running out of soldiers and taxpayers."

"Naturally," said Cosimo. "The proles always follow whoever offers the shiniest vision and the most shameless promises. The Blessed are offering them a vision of kindness and the promise of eternal life in heaven. That's a tough combination to beat."

"But I've promised them equality and justice here and now!" protested Regis.

"Apparently you haven't delivered," said Cosimo. "Or what you've delivered isn't what they consider equal or just. Your real problem is that you're running out of time. Quit worrying about the Blessed."

"What do you mean?"

"Any prole who was inclined to flee your society wasn't going to help you win the war anyway. Besides, the Blessed are doing us a big favor by absorbing your defectors."

"I don't understand."

"Those who flee to the Blessed are just decent people looking for safe harbor in the Darkness. They see the Christian sect as a kindly option. They're looking for peace not more conflict. The Blessed are less likely to attack you or lust after your power than the Jackals, the Outcasts, or the Caliphate."

"But their agenda doesn't align with ours—"

"That remains to be seen," Cosimo replied. "All factions have their own agendas. And they all need money for their missions and cannon fodder for their conflicts—just like you Elites. Every faction is scrambling for the privilege to use and abuse the proles. My key point, however, is that the Blessed aren't the ones setting up field headquarters in Danville, Virginia."

"But the Blessed believe they have a God on their side! What if they use Him to convince their proles to oppose us?"

"The gods are always on the side of whoever invents them—the Greeks had Zeus, the Romans had Jupiter, the Norse had Thor, the Hindus have Brahman, the Blessed have Jesus, the Muslims have Allah, and you Elites have your Collective. The good news is that the proles never invent gods, they just obey them. Your job is to get them to obey yours. You're not doing well, by the way."

"Which god does the Syndicate prefer?"

"The Syndicate doesn't care which god gets worshipped. They're all useful to us, because their commands to renounce the ego can always be leveraged into obedience, and their zeal can never be pacified. But if you're going to lose your proles to another deity, it's better that it's the God of the Christians. If history is any guide, they'll inspire their proles to fight the Caliphate's proles. If you don't get caught between the two factions, you'll come out ahead no matter who wins. If nothing else, the Blessed will distract the Caliphate while you fight the Outcasts."

"So you're saying the Blessed are really on my side, even if my people are defecting to them?"

"No," said Cosimo bluntly. "You don't have a side, other than mine. You agreed to that a long time ago. But the Blessed have often been on the side of the Syndicate over the centuries. Their desire for self-preservation usually trumps their courage and piety. Every faction has been on our side at one time or another. Even the Caliphate. The Blessed haven't decided yet which side they're on in this civil war. Many of them are theocrats, many of them are collectivists, and some of them still believe in individual salvation. They're a very confused bunch. But the Lord works in mysterious ways, most of which involve money. Always follow the money."

"If the proles followed the money, they would end up at your doorstep," said Regis.

"They'd end up at *your* doorstep," replied Cosimo. "That's called a revolution. I, on the other hand, am invisible to the proles. The Syndicate is hidden in a complex, shadowy world that the proles will never understand or get to see. We don't succumb to revolutions or to the rise of tyrants. We instigate them.

There was a long pause before Cosimo continued. "Win the war, or we'll instigate once again." He hung up the phone.

NINE
TREASURE

> Gold, frankincense, and myrrh
> And other things people treasure
> Are all but baubles on a shelf
> Compared to freedom's wealth
>
> — *The Poems of Dark Sun*

F atima's gypsy caravan astonished Dark Sun.
There were over a hundred horse-drawn carriages decorated with wild, bohemian artwork. People were dressed in exotic yellow, orange, blue, and green patchwork clothing embroidered with intricate paisleys and brocades. Many wore arabesque headbands decorated with fresh wildflowers or costume jewelry. The scene was an explosion of intoxicating beauty. Dark Sun felt like they had magically entered the inside of a rainbow.

Children and farm animals scurried in all directions. Lively music wafted above a constant hubbub of conversation. There was a mouthwatering aroma of meat roasting on a spit. Everyone seemed carefree, as if the Darkness didn't exist for them. Dark Sun shook his head in disbelief as Fatima led them through the ebullient tribe.

She brought them to Osiris, the leader of the caravan. The tall, wiry black man wore denim trousers, a plain white tunic, and a richly colored paisley cloak clasped by an exotic medallion at the neck. He held a shepherd's crook in his right hand, likely for tending the livestock that milled about. His salt-and-pepper dreadlocks were more salt than pepper. His short, graying beard and mustache were well-manicured. He exuded vitality and confidence, even though his weathered mahogany skin showed his sixty-three years of hard living.

His dark eyes hinted at a deep sadness. As a young man, he studied philosophy at a public university in New York. He became infatuated with a radical movement on campus. Like many starry-eyed youths, he was dazzled by visions of utopia and roiled by disgust with current conditions. He wanted to change the world so badly that he engaged in violent protests against what he believed to be a repressive society.

His utopian illusions were eventually shattered. The political leaders he admired proved to be powermongers who misled their supporters into destitution, divisiveness, and chaos. His own efforts to force changes upon the world through domestic terrorism ended in tragedy when his fiancée was killed building a pipe bomb in their apartment.

Devastated, he wandered the countryside in a spiritual fog, dodging the crossfire in the civil war he had played a small role in instigating. His efforts to change the world had resulted in nothing but tragedy and sorrow. He spiraled into a dark depression and contemplated suicide.

In the depths of his despair, he had an epiphany. He didn't need to force others to change in order to make a better world. He needed to change himself. A better world wasn't made through violence or coercion, but through simple acts of kindness and wisdom.

Due to his prior brushes with the law, he had his SIN chip cut out. He chose Osiris as his alias, because in lore Osiris was the god of transition and resurrection. He connected with a few other like-minded drifters. They gradually attracted a diverse band of vagabonds whose lives had been displaced by tragedy, war, or oppression. The nomadic tribe recognized him as their leader and spiritual mentor.

The tribe members weren't gypsies in the sense of being descendants of the ancient Romani people but rather in the sense of being free-spirited itinerants who behaved and thought differently than most. They were determined to lead fulfilling lives despite the savagery of the world around them.

Fatima introduced Osiris to Dark Sun and Dark Moon. She described them as two injured people she found at the site of the mysterious explosion. She prodded Dark Moon to describe the horrific events of the night before. Osiris listened intently as she spoke. He studied the bloodied visitors and frowned with concern. He felt sympathy for the destitute couple, because he had personal experience with such anguish. "Your tale is woeful, my friends," he said after she finished. "There's no greater suffering than the loss of your children."

The couple nodded grimly, fighting back tears.

"It's our custom to help people in such distress," he continued. "Each of us came to this tribe by way of personal tragedy. Perhaps there's something we can do for you. I'll discuss the matter with our Council of Elders. In the meantime, let's take care of your wounds." He signaled to Fatima.

Fatima led the two to a carriage that served as a crude infirmary for the gypsies. A gentle Hispanic matron cleaned their wounds, administered a homemade antiseptic, and applied bandages. Then the couple followed Fatima to her carriage, where they stashed their meager belongings and napped.

That night, a large bonfire roared in the middle of the circled carriages. Pungent smoke drifted lazily over the town center. Gypsies milled about, chatting and laughing in the crisp autumn air. Osiris and Dark Sun sat together on a bench near the fire. The blaze warded off the chill of late September.

"Everyone in your caravan looks so alive," observed Dark Sun as the flames leapt into the dark sky.

"You seem surprised."

"I'm used to a life of drudgery and unfulfilled dreams. We never had much to call our own. And now our kids are gone, and our home is destroyed. We have nothing left but a dark mystery to solve."

"Why do you choose such gloom?" Osiris asked.

Dark Sun frowned. "I don't choose it. Life delivers it. Sometimes brutally."

Osiris raised an eyebrow. "Life certainly delivers disappointment and challenges. It also offers love and opportunity. Look about you."

Dark Sun surveyed the camp. Children were playing hide-and-seek. Revelers danced to guitar music. Others sat around the bonfire drinking beer and wine. Everyone was relaxed.

"I don't get it," he mused. "The world is collapsing, yet your little tribe seems unfazed. Why is that?"

"My college studies were mostly a waste of time," replied Osiris. "But I learned something very important afterward. The only reason to go on living is to love and be loved. Our tribe embraces life because we embrace each other."

"That's it? People just choose to be a happy community, and it magically happens?"

"Usually."

"So if everyone became one giant community, the world's problems would go away?"

"No, things would get much worse."

Dark Sun shook his head. He tossed a stick into the bonfire with more force than he intended. "You speak in riddles."

Osiris laughed. "We choose to live with people that we trust and care for. Usually there are about a dozen such people in our intimate circles. Beyond them are perhaps a dozen times a dozen people we're familiar enough with to value their relationship."

"I can count my close relationships on one hand," said Dark Sun. "And that includes Sparty."

Osiris laughed again. "My point is that we don't love in the abstract; we love people we know. When leaders try to force relationships between millions of strangers, our natural instinct for empathy gets crushed. Generosity is replaced by entitlement. Friendship is replaced by alienation. Accountability is replaced by hedonism. The resulting distrust, hatred, and conflict blow societies apart. I learned that the hard way as a young idealist. Everyone is learning that now in an even harder way."

"So why doesn't your little tribe blow apart?"

"Because we *chose* to band together. Humans aren't the fastest animals in the forest. We don't have big fangs or sharp claws. We don't have armored shells, deadly venom, clever camouflage, pointy horns, or protective quills. We aren't monstrous creatures of brawn and muscle. Alone, we're rather defenseless. The prospect of survival increases dramatically when parents care for their young, friends watch each other's backs, and tribemates freely exchange their talents. There's nothing more natural—or more necessary—than for humans to band together in families and tribes. We're communal beings."

In the background, Dark Sun heard a haunting melody played with violin and flute. He couldn't remember the last time he heard music. Recorded media players had long since disappeared. As the chords danced in his head, he watched some of the gypsies prepare the caravan to depart Independence. They were carrying water bags from the river, packing loads onto their animals, making minor repairs to their carriages, and stocking them with items scavenged from the deserted village.

"Where is your tribe headed?" Dark Sun asked.

"Nowhere in particular," Osiris replied. "Eventually, we'll go everywhere."

"That's exactly what Teema said."

Osiris' face brightened. "She's very astute, which I would say even if she wasn't my daughter."

"Your daughter? She's Arabic—"

"My *adopted* daughter," Osiris quickly corrected. "Not in a legal sense, since laws mean nothing now. After we found Teema wandering alone in the wilderness, starving, and abused, she stole my heart. Now I would give my life for her."

This expression of parental love stabbed Dark Sun's heart like a knife. He tried to hold back his anguish, but the tears came forth through stifled sobs and a constricted throat. The urgency to find his two children struck him like a physical blow.

Osiris, seeing his distress, put an arm around his shoulders. "You're not alone, my friend."

"We've always been alone," Dark Sun replied. "We appreciate your hospitality today, but our sole purpose right now is to find our kids."

"You're in luck," said Osiris. "I discussed your situation with the Council of Elders. They've agreed that our tribe should go treasure hunting with you and your wife. We travel widely and interact with many factions."

Dark Sun looked confused.

"We'll be hunting for three treasures," Osiris clarified. "One is named Curious, and another Cammy."

A smile spread across Dark Sun's bearded face. "Thank you! That's incredibly generous! Dark Moon will be as thrilled as I am to have help." As he spoke, it dawned on him just how magnificent the generosity of the gypsy caravan was. "I can pay you," he said to Osiris. "I have some gold—"

Osiris put up his hands and shook his head vigorously. "No! Though my people come from every race and religion, they're just like you and Dark Moon. They were all lost souls who were wounded by cruel fate. Some were kidnapped, like Teema. Some lost their families in the civil war. Some were seeking asylum from the Elites for supposed crimes. Some escaped from the Jackals and the Caliphate. Some didn't want to disappear into nursing homes. When we found each other, we found meaning. And now, we've found you and Dark Moon. The story of your children is the same as the story of our dear Teema. The elders have agreed that helping to find your children is consistent with our legacy and our mission, because nothing is more vile than human trafficking. We're rovers, so we might as well rove toward wherever your children might be. Keep your gold. Love is the currency of families. You're one of ours now."

Dark Sun shook Osiris' hand. "Your tribe has given a whole new meaning to the word *generosity*." Then he remembered his new friend said that the tribe would be hunting for three treasures. "What's the third treasure?"

"I don't know."

Dark Sun raised an eyebrow. "How will you know if you've found it?"

Osiris smiled like the Cheshire cat. "I don't know that either."

"I don't like your chances."

Osiris chuckled. "It's something of a mystery. I became intrigued about it while listening to the tales of other factions we trade with. The Outcasts have invaded the southern states from their island prison off the coast of Florida. It's rumored they've brought with them a great treasure. I want to find out what it is."

Dark Sun knew a little about the Outcasts. For decades, dictators around the world deported their undesirables to Outcast Island. He envisioned it as a hellish place, a devil's island of the world's worst criminals and rogues, a lawless land of unimaginable danger. "What treasure could those renegades have?"

Osiris sighed heavily. "There's something my tribe wants more than anything else."

"Gold?"

"No, we can trade for that," said Osiris with a glare. "But we can't trade for what we really want."

"What's that?"

"We want to live in a peaceful world safe from the Jackals, the Elites, the Caliphate, or any other faction trying to impose their will on us. We want to live in a world where the colors of our skin and the names of our gods mean nothing to others. We want to live how we choose, where we choose, and with whom we choose. We don't want to constantly wonder if there's a gang lurking beyond the next hill with hatred in their hearts and more guns than us. We want to settle into a real community, a real trading outpost, without the fear of being attacked or robbed. Even in my old age, I cling desperately to the hope that the idealism of my youth can be somehow reconciled with the reality of the human condition. That would be the greatest treasure in all of history."

"And you think the *Outcasts* have the solution?" Dark Sun smirked.

"I know the Elites don't," replied Osiris. "Their culture of coercion, envy, and hatred has plunged us into this Darkness. The Outcasts, on the other hand, are an ostracized people, just like my tribe. I'm fascinated by the waves of jubilant support they're rumored to be getting as their armies liberate millions of Southerners from the tyranny of the Elites as they sweep northward. I want to find out what inspired their passion and success despite their horrific circumstances on Outcast Island.

"And I'm intrigued that they call themselves the Warriors of Pathless Land."

TEN
AUDREY (DARK MOON)

When I let go of what I am, I become what I might be. When I let go of what I have, I receive what I need.

— Lao Tzu, *Tao Te Ching*

Audrey glanced nervously at the clock on the wall.

It was almost one in the morning. She was thirteen years old and was never allowed to stay up this late. Farming families went to bed early and got up early.

But there was a problem tonight. Her Mom and Dad had gone to Independence that morning to buy supplies. They always returned before dark. But not today.

Earlier in the evening Audrey and her older sisters, Katarina and Angelica, had walked down the road to the neighboring farm where her friend James lived. He was the same age as Audrey. His older brother, Kieran, was the same age as Katarina. James and Audrey had a budding but unspoken puppy love between them. Katarina and Kieran had a more serious relationship. There weren't many other teens in the area to develop relationships with.

Tonight's visit by the three sisters wasn't a romantic one. They were gravely concerned about their parents. Rumors were spreading that an armed contingent from the Elites had arrived in Independence to root out a rebel cell embedded near the shopping district.

Their parents weren't combatants in the unfolding civil war, but they were shoppers.

There had been a rumbling of distant explosions that rolled across the open prairie from Independence and an orange glow lit the nighttime sky above the town. The sisters knew something terrible was happening.

When they got to their neighbor's, the three girls begged James and Kieran's father to go to Independence to check on their parents. It was a small farming community, so the father readily agreed to help his longtime neighbors. He and his wife Mary departed immediately on horseback.

They were still gone, after several hours. It was 12:58 AM now. Audrey began to worry about them too.

"This is so awful!" Audrey exclaimed to no one in particular. She was brutally tired. She had reached the end of her patience and composure. Her blue eyes began to swim in tears.

Angelica rubbed her shoulder. "I can't stand it either," she said. "I can't stand any of it. The war is moving closer and closer to us. We can hear the explosions now. Maybe it will engulf us tonight. Who knows what our world will look like after that? I'm praying for Mom and Dad, and for everyone else in Independence tonight."

"What good are prayers?" asked Kieran. He had little regard for Katarina's two sisters. To him, Angelica was a maudlin evangelist and Audrey was an unpredictable nonconformist. "Law and order doesn't come from prayers. It comes from police and soldiers with batons and guns."

Angelica looked at him in horror. She burst into tears. "You're an awful person! The whole world is awful now. That's why I'm leaving for Memphis. I'm going to tell Mom and Dad when they get back!"

Audrey and Katarina were stunned by their sister's surprise announcement. Memphis was the theological and tactical headquarters of the Blessed faction, which was establishing a growing presence up and down the Mississippi. They knew Angelica was enraptured by Christianity, but Memphis was a long way from their ranch in Kansas, in so many ways.

"Will running away to a monastery solve your problems? Or the world's problems?" Katarina asked Angelica with a tinge of acid in her voice.

"I'm not like you or your boyfriend," she replied as the rumble of another explosion boomed from Independence. "I'm not looking to solve the world's problems. I just want to be with people who are kind and good."

The room fell silent as everyone processed Angelica's sudden revelation, which was now piled onto their brutal anxiety about all four parents. Audrey in particular took Angelica's announcement hard. From her simple teenage perspective, the world was becoming increasingly unstable and frightening. Her usual reaction was to cling ever more desperately to the people whom she loved. But the harder she tried to cling, it seemed the more unstable things got. And tonight, the instability was ratcheting upward exponentially.

"You can't leave!" Audrey cried to Angelica. "We need each other more than ever! Especially if..."

She couldn't bring herself to finish her sentence. She glanced at the clock on the wall again. It was 1:17 AM.

Katarina cleared her throat to get everyone's attention. "Since we're all here together, Kieran and I have an announcement to make too."

Audrey glanced at James knowingly. They had talked many times about what was likely to come from their older siblings' deepening relationship. Then she looked away quickly, because she harbored a secret wish about her own future with James.

"We're moving to Washington," Katarina announced summarily. "To join the Elites."

James' jaw dropped.

"How dare you?" shouted Audrey. Something in her snapped. This wasn't the announcement she expected. Her oldest sister had been her playmate, her best friend, and her confidant ever since she could remember, at least up until a couple of years ago when Katarina's relationship with Kieran began to intrude. Since then she had been spending less and less time with Audrey as she and Kieran became increasingly involved in political matters. And now Katarina was leaving the family. For the worst possible reason. At the worst possible time. This was the final act of the destruction of her relationship with Katarina.

Katarina glared back at her coldly. "I can't stand to waste away here in Kansas anymore with so much at stake."

"But that's exactly why you need to stay!" exclaimed Audrey. "Everything's at stake *here*! Many of our neighbors already left for Montana. Angelica says she's going to Memphis. And Mom, Dad . . . "

Once again, she couldn't finish her sentence. She burst into sobs. James awkwardly put his arm on her heaving shoulders. It was now 1:24 AM.

"There's nothing at stake on this godforsaken prairie," Kieran said, coming to Katarina's defense. "The power is in Washington. The power to help everyone. The power to change the world."

"Change the world?" shouted Audrey. "The Elites are blowing up Independence right now! That's where my parents are tonight!"

"Dad is going to hate you for joining the Elites," James said to Kieran, shooting him an antagonistic look that made it clear this decision meant their relationship was over too. "You know where his sympathies lie."

"Of course I know!" Kieran said, his chin held high. "But he's wrong. He's wrong about everything."

"Said every teenager in history," shot back James, who had watched his brother's youthful insolence torment his parents for years.

Kieran moved to pummel his younger brother one last time, but Katarina put a restraining hand on his arm. "History will be on our side," she said soothingly.

"You can't do this to our families!" Audrey exclaimed through her tears.

The sound of footsteps on the porch interrupted their argument. Suddenly, the room went silent. Then the front door opened.

James breathed a sigh of relief at the sight of his parents in the doorway.

Then Audrey screamed. She knew immediately. She knew from the tears in Mary's eyes. She knew from the slump of the father's shoulders. She knew from their reluctance to step into the room, or to even utter a word.

Her familiar world had evaporated in the blink of an eye. Order and chaos had changed places once again. Her innocence was gone.

ELEVEN
OUTCASTS

>We're quite different, you and me
>Thru colored lens the world we see
>Yet we both love and breathe and eat
>Hoping our paths will peacefully meet
>
>— *The Poems of Dark Sun*

It dawned on Dark Moon and Dark Sun that they were looking for a needle in a haystack.

They watched the diverse gypsies prepare to depart Independence. They were grateful for the nomads' help, but finding their kids seemed like an impossible task. The haystack was potentially as large as an entire nation.

The two were huddled together inside what used to be a Greyhound bus stop. The wooden bench was pocked with termite holes, and the awning was rusted through. Along Main Street, golden rays of an autumn sunrise glinted off broken windows and pointless street signs.

Some of the buildings had collapsed, casualties of neglect and attacks by the Elites long ago.

To distract her troubled mind, Dark Moon asked Dark Sun to read aloud from his father's journal. She was curious about it and hoped his soothing voice would ease her anxiety. He opened the book to the spot marked by the white rose and began.

June 9, 2054

They arrested Jed Starnes today.

He was one of the few rebels who refused to carve the SIN chip out of his ribs. He even flaunted his real name, proudly affirming his identity while the rest of us hid behind pseudonyms. He called it bravery. We called it foolishness. It turns out we were right.

If he's lucky, they'll kill him quickly during interrogation. If he's unlucky, they'll banish him to Outcast Island. Rumors are that millions of captured rebels have been exiled there.

The concept of Outcast Island was hatched by world leaders after the collapse of Cuba. It became a hellhole of anarchy and starvation. Refugees fled the island in anything that floated. Many who stayed behind were slaughtered by savage gangs contending for food and dominion.

In the meantime, governments around the globe were battling riots and insurrections, so they needed to purge dissidents and criminals from their societies. Since they didn't have enough prisons to hold them, and they didn't have the audacity to build gulags, they conspired to use Cuba as a dumping ground for their human flotsam. It was better to quietly dispose of their misfits into the Cuban netherworld than to further inflame the uprisings in their homelands with trials and executions of rebel martyrs.

The Cuban dumping ground was nicknamed Outcast Island. Flotillas from around the world jettisoned incorrigibles onto its shores. The World Order, a feckless international body of diplomats, apologists, and appeasers that nominally policed the globe, organized a naval cordon around the island to ensure that the Outcasts could never escape.

I imagine Cuba to be a modern-day devil's island. There's likely no food, industry, or social order. The Outcasts speak different languages, believe in different gods, and are of different races, classes, and cultures. They're surely embroiled in hate-filled battles over scarce resources.

I don't know whether Jed Starnes is dead or exiled. What's the difference? Death and banishment both lead to entropic oblivion. Despite his bravery, Jed couldn't beat entropy, which is the enemy of all living things. Nobody can.

The journal entry ended on the same dour note as the first. "That was pretty dark," observed Dark Moon. "I was hoping for something uplifting. I don't remember your father being so morose."

"Neither do I. He hid it well," replied Dark Sun. He pondered his father's fixation with entropy. He knew from his dad's books that entropy is the cruelest aspect of existence. It continually assaults the order called life. Cell replications cause DNA errors. Accidents damage flesh and bone. Diseases corrupt normal body functions. Toxins ravage organs. After enough damage occurs, cells stop metabolizing glucose and oxygen. Then everything shuts down and the body dies. In the meantime, life is toil. It's a continual effort to extract energy from the environment to create a bodily order that can only be temporary because no order can ever be permanent. Life is pushing a rock up a dreary hill until you can't push anymore. Then it rolls over you, and you become food for maggots.

We're just figurines made of sand, just brief flashes of order and meaning, Dark Sun concluded. We emerge from random bits of matter when we're born, struggle mightily while we're alive, only to become random bits of matter again after death.

Dark Moon snapped him out of his silent despondence. "Curious has a smile touched by God," she murmured. "I need to see that smile again." She looked up at him with red-rimmed blue eyes that stabbed his heart.

He stroked her blond hair. "We'll see it again, Moonbeam." But his words rang hollow in his own mind even before they escaped his lips. He consoled himself by reflecting on his son's contagious smile. It was born of pure joy. The boy was a whirlwind of playfulness. Even when he taunted his sister or swiped a treat before dinner, it was hard to get mad at him. The sparkle in his brown eyes and his array of impish expressions were disarming.

And now he was gone. Dark Sun couldn't stop imagining horrific things happening to his children. He conjured soul-churning images of torture and abuse inside the mysterious vehicle that swallowed them.

Spartacus was vexed by the same anxiety. He circled the bus stop, peering forlornly in all directions, sniffing the pavement for a scent of the two children and his companion Brutus.

Sparty put his head on Dark Sun's lap and looked up at him imploringly. Dark Sun scratched the German shepherd between his ears. "Osiris will help us find Cammy and Curious," he said to Dark Moon. "He even calls them his treasures."

Once the caravan got underway, the movement was cathartic for the two forlorn parents. It implied purpose, which countered the despair of passivity. As the caravan of horses, farm animals, and carriages snaked along the road, Dark Moon began to hope that just beyond the horizon something good would happen, if only by the sheer power of the wandering band's intent. She rode in a carriage with Fatima, who had pinned colorful wildflowers to her headband as a vivid contrast to her dark hair and brown skin. To call it a carriage was something of a misnomer, but there was no better word. The gypsies had scavenged carcasses of vehicles that had been abandoned for lack of fuel. These trucks, vans, and trailers were repurposed as crude mobile homes that were pulled along by horses.

The carriages were adorned with intricate, hand-woven buntings and draperies. The walls were painted with wild bohemian swirls of pastels. They housed an eclectic potpourri of furnishings. Intricately crafted knick-knacks lent a wisp of luxury. Nothing matched, everything was second-hand, and yet the cramped carriages exuded the warm and comforting aura of home.

"Where are we going?" Dark Moon asked Fatima.

"East."

"Why east?"

"If the Elites kidnapped your children, they're almost certainly heading that way. They still have outposts scattered between here and Washington. Osiris is going to chat with some of their agents that he's traded with before. One of them may know something about your children."

It dawned on Dark Moon that she didn't know what lay between here and Washington. She had lost all sense of the constantly shifting American cartography. Her family had hunkered down on their Kansas ranch for so long that they were unaware of which factions now controlled which regions. The ongoing civil war had jumbled everything. The Elites were retreating to their stronghold east of the Appalachians. The armies invading from Outcast Island were aligning with the rebel faction in the South. The Caliphate was conquering the Midwest from their base in Michigan. The Blessed were spreading up and down the Mississippi from their base near Memphis. The Jackals were overrunning the Southwest from their base in Mexico. The Northwest remained an ungoverned refuge for survivalists.

Traditional state borders were hopelessly obsolete. New borders were ephemeral, lasting only as long as an occupying faction could hold a swath of land. The constantly shifting borders were impossible to keep track of, especially since there was no longer a central authority to arbitrate and record such things.

It was fortuitous that Dark Moon and Dark Sun had joined one of the thousands of nomadic tribes. The roving bands served as a thin line of glue that barely connected a fractured society. They facilitated exchange of information and goods between the conflicting fiefdoms. Since the nomads didn't lay claim to any territory, most of the factions interacted peacefully with them.

"Will our journey be dangerous?" Dark Moon asked. She was still haunted by memories of black-clad intruders ransacking their home and snatching their children.

"Probably," said Fatima so matter-of-factly that Dark Moon wondered if she understood her question.

"You're not frightened?"

Fatima looked at her with dark, world-weary eyes. "I've faced almost every evil imaginable, and yet here I am. I've learned not to trust most people, especially men, but I'm not afraid of anyone."

"Not even as we head toward the main battlegrounds of the civil war?"

"No. Wars are mostly a threat to people with attachments."

Dark Moon furrowed her brow. "Attachments? To what?"

"Ideologies. Religions. Territories. Possessions."

"Gypsies aren't attached to such things?"

"We're attached to protecting each other and finding happiness," replied Fatima. "We're also attached to trading, which is how we survive."

Dark Moon thought about life on their farm. Her family's attachments were similar. They yearned to grow food, fend off wild animals, and read the many books left behind by Dark Sun's father. It would have been helpful to trade their extra food for things they couldn't make, but there was no one around to trade with.

"What if others get attached to what *you* have?" Dark Moon asked.

Fatima laughed. "That's the abridged version of human history. There are vile people who'd rather take than trade. Innocent folks have to join with like-minded people to defend against the aggressors. Our tribe stays on the move and offends no one. We trade for guns and ammo, and we're all trained to shoot. Security is an illusion without self-defense. That's why porcupines have quills, turtles have shells, and we have weapons. You'll be trained to shoot, just like the rest of us."

"Will you be training me?"

"No. See that man up ahead?" Fatima pointed toward a stark figure flanking the caravan on horseback alongside a shapely female rider with fiery red hair.

Dark Moon examined the tall, broad-shouldered man who had unruly brown hair billowing from underneath a cowboy hat. He wore jeans and a leather vest. He had a pistol holstered on his hip and a rifle sheathed in his saddle. The man turned and stared directly at Dark Moon, as if sensing her gaze. She shivered at the harshness of his chiseled face and the chill of his cold stare.

"Who's he?" she asked.

"Hawkeye," replied Fatima. "He's from Appalachia. He's a man of few words and fewer weaknesses. He was trained by the Elites to be an assassin. The Elites originally deployed him in the Middle East to assassinate terrorist leaders. Then he was assigned to hunt dissidents in America. Being ordered to kill fellow citizens shattered his blind patriotism. The only apparent crime of his victims was that they disagreed with the direction the Elites were taking the country. Once he realized he was murdering innocents, he fled. He defected and joined our caravan many years ago. Osiris trusts him with his life."

"Who's the woman riding with him?" Dark Moon asked.

Fatima frowned. "Ruby. She's trouble. She's Hawkeye's girlfriend. She also defected from the Elites. She was an interpreter at the World Order building in New York. Some say she was really a double agent who used her sexuality for personal gain. She led a life of adventure, hedonism, and rich perks. Her duplicity was eventually discovered, but she fled before she could be captured. She wandered the country with other defectors who became involved with contraband dealers in order to survive. She met Osiris when he traded drugs acquired from the Jackals for weapons she and her cohorts had acquired from the Caliphate. He saw something in her that no one else did and invited her to join the caravan. She was attracted to Hawkeye immediately; she felt safe in his company, and he had a certain animal magnetism. He's a simple man, though, and Ruby often blurs the lines of their relationship when she flirts with other tribe members. Nobody trusts her, except Hawkeye and my father. I think they're both naïve."

Fatima and Dark Moon rode in silence for a while, watching the Kansas prairie roll by. They saw scant evidence of civilization, except for an occasional abandoned farmhouse. After many miles, the caravan veered south. "I thought we were heading east," Dark Moon said.

"We have to head south into what used to be Oklahoma to pick up old Highway 44. After that we'll head east again toward St. Louis to cross the only remaining bridge across the Mississippi."

"Is Oklahoma safe?"

"No," replied Fatima sharply. "It's controlled by the Mexican drug lords. They're human traffickers, which I know from personal experience. But Osiris is hoping they might know something about your children."

Dark Moon's heart raced. She was tantalized by the prospect of getting information about Curious and Cammy. She was terrified that the information would be awful. She had heard horrific tales about the Jackals years ago, and Fatima had said she was raped by them. Her whole body tensed. She dreaded the potential for more conflict, but time was running out and they had to do something . . . anything to find her children.

They rode in silence for a while longer. Just when Dark Moon was becoming mesmerized by unbroken miles of prairie grass, she spotted a dust plume shaped like a rooster tail on the horizon. It was a rare but tell-tale sign of vehicles racing across the land.

Fatima spotted the dust plume too. Her face suddenly went grim. She reached inside her tunic and pulled out a pistol with practiced swiftness.

TWELVE
ZEROES

Law has ceased to be an antidote for chaos; it has become chaos.

— Joseph Sobran

The vehicle suddenly stopped.

Cammy heard their two aggravated captors talking outside the rear door. She slid beside Curious, ready to shield him. The last time the injured men opened the door, they threatened to beat him if he didn't stop crying.

The locking mechanism turned. The door opened, and daylight poured in. Cammy squinted against the sudden brightness. A silhouette loomed in the doorway. As her eyes adjusted, she saw that the man had something in his hand.

"Are you going to kill us?" she asked. It was the first time she had spoken to them.

"That depends." The man peered into the semi-darkness. His gaze lingered where Curious lay curled in a heap of army blankets. "Will that brat ever stop crying?"

"He's crying because you broke his leg! Why are you doing this to us?"

A malignant smile creased the shadowed face of her captor. "I was ordered to. That's all the reason I need."

Cammy rose to her knees, the sunlight reflecting off her fierce blue eyes. Her platinum hair was a wild, tangled mess. Her fists were balled. "Where are my parents?"

The man eyed Cammy up and down, staring where he shouldn't for much too long. Cammy's eyes had adjusted, so she could see the vague outline of a jagged scar marring his cheek. "They're gone, bitch," Scarface said. "They can't protect you now."

Cammy wrapped her arms across her chest and sank back to the floor, frightened by the lecher's ogling. She suddenly felt like a mere object, a dehumanized plaything of mysterious others. It was as if she had been living in a snow globe her whole life. This was her first time getting a glimpse of the giant alien world that existed outside their ranch in Kansas. It was populated by vile creatures who seemed eager to flip her snow globe upside down and shake it for their perverse amusement.

"I hate you!" Cammy spat out.

Scarface laughed. "You're a stupid little girl! It don't matter what you think or feel. You two are just zeroes, sitting in your own piss and wondering if you're going to live or die."

"I'm not a zero!"

"Tell me that after I have my way with you."

A deep voice came from behind her tormentor. "Give it a rest, asshole. We're on a deadline, and our mission is fucked up enough already. The sooner we get back, the sooner we get patched up."

Scarface saluted his accomplice with his middle finger and then turned back to Cammy. "This ain't over, sweetie. I'll be thinking about you. A lot."

Almost as an afterthought, he looked at the brown paper sack he still held in his hand. He paused for a moment as if debating with himself. Then he tossed it toward Cammy. He slammed the door shut with a resounding clang.

In the darkness, Cammy stared where the sack had landed. She wished it would disappear, even though she couldn't actually see it anymore. But then a new smell intermingled with the miasma of urine and feces that suffused the compartment. It was the aroma of food.

Suddenly, Cammy had a glimmer of hope. For some reason, the captors wanted to keep her and Curious alive.

Maybe they weren't zeros after all.

THIRTEEN
JAMES (DARK SUN)

> Dark times lie ahead of us, and there will come a time when we must choose between what is easy and what is right.
>
> — J. K. Rowling

"What are you doing, Dad?"

James had just come down the steps into the basement of their ranch, looking for his father. He knew to look there, because his Dad had been spending a lot of time in the basement lately. He was surprised, though, to see his father hurriedly conceal something. He had a guilty look on his face.

"I'm doing what I should have done a long time ago," his father replied. He looked at his seventeen-year-old son sadly.

"Dad, are you okay?"

His father looked alternately at James and the floor, as if wrestling with whether or not to reveal something of great importance. "I've never been better."

James noticed an unfamiliar grey metal container on the floor. "What's in there?" he asked, pointing at the box.

"Nothing. Yet."

"There's more trouble in Independence today," said James. "Rumor has it that the Elites are searching for rebels again. Is that what's bothering you? I know you've been going to meetings—"

"Kieran and Katarina are leading the search party," his father observed darkly. "But everything is as it should be. James, I think you should go visit Audrey today. You know how nervous she gets when the Elites show up here. I don't think she's ever gotten over the death of her parents."

"She hasn't," James agreed solemnly. "She'll be haunted by it forever. Almost everyone dear to her is gone. I think she's afraid we'll be next. And she's never forgiven Katarina for joining the faction that killed their parents."

"Nor have I forgiven Kieran."

"Dad, I wish you'd stop going to those meetings—"

"Go see Audrey. Now!"

There was something in how his father said these words that alarmed him. It was almost as if his dad knew more than he was willing to tell. Far more.

"Dad, is there something I can do to help—"

"James, listen carefully. I've tried hard to teach you everything I know. Finish reading all of the books I've stashed. I've collected them at great personal risk. Promise me you'll read every one. That's the only thing you can do for me now."

"That seems rather useless, with the Darkness and all—"

"That's precisely why those books are so important!" his father said with blazing eyes. "People will need great wisdom to overcome the Darkness."

James swallowed hard. A part of him wanted to believe that there was wisdom and heroism in his future. The bigger part of him looked at the unfolding tragedies all around them and saw a future filled with sadness and catastrophe. "I'm afraid you're going to be disappointed in me."

"That's entirely up to you. As Chesterton told us, life glitters like a diamond, but is as fragile as glass. Glitter or break. It's your choice. It's the only real freedom we have."

"Your choices haven't accomplished much!" James lashed out in frustration. "You're hiding here in the basement while the thugs search for rebels." He paused, then his eyes widened. "You know they're coming for you, don't you—"

"You're absolutely right about my lack of accomplishments," replied his father with his head held high. "Remember this moment. Remember that we don't exist to live on our knees. Remember that life glitters like a diamond. It will help you understand what's about to happen."

James looked at him with grave concern. It seemed that his father had lost touch with reality. James felt helpless. "I think you're right about what you said earlier. I should go check on Audrey." He abruptly went upstairs, put on his coat, and trudged out the door into the November snow. His girlfriend had been staying with an aunt since the death of her parents, but her heart lay with his family. She spent most of her time hanging out with James and studying with him.

His father remained in the basement, frozen in his chair. He stared in the direction of his departed son. He shook his head, wistfully noting the lack of a proper goodbye. After a few moments, he turned back to the journal he had covered up when his son intruded.

Hours later, after the Elites' thugs finished their searches and left the area, James returned home in the darkness.

His mother met him at the door. "The blackshirts took your father away," was all she said before collapsing into his arms in tears.

Two brutal thoughts assaulted him as he held his sobbing mother. Life is as fragile as glass. And he had ruined the goodbye that his father somehow knew was necessary.

FOURTEEN
JACKALS

> Beware devils without souls
> Brigands, hearts dark as coals
> Hunters, raptors, carnivores all
> Waiting hungrily for prey to fall
>
> *— The Poems of Dark Sun*

Hawkeye spied the dust of approaching vehicles.
He spurred his horse to a gallop, and then fell into pace beside Osiris, who was chatting in the lead carriage with Dark Sun. Hawkeye gestured toward the southern horizon. Osiris looked across the sere landscape and nodded in comprehension.

Osiris signaled for the caravan to halt. He and Dark Sun jumped to the ground; Spartacus followed. Hawkeye dismounted from his horse. The two gypsies readied their rifles. Other gypsies poured from their carriages, alarmed by the sudden halt.

Four ancient Humvees with turreted machine guns emerged into clear view at the leading edge of the gritty dust cloud. The vehicles slowed to a stop about fifty paces from Osiris and Hawkeye. Armed men leapt from the Humvees and pointed their guns at the caravan. Others manned the machine guns. A hundred gypsy rifles aimed at them in response.

A swarthy, barrel-chested man strutted toward the head of the caravan, unconcerned about the rifles pointed at him. His leather-vested torso was crisscrossed with bandoliers. An unruly mane of black hair overflowed a black bandana. Jagged scars disfigured his bare arms and mustachioed face. His shoulders were covered with MS-13 gang tattoos.

"¿*Quien eres tu?*" he asked in a gruff Hispanic accent.

Osiris stepped forward. "I'm Osiris. This is my gypsy tribe. Who are you?"

"*El Asesino*," the man grunted. Scowling, he switched to English. "You're trespassing."

Osiris gestured toward the four turreted machine guns aimed at him. "Is this how you welcome peaceful traders to Oklahoma?"

"This isn't Oklahoma anymore," El Asesino snarled. "It's Republica del Norte now. Go back where you came from."

"We mean no harm," persisted Osiris. "What faction are you with?" He was quite certain he knew based on the bandit's tattoos and his vehicles, which were owned only by sophisticated outlaws and the Elites.

El Asesino held his chin high. "The Jackals. You must leave. El Norte is ours once again."

Osiris nodded slowly, buying time to think. The Jackals were a violent cabal of Mexican and Central American drug lords. They were the marauding vanguard of a Hispanic tidal wave that had poured across the undefended southern border into Texas, Arizona, New Mexico, and now Oklahoma. Mixed among them were Islamic radicals that used the southern border as a gateway to a collection of jihadist cells further north that eventually coalesced into the Caliphate.

The migration happened so fast and on such a large scale that the political structure and culture in the southwestern states perished in its bow wave. It was akin to how the barbarians overran ancient Rome—the invaders didn't become Romans, the empire simply weakened and then collapsed under their pressure.

Ironically, the immigrants poured into the same area that Mexico had ceded to the U.S. in 1848 at the end of the Mexican-American War. Most of the Mexicans already living in the El Norte territory in 1848 remained after it was ceded, because it had been their homeland for hundreds of years. The towns, rivers, and other geographic features of the southwestern states retained their Hispanic names after America took possession.

When Hispanic immigration into the Southwest mushroomed during the twenty-first century, non-Hispanic Americans began retreating to states north and east. Because of these demographic, cultural, and linguistic shifts, the region was slowly alienated from the rest of the country. By 2053, it had been conquered by Hispanics without a shot being fired. The civil war raging in other regions of America prevented the Elites from deploying troops to halt the annexation.

The new El Norte region in America was ungoverned. The Mexican government had collapsed decades before due to corruption, gang warfare, and civil unrest. During the ensuing anarchy, millions were murdered, and a rapacious mafia known as the Jackals arose. The loose confederation of drug lords and human traffickers now controlled Central America and the lawless territory that used to be the Southwestern United States.

The Jackals had no political structure beyond gangland rules. They had no practical restraints on their brutality. Right or wrong was determined by whoever wielded the most vicious force. They were merciless oligarchs hell-bent on acquiring wealth and earthly delights. They spread their gangland despotism mile by brutal mile as they migrated northward, much like how Genghis Kahn's Mongolian hordes swept across Asia centuries before.

Osiris had nodded his head in stony contemplation long enough to formulate a strategy. "I assume you know El Chapo," he said to El Asesino.

The mention of El Chapo startled the bandit. El Chapo was the shadowy kingpin of the Jackals. He was a dark, brooding, killer magnificently fit to lead a ruthless cartel of gangsters. El Asesino took a slight step backward. "You know him?"

"I've traded with him many times," said Osiris. "Those weapons you're aiming at us probably passed through our hands."

The bandit squinted at Osiris. "Prove it!"

"Look at the base of your rifle stock. You should see a tiny emblem of an eagle etched there. That's the mark we emboss on the weapons we trade."

El Asesino examined his rifle butt. He grudgingly nodded his assent to Osiris. A thin smile cracked his scarred face. "Then we're not enemies. Why are you here?"

"We're heading to St. Louis to cross the Mississippi. We're searching for two kidnapped children." Osiris beckoned Dark Sun. "Describe your kids for this gentleman. Maybe he knows something."

Dark Sun described Curious and Cammy in detail, feeling sharp pangs of anger as he did so. Fatima had told him and Dark Moon that she was raped by the human-trafficking Jackals as a young girl. He couldn't help but picture this vulgar man doing something horrific to his own daughter.

El Asesino glared at Dark Sun. "You have *two* kids?"

"Yes."

"That's illegal in your stupid country," smirked the bandit.

"I don't care," Dark Sun replied.

El Asesino eyed Dark Sun. His hesitation made Dark Sun suspect he knew something. "I can't help you," the bandit finally grunted. "I haven't seen your runts."

"They were snatched two days ago from Kansas," said Osiris. "We suspect the Elites took them. If so, they must have headed toward the bridge at St. Louis."

The bandit hesitated again. "A military vehicle raced through here heading west three days ago. We followed it to make sure it left El Norte."

Osiris raised an eyebrow. "Did it return this way?"

"I don't know, Señor." He shrugged his shoulders nonchalantly.

Dark Sun's heart raced. He was certain El Asesino knew more. The gangster's body language made it seem like this was a game. Dark Sun loathed the way such animals propagated violence and mistreated children like young Fatima. He shuddered, then clenched his fists. He didn't believe that a predator like El Asesino could tell the truth. The rage percolating inside him for the past two days erupted. "Did anybody try to sell two kids to your faction?" Dark Sun blurted out.

El Asesino scowled. "What are you accusing me of?"

The bandit spat on the ground and turned his back. Then he spun to face Osiris again. "You're a black man. The gringos abused your race even more than they abused mine. Why are you helping him?" He gestured disdainfully toward Dark Sun.

Osiris waved his arm toward the long line of gypsies watching the drama with great interest. "As you can see, I help people of all races. There will never be peace in the world until our differences in color and creed no longer inspire hatred and violence."

El Asesino unleashed a guttural laugh. "There will always be violence," he replied. He climbed into a Humvee and gunned the engine. His henchmen followed, roiling up another dust storm.

The gypsies made camp for the evening. Dark Sun was in a foul mood. He was frustrated that the sun was setting on another day without clues about his children. He wandered away with a lantern and a blanket to find some solitude and to read the next entry of his father's journal. He climbed a hill overlooking the camp. He opened the journal to the spot marked by the white rose.

. . .

JAMES KEENA

June 16, 2054

My youngest son asked me today what he should be when he grows up.

The question was hard to answer because the future is dark and uncertain. So I lied. I told him to keep studying my books, because the world will need wise men. I should have told him to be an undertaker because their services are in high demand in this shitty world.

People pretend the world is moving forward, but it's sliding backward. I laugh when I read old predictions about the glorious future that has become our profane present.

Earlier generations predicted that we'd be coddled by marvels of technology by now. Robots would do our bidding, machines would do our thinking, and starships would explore the cosmos. They imagined we'd be awash in creature comforts, people would live longer, and peace and prosperity would be our perpetual heritage.

They were dead wrong.

Sure, we developed clever robots, brilliant thinking machines, and sophisticated starships. But of what value are robots if we're just as subservient to masters as the automatons are? How are we different from thinking machines if the Elites monitor all our thoughts and try desperately to control them? Of what value are journeys to other planets if we can't live peaceably on this godforsaken one?

The robots, thinking machines, and starships are now useless contraptions, made obsolete by civil war and a dysfunctional society.

We succumbed to the vain delusion that society was animated solely by machines and by the methods of distributing their output. We forgot that our real vitality was the ambition of flesh-and-blood individuals to invent, craft, and develop our abundance.

We were once the most productive country in history. Then our society cannibalized itself. We taxed away income, plundered assets, and demonized success. We bit the apple of government succor and crawled into cocoons of parasitic victimhood. A couple of generations later, the inevitable result was catastrophic poverty. We reduced ourselves to beggary.

Our country forgot that entropy is a buzzard, a vulture, a jackal. It skulks in the background of life, waiting for prey to falter. Machines will break down without repairs and fresh parts. Prosperity can't survive sloth, envy, and finger-pointing. Darkness awaits societies that don't reward achievement, risk-taking, and innovation.

Abundance doesn't fall out of the sky like manna from heaven. Continual effort is required to keep entropy at bay. For progress to happen, more value must be created than consumed.

Today's world isn't the glorious marvel that futurists once fancied. The present Darkness is a cesspool of moral, intellectual, and economic austerity.

What do I tell my son the next time he asks about the future? The truth is that things are only going to get worse.

Dark Sun had an eerie feeling reading about himself as written by his father thirty years ago. His dad seemed a lot smarter now and had an uncanny prescience about the future.

Dark Moon and Spartacus ascended the hill. She slid quietly beside him onto the blanket and nestled her head on his shoulder. Spartacus lay down next to them. Dark Sun extinguished the lantern and reached his arm around her. They sat motionless, grateful for their shared intimacy in an increasingly alien and frightful world.

They gazed at the gypsies below, who were going through their evening routines. A small band of musicians struck up a tune. The melody floated up into the night air. The haunting music was soothing; it momentarily masked their fear and pain. Dark Moon nestled deeper into Dark Sun's embrace. They swayed in unison to the hypnotic music.

The gypsies began to dance; a few at first, then many more. The music became upbeat and more frantic. The gypsies twirled and cavorted at the behest of the infectious strains. The wild, fanciful music of the gypsies was all that was right with life. More precisely, it *was* life. It fulfilled the need to triumphantly drink nectar wrested from a hostile environment, to celebrate the sensual nature of being, to answer the question "why" with a resounding "for the sheer joy of it!" The beat of the music and the beat of the gypsy hearts were as one.

A particular dancer caught Dark Sun's attention. It was Ruby, the red-haired sprite. She gyrated with magnificent athleticism. She arched and leapt like an acrobat. Many men paused to admire her sensual movements. She spun an erotic symphony of lithe choreography and come-hither gestures. Dark Sun was mesmerized by the primal allure pouring from her.

Dark Moon noticed the hypnotic dancer too. She also noticed the effect that Ruby had on her husband. The magical spell of their intimacy evaporated into the thin air like a dream interrupted by a loud noise. A chill swept over her as the September night pressed upon them. She remembered her missing children and their desperate situation.

"Do you remember how Cammy danced?" she asked, hoping to distract her husband from Ruby and to divert her own mind from her despairing thoughts.

The question had its intended effect. Dark Sun's head filled with images of his daughter twirling like a ballerina, prancing and giggling as if yesterday and tomorrow meant nothing, as if that very moment was the most important in all of existence. He saw her smile, a gorgeous neon splash of unadulterated joy that lit up the world. He saw her blue eyes glittering with the twinkle of a thousand hopes and dreams. He imagined her plunging into his waiting arms when she ended her wild dance. He heard her whisper "I love you, Daddy."

In the dreamlike imagery of his beautiful daughter, he saw part of the answer to his father's despondent musings about entropy. Life is more than an endless descent into death and darkness. How else to explain the look on Cammy's face as she hugged him? How else to explain the emotional jolt of her whispered love? How else to explain the bittersweet tears in his eyes right now?

Dark Sun hugged Dark Moon again. They laid down on the

blanket as the music played on. Sparty curled up alongside them. The two lovers fell asleep on the barren hill in each other's arms, momentarily oblivious to a sinister world that they were just beginning to discover.

FIFTEEN
INNOCENCE

> How cheerfully does the crocodile grin
> How neatly spreads his claws
> And welcomes little fishes in
> With gently smiling jaws
>
> — Lewis Carroll

Pain shot through Curious' shattered leg like a lightning bolt after the truck jounced over a bump in the road.

He gritted his teeth and swallowed a yelp. He was deathly afraid that Scarface and his cohort would make good on their repeated threats to beat him if he wailed again. He saw how Scarface had ogled Cammy and called them zeros. He saw their bloody injuries from the battle at the ranch. He knew that more violence could erupt at any moment. He was determined not to be the trigger.

They had overheard their captors talk about the big river. He guessed it was the Mississippi, which meant they were heading east. It also meant they were moving farther away from their mom and dad.

His physical condition was grim. He had soiled his pants several times, but the urge to relieve himself had subsided because the thugs had given him little food and water. He was assaulted by his own stench, even though he was accustomed to such odors from mucking the stalls in the barn.

The physical suffering wasn't his biggest challenge, however. His wiry body was toughened by the rigors of their rustic lifestyle. He had been injured many times, either from misadventures in the woods, carelessness with tools, or mishaps with animals. He could deal with physical pain.

It was the psychological trauma that was wrenching his soul. Their claustrophobic predicament was so tortuous that he often believed he was having a nightmare and would awaken soon to his normal life. But the horror just became worse each time he realized he wasn't dreaming. In his delirium he wondered many things. Were Mom and Dad still alive? Where were he and Cammy being taken? Why had they been kidnapped? Were they going to be killed? He mulled these questions over and over. His imagined answers became increasingly morbid.

The greatest mental torture was his loss of innocence. Other than natural misfortunes, his life had been a wondrous blend of natural beauty, freedom to roam, food on the table, a loving mother to salve his wounds, a father who played with him and taught him things, and nary a soul other than Cammy to irritate him. This was his first real encounter with pure evil. His crushed spirit hurt more than his shattered leg. His parents had warned him that the world wasn't a safe place, but being thrust into the hands of such vile and irrationally violent people was terrifying. His horror was amplified by the realization that if there was one set of evil brutes, there might be a whole world full of them just beyond their cloistered ranch. It opened his naïve eyes to a dystopian world driven by forces that he had no desire to understand. He longed for the comfort of his mother and father, though he would never feel safe again.

The evil he was experiencing now was infinitely worse than the imagined monsters under his bed. Those illusory creatures had never actually materialized to do him any harm. But the monsters tormenting him now were very real, and it was possible that they were part of a larger horde of demons that lurked everywhere.

Even if the monsters under his bed had been real, he knew his parents were just a shout away. But now they were far away, or perhaps dead.

He was no longer certain of his place in the universe. His heavenly world of familial love and glorious farm life had suddenly become incomprehensible and terrifying. It was now full of horned devils with fiery eyes and flitting tongues. His tissue-paper murals of placid meadowed scenery had been ripped away to reveal the brimstone inferno of a hell that had been lurking behind the fragile veneer.

The scream that he had suppressed from the pain in his leg suddenly erupted from his throat with the force of a bullhorn. The scream wasn't triggered by pain, but by the putrid thoughts worming through his brain.

The sudden shriek startled Cammy from her own reverie. She rushed to put her hand over her brother's mouth lest his screams stoke the ire of their captors once more.

But it was too late.

SIXTEEN
BANISHMENT

> To survive is to belong
> As a tribe we are strong
> Miscreants to the outside must go
> Cruel death they will surely know
>
> — *The Poems of Dark Sun*

Spartacus nudged Dark Moon insistently with his snout. It was dawn and she and Dark Sun had slept on the hill outside camp all night. Dark Moon heard the ominous growls that had spooked Spartacus before she was fully awake. The menacing sounds were close at hand in the dense ground fog.

Dark Sun was still asleep. Dark Moon jabbed him with her elbow. He jolted awake and saw the panic in her face. He heard the beastly snarls and realized they were in mortal danger.

In his quest for solitude last night, Dark Sun forgot that predatory animals roamed the countryside. When the economy collapsed years ago, desperate people released their pets back to the wild to shed mouths to feed. The descendants of these abandoned cats and dogs became feral as they grappled with survival. He also forgot to bring his father's pistol with him.

Dark Sun counted nine large silhouettes slowly circling them. The feral dogs edged closer as they stalked the couple. Spartacus barked ferociously, but the intruders were unfazed. When the muscled brutes emerged from the fog into clear view, Dark Sun could see the blood lust in their eyes and their bared fangs.

The leader of the pack crouched low, nearly scraping the ground with his belly as he inched toward them. The rest of the pack followed his lead, ready to pounce.

Dark Sun quickly threw his body between the attackers and Dark Moon. His abrupt movement incited the leader. The beast leapt at Dark Sun, pushing him atop Dark Moon. He screamed as sharp claws tore through his shirt and carved furrows into his back. Fangs pierced his shoulder and neck as the monster's jaws clamped down. The other dogs scrambled to join in the kill, barking in the frenzy of a hunt.

Spartacus leaped at the leader of the pack. He sunk his fangs into its neck, ripping and twisting, trying to tear the beast off Dark Sun. Dark Sun was unable to wrench free from its vicelike jaws because his arms were propping his own body as a shield atop Dark Moon.

Suddenly, gun shots reverberated. The beast assaulting Dark Sun yelped shrilly and flew off his back. Spartacus was carried away along with it, his jaws still engaged with mortal vigor. The other dogs bolted, spooked by the rapid thunderclaps of gunfire.

The beast that attacked Dark Sun lay dead a few feet away. Two other dogs were also splayed on the ground.

Dark Sun and Dark Moon whipped their heads toward the source of the gunshots. They saw Hawkeye and Fatima approaching in the thinning fog with rifles leveled.

"Are you okay?" Hawkeye hailed.

"Barely," Dark Sun grunted through clenched teeth. He felt blood seeping down his neck and back. He glanced at the inert dog that assaulted him. "Nice shot."

Hawkeye shrugged, chewing on a blade of grass. "That's what I do."

"How did you know we were here?" asked Dark Moon. She was trembling from their close brush with disaster. She stroked Spartacus, who nuzzled her.

"Teema alerted me that you were missing after she did her morning rounds. We heard the dogs and rushed up the hill."

"Thank you for saving us," said Dark Sun. He winced as Dark Moon anxiously examined his wounds.

"The wilderness isn't safe for romantic getaways," Hawkeye admonished coldly. "Don't leave the caravan again without protection."

Dark Sun nodded sheepishly.

"We need to hurry back to camp," Fatima interjected. Almost as an afterthought, she eyed Dark Sun's wounds. "You need medical attention."

Hawkeye chuckled. "Tell them why you're *really* in a hurry."

Fatima glared at him. "One of our men was accused of raping a young girl last night. Osiris is gathering the Council of Elders to decide his fate. I have a particular interest in seeing rapists brought to justice." She spun and walked away briskly.

The rest of them clambered down the hill behind her. Dark Sun hustled to the caravan's crude infirmary for medical attention. It would be nothing more than a thorough cleansing with whiskey, and then the application of homemade herbal poultices.

Dark Moon left Dark Sun in the capable hands of the nurse, Isabella, and accompanied Fatima and Hawkeye into a grassy space circled by carriages. She saw a sea of grim faces already gathered there.

Six elderly men and women of various ethnicities sat in a semicircle inside the ring of humanity. Osiris sat facing the six. Near him stood a haggard man who was bound with rope. Two burly guards flanked the prisoner, who was shaking like he had palsy.

"What's happening?" Dark Moon whispered to Fatima.

"Those six are the Council of Elders," she whispered back. "They're the jury. Osiris will be the judge."

Dark Moon was fascinated as Osiris administered common law justice. He was brusque and efficient, asking short, direct questions, and allowing only short, direct answers. After a handful of witnesses were queried, it became clear that the suspect was in trouble. Not only was he caught in the act of raping the girl, this was not his first crime against a fellow gypsy.

The accused was instructed to make his defense. He stammered, both from fear and from lingering drunkenness. He had no rebuttal against the damning testimony. His meager claim was loss of self-control from intoxication.

The process took less than ten minutes. Osiris instructed the elders to make a quick but just decision. The Council murmured, gestured, and nodded for several minutes. Then, the eldest arose and pronounced, "We've reached a verdict."

"Announce it," Osiris instructed in a loud voice.

"We find the accused guilty of rape," the jurist declared.

Osiris nodded solemnly. "What punishment do you propose?"

"None of our women will feel safe around this convict. And this isn't his first crime against our tribe. Therefore, we recommend banishment."

The onlookers gasped. "So it shall be," Osiris declared. "Bailiffs, administer the sentence."

The wretched prisoner was wild-eyed and apoplectic. He frantically begged for mercy as the two guards dragged him through the encircled gypsies. His frenzied pleas became fainter and more incoherent as he was hauled up the same hillside that Dark Sun and Dark Moon had recently escaped from. The bailiffs abandoned him there. They warned that if he attempted to return to the caravan, he would be shot on sight.

"Why was he begging for mercy?" Dark Moon asked Fatima as the last echoes of the castoff's pleadings hung in the morning air. "Banishment seems rather lenient for such an awful crime."

"Rape is horrible," agreed Fatima. "But so is banishment. Without the help of families, friends, and tribemates, banishment is basically a death sentence. Survival is difficult, and suffering is certain."

Fatima's words rang true to Dark Moon. To be banished was to be deprived of shared skills and communal support. It was to be lowered into the basest scramble for food and protection with only crude tools and weapons. It was to fear the howling of wolves without an ally for protection. It was to feel the icy cut of the wind without a warm embrace. It was to mourn every misfortune without consolation. It was to hear the hollow echo of every thought unanswered by another sentient being. Dark Moon shuddered. "Won't he just join another tribe?"

"If he survives long enough to find a sympathetic tribe. But he'll probably offend them too. His weak character is his enemy, not other people. No matter which faction took him in, it would likely be a living hell. The Jackals would force him to deliver drugs. The Caliphate would make him a slave. The Elites would make him a foot soldier in the civil war. He's a man without community, friends, or family. He'll eventually become unwelcome even to himself."

While Fatima was speaking, Dark Sun had quietly returned from the infirmary and sidled up beside Dark Moon. She eyed his bandages with sympathy and slipped her hand into his.

In a strange way, Fatima's words reminded Dark Sun of his favorite pastime with Curious. They loved to play catch, using any sort of ball they could make. There wasn't any real purpose in the simple activity, but it created a powerful bond. What was there to life without someone to reflect his own existence through interaction? It would be like throwing a ball to an imaginary being. The ball would just land and roll to a stop. A life alone is as devoid of meaning and purpose as any other lifeless object in the universe. It occurred to him that meaning isn't intrinsic to the mere state of being; it exists only in the hearts and minds of people as they relate to each other.

These thoughts put Dark Sun in a contemplative mood. He excused himself to explore another entry from his father's journal.

While everyone else rehashed the morning's unusual events, he settled into the privacy of Fatima's carriage. He opened the book to the spot marked by the white rose.

July 30, 2054

Jed Starnes haunted my thoughts today. It's been over a month since the Elites captured him.

When they took my best friend, they took a part of me. I used to think of myself as an island in the vast sea of humanity, but I've learned that I'm not just me. I'm me and Mary. I'm me and my two sons. I'm me and my friends. But now I'm no longer me and Jed. A part of me has died.

Jed's demise exposed some of humanity's cruel self-deceptions. Everyone wants to live forever. Everyone wants their stories to end happily. Everyone will be disappointed. Just like Jed.

We cling desperately to these self-deceptions. We've taken extraordinary measures to perpetuate them. We've constructed layers of protective shells, on top of those already evolved by nature.

Nature armored us with biological shells. Cells protect our DNA. Organs nourish our cells. Our skeleton shields our organs. Our skin surrounds and protects everything inside.

As the human intellect matured, we crafted external shells, such as huts, houses, and fortified cities, to augment our biological shells. We also developed elaborate societal shells—tribes, armies and governments, laws and economies.

We thought these protective shells would guarantee us long lives and happy endings. But then diseased thinking set in. Misguided philosophers convinced people that society is a collection of human cells, just like each person is a collection of bodily cells.

It was a tragic mistake.

Inside each person, every cell acts harmoniously with all others. Their fates are intertwined, and their interests are indivisible. The cells don't have their own brains. Rather, each person has one brain and one nervous system to coordinate all of their cells.

Outside of each person, the layers of societal shells are less harmonious than the cells inside the body.

Families, which are the closest external shells to each person, have some harmony. Parents and children have an evolutionary imperative to bond with each other. Family activity is synergized by intimacy and natural interdependence.

The next layers of shells, such as friends and neighbors, are less interdependent than immediate family. There are as many minds as people in these circles, with just as many perspectives, fears, and ambitions. It's not possible to achieve complete harmony of thought and action in these small communities. They are rarely as intimate as nuclear families.

The distant shells called cities and states have even less harmony among the individuals who live in them. Millions of people differentiated by geography, creeds, cultures, and ambitions are as alien to each other as are fish in the ocean. Such strangers rarely act in cohesion.

This is where our elitist politicians and professors led us down the path to oblivion. They postulated that one societal "brain"—one leader or government—should control all activity between people, just as one brain controls the cells inside each person. They theorized that people were merely cells in a larger whole, that life and meaning were not individual concerns but collective concerns. They insisted that there be one social dream and one social ambition.

These elitists preached "to each according to his need," even though it was impossible to know who "each" was among the millions in society, or to properly judge their "need." They preached "everyone is their brother's keeper," even though the "brothers" were often strangers hundreds of miles away, and it was never clear how they could be a "keeper."

When the collective became more important than each individual, totalitarianism was inevitable. Once the elitists were granted power to "harmonize" everyone, the Darkness followed. Effective relationships aren't a function of force; they're a function of free choice. Individuals are unique and sovereign; they're not anonymous cogs in a giant human Borg being programmed for collective "perfection."

We're communal beings, but the smaller the community, the closer the relationship. When local communities are subsumed into larger entities, it's hard to love and care for everyone equally and sincerely. In this sense, love isn't scalable. Trust isn't scalable. They work better on a smaller, more intimate level.

Some say that banishment is the worst possible fate. I'm beginning to think that the opposite—forced inclusion—is worse. Even though collaboration is important, everything goes to shit when it's forced. The societal shells originally created to protect us instead become our greatest enemies because they require force to properly "synergize" every person.

Jed Starnes was simply trying to live his life as he wanted. The Elites had a different plan for him. He objected to it, and now he's gone.

Dark Sun dropped the journal onto his lap. In the solitude of Fatima's carriage, he imagined he could still hear the screaming of the banished rapist echoing from the hills. He shivered, partly from the morning chill but mostly from anxiety about a world he still didn't understand, even as a grown man.

Osiris sidled up to the carriage and poked his head inside, interrupting Dark Sun's introspection. "Don't look so glum, my friend. It's time for us to break camp and resume our journey. Curious and Cammy await!"

Dark Sun raised his head. "Who's right?" he asked the sage. "Teema, who said that banishment is the worst of all fates, or my father, who wrote that absolute inclusion is worse?"

Osiris smiled, recalling endless college debates about such conundrums. "Maybe they're both right. The great treasure for humankind will be to figure out how to peacefully reconcile the individual with the collective. But that's my quest, and it can wait for another day."

"At least we survived the feral dogs and the Jackals," said Dark Sun.

"Things will only get tougher once we cross the Mississippi," Osiris said darkly. "The Caliphate and the Elites are on the other side."

SEVENTEEN
ELIJAH (OSIRIS)

Nobody can give you freedom. Nobody can give you equality or justice or anything. If you're a man, you take it.

— Malcolm X

The jail cell door clanged shut.
Elijah was brutally familiar with the sound. A lot of black men were. That's one of the reasons there was a resurgence in 2040 of the violent Black Nationalist movement that had spawned so much discord in the 1960s. The reignited movement enraptured Elijah. It also amplified the social unrest that was tearing the country apart.

Elijah was one of many disaffected black students at Colombia University in New York. He was nominally studying philosophy, but his practical education came in the form of protests, sit-ins, and clandestine violence against what he believed to be a repressive society. His cultural icons convinced him to proudly carry their tribal banner of racial animus into society's political arena.

His father had been a passivist Baptist preacher in the mold of Martin Luther King, Jr., but Elijah rejected passivism as feckless surrender. Where were the promised forty acres as recompense for the centuries of slavery? The renewed Black Nationalist movement demanded modern reparations in the form of cash, food, housing, transportation, and employment. They believed that a socially just nation should naturally provide for the disadvantaged.

"Welcome back," said Sam, as he closed the heavy door. Sam had been a police officer for many years and had come to like the tall, wiry revolutionary who found his way into this cell with regularity. He didn't agree with Elijah's violent methods, and he knew he could never see the world through the eyes of a black man. However, he shared Elijah's deep-rooted disdain for the Elites who were taking the nation down a dangerous path. Sam also had a sense that there were hidden forces working to pit the races and classes against each other, for some purpose he didn't understand. Sam wasn't an anarchist, but he had an affinity for those like Elijah who were. Someone had to do something. The country was on the verge of civil war. People were being played by the Elites and were now killing each other.

Elijah looked down at him with frightened eyes. "I gotta get outta here, Sam." It was an unusual plea, given that Sam was a police officer.

"Of course," replied Sam. "But you keep coming back."

"It's different this time."

Sam could see that something was indeed different. Elijah normally had a confident swagger. His tall frame and fearless demeanor stood out in a crowd. Perhaps that was why he was often the target of police when he was in the midst of a disturbance. But tonight he was jittery and distracted. His reddened eyes showed fear. Something was seriously wrong.

"Elijah, what's going on?"

"A friend told me there was an explosion while I was at the protest tonight."

Sam shrugged his shoulders. "That's not unusual on the nights that you end up here."

"It wasn't me this time. I have to make a phone call."

"I already called your lawyer," Sam said. "I have him on speed dial."

"I don't need a lawyer. I need to call Diana. Now."

Sam paused. There was a desperate plea in Elijah's eyes. It wasn't the plea of a prisoner to a jailor or the plea of a black man to a white man. It was the plea of one man to another. It was the plea of a man who loved his woman.

Sam opened the jail cell. "Make it fast." He led Elijah to a desk where there was a phone. Elijah keyed the number and then listened. Elijah's eyes grew more sorrowful as it kept ringing. The call cut over to Diana's voice mail. Sam heard her recorded sing-song voice. Elijah dropped the receiver onto the desk.

"I have to go," Elijah said forcefully.

"You're a prisoner!"

Elijah looked at him in a way that shook Sam to his core. "My friend said the explosion was at my apartment. Diana was there with some others. I'll be honest; they were making nail bombs. Something must have gone wrong."

"Jesus!" exclaimed Sam. His head spun with a maelstrom of emotions. He was the ranking officer this evening and had a job to do, and Elijah had a long history of breaking the law. But Sam had met Diana several times during previous run-ins. She was a bright, effervescent woman. Her personality reminded Sam of his own daughter, who had died in a car accident two years prior. And with the growing civil unrest and the first skirmishes of the civil war, he wasn't quite certain about who was right or wrong in the whole mess. Someone somewhere seemed to be pulling the strings and getting rich off instigating the ordinary folks who were killing each other in the streets.

"Please," Elijah begged. "Let me go. Diana is everything to me."

Sam looked down at the badge on his uniform and the gun in his holster. He thought about the oath of office he had taken under the auspices of the Elites. It was no longer clear to him what it all meant. He shook his head in confusion and then pushed Elijah toward the front door of the precinct. "Just promise me one thing. Don't ever come back."

Elijah turned to flee, then looked back at Sam. In the instant that their eyes met, they both realized they were on the same side of a conflict that neither truly understood. And neither knew who was on the other side. Elijah nodded his appreciation to Sam, and then flew out the door.

Sam stared at the door for a few more seconds. Then he looked down once again at his badge and his gun. He slowly unpinned the badge and unbuckled his holster. He laid the badge and the gun on his desk. Then he fled into the Darkness through the same door that Elijah had.

Elijah caught a cab to his home. When he arrived, there was a tumult of activity. A fire raged in his apartment building. Emergency vehicles were everywhere. The area was cordoned off by police tape. A crowd of onlookers gaped at the disaster.

He elbowed his way to the front of the ranks. Bodies were being wheeled out on stretchers to waiting ambulances. The first four casualties were men. They were bloodied but still alive. One of them locked eyes with Elijah and seemed to apologize with his gaze. A fifth body was carried out under a blood-stained sheet. He couldn't tell who it was. But then he saw the sneakers protruding from the sheet.

Red sneakers. Diana's sneakers.

That image was seared into his brain forever. The suddenness and brutality of his soulmate's slaughter tore him apart. Death is so final, so irreversible, and so terrible that it can transform the survivors in an instant. The idea that people were dying in the social turmoil had been a clinical concept for Elijah before. But in this horrible moment, it was a reality so stark and life-altering that it drove him to madness.

It drove him to madness because he was the cause. Death had meant little to him when he and his fellow conspirators dealt it to others. But for every action there is a reaction, and the echo of his callous violence resounded in the form of Diana's blood spilled in his own apartment. His political and social hatred was a one-way ticket to tragedy. He was overwhelmed by a sudden desire to rip that hatred out of his own heart.

He couldn't bring Diana back to life, but maybe he could save his own.

He fled the scene not so much to avoid getting recaptured but to escape the ghosts that now haunted him. He sprinted toward the subway, but he couldn't evade the ghosts. The ghosts were hounding him: the ghost of Diana's young life cut so short by the violence he propagated, the ghost of the hateful person he no longer wished to be, the ghosts of the angry factions trying to grind each other into dust.

He took the subway as far as he could and then hitchhiked the rest of the way out of the city. There was nothing there for him anymore. There was nothing anywhere for him.

As he wandered the countryside, he came to the realization that he and millions of others had been played like pawns by some monstrous unseen power. He would never forget the look in Sam's eyes when he let him go. It transcended race, creed, and class. Sam seemed to genuinely care about him as a human being. So who was driving this madness? For what reason? Whoever was pulling the strings the result was always the grave for the pawns, after they had utterly wasted their lives.

Elijah was determined to fully discover that seed of essential humanity that bound he and Sam for that brief moment. He became determine to make it grow. He became determined to bring people together rather than to tear them apart. He became determined to stand like a man against the unholy forces that had made his life a misery, ended Diana's life, and spun the world forever in turmoil.

And he was going to do it one lost soul at a time. Beginning with his own.

EIGHTEEN
DESTRUCTION

> Contradictions do not exist. If you perceive one, check your premises.
> One of them is wrong.
>
> — Ayn Rand

The pungent cloud of smoke wafting across the table toward Regis was an irreverent reminder of his subordinate position. Cosimo sported his usual expensive suit, arrogant mien, and dark intentions.

"Put that noxious thing out!" insisted Regis. "This is the Situation Room. Your smoke could trigger a serious alarm."

"Don't push the wrong button if it does," Cosimo said as he ground his cigarette out on the table. Then he lit another. "The Outcasts are marching toward Richmond. Have you looked at a map? It's not far from here."

Regis' armpits were stained with perspiration. This wasn't going to be a pleasant meeting. "This civil war was your idea," he offered as a meager excuse.

"It was the Syndicate's idea."

"That doesn't make it good."

Cosimo inhaled deeply, eyeing Regis like a drill sergeant scrutinizing an insolent plebe. He blew out a plume of smoke and said, "The Syndicate's ideas are neither good nor bad. They're just part of nature. Like a lion eating a gazelle."

Regis held Cosimo's stare for a brief moment, then looked away toward a bank of computer screens. He didn't feel inferior to many people, but Cosimo's secretive, acidic attitude intimidated him. "I don't understand how the bloodshed and mayhem of war helps the Syndicate."

Cosimo waived his hand. "The Syndicate doesn't desire bloodshed and mayhem per se. We prefer a peaceful, submissive world."

Regis shook his head in confusion. "Then why the war?"

"Everything else we tried failed."

"Failed? Failed to do what?"

Cosimo flicked his ashes onto the floor. "Destroy America."

Regis bolted upright. "But I'm the president!"

"I know. The Syndicate thought your feckless leadership alone would destroy the country. That's why we backed you, when there were elections. That's why we supported your political positions, even though socialism is a proven failure that destroys everything it touches."

Regis shivered. "That makes no sense."

"It makes sense if our goal is to bleed America to death. But your socialism was taking too long. That's why we also abetted the rise of radical Islam here."

"You thought that Caliph Timur and his jihadists would destroy America?"

Cosimo shrugged and blew a smoke ring. "The idea seemed reasonable at the time. They have no respect for the laws or ethics of western civilization. Their Medieval theocracy has ruined every other country its infected. Radical Islam is a nihilistic cult of death that's violently opposed to democracy, which is why we supported it."

Regis paled. "Who else have you supported?"

"El Chapo and his Jackals. They're like cockroaches. They don't follow any rules, and they're impossible to kill. We aided the tidal waves of gangs, drug runners, and human traffickers pouring across the southern border. We hoped that making your welfare state available to an influx of victims, criminals, and anarchists would destroy America."

A look of horror washed over Regis' gray face. "Why are you telling me this?"

"You said you wanted a peek inside the Syndicate. This is your peek."

Regis fell silent as he tried to make sense of everything. Cosimo enjoyed the tension in the air and the loss of blood from Regis's face. He mercifully broke the silence. "The Syndicate instigated the civil war to set America on fire in case none of the factions we backed succeeded on their own. We turned hordes of true believers into weapons of mass destruction against each other."

"Why do you want to destroy America?"

Cosimo pointed toward the Stars and Stripes hanging in the corner of the Situation Room. "The Syndicate hates the concept of America. It's the true evil empire. Our worst nightmare is a country that breeds independent, free-thinking people. They're impossible to rule. In this regard, the Syndicate has much in common with socialists, but we're not socialists. We have much in common with the Caliphate, but we're not Islamic. We have much in common with the Jackals, but we're not anarchists. All of us want to obliterate America's smarmy blather about freedom, constitutions, and individual sovereignty."

"So this civil war was meant to be America's death knell from the beginning?"

Cosimo's steely gaze bored through Regis's eyes. "Yes, and you Elites were supposed to be our surrogates ringing that death knell. Unfortunately, the Syndicate didn't expect your incompetence, nor did we anticipate the invasion of the Outcasts during the middle of the war. Their faction is a wild card completely beyond our control. And you're losing to them. That's unacceptable."

"If you don't give a shit about any side in this war, why is it bad for the Outcasts to win?"

"For the same reason that it would be bad for gazelles to eat lions. It would upset all of nature and all of history. Just like the early Americans, the Outcasts by their very nature would be impossible to rule. That's why you must defeat them. The Outcasts don't fit into our equation. If they win, they'll ruin everything we've fought for over the centuries."

"That's what you came here to tell me?"

Cosimo shook his head slowly. "No, I came to give you fair warning. Your performance has been abysmal, so I'm considering taking matters into my own hands."

Regis's heart skipped a beat. "What would that involve?"

"Not you."

NINETEEN
MOTHER

Mother is the name for God in the lips and hearts of little children.

— William Makepeace Thackeray

When the vehicle imprisoning Cammy and Curious arrived at the western shore of the Mississippi River, it had to be loaded onto a barge for transport across the vast expanse of water. The kids heard loud haggling outside their compartment between their captors and some rivermen who were arranging the transport. They whispered conspiratorially that they should bang on the sides of their compartment and shout to draw attention to their plight.

But then they heard the rivermen order their captors to open the rear compartment for inspection. The rivermen suspected that contraband was being smuggled, and they wanted to claim a share. They heard Scarface object vehemently, but he was told in no uncertain terms that his vehicle wouldn't be loaded onto a barge without proper inspection.

Scarface unleashed a stream of desperate, salty curses. There was a brief scuffle. Suddenly, the door was unlocked and pulled open. Curious and Cammy recoiled from the shock of daylight pouring in. The inspector recoiled from the stench that poured out in the other direction. He shined a flashlight into the compartment.

Their hearts froze. There was no certainty that the inspector shining the flashlight at them was a Good Samaritan. It was possible that the bald, barrel-chested man was even more of a villain than their captors.

They learned two things in the instant that their eyes adjusted enough to see clearly. The brown-robed inspector was disappointed in the nature of the contraband he had just discovered. And he was wearing a large gold crucifix. Cammy was thrilled by the sight of the crucifix. Surely this pious man and his compatriots would save them. "Help us!" she whispered, fearful of spooking Scarface and his accomplice. Curious felt a wave of euphoria from the thought of possible escape.

The inspector locked onto Cammy's imploring stare. He was mesmerized by her frightened blue eyes and her unholy mane of tangled hair. Then his gaze shifted to Curious, who was a sodden mess of excrement, and whose broken leg was splayed at an obscene angle. The monk froze at the unexpected sight of two children who had been reduced to an almost sub-human state.

An ominous tirade from Scarface about the almighty power and ruthless vengeance of the Elites broke the spell. A seagull squawked sharply three times, just above their compartment. The Blessed monk tore his eyes away from the kids. At first, he looked afraid and then the fear turned to shame. He did a hasty sign of the cross and swung the door shut with a violent thrust.

Cammy screamed and pounded on the walls, but Curious knew it was futile. The look in the monk's eyes told him everything he needed to know. He was an unrighteous man with little courage, driven by self-preservation. There would be no rescue that day by the river. Awful monsters roamed the planet, and his perfect world of warm milk, cool streams, and unconditional love was over. No more would his mother tuck him into bed. Those had been his most precious moments. He often pretended to be sleeping as she stroked his hair, kissed his forehead, and cooed sweet nothings into his ear to gently transport him to a comforting world of pleasant dreams. Her love for him was the most powerful, unconquerable force in the universe. The nightly ritual triggered such a tidal wave of contentment that he grew up with no comprehension of the harshness of their lives. He had no sense of the deprivation that his parents labored mightily to overcome. He knew only one thing in those moments. The bliss of family life.

He realized now he was living in hell.

It took about an hour to cross the river. The ride on the smooth water brought some relief to his leg. On the other side, though, the jarring of the truck as it ran roughshod over the washboard roads tormented his broken leg. They could tell the pace had quickened. Their captors no longer stopped to give them food or water. His throat was parched, and his belly begged for nourishment. His skin burned from the acid of his feces and urine. And they were moving deeper into danger. They had overhead the monk at the river warning Scarface about the horrors of something called the Caliphate. People were being beheaded and crucified, which meant that even if he and Cammy could somehow escape their vile captors, there would be no safe haven for them.

He thought of only one thing now. As the pain shot up his leg, he wished his mother was there to make it go away. As hunger raged in his stomach, he wished his mother was there with a hot serving of her delicious braised chicken. As thirst tortured his desiccated throat, he wished his mother was treating him to a soothing cup of honeyed hot water. Oh, how he wished she was there to wrap her arms around him and tell him everything was going to be okay.

He was trapped in a world of peril and dark mystery from which there was no apparent refuge, except through an escape hatch in his mind.

And so he fled through the mental escape hatch to his mother, ignoring the unthinkable possibility that she might already be dead. He fled to a Christmas morning in the past, where candied apples beckoned on the table, a fire crackled in the hearth, homemade presents teased underneath a crudely decorated pine tree, and unbeknownst to him, his mother bravely hid her exhaustion.

He fled to other moments of joy, to memories of his mother's angelic voice crying out, "dinner!" He fled to the glory of her lavender scent and the radiance of her infinite smile. He fled to her calming assurance that he was safe and loved for all eternity.

The vehicle stopped abruptly, jarring Curious from his make-believe world into the reality of pain and fear. He heard footsteps. The door of the rear compartment sprang open. A blast of light poured in, accompanied by a gust of cold air that told him winter was on its way.

Scarface loomed in the doorway. "You're someone else's problem now," he snarled. Curious heard the staccato footsteps of others approaching.

Scarface jerked erect and saluted with fear in his tired eyes.

TWENTY
VICTIMS

> You claim to have a soul
> Yet let others take control
> Assert your will and be freed
> Or your spirit you will cede
>
> — *The Poems of Dark Sun*

Osiris hoped that the last bridge across the Mississippi River was still intact as the gypsy caravan lumbered toward St. Louis. The weather was crisp and dry, but a bitter northwest wind was a harbinger of winter. Their journey had been a lonely affair for days since their brush with the Jackals. Motorized vehicles had all but disappeared in the Great Plains, and travel by foot was dangerous. Almost everyone had fled the region to the survivalist enclaves in the Northwest or the rebel underground in the South.

Most of the road signs they passed were corroded beyond recognition. The few readable ones displayed faded information that was now irrelevant, taunting humanity about its collective folly. What did Coke taste like? Did McDonald's really sell billions of hamburgers? Was there really enough gas for all of those gas stations to sell?

The shoulders of the crumbled road were overgrown with weeds and saplings. Insects and tiny critters laid claim to the rubble of the highway with their nests. "It's over," the ghost of America seemed to whisper.

When they neared the outskirts of St. Louis, their solitude was interrupted by someone walking alongside the road in the distance. As they neared the hiker, they saw that it was an emaciated woman dressed in rags. She plodded along with a fixed gaze that suggested she was oblivious to the approaching caravan. She was alone, a defenseless soul adrift in a dangerous world.

Osiris halted the caravan when it came up beside her. The woman didn't appear frightened. She looked up at Osiris perched on his carriage. He felt invisible as he returned the stare of her dark, lifeless eyes.

"Are you lost?" he hailed down to her.

"Yes," she murmured. Her meaning sounded eerily different than his question intended.

"Where are you going?"

"Away." The gaunt woman glanced wistfully toward a distant horizon.

"From?"

She pointed to the city behind her. "Them. The Victims. Nothingness."

Osiris nodded in understanding. She wasn't just fleeing a city called St. Louis, she was fleeing an environment nicknamed a "reservation." The slang had evolved to describe cities where the people had been patronized, overprotected, and insulated from personal responsibility for so long that their ability to survive as independent adults had atrophied.

Their plight reminded Osiris of a quip he had read in college: "Any bird that has learned how to grub up a good living without being compelled to use its wings will soon renounce the privilege of flight and remain forever grounded." Generations of these urbanites had traded their votes to politicians in exchange for the crack cocaine of victimhood and the ecstasy of handouts. The cities they lived in were designated as protected zones after their learned helplessness spanned multiple generations. The classification was similar in purpose to the reservations set up for Native Americans two centuries before. The people who lived in the modern reservations called themselves Victims.

Osiris studied the gaunt, emotionless woman. Her most striking feature was that there was nothing striking about her. It was as if she had inherited the average of every human characteristic. Her homogenous appearance and her blank stare made her look like a walking dead person. Perhaps she had never been born, in the sense that people who are truly alive come into the world full of hopes, dreams, and possibilities. He felt pity. "What's your name?" he asked gently.

"Society's Child," she replied in a monotone.

Of course, he thought, although it wasn't clear if her answer was satire or her real name. He felt a twinge of guilt, wondering if his youthful radicalism was somehow complicit in her situation. "So, you're fleeing the reservation?"

She hesitated. Osiris sensed a feeble flicker of spirit still alive underneath her catatonic demeanor. She appeared to be fighting through a lifetime of adverse conditioning. It was almost as if speaking her mind was an unnatural act. Finally, with a barely discernable twinkle of humanity in her eyes, she said, "I'd rather roam in the wilderness than continue to suffocate back there."

"It's dangerous out here," Osiris said, knowing that in the Darkness, a lone woman would be like an armadillo without a shell. "You won't survive long on your own."

"I'm not afraid to die. You can't be if you've never lived. Besides, it's more dangerous in there." She gestured toward the reservation.

"Please, ride with us," Osiris said out of the soft spot in his heart. "We're headed toward the bridge. We can protect you." He extended a weathered black hand down to her.

She studied it as if judging whether it represented good or evil. She shrugged, then grasped it. He pulled her up onto the seat beside him. He signaled for the caravan to move.

They rode in silence as Osiris gave her time to grow comfortable in his presence. When they neared the first decrepit buildings on the outskirts of the city, she finally spoke. "Don't go through St. Louis to get to the bridge. You'll be attacked."

"Our caravan is well-armed," Osiris replied.

"You're prepared to fight enemies who care if they live or die but not ones who don't."

This made him wonder if things had deteriorated since his last passage through St. Louis. That was many years ago, and it was nerve-wracking even then. "Tell me more," he said.

She hesitated. "The bureaucrats were our parents for a long time," she began. "But they orphaned us when they ran out of money. They don't even bother to put SIN chips in our babies anymore. We're desperate to blame someone for our plight because that's all we've ever done. But there's no one left to blame, unless strangers wander through. We reckon that our plight must surely be their fault, so we attack them. We take everything they have because that's all we know. Afterward, we sink back into the nothingness of our lives, until the next strangers come through. I'm warning you to stay away."

Osiris had last ventured through St. Louis many years ago. He had noticed Victims eyeing his tribe with far too much interest even then. They stared at him from broken porches, graffiti-defaced houses, weed-infested yards, and sidewalks littered with debris. They were poised like vultures, silently waiting for the right moment to scavenge. Perhaps anarchy and bloodlust ruled their lives now. It was rumored that the reservations had become black holes—visitors went in but never came back out. Even the drug lords had stopped sending their runners into these toxic cities.

"Okay," said Osiris. "Then how do we cross the Mississippi? The only bridge left is in St. Louis."

"Head south along the river," she said pointing to the right. "I've heard there's a spot where barges will ferry you across."

"South it is," Osiris said as he turned his wagon. Following Osiris' lead, the caravan swung in that direction, putting behind them the tarnished Gateway Arch that used to celebrate America's westward expansion.

"I'm glad you're coming with us," Osiris said. "Why are you called Society's Child? It's an unusual name."

"Everyone in my generation is called Society's Child."

Osiris suspected she was kidding, but he played along. "If you all have the same name, how do you tell one person from another?"

"Names don't matter. We're all alike now. We all wear the same clothes, although you can hardly tell anymore," she said as she swept her thin arms in a half-hearted flourish over her tattered rags. "I'd be shunned if I tried to be unique. My grandparents had fanciful names and dressed wild and flashy, as if they were special. But it was all superficial. The flashy things were just empty status symbols. It was a showy, shallow form of self-esteem. As time went on, even that was stifled by an unseen force that's hard to describe. There was a gradual erosion of individual identity. All references to race, religion, gender, and physical differences were banned. People sacrificed their uniqueness for equality. They surrendered their specialness to victimhood. It became simpler to just give everyone the same name. And now everyone my age is called Society's Child."

Osiris looked at her sadly. "My dear, you are indeed lost, in so many ways. I understand why you want to flee the reservation, but you'll keep running forever if you don't get to the root of the problem."

"The root runs deep."

"Indeed," said Osiris. "But you have to start somewhere. You need a fresh identity, untainted by the past." He paused, thinking of a symbolic gesture that would properly anoint this change in her life. A baptism came to mind. "From now on, we'll call you Eve."

She looked at him with a glimmer of interest. "Eve?" she asked.

"The name symbolizes a pure spirit." He placed his hand on her forehead. "Abandon the original sin called the past. Erase it from your memory. Only by rejecting the conditioning and grievances of the past can you become the person you dream of. Spend your energy and emotion on the present, with a view toward the future. Open your eyes to a new world. Open your heart to joy. Embrace the glory of existence. Be proud of who you are, and who you can become."

"I *want* to be proud," Eve said. "I *want* to be respected. I *want* to be loved. I *want* to be wise. I *want* to be brave. I *want* to be happy." She paused, staring into the distance. "But I don't know *how*. My grandma used to tell me stories about how life used to be. They kept her in a room upstairs. They called her senile, but her stories were wonderful to me. She taught me to read old forbidden books that she hid in the attic. They were all burned after she died. My favorite was *The Adventures of Huckleberry Finn*. Maybe it was because we lived near the river. Maybe it was because the characters seemed so *alive*. After grandma died, I began drawing birds. Birds are beautiful. There are so many different kinds. And they're not afraid to fly anywhere they wish."

Osiris took hold of her hand. That she had read books of old while enduring the suffocating conformity of a reservation explained the turmoil in her soul. "Everything you wish for is possible, my dear," he said. "If you want to be respected, respect yourself. If you want to be loved, love. If you want to be praised, be praiseworthy. If you want to be wise, observe. If you want to be brave, dare. If you want to be happy, embrace the joy that abounds in existence. Living isn't a passive state of *being*. It's an active state of *doing*. It requires saying 'I will' not 'I can't'."

Eve looked at him with eyes that were wide with fear. "I'm afraid that saying 'I can't' is a habit that's going to be very hard for me to break."

"Maybe," replied Osiris. "It's true that you came from a culture where achieving the status of victim was held in higher regard than actual accomplishment. But here's the key: You have complete control over your life because you have complete control over how you respond to the forces that press upon you. We are all conditioned by our experiences, our cultures, our parents, our schools, and hosts of other influences that give rise to personal mythologies. But we can choose, if the effort is worth it, to question each of those and to think differently. Seize this opportunity for rebirth. Take control. Become everything you want to be. I can help you, if you like."

After this ad hoc baptism, they had a long, spiritual conversation. Eve even smiled a few times. Osiris shared with her his own life story, including the depths of his depression and the metamorphosis that emerged from it. His compassion and empathy seeded a bond that drew her into the family of the caravan.

He had nurtured this same bond with other runaways he had rescued over the years. He had learned long ago during his fruitless years of radicalism that it was impossible to save everyone. But if he could help just one hopeless person, it made a difference.

To the lost soul, and to him.

As the caravan clattered toward the river, Dark Moon and Dark Sun laid next to each other in Fatima's carriage. Dark Moon burrowed into the warmth of his embrace, trying to melt her icy dread about Curious and Cammy. Every thought of them was colored by morbid images of suffering and tragedy. Even though the caravan was moving, it didn't feel like they were getting any closer to rescuing them. At times she could hardly breathe under the weight of her worry.

Dark Moon's children were always miraculous to her. As she lay in her husband's arms, she reminisced about the magical day when Cammy was born. When she first held her wet and wriggling baby girl, she marveled at her own ability to create new life. Somehow, her maternal body had organized random bits of matter into a new person. It was more than new flesh and blood that she brought into the world. It was a person, a pure soul, so naïve to the harshness of reality, so unconditioned by the imprint of history, that she was reluctant to let go of their first hug. She was certain it would be her little girl's last moment in a state of perfect innocence.

In Cammy, Dark Moon had created something *new* in the universe, formed *from* the elements of the universe, endowed with the ability to *change* the universe. She was fascinated by the emergence of this new personality with her own dreams and the ability to *act* on those dreams. Magical though it was, it had happened countless times throughout history—billions of new personalities had been born, each with their own dreams and the ability to *act* on those dreams. This powerful tidal wave had the potential to transform all of existence no matter what dragons lurked in the dark netherworlds.

She remembered when they named Chameleon. She felt an immense responsibility, because conferring a unique identity was a sacred task. It distinguished her newborn from all the other stars in the human galaxy. It signified that her beautiful baby girl was now a separate person, with her own desires and ambitions. It awed her that she could make such a thing possible. These recollections warmed her soul a bit. She nuzzled with Dark Sun until she fell into a rare deep sleep.

Dark Sun took advantage of the quiet interlude to read the next entry in his father's journal.

September 20, 2054

James stared into the distance today, like teenagers often do. He was frowning. Perhaps he's finally sensing his daunting future. I had no optimism to share with him. I feel terribly inadequate as a parent.

Even our rebellion against the Elites seems inadequate. We're not so much rebels without a cause as we are rebels without a plan. That makes us no different than teenagers. Or anarchists.

When I last scribbled here, I speculated that absolute inclusion was worse than banishment. This realization helped me clarify the purpose of our rebellion.

The Elites desire rigid control of minds and bodies. Their state-implanted SIN chips, their state-administered education, their state-controlled media, their state-rationed services, and their state-managed economy are all societal umbilical cords linking everyone to a bureaucratic placenta.

The result of this absolute inclusion is absolute dependency. When people aren't allowed to act and think on their own, when they're excused from securing their own basic needs, and when they aren't held responsible for the consequences of their decisions, the result is perpetual decline. Adults regress back to childhood as bureaucrats smother them like overprotective helicopter parents.

Millions of adults are now perpetual children who are incapable of caring for themselves. They've become addicted to short-term gratification. They know games but not work. They know hedonism but not investment. They know fun but not happiness. They know victimhood but not success. They know slogans but not truth. They know pop culture but not morality. They know fantasy but not cause and effect.

They've been coerced into a psychological Neverland. The state is their Peter Pan, and they're the Lost Boys wallowing not in fantasies of mermaids, fairies, and pirates, but in the mind-numbing delirium of video games, social media, porn, and drugs.

The Elites reject religion as the opiate of the people. However, their philosophy of child-like dependence on the state is an even more powerful opiate. The Elites are mystics just like the theocrats. Their myth is that unseen fairies and elves will magically provide life's necessities without any personal effort.

It's the biggest of all the Big Lies because entropy continually erodes buildings, roads, cities, cultures, and the human body. The challenge isn't to figure out how to divide things up equally, as if goods and services magically appear out of thin air. The challenge is to figure out how to continually create and renew things. Entropy is always the enemy.

The backbone of society is crumbling. The black hole of absolute dependency is devouring competence, achievement, and self-esteem. It's a spiritual suicide. Is it any wonder that so many modern Lost Boys are remorseless psychopathic thieves and killers, or suicidal?

My oldest son Kieran has already fallen under the spell of the mythology of the Elites. He's a Lost Boy now. I need to save my youngest son, James, from the same fate.

His girlfriend, Audrey, seems to have her head screwed on right. She studies my books with more enthusiasm than he does. Maybe she can lead him down a more fruitful path someday.

Dark Sun closed the journal and smiled at the reference to Dark Moon. She was indeed a better student than he was. But what did it matter now? Society had completely collapsed. The divisions between the factions in America were now vast philosophical chasms that seemed unbridgeable.

This hadn't dawned on him before because he had been isolated in Kansas most of his life, disconnected from world events. He had read many of his father's old books, but there was no substitute for real-life experience. Comprehension was finally seeping in, three decades after his father had observed him staring blankly into space.

Dark Sun felt moved by something he couldn't define. Essential forces were welling up inside of him, pushing against his insides like a hatchling pecking at its eggshell.

He wondered what the hatchling might become.

TWENTY-ONE
FATIMA

When plunder becomes a way of life for a group of men in a society, over the course of time they create for themselves a legal system that authorizes it and a moral code that glorifies it.

— Frederic Bastiat

"Here's your gold."

Fatima dropped the three small gold bars onto the red soil outside an adobe hut in the hills near Amarillo, Texas. The young girl had just returned from delivering fentanyl to a gang leader in the suburbs of the decaying city. The gold bars lay at the feet of Miguel, one of the hundreds of strongmen who coordinated drug deliveries in the worldwide narcotics empire of El Chapo and the Jackals.

Miguel glared at her. The brown-skinned beauty was one of his best drug runners. She was fast, smart, and fearless. But she was also the biggest thorn in his side. "Show a little respect, bitch."

"Earn some," Fatima snarled. She was covered in sweat and dust from her long hike and was in no mood for more abuse. Her life had been miserable ever since her kidnapping. She had been sold by the Elites to the Jackals, who fed and protected her, as long as she delivered their drugs and returned with their gold. But to the Jackals, who were the most heinous human traffickers in the world, protection merely meant that they kept her alive as a useful possession. It did not mean that they sheltered her from mental and physical abuse.

Miguel rolled up his sleeves, baring his muscled biceps. It was a subconscious habit whenever he became angry with her. It advertised his gruesome MS-13 tattoos and made it easier for him to hit her. "You filthy Arab. How about another lesson in respect?"

Fatima stood her ground defiantly. "A man who abuses women doesn't know the meaning of the word *respect*."

Miguel snorted. He was amazed that an indentured female drug runner had the gall to challenge him, especially when there wasn't a soul around to come to her aid. Didn't she know her place in this world? "If your Muslim overlords didn't respect you, why should I?" he asked rhetorically.

Miguel's joust hit home. The Caliphate's treatment of Fatima and her mother, Ayaan, was so brutal that they had to flee their own faction years ago. Ayaan had been raised as a devout Muslim, but she could never reconcile the core tenets of her faith with its misogynistic practices of female genital mutilation, forced child marriages, hijabs and burkas, and stonings and honor killings of women. She also couldn't reconcile herself with the growing violence against heathens as Timur and his jihadist Caliphate conquered more and more territory in America.

Ayaan, who had been born in Yemen but migrated to America to flee the violence there, ironically had to also flee the rising Caliphate in America with Fatima and her brother. Ayaan was a brave and stubborn woman. She risked her life and that of her children by becoming a vocal critic of the Wahhabi faction of Islam. She couldn't stand for its violent radicalism anymore. It contradicted her desire for a life of peace. She considered the American Caliphate to be a military and political abomination of Islam that was more fascism than it was religion. It seemed to her to be a misogynistic cult that was less concerned about truth and the salvation of souls than about subjugating heathens, women, and territory to a purified Islamic State. To her, it was morally incompatible with a world that should instead be striving for peace, inclusion, and the protection of all people, most especially defenseless women and children.

Ayaan drew the attention of the Elites, not for her religious apostacy but because she violated the One Child policy. As punishment, they kidnapped her children and sold them in separate transactions to the Jackals in exchange for gold.

Fatima lost her faith not only in the religion of Islam but also in the ability of male leaders to act justly. For her, life appeared to be a cruel jest intended solely for the submission of innocents, especially women. She hated both the Caliphate and the Elites. And now she hated the Jackals.

She never saw her brother again. She heard that her mother was traded by the Elites to the Caliphate, in exchange for a high-ranking official who had been recently kidnapped and held for ransom under threat of beheading. Fatima didn't know the ultimate fates of her mother or her brother, but she assumed the worst. Her mother had likely been stoned to death for her apostacy, and her brother was probably killed delivering drugs for the Jackals.

As Fatima ruminated on her past, she became vaguely aware that Miguel was staring at her much too intently. He eyed her body from head to toe, pausing to ogle far too long at her budding womanhood.

"How old are you now, pretty little Arab?" Miguel asked as he looked around the small village. There was no one else in sight. Everyone was away, making their assigned deliveries.

Fatima began to shake. She knew this day had been coming for a long time. It came for every captive female drug runner when they reached their teens. Many of them had shared their gruesome stories with her. "I'm eleven," she lied. She was thirteen.

"Close enough," grunted Miguel. He grabbed her and put a filthy, calloused hand over her mouth. He dragged her into the adobe hut and slammed the crude wooden door shut. The outside world disappeared. The next half hour was everything Fatima had dreaded and worse. The pain was excruciating, and the blood was terrifying. Her entire life scrolled in her head during the ordeal. Miguel's obscenity was just a violent exclamation point on a slow, tortured script that had been leading up to this denouement for a long time.

She hated Miguel violating her body and her spirit. She hated the vile stench of the pig who pinned her with his grotesque body and grunted like a mindless animal. She hated her nakedness and vulnerability. She hated her helplessness and humiliation. She hated a world full of male-dominated factions that treated women as objects and playthings. She hated her unstoppable lust for revenge that overwhelmed the goodness in her soul.

When Miguel was finished, he stood up and buckled his pants. He said nothing to Fatima, because she was nothing to him. He turned for the door.

It was one abuse too many for Fatima. It was so intolerable that life had just lost all of its meaning for her. She thought of her mother and the abuse she must have endured. She thought of her brother and the hatred surged in her veins. Through her tears, she spotted a wrought-iron poker lying next to the wood-burning stove. She scrambled to her feet, grabbed the poker, and swung it at Miguel's head with as much ferocity as she could muster.

The hook part connected with Miguel's temple. He collapsed to the dirt floor like a sack of potatoes. Blood oozed out of the wound onto the soil. Fatima stood frozen in shock. She dropped the poker, leapt over the dead body, and tore open the door. She ran partially clothed to her own hut, washed away the horror of her ordeal, and threw on some clothes. Then she ran harder and faster than she ever had in her life.

She had no place to run to, but she had everything to run from.

After an hour of rushing deeper into the desolate hills outside Amarillo, she paused to rest. As she squinted into the setting sun and examined the barren landscape around her, three realizations hammered her.

She was utterly alone in a dangerous world.

There was no hope for a society where women would be honored and protected.

And she would never again be the victim of any man.

TWENTY-TWO
SCHIZOPHRENIA

> Some claim Jesus said this
> Others claim Jesus said that
> Something terrible is amiss
> With the confusion He begat
>
> — *The Poems of Dark Sun*

The gypsy caravan reached one of the great divides in America.
They arrived at the docks where riverboats piloted by the Blessed ferried passengers and cargo across the Mississippi. The muddy water smelled of silt and decomposed vegetation carried from a thousand miles upstream. Herons and gulls glided above the sandbars dotting the river. Its banks were striated with flood lines and bounded by vast expanses of trees radiating glorious fall colors. The relentless flow of water from a seemingly limitless source created an aura of timelessness.

Osiris dismounted his carriage and headed toward the shoreline. A rotund man in a hooded brown robe ambled over to engage him. He wore a white mantle emblazoned with a red cross. A large golden crucifix dangled from his neck.

The man pulled his hood down, revealing a round, shaven head. "Do you and your companions wish to cross the great river, my son?" he asked with syrupy hospitality.

"Yes. I'm Osiris, leader of this gypsy tribe."

The barrel-chested cleric bowed with his hands folded in front of his chest. "I'm Bernard, a humble monk of the Blessed."

The Blessed was a faction of Christians impassioned by righteous aversion to the hedonism, brutality, and godlessness of the other factions. Their goal was spiritual salvation, for themselves and often for others. They plied the Mississippi, trading goods and recruiting converts.

Osiris was wary of Bernard, simply because he was wary of all organized religions. Conflict between the various creeds was common. Most of the recent conflicts involved radical Islam, but nearly all organized religions were tainted by legacies of coercion and abuse that included wars, genocide, human sacrifice, slavery, torture, and extravagant edifices built on the backs of peasants.

The rivalry between the Blessed and the Islamic Caliphate was one of the major fault lines in the current civil war. The Blessed saw themselves as modern Crusaders akin to the medieval Knights Templar. They were a paramilitary organization commissioned by Pope Pius XIV in 2058 to collect tithes, recruit missionaries, and wage a holy war to retake the U.S. territories that the Caliphate had overrun. Christians from all denominations rallied to their cause.

Their efforts were an echo of the Christian crusades to wrest Jerusalem from the Muslims a millennium ago. The Blessed wanted to establish a Christian theocracy in America, just as the Caliphate wanted to establish an Islamic theocracy. Many people were dying in the theocratic crossfire.

Bernard's eyes wandered to the other gypsies who had strolled down to the riverbank. His gaze fixed on Fatima. "Crossing the river isn't free," he said to Osiris. "My price is that exotic brown woman with the black hair and dark eyes."

Fatima pulled a pistol from her tunic and aimed it at the monk. "Do I look like an object to you?" she sneered. "The Caliphate treated me like an object with their Shariah law. The Elites treated me like an object when they sold me to the Jackals. The Jackals treated me like an object when they raped me. So is it your turn now?"

Several brown-robed monks drew pistols from their vestments with surprising alacrity and rushed to Bernard's side. Hawkeye stepped in front of Fatima and leveled his rifle at Bernard. Osiris slipped in front of Hawkeye.

"Explain yourself," Osiris growled to Bernard.

Bernard spread his arms in a conciliatory gesture, as if addressing his congregation instead of strangers he had just angered. "My proposal is simple. You need to cross this river, and my tribe needs more members. The Lord has instructed us to be fishers of men . . . and women. We're fighting the Caliphate for the soul of this land, and wars require multitudes. Besides, that Arabic girl looks like how I imagine Mary Magdalene did. We can help her achieve redemption. A life amid the Lord's grace would be far better for her than the sin and debauchery of your gypsy lifestyle."

Osiris stepped forward and towered over the rotund cleric. "Women aren't bargaining chips," he snarled. "No one should ever be. Make a more civilized proposal!"

Bernard stepped backward and slipped on the muddy bank. His fellow monks quickly reached out to help him regain his balance. "You heathens are going to hell," he said smugly, although there was now fear in his eyes. "Unless you repent and pay homage to our Lord."

"This world is already hell!" Osiris retorted. "Your empty prayers, rapturous hymns, and pious rituals accomplish nothing. If that pixie dust was worth a damn, the Darkness would never have descended upon us. We'll swim across the river if we have to!"

"Then swim!" Bernard shouted. "I won't help heathens who won't help us save humanity from its sinful ways."

"There's no shortage of factions wanting to save humanity," replied Osiris. "I used to be part of one, and I ran like hell from it. The real question is how to save humanity from everyone who wants to save humanity. You Christians don't even know which side you're on! Some of you supported the socialism of the Elites. Some of you provided sanctuary for the Jackals pouring across the border. Some of you supported the immigration of the jihadist theocrats from the Middle East. And I'm sure some of you are chomping at the bit to tell the rest of us how to live our lives. And now our society is at war with itself!"

"You misunderstand!" protested Bernard. "Life is hard, so people need the strength of God to lift them up, carry them forward, and quiet their fears. They yearn for the joy and gratitude that comes from our way of life, especially after death. In return, they just have to follow the commands of the one true God—"

"I don't see a god standing on this bank," Osiris interrupted. "I only see *you* claiming to speak for one. Life is indeed hard, but all evil begins with prideful people trying to impose themselves on others. I learned that lesson the hardest way possible. If your god was truly merciful, he would instruct you to leave everyone else alone. Why do you insist that your doctrines become those of an entire nation? It makes you no different than the Caliphate or the Elites."

"Because we're the *moral* faction. We're the *Blessed*, for God's sake! It's our divine destiny to lead the other factions to peace and salvation."

"*Every* faction thinks they're moral," replied Osiris. "*Every* faction thinks all others are wrong. *Every* faction sees what they want to see and ignores what they want to ignore. Your uncompromising religion drives you to insinuate Christianity into government and to insist that everyone else be bound by its tenets. Such unyielding attachment to dogma is why there's so much tribalism and conflict in the world. Death, not truth, is often the result."

"There's so much conflict because people like you hate Christians!" said Bernard.

"My hatred is generic," replied Osiris. "As the descendent of a slave, I hate *everyone* who claims the right to tell me how to live my life.

I admire the Christians I've met who pursue their *own* salvation. They inspire me through wondrous examples of personal generosity, and through their courage to live their lives according to their personal convictions no matter how difficult their circumstances. The world is better for such saintly believers. My disdain isn't for the principles of Christianity. I simply despise those Christians who try to force me to conform to their convictions and who use their schizophrenic religion as a cudgel against the rest of humanity."

Bernard fussed with his mantle that had become askew. "You think too much. You must have faith in the Lord. How else can you know right from wrong?"

"You think too little," replied Osiris. "How do you know which of your beliefs are right and which are wrong, if you're unwilling to think critically? Maybe that's why you can't make up your mind about whether to be on the side of the socialists, the anarchists, or the people. Maybe that's why the owner of my slave ancestor was a devout Christian. Theocracies don't encourage people to freely discover truth, they peddle dogma that may or may not be true. Everyone is fallible—including you and your leaders."

Bernard was aghast at the tall black man who was lecturing him. "Such heresy is why the Blessed must be victorious! There will be chaos if common people are allowed to decide right from wrong. Who knows what lurks in the dark hearts of you godless heathens? Everyone must learn to accept the supreme will of God! No one should challenge the established orthodoxy!"

"We have to cross this goddamn river!" Dark Moon shouted. Time was her enemy, not Osiris' indignation or the ruminations of an obscure monk.

Bernard cringed at her blasphemy and then shrugged his shoulders. "I'm sorry. The Lord is merciful to his followers but vengeful toward heathens. If you won't help restore America to the Christian roots that made it great, we won't help you."

"Christianity made America great?" exclaimed Osiris. "The very same Christianity that brought inquisitions, slavery, and crusades to the world? The very same Christianity that the Pilgrims fled when they came to America? If Christianity made America great, why didn't that same greatness burst forth everywhere? Christians held sway in Europe for over a thousand years, yielding nothing but wars, dictators, and oppression of women and minorities. The colonial powers of Europe exported Christianity around the globe with missionary fervor, yielding nothing but slavery, barbarism, poverty, and the slaughter of indigenous people in Mexico, the Caribbean, South America, Russia, Africa, and India. The Middle East, which was the birthplace of Christianity, has seen a never-ending succession of religious wars and bloody intolerance!"

"Good Lord!" blurted Bernard as he did a sign of the cross. "Then what, in your godless opinion, made America great?"

"A *separation* of church from state. It wasn't until nations granted sovereignty to individual people rather than to kings and bishops that greatness finally emerged on this planet."

Suddenly Eve stepped forward. She was anguished by the dread and panic on Dark Moon's face as the debate raged. "I'll join your faction," she offered to Bernard. "Let everyone else cross the river. Will that please your god?"

"I won't allow it!" shouted Osiris.

Eve glared at him. "It's not up to you! I'm done letting others decide things for me. Life with this righteous monk can't be worse than the life I came from. Consider my sacrifice a gift to your tribe, as thanks for my rebirth." She winked at Osiris. He suddenly understood that she intended to run away from the Blessed at her first opportunity, just as she had run from the Reservation. Turning back to Bernard, she said, "I'd love to join your faction. Maybe I can even become a priest."

Bernard smiled at her with cheesy satisfaction. "Your sacrifice is pleasing unto the Lord. We don't, however, allow women to become priests." Turning to Osiris, he said, "She is sufficient payment for your transport across the river. Our Bible will teach her compassion and right from wrong. Another fresh mind to mold with our sacred doctrines."

"You mean another fresh mind to stop from thinking independently," said Osiris. "The world is full of intellectuals, politicians, and priests eager to mold minds with sacred doctrines. So why are we mired in the Darkness? It's not for want of intellectuals, politicians, and priests."

"The Blessed are the world's only hope in this Darkness. It is only with the protection from God and the promise of heaven that people can have the courage to do the right things and to fight evil."

Osiris shook his head. "If someone obeys an omnipotent god who has the power to cast sinners into hell, is it the highest form of morality or the lowest? Is it even a moral act or simply surrender to coercion? Likewise, if a man is fearless in this life because a god promises him eternal heaven in the next, is that the highest form of courage or the lowest? Is it even courageous, because the implication of the promised eternal life is that no real harm will come in the long run?"

Bernard ignored him. He had what he wanted. Osiris remained silent. He knew the monk was incapable of a sublime discussion about morality. He also knew the cleric couldn't hold the reborn Eve for long. When the monk reached for Eve's hand, Dark Sun blurted, "Hold on! I've got something you might want instead of her." He reached into a pouch and extracted a shiny bar that grabbed the attention of the bald cleric.

"Is that gold?" Bernard asked, his eyes transfixed on the gleaming metal in Dark Sun's open palm.

"Yes. Take it as payment instead of Eve. It's a fair deal—everyone is satisfied, and no one is sacrificed. If your god is worth a damn, he'll be proud of you."

Bernard bowed his head. "I'll pray to him for your soul, my son."

Dark Sun sneered. "Don't bother. Like Osiris, I'm worried that this shitty world is partly the result of your prayers."

The monk scowled. He looked at Eve, then at the gold. He reached for the gold.

Dark Sun withdrew his hand, curling his fingers around the gold bar. "One more thing. Since your ferries are the only safe way across the river, you probably see almost everyone who crosses." He described Cammy and Curious, explaining that they were being transported as captives. "Have you seen them?" he demanded.

The monk studied Dark Sun. His gaze drifted down to the gold in his clenched fist. A wave of shame washed over him. Dark Sun's heart pounded in his chest. "Answer me!" he cried with impatience.

Without lifting his eyes from the gold, Bernard said, "I saw them recently with two soldiers. We ferried their vehicle to the East shore."

Dark Moon squealed as she tore through the tight circle of gypsies around the monk. "My God, were they okay?" she asked.

"The soldiers were injured, but I think they'll survive."

Dark Sun shot him a murderous look. "She was asking about our children!"

Bernard blushed. "The boy was badly injured. The girl never let go of his hand and never took her eyes off him. I've never seen such compassion." After a brief hesitation, he added, "I've never seen such fear, either."

Dark Moon cried and smiled at the same time. Her kids were still alive! "Where were they taking them?" she pleaded between sobs.

The monk shrugged. "I don't question the Elites."

Dark Sun was stunned. "You saw a wounded boy and a young girl in the hands of those thugs, and you didn't challenge them?" In Bernard's callousness Dark Sun could see how many Christians had looked the other way during the Jewish holocaust in the twentieth century and the Chinese genocide of Muslims in the twenty-first.

"I give to Caesar what is Caesar's." The monk made another sign of the cross, perhaps to seek forgiveness, or perhaps to ward off Dark Sun. His eyes fell once again to the gold bar in Dark Sun's fist. "We need worldly resources to carry out the Lord's divine plan. We need soldiers to defend the faith. We need cathedrals to exalt him. We need missionaries to spread his word."

"Truth doesn't come in the form of armies, buildings, or myths." Dark Sun dropped the gold bar into the silt at Bernard's feet. He recalled Matthew's words two millennia ago about the Pharisees: There are far too many hypocrites who appear beautiful on the outside but on the inside are full of dead men's bones.

The monks helped the gypsies load their menagerie onto several ferries. It took an hour to get the carriages, livestock, and horses up the ramps and safely stowed. The shallow-bottomed boats pulled away from shore with their steam-driven paddlewheels thump-thumping the rippled surface of the river. The gypsies lined the railings to view the grandeur of the Big Muddy.

Dark Sun glanced at Dark Moon, Fatima, and Eve. The three women were leaning against a railing, chatting. He noticed that Eve was somehow changed from the lifeless woman they had encountered earlier in the day. It was as if she had discovered she could live like the characters in her grandmother's old books. Her eyes sparkled. She laughed. She even sang a bluesy song. Her transformation was remarkable.

Dark Sun smiled and looked out across the great river. He noticed that Spartacus was pacing back and forth on the deck, staring toward the Illinois shore too. The German shepherd's fur bristled, and his hackles were raised. The dog was spooked, much like how animals can sense an impending natural disaster.

Dark Sun felt his own skin crawl in sympathy. He recalled Osiris's prediction that circumstances east of the Mississippi would change his perspective on everything.

TWENTY-THREE
STRANGER

> When the night is darkest and cold
> Long after the dread bell has tolled
> Comes a strangely haunting clue
> For the confusion blinding you
>
> — *The Poems of Dark Sun*

After the ferries landed on the other side of the Mississippi, the caravan rejoined Highway 64 and headed east toward Washington, the capital of the Elites. Leaves fell in earnest from the trees carpeting the rolling hills as autumn's colorful pageant wound down. A cold wind blew from the northwest. It reminded the tribe that they needed to cross the Appalachians before snow choked the passes.

Osiris was vigilant in his lead carriage because Southern Illinois had become a perilous no-man's-land. Many warring factions were trying to gain footholds there. The Blessed pressed inland from the Mississippi. The Caliphate pressed southward from the upper

Midwest. The Jackals pressed northeast from El Norte. The Elites still had spies and tactical units in the region.

But the most virulent force was the rampaging Outcast army charging northward across the ancient Mason-Dixon Line. In the fog of war and in the shadow of the Darkness, the insurgents had mounted a Sherman-like march across the South and into the Midwest.

This was a stunning turn of events in the civil war. Decades ago, the nations of the World Order maintained a naval cordon around Outcast Island in order to prevent the incorrigibles from escaping. When economic turmoil and a spate of civil wars exhausted the world in the mid-twenty-first century, the naval blockade was abandoned. It was considered a waste of resources since the Outcasts had never mounted a visible threat.

Shortly thereafter, under cover of the Darkness, the Outcasts in Cuba invaded the other Caribbean islands. They also invaded the surrounding coasts of Latin America. These territories became prolific sources of human and natural resources. In late 2083, an Outcast naval flotilla launched massive amphibious assaults on Florida. By early 2084, the Outcasts, a diverse people who called themselves the Warriors of Pathless Land, had overrun the old Southeastern states with sophisticated mechanization and technology.

Seemingly overnight they became the most potent faction challenging the Elites. The conflict between the rebels and Elites on opposite sides of the old Mason-Dixon Line was eerily reminiscent of the first Civil War between the North and South in old America.

The onrushing Outcast armies were embraced by the fiercely independent Southerners, who resented the domination of the Elites and who still remembered the brutal humiliation their forefathers suffered in the aftermath of the first Civil War. As the Outcasts liberated city after city from the Elites, celebrations erupted to welcome the victorious soldiers.

Osiris hadn't encountered any Outcasts in his many travels. However, he was intrigued by anecdotal stories he heard about a great treasure of theirs. Some of the rumors hinted at a vast horde of gold, others at a potent new military technology.

Osiris suspected the treasure was different. Something powerful had inspired the Warriors of Pathless Land to rise like a phoenix above the tumultuous religious, political, ethnic, and class conflicts in the hellhole called Outcast Island. He hoped to meet some Outcasts as the caravan headed toward Washington so that he could learn more about their vaunted treasure.

Osiris thought it ironic that Illinois was such a battleground. Back when America was a prosperous nation renowned for its unshakeable solidarity, the Illinois city Peoria was the allegorical center of the country. Now, Peoria was ground zero of the shattered union. It was the epicenter of a mad scramble for territory, minions, and ideological influence.

After two days of wary travel across southern Illinois, Osiris sent a small reconnaissance party ahead on horseback to probe a nearly abandoned town called Mt. Vernon. Osiris knew of an Elite outpost there.

Ordinarily, the gypsies steered clear of such outposts. Encounters with the Elites were always uncertain propositions. Some of their agents were apolitical and simply wanted to trade contraband. Others harassed wanderers with trifling charges of violating obscure laws. Years ago, such zealots tried to arrest members of Osiris's caravan as a pretext to extort ransom. The attempt ended in gunfire and casualties on both sides.

At the Mt. Vernon outpost, however, Osiris had traded several times with an agent of the Elites who called himself Stranger. He was disenchanted with his own faction, but remained in their employ for lack of better options. He was a non-conformist in a cult of rule followers. His prodigal attitude would have had dire consequences if he wasn't stationed in such a remote outpost.

The scout party returned the following day. Osiris was relieved to see Stranger was with them. He hoped the agent had information about Curious and Cammy. If Bernard's account was correct, it was possible that the two were transported through Mt. Vernon after crossing the Mississippi.

Stranger was tall, thin, and taciturn. He was physically fit for a man in his early fifties, although his short hair was receding and turning gray. He was dressed in jeans and a black T-shirt. His face was salt and peppered with a stubbly beard. A cigarette dangled jauntily from his lips. He had a furtive demeanor that was amplified by his mirrored sunglasses. He continually scanned his periphery for potential threats. He was on a razor's edge, poised like a giant cat ready to pounce toward safety at the first sign of a threat.

He distrusted everyone and rightly so. When he was a young boy, his parents were drug addicts, caught up in a brutal opioid epidemic that devastated millions of families. He was raised in a loveless realm by his derelict parents and then by state agencies after he was orphaned.

Accustomed to living without rules and bred with an open disdain for civil authority, he became a street thug. Survival was precarious, but with guile, wit, and daring, he eventually reached adulthood. After several stints in prison, the DEA recruited him to help stage drug stings in exchange for parole. He excelled at the gritty undercover work. He was eventually hired as a full-fledged secret agent in the Department of Homeland Security. His amoral character and lack of intimate relationships were perfect attributes for this career.

Osiris assembled Hawkeye, Fatima, Dark Sun, Dark Moon, Ruby, and the Council of Elders to chat with the visitor. Stranger toked on a joint that Osiris had given him as his usual greeting gift. The visitor spoke first. "You're in dangerous territory," he said in a gruff voice.

"More dangerous than having my house blown up and my children kidnapped?" asked Dark Sun.

Stranger looked at him blandly and exhaled a pungent cloud of smoke. "Maybe. The Caliphate is on a rampage. They captured Champaign a couple of weeks ago."

"That's bad," said Osiris. "Tell us more."

Stranger described the jihadist threat in detail. Led by a brutal

Caliph named Timur, they subdued Champaign with their usual tactics. Some of the Christians who refused to submit to Islam were herded into the city's churches and burned alive. Others were publicly beheaded. Priests who defiantly wore crosses and collars were crucified. Young girls had their genitals mutilated. Some of them were forced into sexual slavery. Homosexuals were stoned to death.

The Caliphate established Sharia law in Champaign, outlawed all political parties, and banned all Christian customs. It proved to be as inimical to Christians as Nazism was to Jews. They set up madrassas for Islamic indoctrination. Their teachings included intolerance of heathens and the glorification of militant suicide as the ultimate worship of Allah.

According to Stranger, their goal was to expunge infidels from the planet in a relentless expansion of Islam. No atrocity was beneath the radicalized immigrants from Iraq, Iran, Syria, Saudi Arabia, Indonesia, Somalia, and Yemen. They were a genocidal threat to every other creed. They boasted they would someday raise the flag of the Islamic State over the White House.

"I wouldn't bet against it," Stranger said, wrapping up his assessment.

"It would just be one tyranny replacing another," replied Fatima. "That's been the story of my life."

Stranger raised an eyebrow at the Arab girl. He looked with concern at Osiris.

"She ran away from the Caliphate," Osiris assured him. "And she ran from the Jackals. She's not a threat. Nobody in my tribe is."

Stranger nodded. "The Caliphate isn't the only faction you guys should worry about. The Outcast army is surging northward. Anyone caught between them and the Caliphate is in for a shit storm. We're packing up our outpost in Mt. Vernon to retreat further east."

Osiris leaned forward. "Tell me more about the Outcasts."

"Steer clear of those renegades," said Stranger. "They're the spawn of demons. It's a shame they didn't devour each other on their island hellhole."

"But why didn't they? How were they able to build a navy capable of amphibious assaults and armies capable of sweeping across the South?"

"If you believe the legends, they have a great leader."

Osiris leaned forward a bit more. "Who is he?"

"We don't know—yet," replied Stranger. "The Outcasts use a code name for him, which is simply the letter J. Then he suddenly blurted, "Damn it! I shouldn't have come here. You're in danger and now so am I!"

"What are you raving about?" asked Osiris.

"See that bird over there?" Stranger asked discretely tilting his head toward Osiris's carriage.

Everyone looked. They saw that there was indeed a large crow perched on the roof.

"Shoot it," Stranger muttered under his breath. "Now!"

Osiris wrestled with the absurdity of the bizarre command. He considered the possibility that his visitor was hallucinating from narcotics. He decided to humor him, so he nodded a silent command to Hawkeye who stood, aimed his rifle, and pulled the trigger. The crow exploded in a cascade of metal fragments and electronic debris. Everyone swung their heads toward Stranger in surprise.

"It was a drone." He threw his joint on the ground and paced like a caged lion. "I've learned to spot them. They look like birds, but they don't move like birds."

"What's a drone?" asked Dark Moon.

Ruby jumped into the conversation. "It's a remote-controlled flying machine used for spying and unmanned attacks. Most have high-definition cameras and sensitive microphones."

Dark Moon looked at her in surprise. "How do you know that?"

Ruby met her stare without flinching. "I know a lot about the surveillance tools of the Elites. I used to be their interpreter in the World Order."

"I heard you were many other things, too," replied Dark Moon.

Ruby's murderous glare was cut short when Stranger declared, "I'm leaving. I've been compromised! And you can bet your asses someone's compromised all of you. There's a reason that drone was spying on your caravan. Which of you is a double agent?" He turned toward Ruby, who had just admitted being a former Elite.

Osiris stepped between Ruby and Stranger. "I trust everyone in my tribe—completely. If you're alarmed, you should go—"

"Wait!" shouted Dark Moon. She rushed up to Stranger and probed his face with mournful eyes. "My children—have you seen them? A boy and a girl held hostage in a military vehicle—?"

"No!" he snapped. "If the Elites snatched your kids, something terrible is going on. We don't waste resources on trivial kidnappings and frivolous drone surveillance. I don't know who you pissed off, but I don't want any part of it. I'm outta here!"

"But why would they do such a thing?" begged Dark Moon. "We haven't hurt anyone!"

Stranger paused, suddenly mesmerized by the pain etched in her face and the anguish welling up from deep inside her. He felt an unfamiliar glint of caring. He briefly lifted the emotional shield he had carefully constructed around his heart since his youth. "It may not be you who pissed them off," he said softly. "Our secret service often targets the relatives of our enemies. Collective punishment based on collective guilt. Just another facet of our worthless collectivist philosophy."

Dark Moon fought back tears of frustration. "We haven't seen our relatives for decades."

"For whatever reason, you're in the crosshairs of the Elites." He paused as if wrestling with an inner turmoil. Then he turned, mounted his horse, and galloped off.

———

After Stranger fled, the gypsies arranged their carriages in a fortress-like circle for the night. Many of them were on edge as they performed their evening routines. Stranger's ominous words about the impending clash between the Caliphate and the Outcasts unnerved them, and the bizarre encounter with the drone left them wondering what other surprises lay ahead.

After dinner, Dark Moon and Dark Sun snuggled in Fatima's carriage. Suddenly, Dark Moon began sobbing in his arms. "Will we ever see our kids again?" she asked.

"We're doing all we can to find them," he consoled. Deep down, however, he was concerned about the onset of winter, the caravan's slow progress, and Stranger's ominous words. "Go to sleep, Moonbeam. Dream of a happier time and place. I'll keep watch." He kissed her cheek and then went outside.

Keeping watch was unnecessary because Hawkeye and his deputies circled their perimeter in shifts each night. However, he felt a need to contribute to the security of the tribe even though he wasn't trained as a soldier. Such delusions kept him from despairing that his whole life was superfluous. He also enjoyed the opportunity for quiet contemplation.

After an hour of uneventful watch, Dark Sun saw the official patrol circling toward his side of the camp. He took a short reprieve from his vigil to read from his father's journal by lantern light.

October 13, 2054

It's my brother's birthday today, but I won't celebrate. A year ago, the Judas slithered away from our village and joined the Elites.

He and I grew up together. We laughed together. We cried together. We said we'd always be there for each other. He was my best friend in a world where friendship is hard to come by. And now, I feel only disgust. He turned his back on our family and our village. For what? Righteousness? Power? The whole country has chosen sides, and it's tearing everyone apart.

Dark Sun paused. Something in the darkened prairie teased his attention. He listened for a moment, but he sensed nothing. He continued reading.

Deep down, I suspected that my brother would defect. He admired the iron-fisted way the Elites enforced their dictates. Right and wrong for him were what the Elites declared them to be. He believed that truth came from the aristocratic decrees of bureaucrats, not from facts or logic.

He genuflected to the gospel of the Elites that was being spread in the public schools, by the mass media, and throughout the complicit popular culture. He believed the only way a society could embrace a common understanding of right and wrong was to default to the definitions pushed by the aristocrats.

This secondhand view of morality is very shallow. Unfortunately, too many people yearn for a savior, authority, or culture to formalize the truth for them. They forget that this burden is entirely their own. Official orthodoxies merely constrict truth and impede further inquiry.

To my brother, the rest of us in Kansas are rogues and anarchists. He hates that we dispute the official version of right and wrong. In his mind, "commoners" deciding such things would be chaos. Only Elites with high IQs and dazzling academic credentials, backed by a central authority, can establish truth for everyone else.

Dark Sun paused again. He was certain he heard something beyond the carriages. He stood up and looked around. He could see the regular security patrol on the other side of camp. They didn't seem alarmed, so he went back to the journal.

So my brother became an Elite and ceased being one of us. It's rumored that he joined the Department of Homeland Security. It was originally created to fight foreign terrorists during the rise of radical Islam. Then it morphed into a secret police force that squelched internal dissent and harassed dissident Americans.

The government stopped protecting us from the terror of foreign monsters. Instead, it started protecting itself from the "terror" of people objecting to its bureaucratic intrusions. It was no longer a government of the people, by the people, and for the people. It became a government against its own citizens.

A bureaucracy is just like any other tribe. It instinctively circles the wagons to preserve itself. Bureaucrats become addicted to their authority and control, seeing everyone else as instruments of their selfish aristocracy. This curse rears its ugly head at every level of bureaucracy, from the smallest village council to the grandest chambers of the federal government.

This latent seed of despotism is inside us all. As the Russian novelist Solzhenitsyn put it, "The line dividing good and evil cuts through the heart of every human being." Everyone has the urge to impose personal wants, needs, and beliefs on others. This urge for personal purpose to become public purpose may be the root of all social conflicts.

Since this seed is in everyone, it's in every government agent. But the potential evil of a government full of corruptible agents is far greater than the evil lurking in any one person. The potential despotism of a government is equivalent to the unchecked authority and money at its disposal. The only way to limit this exposure is to starve government of authority and money, just as the only way to kill cancer is to starve it of blood and nutrition.

The Elites don't understand the simplest truth: entropy is the supreme ruler of the universe not them. Entropy doesn't heed their commands. It doesn't flinch at their guns. It doesn't give a shit about their dogma.

All things will pass away. The regime of the Elites is slowly self-destructing. But what will emerge after it collapses?

Just as Dark Sun finished, he thought he heard a faint voice outside the camp. He listened intently. There was nothing but the breeze rustling the dry prairie grass and an owl hooting in the distance. Still, he sensed someone was out there. The skin on his neck prickled. He extinguished his lantern.

He heard it again, this time much nearer. "I want to approach you," said the husky voice. "I'm unarmed."

Dark Sun pulled his father's pistol from his waistband. The gun shook in his hand. Being a night watchman seemed like a noble idea, but he was wretchedly unprepared for an actual encounter.

"Move slowly with your hands up," he commanded to the disembodied voice lurking in the darkness. The nervous catch in his voice betrayed his false bravado.

A shadowy figure swished through the long grass with arms stretched skyward. Dark Sun aimed his gun erratically at the phantom while he relit the lantern with his free hand. The flame flickered to life, bathing the visitor with light. It was Stranger.

Dark Sun pointed his weapon at Stranger's chest while he scanned the dark prairie for other intruders. He was afraid more Elite agents were out there. "Are you alone?" he asked.

"More than you know," Stranger replied.

"What do you want?"

"First, I want to put my arms down."

The man was in such a vulnerable position that Dark Sun judged there was little risk. "Okay, put them down. What do you want?"

"I'm not sure. The spying by the drone earlier today forced me to reevaluate my situation. At first, I was afraid I'd be punished for meeting with your tribe. But as I thought about it, the very notion that I had to fear such a thing was profoundly damning. It made me realize that I've been a stranger in my own faction for far too long. I no longer want to be with the Elites. They know only distrust, threats, and coercion. I've always despised them. I just needed an opportunity to abandon them."

"Why come here? The Elites seem to be out to get my wife and me."

"Where else would I go?" Stranger gestured toward the endless prairie. "Earlier today, I was shocked when Osiris said that he completely trusted all of you. You can't *all* be trustworthy because someone has betrayed your tribe. That means your relationships are so valuable that he would stubbornly defend them, even in the face of evident treason. It's the opposite with the Elites. Treason is assumed, and constant proofs of loyalty are required. Where your tribe trusts, the blackshirts eavesdrop and entrap. To them, relationships aren't sacred commitments born of intimacy. They're unstable alliances born of conspiracy, deceit, and extortion."

"I'm sure you've known that for years—"

"But I never stared directly at the naked truth of it before. That happened when I looked into your wife's eyes. Underneath her immense pain and suffering, I saw a love for your lost children that was overwhelming. I saw in her the mother I never had. A dam of pent-up longing burst inside me. It's been so long since I've cared for anyone or anyone has cared for me. Caring isn't possible in the dystopian realm of the Elites. You can't truly care for millions of anonymous strangers. And you can't even care for the people you do know. They might be informants, or they might be using you as a pawn in their struggle for political favor. You experience the opposite of caring. You become permanently callous. You become numbed by constant indoctrination and anesthetized by sterile bureaucracies. In the shadow of the state, you shrink to nothing. The social tethers connecting people snap."

Dark Sun waved the gun at him. "Where are you headed with this?"

He flopped his arms in a gesture of shame and humility. "After witnessing Osiris's unconditional trust and your wife's humanizing agony, I knew I could never be truly alive if I remained with the Elites. I want to join your tribe. I'll never be a saint, but I can at least become a real person with real relationships. I've never had them, not even as a child." He paused, then added, "I think I can help you find your children. Maybe I'll find myself in the process."

Dark Moon had been awakened by the intrusion. As she walked

toward the commotion, she heard much of the confession that poured forth from Stranger. "Join us!" she exclaimed to the surprise of both men. Her motherly instincts fueled a powerful desire to help a tortured soul who had no place to go. She sensed he had cracked open a spiritual door that had been wedged shut for decades. She was also intrigued by the possibility of help in finding their children.

Dark Sun was moved by his wife's confidence and empathy as she welcomed Stranger. The lantern light reflected off her tousled platinum hair. It cast a shimmering aura, like a spiritual beacon piercing the dark void of eternity. Despite the darkness of the night, the darkness of their plight, and even the Darkness of society, it struck him that the pseudonym Dark Moon didn't seem quite right anymore. She was alive and glowing in a way that he had almost forgotten to be possible in the wake of their tragedy.

In her sudden exchange with Stranger, he saw an unconditional acceptance that elevated her. In a way he couldn't fully comprehend yet, it elevated all of humanity.

His heart sang with love.

TWENTY-FOUR
ILLUSION

His mind is not for rent
To any god or government

— Rush

Regis threw his empty whiskey glass at the fireplace in the Laurel Lodge. It sailed past Cosimo's head and crashed against the stonework in a spectacular shower of shards. He was surprised at his own audacity and even more surprised that he didn't fear the consequences.

Cosimo didn't flinch, but his expression changed. He calmly drew on his cigarette, studying Regis like an exhibit in a wax museum. "I see I hit a nerve," he said.

"Hit a nerve? How many times do I have to hear that I'm failing? How many times do I have to hear that my role is merely to follow your orders? I'm one of the most powerful people in the world! I deserve to know what the hell's going on!"

The two men were seated in a secure conference room at Camp David, which was located in the wooded hills of the Catoctin Mountains in Maryland. The site served as both a presidential retreat and a military installation. Regis was spending the bulk of his time there since the Outcasts were bombing Washington every day now.

Cosimo extinguished his cigarette and paced the room. His subordinate was clearly at a crisis point. The whole world was at a crisis point. He had two choices. He could dispose of Regis, like he had disposed of so many failing subordinates before. But the military situation was on a hair trigger and disrupting the leadership of the Elites now would threaten the plan. He needed to temporarily assuage Regis until there was a better time to arrange his demise.

"You're right," Cosimo said, lighting another cigarette.

Regis did a doubletake. That was the last reaction he expected. "I am?"

"Yes. You deserve to know more about what's going on. So I'll tell you." Cosimo strutted to the bar. He poured a double shot of Jameson's and handed it to the president.

Regis accepted it. He appreciated the conciliatory gesture but knew something was off-kilter. He felt a wave of apprehension.

"Think of power like Matryoshka nesting dolls," Cosimo began. "There's always one doll inside another, until you get to the one at the core. The dolls of the outer shells are just for show."

"Are you the doll at the core?" Regis asked. The whiskey was calming his jangled nerves.

Cosimo smirked. "I wouldn't be wasting my time here if I was. Ten people are at the core of the Syndicate. They're the only ones who know the full extent of the plan. They're called the Deka, or sometimes the Hidden Hands because they're the ten digits who manipulate everything. The Deka is the ultimate authority. Humankind is destined to submit to them. You'll never know who they are. I'm not a member of the Deka, yet. Maybe when one of them dies."

Regis looked puzzled. He was familiar with democracies and dictatorships, but nothing like what Cosimo was describing. "How do you get selected to the Deka?"

Cosimo looked at Regis with eyes dark as coals. "There's fierce competition for that honor. I won't be selected if I fail at my current mission. At the moment, I'm failing because you're failing. The Deka always punishes failures. And shit travels downstream."

Regis set down his whiskey. The icy pall of fear returned. He felt like he was in the crosshairs of something abominable.

"The Syndicate is a worldwide alliance of thousands of influencers," Cosimo continued. "The Deka hires the influencers. The Syndicate isn't bounded by any nation, religion, or ideology. It's an economic alliance—less than a thousand people control 90 percent of the world's wealth. Our only interest is the power to acquire and control wealth. Our only loyalty is to each other. Once an influencer is hired by the Syndicate, there is no opting out. The recruit will never know the inner workings, but the perks are fabulous. The Syndicate creates and destroys empires. It has reigned for centuries. All lesser rulers are granted the illusion of power at our behest. Including you."

Regis was certain now that something was off-kilter. "Are you an influencer then?"

"No, I'm a centurion. There are a hundred centurions who serve as consiglieres for the Deka. There are ten of us for each one of the Hidden Hands. We call ourselves the Golden Hundred. Our job is to coordinate the activities of the influencers to execute the Deka's directives. My current mission is to destroy America."

Regis squirmed uncomfortably. "What's my role in this?"

"Obviously you're not a member of the Syndicate. You're not even one of our thousands of influencers. That means you're not nearly as powerful as you or the proles think you are. You're merely one of the Matryoshka dolls in the outer layers."

"Who are your influencers?"

"You might guess who some of them are, but you'll never know for sure. We've positioned them around the world in the financial institutions, tech companies, academia, media, governments, courts, secret police, churches, popular culture, state departments, and military. We use these embedded influencers to maintain control of all factions and all strategic institutions, and to stay aware of all trends and conspiracies. For example, you're being monitored by a number of our influencers every day. Some of their reports are very interesting."

Regis blanched. "Are these influencers what some call the Illuminati?"

Cosimo laughed. "No. We've propagated a number of such conspiracy theories to confuse those who might suspect our influence on world affairs. We've seeded enough of these outlandish theories, spread by enough fringe lunatics, that nobody really believes any of them. No one wants to be tainted by lunacy, and everyone prefers to believe they're part of a sane world they can actually control. The fringe lunatics call us the Illuminati, the Council on Foreign Relations, the Bilderberg Group, the Bohemian Club, the Deep State, the Skull and Bones, the Rothschilds, the Trilateral Commission, the Elders of Zion, the New World Order, and the Freemasons. Those are all blind guesses seeded by our clever mis-directions. But a shadow government such as the Syndicate does exist, and it intends to become master of the universe."

Regis shook his head slowly. "So the goal of this fabulous ruse is to create one world government?"

"The Syndicate already governs the world. Behind the scenes, the Deka has pulled the strings of emperors, kings, generals, and theocrats for centuries. Recorded history is a mere shadow of reality. The real history of the world is a sordid tale of international crime, bribery, mass murder, secret alliances, deep states, regicide, and false-flag operations, all of which have been necessary for the Syndicate to control everyone else. Our hand is in everything, but we remain invisible, despite the fruitless efforts to name us. We are everywhere, yet we are nowhere. We shall remain hidden until that time when no earthly force can counter us."

"Why am I not a centurion or an influencer?" asked Regis. "I'm the president! Surely, I'm one of the most powerful people in the world."

"We did indeed need a strong fascist leader to pose as the savior of the American proles. You were valuable to us in that regard, but you were never powerful. You're not leading; you are being led. And now your country is being led into the abyss. Your dwindling power will last only as long as I countenance it. None of the apparent political or religious leaders of the world are members of the Syndicate. That would defeat our strategy, which is to position ourselves as an unstoppable force of hidden power brokers. It would give too much knowledge to those who could compromise us. It would position us too close to the proles."

Regis wanted to crawl out of his skin. "Why should I continue being part of this farce?"

"Because your conceit makes you drunk with your illusory power and prestige. You've proven throughout your career that you would sacrifice everything, including your integrity and the welfare of your constituents, to bask in the glow of your exalted position. The desire to be important is your deepest urge. Every man like you aims at power, and every man like you would become a dictator if he could. The mob believes that you have the power of a king, and they're willing to be your beasts of burden. That's sufficient gratification for the likes of you. But not for us. You're one of *our* beasts of burden. You are content in that role because we've fulfilled all of your narcissistic desires."

"And if I revolt?"

"You're in far too deep to quit now. We decided when it was time for Napoleon to come and go. We decided when it was time for the Soviets to come and go. We decided when it was time for the National Socialists to come and go. We decided when it was time for the Islamists and the Jackals to terrorize the world, and we will decide when it is time for them to go. Likewise, we decided to give you the power that you now enjoy."

Cosimo smiled and then turned for the door of the Laurel Lodge. "You need to win the civil war quickly," he said as he walked away. He looked back over his shoulder at the president. "Because we also decide when it's time for you to go."

TWENTY-FIVE
ENCOUNTER

> Rip joy from the jaws of death
> Priceless is every fleeting breath
> But the hope for joy will be in vain
> If innocents are abused or slain
>
> *— The Poems of Dark Sun*

Dark Moon wakened Osiris.

She pled with him to allow Stranger to join the tribe. Osiris grumbled at the late-night inconvenience, but he relented, knowing that the intrusion by an Elite had to be addressed. He summoned an unusual midnight session with the Council of Elders.

The rest of the gypsies were awakened to witness the event. They gathered around a refreshed bonfire. Stranger sat cross-legged in front of the elders. A wave of nakedness washed over him. If the elders rejected him, he had nowhere else to go. He felt the chill of desperation.

Osiris began the proceedings. "My friend, explain why you want to join our tribe."

Stranger paraphrased his earlier words to Dark Sun. He added that he feared retribution from the Elites because the avian drone had likely spotted him AWOL from his post, consorting with undocumented proles. And now that he had defected, he would be considered a criminal. If he was recaptured, the Elites would accuse him of theft of self, the same crime that slaveholders charged runaway slaves with two hundred years ago.

The elders nodded their heads and murmured approval. "Why should we trust you?" Osiris asked.

Stranger opened his arms in a submissive gesture. "I'm unarmed and at your mercy. I've lost my way and need to find a different path. I'm pleading for a chance to *earn* your trust." There was more head nodding from the elders. Most of them had been in similar predicaments before they joined the caravan.

"How well can you shoot a gun?" Osiris asked.

"I learned from street gangs when I was eleven. The Elites made me an expert."

"Are you willing to kill to defend the tribe?"

Stranger flinched. "Yes, but killing is a last resort for me now. As a youth, I was intoxicated by the notion of using force to get what I wanted. However, I've learned that the most important things in life can't be obtained with force. Force can't make someone trust you. It can't make someone love you. It can't even make you like yourself. After a lifetime of bullying others, I'm unloved and unwanted. I'm back where I started as a kid."

Osiris nodded. "No more questions." He caucused briefly with the elders, then announced to Stranger, "Welcome to our tribe! But you need to pick a more fitting pseudonym. You're among friends now."

Stranger furrowed his brow. "I want to be called Saul," he said.

"Saul?" echoed Osiris quizzically. "Is that your real name?"

"No, my real name belongs to the Elites. I want to name myself after the man who had the greatest epiphany in history."

Osiris cocked his head and looked puzzled.

Stranger chuckled. "Saul of Tarsus, from the Bible. He later became Saint Paul."

"You don't strike me as the saintly type."

"Obviously," replied Stranger. "But I'm like Saul in the sense that he was an imperial agent until he realized he was playing for the wrong team. I wasn't struck blind like he was on the road to Damascus, but I was blind to the truth for a long time. I haven't been saintly so far, but I'll try. Consider me a work in progress."

Osiris shook his head and smiled. He waved his arm in a majestic arc over Stranger's head and solemnly pronounced, "From this moment on, you are Saul!" Many of the gypsies cheered, pleased to see an Elite agent repent and show some humility. Some remained silent. Saul's induction meant there was another former Elite in their ranks. Fatima in particular was rankled. She usually was whenever the tribe inducted a new member from one of the factions that had abused her and her family.

"One more thing!" Osiris shouted over the din.

Saul could tell by the bemused faces around him that this interruption was expected. He looked at Osiris in confusion.

"You have a SIN chip in you."

Saul's hand went subconsciously to his rib cage. It dawned on him that the Elites could still track him.

"It must be removed."

Saul's face turned ashen. "How?" His voice was almost inaudible.

"It won't pop out on its own. One of my men is a surgeon—sort of. Are you ready?"

Saul's throat constricted and his knees weakened, but he knew he had no choice. He took a deep breath to steady himself. "Give me some whiskey and something to bite on."

Osiris gestured to an aide, who rushed off to gather the requested items. When the aide returned, Saul took several long swigs from the whiskey bottle. The aide handed him a leather strap. Saul clenched it between his teeth and mumbled, "I'm ready."

The "surgeon" directed Saul to remove his shirt and lie on a blanket. Four other gypsies pinned his arms and legs to hold him steady. Lanterns were positioned to illuminate the procedure. The surgeon poured whiskey onto Saul's abdomen and scrubbed it. He scrubbed his own hands and then the blade of a knife.

Without warning, he jabbed the blade into Saul's abdomen. Saul convulsed violently, almost breaking free from the restraint of the four gypsies. The leather strap muffled his scream. The surgeon waited for Saul to stabilize, then he maneuvered the knife under Saul's first rib. He inserted a finger into the wound. With practiced skill, he found the SIN chip and extracted it from the bloody slurry of flesh.

Osiris smashed the device with a hammer.

Saul was unaware of the successful extraction because he had fainted. The surgeon washed out the wound with more whiskey and then stitched it with a crude needle and string. A short time later, Saul wafted into consciousness, pale as a ghost and moaning in confused agony. Osiris knelt beside him, his graying dreadlocks partly obscuring his face. He patted Saul's shoulder and said, "Congratulations! You're one of us now."

By morning, Saul had recuperated enough to chat with Osiris over breakfast. The discussion turned to the caravan's travel plans.

"It's not safe to continue east," Saul warned. "One of our outposts along I-64 was attacked by the Caliphate two days ago. All six agents were beheaded. Their bodies were nailed to wooden crosses. Head south instead."

Osiris frowned. He didn't want to expose his tribe to the ruthless barbarism of the Caliphate, but a southern detour would delay their journey. As he weighed the two options, he thought of Curious and Cammy in the clutches of the Elite thugs. He recalled stories Fatima had told him about her captivity by the Jackals years ago. It was the rape that horrified him the most. He shuddered. He couldn't prolong the kids' ordeal, no matter the risks.

"Thanks for the warning, my friend. But time is of the essence. We'll continue eastward."

"Then break camp immediately," advised Saul. "This region is like old Poland—every army is itching to invade it. With luck, you can slip through the narrowing gap between the Caliphate and Outcast armies. But even if you do, you'll be heading directly toward the Elites."

"We have no choice. They have Curious and Cammy." Osiris stood up. "Let's move!" he shouted to gypsies milling around him. "We leave in fifteen minutes!"

The tribe headed east on old I-64. During a week of travel, they passed several Elite outposts that were abandoned in anticipation of the impending mayhem. The caravan plodded along as fast as their entourage of farm animals would allow, which was distressingly slow. They had covered barely two hundred miles since meeting Saul at Mt. Vernon. The last few leaves were fluttering to the ground like giant umber snowflakes. Winter was looming, and they had a long way to go.

On a chilly morning, they entered a densely wooded area in southern Indiana. Dark Moon was still asleep in Fatima's carriage, so Dark Sun hustled to the front of the caravan to chat with Osiris. As he jogged along the line of rattling carriages and ornery animals, he became acutely aware that no sounds came from the woods. It was as if all the woodland creatures had fled an impending storm. After he climbed into the seat beside Osiris, he said, "It's unusually quiet."

"It's very strange," agreed Osiris, scanning the forest on both sides of the road. He peered into the eerie, translucent fog. "Something's wrong."

"Are we lost?"

"Worse," said Osiris with rising alarm. "I think we've been found—"

"Yee-aay-ee! Allahu akbar! Yip-yip-yip! Allahu akbar!" screamed the mounted horsemen who galloped at them out of the foggy woods. The black-robed attackers wore turbans on their heads and masks covered everything but their dark, murderous eyes. They brandished glinting scimitars and blazing torches.

The lead horseman held aloft a black jihadist flag with white Arabic lettering that translated as "Islamic State: Submit or Die." Behind him another horseman held aloft a banner with a beatific image of the Caliph Timur wearing a silken black turban.

Osiris shouted a warning to the caravan, but his voice was lost in the din of pounding hooves and blood-curdling shrieks of "Allahu akbar." His warning was unnecessary. The sudden cacophony of the Caliphate attack alerted everyone to the unfolding calamity. Gypsies in various stages of dress leapt from their carriages with rifles and pistols at the ready. As the first of the stampeding horsemen assaulted the carriages with scimitars, the gypsies fired in defense. In the blink of an eye, the forest was transformed into a frothing combat zone.

The jihadists had the advantage of surprise. Their rampaging horses overturned several carriages, scattering children and contents to the ground. The attackers hacked three gypsies to death in the first instant of the battle. Horses trampled two others to death. Torches were thrown into carriages. Fire quickly spread to the dry brush and fallen leaves alongside the road. The sulfurous smell of gunpowder and the pungent smell of burning wood wafted over them.

Dark Sun froze briefly, but then his adrenalin kicked in. He fired wildly toward the mass of charging horses, flying robes, and slashing scimitars. A hundred other gypsy gunners launched volleys into the blinding mayhem. Gunshots, screams, clanging metal, and pounding hooves rent the morning air.

The battlefield was soon littered with a horrific composition of Bedouin and gypsy carcasses. The slaughter was so quick and ghastly that it seemed like a scene from a graphic movie.

A jihadist grabbed a screaming gypsy girl by her hair. Abruptly, he slashed her throat. The girl dropped to the ground, writhing in a pool of her own blood. The jihadist hacked at her neck again, completely severing her head. He held it up like a gory trophy, howling epithets in Arabic.

A wounded horse careened into Dark Sun and smashed him to the ground. He hit his head hard and momentarily saw flashes of light in his brain. When he regained his vision an arm plopped near his face, with a tangled mess of bone and tendon at the severed end. A bloodied horse tumbled past him, neighing furiously and kicking wildly in an acrobatic death throe. A wayward bullet hit the ground and kicked up debris into his beard. He heard Osiris howl in pain from a scimitar slice to his back.

The sound of impossibly loud machines rose above the battlefield, adding to the pandemonium of the roiling conflict. Their powerful engines spun vortices of dirt into the air, blinding the combatants. Brilliant flashes of light lanced like lightning bolts. The screaming and howling intensified. Dark Sun believed that this glimpse into the depths of hell portended his death.

The battle stopped as abruptly as it began. Dark Sun's heart skipped a beat. Amid the cyclonic swirls of dirt, he saw the attackers galloping off in terrified retreat. He felt someone lift him to his feet. He steadied himself and squinted through the squall of dust. He saw something incredible.

Six hovercrafts levitated above the crippled caravan. Two others thundered past just above the tree-tops, firing staccato pulses of blazing lightning bolts at the fleeing jihadists. The thrust from their giant props thrashed the tree branches like palm fronds in a hurricane. The surviving gypsies gaped in awe at the otherworldly intruders who had just saved them from total catastrophe.

The six hovercrafts descended to the ground, triggering fresh squalls of dust across the battlefield. Armed soldiers leapt out. One of them spied a knife-wielding Bedouin slinking behind a burning carriage. He raised his weapon and pulled the trigger. A blinding shaft of light tore through the jihadist's body, rendering it into a contorted mound of seared flesh. The laser beam was as eerily soundless as the victim's death.

Osiris confronted the mysterious intruders. "Who are you?" he grunted, oblivious to the blood stain spreading across the back of his own shirt.

A clean-cut officer stepped crisply in front of his soldiers. "I'm Captain Chavez, commander of the Sixth Expeditionary Force. Who are you?"

"I'm Osiris, leader of this gypsy caravan . . . what's left of it." He squinted as if the white, black, and Hispanic soldiers arrayed in front of him were mirages. "Are you Outcasts?"

"That's a matter of perspective," said Chavez sharply. "We call ourselves the Warriors of Pathless Land. Today, you can call us the cavalry."

Osiris cracked a pained smile. "Thank you for saving us," he said softly.

"It was an accident of fate," said Chavez coldly. "We were scouting the Caliphate army. We saw a mounted contingent slink into the woods an hour ago. When they ambushed you, we counterattacked. The truth is, if we didn't kill these jihadists in today's fight, we were going to kill them tomorrow."

Just then, Eve ran up to Osiris. She was breathless and hysterical. "Teema is dying!" she screamed between gasps. "Come with me!"

Osiris and Dark Sun sprinted behind Eve through an obstacle course of dust-covered corpses. When they neared the last carriage, they saw Dark Moon and several gypsies kneeling over a fallen body. The mourners yielded their vigil just enough to make room for Osiris, who fell to his knees beside his adopted daughter.

Blood gushed from a savage gash in Fatima's heaving abdomen. Her hand still gripped a pistol. Much of her body was covered with a macabre paste of dirt and blood. Blood gurgled from her lips as she tried to speak. Her terrified eyes told Osiris everything she couldn't say, and everything he didn't want to hear.

"God damn it!" cursed Osiris. A horrific image of Diana's red sneakers protruding from a white sheet flashed through his head. He looked like he had aged ten years in the last few moments. "Do something!" he screamed. He frantically looked from face to face at those arrayed around him.

Captain Chavez, who had followed the rush toward Fatima, put a hand on Osiris's shaking, bloody shoulder. "Answer two questions correctly, and my team will help the Arab girl and all of your other wounded."

Osiris gaped dumbly, as if the Outcast commander had spoken in a foreign language.

"Caution is necessary because we have no idea who you are," Chavez persisted. "How does your tribe make its living?"

The question bewildered Osiris, but he was at the captain's mercy. "We're gypsies. We're mostly self-sufficient. We trade for the things we can't make ourselves."

"Excellent," interrupted Chavez. "It means you understand and value freedom. Who do your people swear allegiance to?"

Osiris fumed at the senseless delay. "We're loyal only to each other," he spat out hastily. "We don't do the bidding of gods or dictators."

"Then we're not enemies. Our mission is to save the innocents in old America. We'll load your injured into our hovercrafts. Our medics are equipped to perform emergency procedures during the flight to our provisional capital in Atlanta. We have outstanding medical facilities there. We'll return your injured mates back to this very spot after they're healed, since it doesn't look like you're going anywhere soon. Let's plan on exactly two weeks from now. Our soldiers will secure the area, so you should be safe from further attack." Captain Chavez barked corresponding orders to his men.

Osiris scooped his arms under Fatima's limp body and gently lifted her, ignoring the searing pain in his back. She was unconscious now, but still breathing. Two soldiers arrived with a stretcher. Osiris laid her failing body onto it.

He tenderly pried her fingers from the handle of her pistol. As he kissed her forehead, he saw a wisp of a smile grace her bloody lips. His eyes were wet with tears as he confronted nature's most perverse horror, which is a parent losing a child. "I love you, Teema," he murmured.

The stretcher-bearers transported Fatima into the bowels of a hovercraft. Osiris followed behind and as he started to ascend the ramp, Dark Moon tugged at his bloody tunic. "You have to stay here," she said. "The tribe desperately needs your leadership. Dark Sun and I will be of little use here, so we'll go to Atlanta with Teema and the other injured. I promise to protect her as I would my own children. It's our turn to help you. The search for our kids is stalled anyway, because it's going to take time to piece the caravan back together."

Osiris looked to Dark Sun for disagreement. Dark Sun was quietly admiring the decisive demeanor of his wife. He knew how desperate she was to rescue Curious and Cammy. He knew every minute of every day she felt their pain and fear as if her own. Therefore, he knew how much fortitude it took for her to focus now on helping Fatima and Osiris.

"She's right, Osiris," Dark Sun said. "Stay with your tribe. You're the only one who can lead them through this disaster."

Osiris wiped a tear and then nodded. "Bring them all back safely," he pleaded. "When you return, I'll move heaven and earth to find your children."

Dark Sun and Dark Moon hustled to gather their few personal effects for the trip to Atlanta. Eve and Saul trailed behind them performing battlefield triage, pointing out to the Outcast medics the casualties that needed assistance.

Dark Sun stopped in his tracks. A short distance from Fatima's carriage lay Spartacus, bleeding profusely. His front leg had been hacked by a scimitar. Dark Sun ran to his canine companion, hoping to find a way to save him. But when he plunged to the ground beside the dog, he knew it was for naught. Spartacus had lost a horrific amount of blood. His breathing was shallow and intermittent, and his body was convulsing. His jaws were clenched onto a bloodied swatch of black robe.

Saul put a hand on Dark Sun's shoulder. "I'm sorry, but you have to do the humane thing."

Dark Sun nodded somberly. He pulled his pistol from his waistband. Eve and Dark Moon turned their backs in anguish. Dark Sun stroked Spartacus between his ears one last time. The dog attempted to lift his head, but it fell back to the ground. With bitter tears in his eyes, Dark Sun grimaced, pointed the pistol, and said, "You don't deserve this. No living thing does." A shot rang out; it was over. He somberly noted that they now had one less connection to their past. Or maybe it was their last.

Dark Sun and Dark Moon gathered their things from Fatima's carriage and ran back to the hovercrafts to go to Atlanta. A profound wave of darkness washed over them. What did it matter where they went now? It seemed like they were battling a demonic hydra that sprouted new heads every time they cut one off. There was always a virulent faction just around the next bend ready to snatch something from them.

Their grim circumstances reminded Dark Sun of a fable about two baby calves who were still inside their mother's womb. One calf asked the other, "What do you think life will be like outside this womb?" The other replied, "We will graze forever in an endless meadow beside our loving mother, munching tender clover and drinking from a cold, clear stream. What do you think it'll be like?" The first calf said, "I fear that we'll be penned in tight quarters, fed disgusting food, and injected with hormones. Then we'll be clubbed in the head, ground into a gooey mess, and fed to vulgar hominids." The other said, "I like my guess better." The first calf concluded, "Of course. Most sane calves would."

Dark Sun no longer knew whether he was sane or insane. What other fiendish demons lurked in their future? What was left for the demons to take? How long before he and Dark Moon were clubbed in the head by vulgar hominids?

They climbed into the Outcast hovercraft. The ramp closed like a prison door behind them.

TWENTY-SIX
REGIS

Power into will, will into appetite; and appetite, a universal wolf.

— William Shakespeare

Regis drank in the applause like a sponge soaking up a messy spill.

After finishing his speech at a pig and corn roast in Des Moines, he waved to the audience and headed backstage. His promise to double the federal corn subsidy was a stroke of genius that he conjured up on the bus ride to the auditorium. He took off his John Deere hat and tossed it into a nearby trash can. His stomach rumbled from the plateful of pulled pork that he now regretted eating. He never ate such swill at Yale or on Martha's Vineyard.

"Nice performance," said a tall man who suddenly emerged from the shadows. "You should have been an actor. Or a magician."

Regis was taken aback. His usual entourage of speechwriters, publicists, policy wonks, and social media mavens were nowhere in sight.

Perhaps they were already on the bus waiting for him to embark on the next leg of their 2036 presidential election campaign swing. They were headed to the University of Dubuque, where he would propose free college education for all. He felt a sudden wave of insecurity being alone with this strange man in the expensive suit who blocked his exit. The intruder wasn't yielding. Or smiling.

"Who are you?" Regis asked.

The mysterious man had dark hair that was slicked back. He had a well-manicured mustache and beard that gave him a debonair appearance and an air of wealth, despite his relative youth. He took a long draw on his cigarette. "You can call me Cosimo."

"That's an unusual name." Regis often lost much of his eloquence when the teleprompter was off.

"I'm an unusual man."

There was an awkward silence as Regis looked around the darkened space for any sign of his entourage. Even his security guards had mysteriously evacuated the backstage. He and Cosimo were utterly alone. He considered crying out for help, but that seemed pathetically unpresidential, especially in Iowa.

"What do you want?" Regis finally asked.

"I want what you want, Senator. I want you to be the next president of the United States."

"I'm afraid you're going to be disappointed," replied Regis. "I'm buried pretty deep in the polls."

"Which is where you will remain, if you don't accept my help."

Regis studied Cosimo's immaculate suit and the well-coiffed hair. He noticed his jeweled ring, which featured a snake encircling the globe. Perhaps the interloper had lots of money, which is what Regis desperately needed right now. It cost billions of dollars to put a person in the Oval Office, which was more than NASA spent to put a person on the moon. Grifting for campaign funds was in Regis' comfort zone, so his insecurity began to wane. "What help are you suggesting?"

"I'll get to that in a moment," Cosimo said. "First, let's verify your presidential qualifications."

Regis launched into the practiced cant of his public persona. "I graduated Magna cum Laude from Yale. I've been in public service my whole life. I've been a US Senator for eight years. I sponsored bills to reduce the voting age to sixteen, fund free health care for all, guarantee everyone a living wage, ban fossil fuels, open the borders to foreigners, nationalize the Big Tech companies, and put labor union leaders on the boards of every corporation in America. I've been endorsed by the League of Women Voters, Planned Parenthood, La Raza, the NAACP, the labor unions, and the Southern Poverty Law Center."

"Perfect," replied Cosimo with a hint of snark. "But those aren't the qualifications I'm interested in. They'll earn you eighth place among the other pious poseurs running for your party's nomination."

Regis looked puzzled. "What qualifications are you looking for?"

"Let's go through them. Are you a true believer in your cause, whatever it is?'

Regis puffed out his chest. "No one is more committed to helping victims and the underclass than I am. I've dedicated my whole life to serving their needs!"

Cosimo smiled for the first time. "Yes, I suppose you come into contact with many of them at your country club. It's important for you to be a true believer. That's the only way you'll be able to credibly sell the necessary illusions. How well can you lie?"

"You be the judge," said Regis. "Did you hear that applause from those farmers? They actually believed I knew the price of a bushel of corn in the Chicago commodities market. They even believed my plan to drive those prices up would actually work. As far as I know, corn grows on a tree."

"Your performance was indeed impressive. Such duplicity will be important in the future. Is there anything you're unwilling to do to become president?"

Regis fell silent for a moment. "I won't commit murder. And I'll never promise to cut a government program. I was born to be president. I desire nothing else. My parents groomed me for it, to the point of naming me Regis. My dad orchestrated my political career using his connections, but I think he's reached the limit of his influence. He's no Joe Kennedy."

"His meager influence ends where mine begins," said Cosimo. "I've been studying your career for several years now. I think we can work well together. If I help you win the presidency, will you be loyal to me above all others?"

"In order for me to change the world, I have to become president. If you can make that happen, I'll do anything you ask in return—short of murder and spending cuts." Regis paused as a look of confusion washed over his face. "What organization do you work for?"

"It's called the Syndicate. It's a worldwide network of kinship and solemn trust. I'm not at liberty to disclose any other details."

"Then how can I be certain that this is a serious deal, and that you'll hold up your end of our bargain?"

Cosimo flicked his cigarette butt away. "When you return to your hotel room tonight, check the balance in the bank account of your PAC. It will be $100 million greater. That's merely a down payment. We will commit any additional funds that are necessary to get you elected, as long as you continue to demonstrate your loyalty and worthiness. Our Influencers will also provide whatever media and cultural support is necessary to frame your candidacy in the best possible light, and to frame the candidacies of your opponents in the worst possible light. But understand that if we shake hands today, it will be the point of no return. You will have a grand career and a wealthy lifestyle. But the price will be absolute, unconditional loyalty to me. In everything."

"And if we don't shake hands?"

"You will be nothing more than a minor footnote in history, and no one will believe that this private conversation in a darkened auditorium in the middle of Iowa ever occurred."

"What's in this arrangement for your organization?" asked Regis.

"The same thing that's been the Syndicate's objective for hundreds of years."

"Which is what?"

"Influence," replied Cosimo. "We like to have our fingers on the pulse of the major players around the globe."

Cosimo stuck out his hand expectantly.

Regis stared at the proffered hand in amazement. He was bewildered by this sudden intersection with destiny. He was intrigued by this peek into a world of stealthy undercurrents he had heard only vague rumors about. Cosimo's extended hand seemed to him like the serpent holding a shiny apple in the garden of Eden. Regis was mesmerized by it, just as Adam and Eve were tantalized by the Tree of Knowledge. Everything he ever wanted was within his reach, including the opportunity to help shape America in his own image.

He grabbed Cosimo's hand as if he were grabbing the actual power and notoriety he had always lusted for.

The edges of the jeweled snake on Cosimo's ring dug into his fingers.

It felt good.

TWENTY-SEVEN
INTERROGATION

The answer is always there
When the soul is laid bare
Think deeply about the sublime
True wisdom will come in time

— *The Poems of Dark Sun*

Inside the hovercraft, a medic worked feverishly to stabilize Fatima. Dark Moon knelt beside the unconscious young woman, holding her hand and whispering encouragement into her ear. Dark Sun stood behind her, reveling in the beauty and grace of Dark Moon's maternal manner. He had witnessed her remarkable ability to ease suffering countless times when Curious and Cammy got hurt, which happened quite often for the young tree-climbers and outdoor adventurers.

Dark Sun was pushed aside by medics scrambling to tend to the wounded. He retreated to a corner of the craft. He pulled his father's journal out of his satchel and began reading the next entry.

December 12, 2054

I'm staring at a faded picture of my two sons wrestling many years ago. It was a normal thing for brothers to do, but I look at it differently now. Kieran is on top, rubbing his brother's head with his knuckles. Kieran often bullied James, who took his beatings meekly.

The faded picture is an allegory for the modern world. Today, Kieran is an Elite. The Elites are shameless bullies who impose themselves on people who are too willing to turn the other cheek.

True to form, the Elites came looking for our guns again today. Their agents sweep through the area monthly. They know if we're armed, we'll continue to fight back. Bullies prefer defenseless victims.

When they find guns, they punish the transgressors, using their spurious laws as cudgels. They also punish people for hoarding banned books. They consider them to be intellectual weapons. Such oppression is the very reason that citizens should be armed, regardless of any laws to the contrary.

The bullies ignore the reality that life must be constantly defended. The threats range from bacteria and viruses at the micro level, to carnivores, villains, storms, and a host of other dangers at the macro level. These are all manifestations of entropy's continual assault on living beings.

Defending life is so fundamental that it supersedes all law and all social conventions. The right to defend is synonymous with the right to life. They're inseparable.

The most severe threats to humans are other humans. We attack each other because of religious, political, and cultural differences. We attack each other out of greed, hatred, and a host of other psychological afflictions. Usually, we attack others who aren't "us."

Sometimes we're attacked by the authorities who are supposed to protect us. When citizens are disarmed, atrocity and genocide follow with alarming frequency, as the disarmed citizens of Stalinist Russia, Maoist China, National Socialist Germany, and the Socialist European Union learned.

Disarming innocent people is like ripping the shells from armadillos or stripping the quills from porcupines. The naked creatures are left to cower helplessly, waiting for inevitable harm, captivity, or death.

Even though we delegate the use of defensive force to the police and military, we must never cede the right to our own self-defense. We can never have absolute assurance that the police or military will perform their duties or arrive in time. If we rely solely on them to protect us, we will be defenseless if they become monsters, as they sometimes do. The right to bear arms is ours by our very nature as humans who require constant defense to survive.

This right precedes governments and can never be rightfully abrogated by them, though they've all tried and will forever try. Our own government found a hundred pretexts to defang the Second Amendment. Then the Constitutional Convention in 2041 eliminated it entirely. However, there are millions of outlawed guns hidden around the country. We have a right to protect ourselves from bullies who torment us. As the Jewish sage Hillel asked, "If I am not for myself, who will be for me?"

The Elites are committing the ultimate treason—they're attacking us, rather than defending us. We're resorting to the most basic political right, which is the right to revolt against abusive leaders. The weapons necessary to enforce this inalienable right are the only antidotes to a world teeming with tyrants. As George Orwell put it, "That rifle on the wall of the laborer's cottage or working-class flat is the symbol of democracy."

That's the lesson James must learn, or else the Kieran's of the world will always have their way with him. So far, he doesn't seem to be getting it.

Dark Sun set the journal down. He pulled from his waistband the pistol his father had unknowingly left him. He turned it over in his hands slowly, examining it as if he had never seen it before. He was beginning to see the world through different eyes. He was starting to get it. Something powerful was fermenting in his heart as the hovercraft sped toward the new citadel of the Warriors of Pathless Land.

The young medic and his aide continued working on Fatima. They paused periodically when turbulence shook the hovercraft. Dark Moon wiped away a tear that had dripped onto Teema's forehead. Then she brushed dirt and leaves from Fatima's dark hair. The aide tried to usher Dark Moon away, but she shrugged him off. She had sworn to Osiris that she wouldn't leave Fatima's side.

It was ironic to Dark Moon that fate had given her this opportunity to help the woman who had rescued her and Dark Sun after the attack on their home in Kansas. It struck her that life is a series of karmic events in which everything is somehow connected to everything else. Karma had now cast her among the Outcasts.

The medic dropped an instrument. It clanged sharply on the floor, startling Dark Moon. She eyed him up and down, intrigued by this close encounter with an Outcast. He was tall and lean, filling out his impeccable white smock smartly. His hair was brown, with a hint of red. He looked too young to be a doctor, but his manner was confident and professional. He had a radiant, innocent face that seemed permanently poised on the verge of a smile. His striking brown eyes made him warm and approachable. To Dark Moon, he looked like she imagined Curious would as an adult. She winced, unsure if Curious would survive long enough to become one.

"What's your name?" she asked, when the medic paused during more turbulence.

"Kerry Kozlowski," he replied with an air of distraction. He studied digital displays on the sophisticated equipment monitoring Fatima. "What's yours?"

"Dark Moon. Is Kerry Kozlowski your alias?"

He glanced at her quizzically. "That's a strange question. Why would anyone mask something as essential as their identity?"

Dark Moon winced. The medic's question reopened a deep spiritual wound that she had cauterized years ago. She used to have recurring nightmares about the sacrifice of her real identity, which had been necessary to elude the prying eyes of the Elites. In her nightmares, she was adrift in a surrealistic world of blank faces that floated in a dark void that had no up or down, like marooned astronauts adrift in deep space. She had no sense of who these drifting faces were. She had no idea who she was. There was no purpose to anything. It was like being in a coma while aware. It was as if her ego had died but her mechanical brain was still alive.

The recurring nightmares reflected her stark fear of a perpetual state of being alive and yet not *being*. It was hard to condense this terror into concise enough words to properly answer Kerry's question. All she could manage was, "I don't *want* to hide my identity. I'm . . . afraid."

"Of what?" The medic paused, waiting for his aide to prep some instruments.

Dark Moon thought for a moment. "Others," she replied hesitantly.

"Your husband? Your family? Your friends?" His questions were colored with sarcasm.

"No, of course not. I love them. I'd trust them with my life."

"Then who do you fear?"

"Everyone else, I suppose. Elites. Jackals. Jihadists."

"They arouse such fear that you hide your very identity?"

"They have gangs, guns, armies, secret police . . . and kidnappers."

"They must not have *complete* power over you. You removed your SIN Chip."

"How do you know that?" His observation reminded her to be cautious of the strangers invading from Outcast Island.

Kozlowski pointed to a device mounted on the ceiling. "We scan for SIN chips in our vehicles and buildings. Any Elites trying to infiltrate would be flagged immediately. Ironically, they used the SIN chips to keep track of rebels, and now we're using their chips to keep track of them. You were brave enough to surgically free yourself from their electronic shackle. Maybe someday you'll be brave enough to reclaim your real identity."

"How are you so brave?"

Kozlowski laughed, flashing an intoxicating smile that once again reminded Dark Moon of Curious. "I often get told I'm not brave enough. I've been more lucky than brave. My parents had the good fortune to be rejected by your dysfunctional world. I'm what you call an Outcast, remember?"

"I suppose my husband and I are Outcasts too," Dark Moon conceded. "We've joined a roving band of misfits."

Kozlowski nodded toward Fatima. "For a misfit, your daughter is very beautiful."

"She's not mine. But my daughter was beautiful too." Dark Moon felt a sharp pang in her heart for speaking of Cammy in the past tense.

A shrill alarm blared. "We're descending into Atlanta," said Kozlowski. "We have to prep our patients for transfer to the hospital."

Dark Moon looked out the windows. In the distance, she could see a massive city to the right, and a mountain shaped like a giant stone to the left. A sculpture carved on the face of the mountain depicted three rebel civil war leaders from two centuries before. It never ends, she thought to herself.

Moments later, the hovercrafts alighted on the roof of a military hospital. Fatima and the other wounded were hastily wheeled down a ramp by medics. They were flanked by soldiers barking out instructions. Dark Sun and Dark Moon hustled behind them. Everyone piled into a freight elevator that descended into the bowels of the building.

The frantic entourage poured out of the elevator toward a set of doors that were marked Emergency and were guarded by armed soldiers. Kozlowski waved his hand over an electronic scanner. The doors swung open and the procession of medics and gurneys scrambled through.

Dark Sun and Dark Moon attempted to follow, but a burly black guard shouted "Stop!"

The couple froze in place. The guard studied the two strangers dressed in bloody, tattered civilian garb. It was obvious they didn't belong in a military facility. "Who are you?" he asked with a Jamaican accent.

A soldier who had flown with them from the battlefield stepped forward to explain. "They're companions of the casualties who were just wheeled into Emergency. We flew them here from the combat zone in Indiana."

The guard continued to eye the bedraggled interlopers. "Are they from the Elites? The Caliphate? The Jackals? It's reckless to bring—"

"Captain Chavez of the Sixth Expeditionary Force authorized it," interrupted the soldier. "It was an act of mercy. They're from a tribe of gypsies that were being slaughtered by the Caliphate until we intervened."

"Have you searched them?"

The soldier stiffened. "No. We had to hurry. Many were dying—"

"Damn it! Have you forgotten what the mainlanders did to our ancestors? Search them!"

"We'll save you the trouble," volunteered Dark Sun. "We're not a threat. Here, I'll give you my pistol and knife until we're ready to leave."

When he reached for his weapons, the guard leveled his gun at him. "Stop! Put your hands up!"

Dark Sun complied. Another guard frisked him and Dark Moon from head to toe and extracted their weapons.

"Scan them and their bags," growled the guard.

A guard pulled an electronic device from his service belt. He waved the coiled contraption over Dark Sun and then his bag. The guard showed the device's display to his partner with a satisfied look. Then he scanned Dark Moon. Nothing. Finally, he scanned her bag. Shrill beeping erupted from his device.

"Search the bag!"

The guard grabbed it and dumped her meager possessions onto a table. He waved the scanner over a tangled wad of clothing. The shrill beeping became more incessant when the device hovered over a blouse. The soldier shook the blouse, and a small object fell to the table with a clank.

The burly guard snatched up the object. It looked like an insect, but no insect would clank on a table. He rolled it over in his fingers to inspect it. "It's a miniature drone!" the guard snapped. He threw it on the floor and crushed it with the heel of his boot. "The bastards are spying on us! Arrest them!"

MPs corralled Dark Sun and Dark Moon. Dark Sun started to protest their innocence but was kneed in the groin to end further dissent. They were blindfolded, bound, and tossed like a sack of potatoes into a military police tram that was stationed outside the hospital. The tram sped away with lights flashing and siren blaring.

After a long ride at high speed, the vehicle screeched to a halt. In the darkness of the rear compartment, Dark Sun and Dark Moon heard the muffled sound of soldiers reporting their situation to officials. They surmised from the dialogue that they had been transported to a prison. Dark Sun leaned his blindfolded head close to Dark Moon's and whispered, "Be completely honest with them. We've done nothing wrong."

He felt her head nod. He could tell from her rapid, shallow breathing that she was terribly afraid. He could hear his own heart thumping. He didn't fear for himself, though. He feared for his children, who might never be rescued now. He imagined them equally terrified in their own captivity, hoping desperately for their parents to save them. He figured they probably still believed that a rescue was forthcoming, because kids think their parents will never fail them. But like a seafarer adrift in a sinking boat, he couldn't even save himself.

The MPs dragged Dark Sun and Dark Moon out of the tram. Dark Moon heard a scuffle and then shouting from guards. During the discordant exchange, she heard Dark Sun yell "I love you," although his voice was trailing off. They were separated now.

Dark Moon was led into the building and through a series of doors and turns. Abruptly, she was pushed into a cold concrete cell, and her blindfold and binds were removed. The steel door clanged shut, leaving her alone with a stainless-steel sink, a toilet, and a grated metal platform that was perhaps a bed.

Hours passed as she huddled in a corner of the cell like a caged animal. She wondered if Dark Sun was being tortured, if Fatima was still alive, and what horrors Curious and Cammy were enduring. She was confined in a suffocating space with every foreboding thought that her disoriented mind could conjure. It was like being in Orwell's Room 101. Her heart beat hard like a clock counting down to doomsday. She was at the mercy of strangers who had no reason to keep her alive. She was powerless to help her imperiled loved ones. Her situation was the perfect incubator for imagining the worst. That's where her mind went.

The door suddenly slid open. "Come with us," one of two armed guards commanded with a Hispanic accent. They led her down a sterile hallway, up two flights of stairs, and then down another hallway. They stopped at an unmarked door and knocked. A muffled voice beckoned them in.

Two armed officers were inside the dimly lit room. Her escorts saluted and left. She stared blankly at the officers standing across the table. The tall, thin one had the name Lopez embroidered on his uniform. The short, stocky one had the name Garcia. They eyed her dispassionately, noting her bloody clothes, disheveled blond hair, and obdurate stare. Lopez pointed to an empty chair. "Sit," he ordered.

She complied. "What do you want?" Her lips trembled as she spoke.

"We'll ask the questions," barked Garcia. "What's your name?"

"Dark Moon."

He glared at her. "What's your *real* name?"

She lifted her chin in defiance. "Dark Moon."

"Your only hope to leave here is to cooperate."

"If you say so," Dark Moon replied softly. "But I'll never reveal my slave name."

"I see." Garcia pursed his lips and furrowed his eyebrows. "Well then, what's your companion's name?"

"Dark Sun. He's my husband."

Garcia glanced at Lopez, got a nod in return, and then stood up from his chair. Dark Moon slid her chair back, fearing violence. "Are . . . are you going to torture me?" Her voice cracked.

The stocky officer circled menacingly to her side of the table. He squatted and looked directly into her eyes. "We don't torture. We need your help."

Dark Moon was caught off guard. "I . . . I don't understand."

"We investigated your situation. Our officers in Indiana confirmed that your tribe was ambushed by the Caliphate. Your wounded companions were sent here by order of a trusted commander. Therefore, it's unlikely that you are part of an organized effort to infiltrate us. That's the good news."

Dark Moon cringed. "And the bad news?"

Garcia stood and began pacing. "The Elites are obviously tracking you. The drone in your clothing was likely navigated there by one of their expert remote pilots. One of your wounded companions revealed that another drone had monitored your caravan earlier—"

"Hawkeye shot it."

Garcia waved a dismissive hand. "It's extraordinary that the Elites would be so fixated on your insignificant tribe. It tells us that you're important to our enemies. That means you're important to us. We need to know more. Tell us your story."

"But you're Outcasts," Dark Moon said, as if this slur justified her obstinance.

"Damn it, woman! You're in incredible danger, and it's not because of us. Since a drone followed you here, we're compromised too. We're going to protect ourselves—with extreme prejudice, if necessary. If you cooperate, we'll protect you too. But we need to know more about your situation. Tell us your story!"

Dark Moon realized she couldn't help Dark Sun, Fatima, or her children by making a quixotic stand in this prison. They could hold her here forever. Or kill her. "Okay, I'll tell you," she conceded.

She recounted in detail the attack on their home in Kansas, the kidnapping of their children, their involvement with Osiris and the gypsy tribe, and their frustrating eastward trek to search for Curious and Cammy. Then silence.

Finally, Lopez said, "There's more to your story than meets the eye. The Elites don't track just anyone with drones. And sending agents to your home in Kansas to abduct your children is done only at great consequence. Why are they so interested in your family?"

Dark Moon shook her head. "I've asked myself that over and over. I have no idea!"

"Were you combatants in the civil war?" he pressed.

"No! We lived in no-man's-land. We have no political allegiance. We just want to be left alone. And now everyone is interested in us."

"Are you connected to any Elites?"

Dark Moon told them about her sister, Katarina, and Kieran.

The two officers looked at each other solemnly. Lopez said, "So the two of you have family members who joined the Elites?"

Dark Moon shrugged. "Yes, but that doesn't justify the assault on our family. I'm sure many other families are in the same situation."

"There must be a connection!" blurted Garcia. "There's a reason the Elites are obsessed with your family. Think!"

"I have!" shouted Dark Moon. "Every waking hour since my kids were kidnapped! If I had a fucking clue, I'd tell you!"

"Tell us your real names," Garcia persisted. "It would help us piece this puzzle together."

"Why are you so damned interested in us?" Dark Moon blurted. "Why are the *Elites* so damned interested? Why does everybody suddenly care about us?"

"We care because our mortal enemies see you as vitally important. That could mean great danger for us . . . or perhaps great opportunity. We need to know!"

"I won't tell you my real name! In a sane world, my true identity would be a badge of honor. But it's not a sane world." Dark Moon angrily pulled aside a torn flap of her blouse to reveal the scar where her SIN chip was removed. "See this? My real identity was tethered to a tracking device monitored by the Elites. It's forever linked to their databases. Before I went dark, everything I did was tracked, scanned, and uploaded. My identity was hijacked. If I surrender my anonymity now, I risk being completely exposed again. I won't do it! Kill me instead—it's the same thing."

Dark Moon dropped her head into her hands and sobbed. Lopez put a consoling hand on her shoulder. "We understand, more than you know. You ripped out your SIN chip because you hated their control. Decades ago the Elites banished many of our people to an island prison because we rebelled against their control. We have the same enemy. Trust us!"

"Trust is very hard in this world," Dark Moon muttered through bitter tears. "I'll trust you just a bit now. You didn't torture me when you could have, and I think your doctors are trying to save Teema."

"She is going to live," Lopez said. "So will the others."

Dark Moon breathed a heavy sigh of relief. "I'm very grateful. But why are you helping our wounded?"

"Because you're not our enemies. Our fight isn't with the American people. We're here to liberate innocent people, not to harm them."

Dark Moon nodded and then looked at the two officers expectantly.

Garcia held her gaze. "We have a proposal for you. I'll be very direct—your end of the bargain will be dangerous."

"Just tell me what I have to do to find my kids."

The officer nodded grimly. "We need to use you and your husband as bait."

TWENTY-EIGHT
LEVIATHAN

If a nation expects to be ignorant and free, it expects what never was and will never be.

— Thomas Jefferson

The massive concrete, steel, and glass edifices in Washington were awesome at first, but Cammy soon tired of the sunless canyons between the tall, sterile buildings, and the endless concrete beneath her feet. The stark contrast with the meadows and woods of Kansas made her feel unwelcome and claustrophobic.

Cammy and her brother were confined to a minimum-security prison when they arrived in the capital. They shared a small, austere cell. She was alone for the first few days, because Curious was sent to a hospital. When he returned to their cell his left leg was in a cast, and he was in a wheelchair.

Once a day they were escorted on walks in the city. Cammy felt great loneliness among the faceless crowds. Strangers didn't acknowledge each other when they passed on the street. Instead, they fixed their gazes on distant focal points, as though nobody cared that anyone else even existed.

Curious was in less physical pain after his surgery, but his spirits were crushed. Cammy did her best to cheer him up, even though she wrestled with the same demons. They were captives in an alien city. They didn't know why they had been abducted. They didn't know the fate of their parents. They missed Brutus and Spartacus. Perhaps they were all dead.

It seemed something was going to be revealed to them soon. A guard had thrown new clothes into their cell. They were ordered to change into them and to tidy up. The guard said that the two of them were finally going to be put to use.

Cammy inspected the simple blood-red smocks. Their only adornment was a royal purple logo just below the neckline, offset to the left. The logo depicted the world cradled in the hands of some unseen person. It had no inscription. The meaning of the logo eluded her. The smocks were identical to those worn by the officious ministers who escorted her and Curious on their brief outdoor walks.

After they dressed, uniformed aides came for them. They were driven by limousine through Washington. They gawked out the windows at an endless sea of beehive-like buildings, where countless people presumably worked. Cammy had no idea that so many people even existed. She also had no idea what work they actually did because she saw no farmland in the city nor anything that looked like a factory.

The limousine pulled up to one of the massive beehives. The monolith towered over them as they approached its shadowed entrance. They were led into a realm of unnatural lighting and hiked past bay after bay of modular cubicles, each identified by a number. They had just strolled past cubicles 3027, 3028, and 3029. She wondered how many such pens were in the building.

Worker bees occupied the drab habitats, staring bleary-eyed at glowing screens. Some of them talked in desultory monotones into their screens. Cammy couldn't discern any purpose in their activity. She shook her head, unable to imagine a lifetime of such banality. She knew if she had to choose between staring at those screens for the rest of her life or shooting herself in the head, the choice would be easy.

She wondered if any of them had ever strolled down a wooded path with a faithful dog by their side. Had they ever pranced barefoot in a cold stream, smelled the earthiness of a flowered meadow after a warm summer rain, breathed the pristine air of an autumn afternoon, or experienced any of the other sensual and spiritual blessings that made existence divine? She wanted to scream to snap them out of their comas, but she knew that an outburst would end badly for her. The Elites were more serious about discipline than her parents.

She noticed that each cubicle had a chart posted by a group called the Committee for Public Information. She quickly realized that the charts weren't measuring the productivity of the workers. They were measuring something called Social Sincerity. The score was a tally of each worker's social media posts, participation in group events, rule compliance, and other indicators of social conformity.

She didn't know what the workers gained or lost based on their score, but it was clear that their scores were important, because there were no other charts posted. It struck Cammy that the clumsy attempt to bludgeon the workers into proper social behavior was perhaps why they had atrophied into drones. Even she knew that sincerity wasn't measured by graphs on pieces of paper. It was measured by hearts in real relationships.

Next to each Social Sincerity chart was a placard with a simple guideline. It reminded the workers that they were free to speak their minds, but the Committee for Public Information would penalize anti-social comments. That seemed deviously vague to Cammy. Were people free to speak or were they not?

Their entourage entered a large room that was very different from the honeycombed pens they had passed along the way. Its purpose was mysterious to Cammy. In it were many contraptions that looked like movie cameras, at least from pictures she recalled from her grandfather's books. Bright lights illuminated what appeared to be a stage.

The two kids were beckoned by an agitated person wielding a clipboard who had been harping about some details of the setting on the stage. "You're late!" the clipboard-holder chastised. "Regis will be pissed if we don't get this done today. Get up on stage. Now!"

Cammy complied. An aide wheeled Curious up a ramp. They were positioned next to an older man and an older woman, both of whom scowled at them. They looked vaguely familiar.

Suddenly, the stage lights momentarily blinded them. A show was about to go on, and Cammy and Curious were apparently the main attractions.

TWENTY-NINE
J

> Hope and salvation followed
> Into the dark abyss we wallowed
> The process of life will connect
> In strange ways you least expect
>
> — *The Poems of Dark Sun*

Dark Sun and Dark Moon were ecstatic.

They hugged tightly, then she placed her hands on his cheeks and kissed him.

Dark Sun smiled and gazed into her teary eyes. "I'm surprised they're letting us go. They didn't get much out of me. I didn't even tell them my real name."

"You were stronger than me," Dark Moon said. "I agreed to cooperate with them."

Dark Sun stopped smiling. "Did they hurt you?" He held her at arm's length and scanned her body for signs of violence.

"I'm okay. They're not the monsters some say they are. I think we can be allies."

"With Outcasts? Are you nuts?"

"We're outcasts too . . . sort of." Dark Moon scanned his body. "It doesn't look like they hurt you, either."

"Just this little pinprick." Dark Sun pointed to a tiny hole in the back of his hand.

"Why did they do that?"

He shrugged. "I don't know. I expected worse." He paused because something she said earlier finally sank in. "What did you agree to?"

"Not to tell anyone what happened here in exchange for being released. They gave me a tracking device so they can monitor our location. We can also use it to send an emergency signal if we get in a jam."

"I don't understand," said Dark Sun. "Why do they care where we are? How is that any different than being tracked by the Elites?"

Dark Moon rubbed her arm. "It's simple. We're clearly important to the Elites. Since the Outcasts are at war with them, they want to use us to foil their scheme. And perhaps they can help us rescue our kids in the process."

"Let me get this straight, Moonbeam. We're going to be lured into contact with the Elites. You're carrying an Outcast tracking device similar to the SIN chip you extracted. And then we'll end up in the middle of a conflict between two powerful factions."

"I think you've got it," she said drily.

Dark Sun shook his head slowly. "You *are* nuts."

Dark Moon threw her hands up in exasperation. "It gets us the hell out of Atlanta so we can search for our kids again! We need to tangle with the Elites anyway. Why not have allies who might help us?"

"Will they help us or use us?"

Dark Moon sighed heavily. "Our options are limited. It's possible that we're just bait, and this will end badly. But the Outcasts rescued us from the Caliphate and healed our friends. I don't think we're enemies." She paused. "I'll take all the help I can get to save our children."

"I don't think Osiris will approve—"

"He won't know. I promised that we'd keep this a secret. The Outcasts are worried that too many people in our tribe have connections to the Elites."

Dark Sun mentally weighed the deal she had agreed to. On one hand, it entangled them in a civil war that they had nothing to do with. On the other hand, it was a tenuous alliance with a very powerful faction that could help take on the dangerous Elites. He reflected on the destruction of their home and the violence of the kidnapping. He nodded his head slowly. Time was running out, and they indeed had no other options.

He hugged Dark Moon again and whispered into her ear, "You did well, my love."

Later that day, Dark Moon fussed over Fatima in her recovery room at the hospital. Dark Sun sensed that she had mentally adopted Fatima as her surrogate child in the absence of Curious and Cammy. He smiled; she had always wanted a third child.

Dark Sun took advantage of the solitude to read another entry from his father's journal. He noticed something strange when he opened it. His shabby white rose was gone. In its place was a new white rose, freshly laminated. He wondered why the Outcasts made the substitution. Maybe it was their way of apologizing for snooping through his things, which they clearly had done. Maybe they had lost the original. He shrugged away a tinge of disappointment at losing his father's memento, then began reading.

January 23, 2055

James and I had a successful hunt today. We bagged three rabbits and a wild pig. Mary was thrilled. It's been a tough winter, and the food in our cellar was dwindling. Every winter seems harder than the last. That's another sign Father Time is sneaking up on me.

We're far better off than those who don't live on a farm. Millions in America are starving, which is ironic in a land that once was the breadbasket of the world. There are rumors that desperate people are eating their dead, just like the first settlers in Jamestown. What a macabre circle our country has circumscribed in four centuries.

The starvation was seeded in 2041 when America held a constitutional convention in Philadelphia. We replaced our old constitution with the World Order's Universal Declaration of Human Rights. It guaranteed everyone the right to food, clothing, housing, education, transportation, and health care. In exchange, people were "bound" to their community.

The goals of the new declaration seemed righteous to many people, but it was essentially a suicide pact. It replaced the very real freedom to act, which is vital for survival, with the phantasm of freedom from economic need, which is impossible. It sacrificed our liberty for the illusions of security and equality. It was the most foolish decision ever made. As Franklin told us, "They who give up essential liberty to obtain a little temporary safety deserve neither liberty nor safety."

To implement the rights asserted by the declaration, at least one of the following conditions had to be true. Condition One: Food, clothing, housing, education, transportation, and health care magically appear out of thin air. Condition Two: The government forcibly transfers the fruits of some people's efforts to others.

After the new constitution was ratified, people learned two awful truths. Truth One: Food, clothing, education, transportation, housing, and health care don't magically appear out of thin air. Truth two: Productive people will object to having the fruits of their efforts forcibly transferred to freeloaders.

Eventually, most hard-working people went dark. They melted into the anonymity of black markets, or they joined the expanding cadre of freeloaders. A slave won't choose to remain a slave forever. What sane person would? When a society incentivizes sloth, it gets more of it. When *a society punishes ambition, it gets less of it. When a society treats everyone as entitled, no one feels responsible. When a society collectivizes ownership, no one owns anything.*

Even though the new constitution guaranteed free food, it delivered mass starvation. Instead of free clothes, it delivered tattered rags. Instead of free homes, it delivered homelessness. Instead of free transportation, it delivered economic paralysis. Instead of free health care, it delivered rationed services and disappearing doctors. Instead of free education, it delivered propaganda, political correctness, and revisionist history.

The new constitution required a coercive state able to impose its will. It ignored the truth that nothing can be called a right if it requires force to transfer something from one person to another.

That's how the Elites came to be our overlords. They originally called themselves democratic socialists. They used flowery platitudes like "progress," "change," "fairness," "equality," and "social justice" to disguise their intrusions on our liberty. After the new constitution was ratified, they dropped their pretenses and called themselves the Elites. They could just as well have called themselves the Masters.

When the power of government expands, it intrudes upon the spontaneous order and creativity of free people. Progress and innovation get stifled. People lose the liberty to act rationally in their self-interest. Then entropy devours everyone.

Entropy is devouring us all now. Our society has descended into gang warfare, riots, and widespread strife between factions that have been stoked to hate each other for decades. Our country has become a third-world hellhole of poverty, wanton violence, tent cities, sewage-filled streets, and nihilism. People now stand in line for bread and toilet paper, as they did in countries we used to mock. They're learning the hard way that producers don't need parasites, but parasites need producers.

Today, James and I hunted small game to keep our family alive. In the future, I may need to hunt bigger game to keep everyone alive.

Dark Sun inserted the new bookmark and shut the journal. His father was emerging as a much different person through his writings than Dark Sun had known as a youth. Perhaps it was because he was now experiencing him through the lens of adulthood. It was spooky, like he had lived with someone else those many years ago.

On the last evening before the recovering gypsies were scheduled to return to the caravan in Indiana, Kerry invited them to a dinner in the hospital cafeteria. It was a farewell gesture, and also a final opportunity for the young doctor to spend time with Fatima.

He was incubating a fascination with the beautiful gypsy girl. He had spent many hours with her during her rehabilitation, and he had introduced her to the hospital's library of books. She particularly enjoyed the private moments when he read aloud by her bedside. Because of his constant ministrations, Fatima recovered quickly. She was still wheelchair-bound though, as a precaution while her wounds healed.

Kozlowski sat beside her while the guests feasted. She fidgeted with her food in silence, but intently followed the conversation that swirled around the table. Kozlowski was peppered with questions about the mysterious Outcasts and the nation they called Pathless Land. She avoided looking at him, even though he was the focus of the discussion.

After her second glass of wine, she began stealing sideways glances at the handsome young doctor. She felt awkward. She admitted to herself that she was infatuated with him. His constant doting during the past two weeks had her attention. But she also knew that trusting another man was a bridge she was unlikely to cross.

After her third glass of wine, the conversation shifted to the capabilities of the Outcast soldiers. This piqued Fatima's interest. She was passionate about self-defense ever since the Jackals abused her. She finally jumped into the discussion.

She steeled herself and looked directly into Kerry's brown eyes. "Is everyone trained to fight in Pathless Land?" As soon as the words escaped her lips, butterflies fluttered in her stomach. She was mesmerized by his warm and welcoming eyes. Her mind was awash with conflicting emotions.

Kerry flashed his infectious smile. "Citizens must be willing to defend a free society, or there won't be one left to defend. Nearly everyone in Pathless Land volunteers to be a soldier, if only part time. We're determined to protect our free society, even if we're standing alone against a world that wishes to kill us. As a wise man once said, no weapon is as formidable as the will and moral courage of free men and women."

"I'm surprised that everyone is trained to fight in your country," said Fatima. As she locked eyes with Kerry, every word she uttered seemed trite or out of place. She couldn't remember ever being this insecure. It was agonizing.

"Surprised?" Kerry looked disappointed. "Being a warrior is a noble calling. That's why we call ourselves the Warriors of Pathless Land. What could be nobler than risking your life to protect those you love and to safeguard everything you hold sacred?"

Fatima suddenly lost the ability to speak. Her tongue was tied. Her lips felt numb. This bizarre paralysis had never happened to her before. Kerry smiled and ignored the awkward pause. "We owe an immeasurable debt to those who take up arms to defend us. When we lay our heads on pillows at night, it's because there's a soldier somewhere laying his head on a cold, damp rock. When we sit beside our warm hearths in the evening, it's because there's a soldier somewhere bivouacking on a wind-swept plain. When we hug our loved ones, it's because there's a soldier somewhere hugging his rifle and fighting the loneliness in his own heart. When we enjoy the freedom to relax or play a game, there's a soldier somewhere whose every sense is focused on an unseen enemy seeking to kill him. When we relish the sound of laughter with friends, it's because there's a soldier somewhere hearing the sudden snap of a twig in the darkness and wondering if it's the last sound he'll ever hear. There's nothing surprising about such nobility."

Fatima blushed. "I only thought it was surprising because everyone in our tribe is trained to fight too."

"Then you understand," Kerry observed solemnly.

"I do, but perhaps for different reasons." Her demeanor suddenly turned serious. "Many people want to take things from us. They want to control our thoughts and actions for their benefit. They want us to worship their leaders. They want us to worship their gods. They want us to worship *them*. Self-defense is the only alternative to submission to the Jackals, the Caliphate, and the Elites."

Kozlowski was smitten by the spectra of emotions that flashed across Fatima's exotic face. "Our views aren't so different. The people in your tribe are much like the castaways in our society. I'll add one more perspective. Not only is the world full of the raptors that you mentioned, it's also full of hate. The Elites hated us enough to banish us. Surely you understand that."

Fatima frowned. "I'm not sure I do."

Kozlowski put his hand on her arm. "I pieced you back together after the Caliphate tried to filet you. Why do you suppose they did that?"

Fatima was pleasantly distracted by his touch. "Because I happened to be in a caravan they attacked?"

"You were in a caravan of heathens, at least from their perspective. Their creed compels them to convert, enslave, or kill infidels. They can't tolerate other religions or any civil authority above their religion. They're obliged to hate you merely for not believing what they do. And their hatred can only be resolved by your submission or your death."

"That's true," replied Fatima. "That's why my family fled the Caliphate and became apostates. My mother and I were second-class citizens in their patriarchal cult."

Dark Moon chimed in. "I don't know the Elites' motive for kidnapping our children, but it does seem like hatred is involved."

"It was the same with us," said Kozlowski. "The Elites didn't deport our people to Outcast Island because they wanted our gold or food. They had the power and the guns to steal those things. They deported us because we wouldn't submit to them. We rejected their propaganda. We rebelled against their tyranny. They hated our existence because we threatened *their* existence. It's the same reason the Muslim jihadists hate us. We're the unrepentant counterpoint to their worldview. We stand in the way of their domination. That's why J teaches that it's important for everyone in Pathless Land to be fighters. When the wolves are deciding what's for dinner, the lambs are better off if they're armed and in a foul mood."

"Who is J?" asked Dark Sun.

"Our leader."

"Tell us about him."

Kozlowski leaned forward. "He was banished by the Elites to Outcast Island. He refused to surrender his humanity to the savagery he found there. He inspired the religiously and ethnically diverse Outcasts to stop focusing on their group differences and grievances. He taught them to embrace their commonalities and to respect everyone's sanctity as individuals. He convinced us that unless we eliminated our tribal urges for political, religious, and cultural coercion, we would grind each other into dust. He established a cohesive society worthy of rational humans, which we now call Pathless Land. Our society gradually spread throughout the Caribbean and the coasts of Latin America and South America. He's leading us to rescue the rest of humanity from totalitarianism."

Dark Sun smirked. He pictured the fictional Big Brother in Orwell's 1984. "Is he a real person, or just a figurehead contrived to frighten your enemies and rally your faction?"

"He's flesh and blood, just like you and me."

"Have you met him?" asked Dark Moon, with undisguised skepticism.

Kozlowski hesitated. "Many times. He's old now, but he still has a spark of life that's instantly contagious. When he speaks, everyone listens, because they sense two things: he's committed to achieving a great vision, and he has no fear."

"Why is he hiding his real identity?" asked Dark Sun. "He must fear something."

"It's a practical matter. The Elites are desperate to unmask and kill him for the same reason the Romans and the Jewish oligarchs crucified Jesus. They're offering 100 pounds of pure gold to whoever delivers J to them, dead or alive."

"Are you ever tempted?"

"That would be impossible for me," Kozlowski replied before abruptly ending the discussion. "Everyone should get some rest, especially Teema. The hovercrafts leave for Indiana early tomorrow."

Everyone bade each other goodnight and headed for their rooms, except Kozlowski. He held his gaze on Fatima while Dark Moon maneuvered her wheelchair toward the cafeteria exit. When the two women neared the doorway, Fatima turned for a final look at the handsome young doctor. Their eyes met. She smiled at him, but her heart was heavy. It was unlikely she would ever see him after tomorrow. Even if she did, their lives were so different. She was a wandering gypsy frightened of intimacy with men, and he was a rebel doctor waging war against the Elites. Any relationship between them could never amount to anything.

She tore her eyes away from his and disappeared into the night.

THIRTY
CARNIVAL

> Life is a parade of grand emotions
> Love, hope, and other such notions
> All exist to animate and bless us
> But laughter is the most infectious
>
> — *The Poems of Dark Sun*

Dark Moon feared the worst.

An autumn sun peeked over the horizon when the gypsies lifted off for their scheduled rendezvous with the caravan. As they flew, Dark Moon was enraptured by the beauty of the landscape below. The world appeared so tranquil when viewed from so high up. How misleading, she thought.

She was concerned about what they would see when they rejoined the caravan in Indiana after their two-week hiatus. She was still haunted by the memories of the mayhem, corpses, burning carriages, and terrified faces. Osiris had looked so haggard and defeated. She expected to see wretched gypsies in a grim dolor, mourning their dead or agonizing over the uncertain fates of the injured who had been sent to Atlanta.

The hovercrafts descended, skimming over a mass of trees carpeting a large hill. When they cleared the crest and readied to land, Dark Moon caught sight of the caravan. Her jaw dropped.

The scene shimmered with revelry. Repaired carriages were redecorated with a dizzying array of colorful buntings. Children ran and played with youthful abandon. Wild game roasted on a spit. Tables were filled with food and drink.

The hovercrafts landed with a windy flourish that rippled the buntings and spun dust in all directions. She saw Osiris standing tall, brandishing a whiskey bottle and a smile as big as old Texas. The gypsies gathered behind him, eager to greet their returning compatriots.

The door of her aircraft opened, and a ramp descended to the ground. A medic began easing Fatima down the ramp in her wheelchair, but she dissuaded him with a scolding glare. She slowly stood up, took a few uncertain steps down the ramp, and hobbled toward Osiris.

Tears welled in his eyes as two weeks of pent up anxiety threatened to burst his heart. He ran to her. They embraced, immersed in the bliss of reunion.

Dark Moon and Dark Sun followed Fatima down the ramp. Osiris released her to the throng of gypsies converging on her. He parted the ranks and hurried to greet his two friends. "Thank you!" he shouted above the noise. "My Teema looks as perfect as ever! I'm forever in your debt!" He hugged Dark Moon and shook Dark Sun's hand like an exuberant father of a newborn.

Captain Chavez descended the ramp flanked by two soldiers. Osiris approached him with extended hand and said, "I can never repay your generosity."

Chavez shook his hand and nodded brusquely. "Promises made, promises kept. That's the bedrock of relationships and societies. Everyone we took to Atlanta is recovering nicely."

"That's the best news I've ever heard," said Osiris. "Please, join our celebration. It's the least we can do for you and your wonderful crew. We have wine, food, and—"

"Thank you, but no," said Chavez. "We're needed for the next phase of our operation against the Caliphate. As soon as your people disembark, we must depart." The captain saluted smartly, then headed back up the ramp into the hovercraft. He passed a line of gypsies exiting toward their waiting tribemates.

Dark Moon looked around the caravan in amazement. "The transformation here is stunning!" she said to Osiris. "You're a remarkable leader."

"I had great help, especially from Eve." Osiris beckoned Eve to join them. "She bandaged, cooked, consoled, and just about everything else. She was a human dynamo of energy and compassion. I may have to adopt another daughter."

Eve blushed. "I suppose I helped a bit—"

"What the hell?" Osiris cut her off and glared in the direction of the recovered gypsies who were streaming from the hovercrafts.

He had spotted among them a stranger carrying a large suitcase and waving farewell to the hovercraft crew. Osiris frowned. Dark Moon and Dark Sun turned to see the source of his displeasure. Kerry Kozlowski was walking toward them, looking very much like he didn't intend to return to Atlanta with his mates.

Kozlowski smiled familiarly at Dark Sun and Dark Moon, then extended a hand to Osiris. "Hello! You must be Osiris."

Osiris eyed the proffered hand and then the suitcase. "Who are you?"

The visitor lowered his arm and shrugged. "I'm Kerry Kozlowski." He paused. "I'm the doctor who treated Teema and some of the other wounded."

Osiris blushed and then bowed. "My apologies. Thank you. My tribemates were apparently in very good hands." Then he gestured toward the suitcase. "It looks like you're planning to stay awhile."

"I'd like to." Kozlowski flashed a disarming, confident smile.

"Who invited you?" challenged Osiris. Kozlowski looked to him like a travelling salesman with a suitcase full of baubles. Some of the gypsies noticed the tension. They fell silent, surprised by the boldness of the intruder.

"No one invited me. I want to join your caravan. I'm an excellent doctor."

Osiris frowned. "You're free to decide that you *want* to join us. We're free to decide if you *may*. Clearly, we haven't . . . yet."

"I can help your tribe," Kozlowski persisted.

"Perhaps," conceded Osiris. They needed a doctor—desperately so. However, he also knew that the world was full of overbearing bullies eager to impose their ideas and ambitions on others. He used to be one of them. "If I let random strangers force themselves on us, we'll become just another commune where drifters show up and live upon the efforts of others. I'm not saying you're like that. I just don't know you."

Kozlowski stood his ground like a well-trained soldier being reviewed by a drill sergeant. "I understand. Teema described the culture of your tribe in great detail. That's one reason I want to join. Please, allow me to earn your trust and respect."

"Won't your fellow Outcasts be angry if you defect?"

"We embrace free association, just like your tribe. There'll be disappointment, but there will be no retribution."

Osiris studied Kozlowski with growing interest. A devious thought occurred to him. When the Outcasts were deciding whether to save Fatima, Captain Chavez quizzed him with some questions. The exercise infuriated him, because his daughter's life hung in the balance. Here was an opportunity to reciprocate. "If you answer a few questions properly, we'll consider letting you join our tribe."

"Fair enough."

"Are you willing and able to help defend our tribe?"

"We're all warriors in Pathless Land, just like everyone in your tribe. The world has abused us with every injury and insult imaginable. I fully understand what's at stake in such a world. If you accept me into your tribe, I'll help defend all of you."

Osiris nodded. "What's the meaning of life?"

"The meaning of life is to give life meaning, a wise man once said," Kozlowski replied. "I prefer happiness over suffering. I prefer the long-term satisfaction of achievement over the short-term pleasure of hedonism. And it's loving and being loved that makes everything worthwhile." He scanned the circle of gypsies until his eyes found Fatima. He smiled at her.

Fatima stared at the ground demurely and kicked a stone. His unexpected attempt to join the caravan both exhilarated and unnerved her.

"Interesting," murmured Osiris. The unspoken interaction with his daughter gave him some insight into Kozlowski's real motive for joining the tribe. "Last question: What's the treasure you Outcasts are said to have?"

Kozlowski flinched. "J decides when and how to reveal our treasure. It can't be easily described, and it's only valuable under certain conditions. I can say this: there's nothing else like it in the world. It's the Rosetta stone for peace on Earth."

"I was hoping to hear more specifics," said Osiris. "But I respect your answer. I'll discuss your petition with our Council of Elders after today's festivities. If they decide against you, you'll have to leave with your mates. In the meantime, you're welcome to celebrate with us."

Kozlowski shook his head. "The crew has to depart immediately. And I can't party right now. I'm a doctor. There are people here who still need medical attention, including you. Dark Sun told me about the injury to your back. I brought along several large crates of medical supplies. Loan me two people to unload them and to set up a makeshift infirmary. I meant it when I said I intend to earn your trust and respect."

Osiris nodded. "I hope the elders decide in your favor, because it's a long walk back to Atlanta. By the way, your answers to my questions were well considered. Did you learn your philosophy from J?"

"J inspires almost everyone in Pathless Land, just as Teema tells me you do with your tribe."

Osiris half smiled at that and waved his hand for people to help Kozlowski get settled.

Kozlowski, Saul, and Eve fabricated a crude infirmary out of materials scavenged from carriages that were wrecked during the jihadist attack. Gypsies with lingering wounds queued for treatment. Eve, who had found her calling as a nurse in the aftermath of the tragedy, assisted Kozlowski.

In the meantime, Dark Moon escorted Fatima to her carriage. Fatima had excused herself from the celebration to get some rest. Deep down, she dreaded being anywhere near Kerry. He had found a way to turn her life upside down, and she wasn't used to such disequilibrium. She asked Dark Moon to stay with her for a while.

Everyone else resumed celebrating the return of their mates from Atlanta. It was a boisterous party. Singing, dancing, and drinking continued deep into the night. Inhibitions evaporated as the wine flowed and the flames from the bonfire teased like a satyr. The gypsies embraced the healing magic that happens when play and laughter replace worry and fear.

After a few drinks, Dark Sun was drawn into the revelry. He felt the enormous weight of the past few weeks lift from his shoulders as he joined in the revelry. It was like he had set down a sack of grain he had been carrying for so long that he forgot how much it weighed. As he danced, he began to understand why the gypsies had chosen to celebrate rather than mourn.

Ruby pirouetted in front of him while he swayed to the rhythm. She writhed in erotic syncopation with the primal beat. Her sensuous movements unleashed a torrent of invitation. Dark Sun was mesmerized by the sexual aura exuding from her voluptuous body. She vamped, undulating her arms and purring the lyrics of the music through pouted lips. She was a red-haired goddess teasing him in the heat of the moment.

Dark Sun's eyes met hers in a regnant stare that blocked out the noisy revelry around them. She moved closer to him. She wrapped her arms around his waist, synchronizing her movements with his. Her warm body rubbed against his. She nuzzled his neck, tickling his beard with her nose. Her jasmine perfume intoxicated him. "I want you," she purred.

Dark Sun was delirious with wine and temptation. As they continued to grind together, he struggled with thoughts he never believed he could contemplate. Somewhere in the haze of his confused brain, he heard himself say, "I thought you were Hawkeye's girl."

"Most of the time." She giggled in a drunken, saucy manner that accentuated her sensuality.

"Isn't he a deadly sharpshooter?" asked the small part of Dark Sun's brain that somehow kept its composure under enormous libidinous pressure.

"Don't worry," Ruby cooed. "He can't aim when he's drunk, and he never remembers anything the morning after. Besides, this is a carnival! Don't you know what that means?"

"I don't know what anything means right now." It was clear to him, however, that Ruby's scurrilous reputation was well deserved.

"Carnival is a gypsy tradition." Ruby's breathy voice was as erotic as her appearance. "For one night, we indulge our primitive instincts. We embrace wine, music, and each other. No inhibitions, no rules. Set yourself free. I'm all yours!" She pressed her lips violently against his. Her warm tongue found his.

Dark Sun was lost in the allure of her sexual energy and the contagion of the carnival spirit. Then images of Dark Moon flooded his brain. A cold wave of guilt and inhibition washed over him. He realized he was following Ruby down a destructive path. He pulled away from their kiss abruptly and retreated to arm's length. "I'm sorry," he said. "I can't do this. I love Dark Moon."

"You can love me too," she persisted.

"No!" he said. "It can never happen."

Ruby's green eyes spit fire at him. She wasn't used to rejection, particularly during carnival. She knocked his hands from her shoulders. "What makes you so special?"

He shook his head to break the spell of lust and alcohol. Everything that was important to him came back into focus. He noticed that Ruby wasn't quite so pretty now that her spell was broken. "Dark Moon makes me special. She's the mirror of my soul. In her reflection, my weaknesses shrink, and my strengths are magnified. She understands my deepest thoughts. She accepts me as I am, for better or worse. She forgives my frailties and my failures, and she inspires me to do what's right and good. In this cold and brutal world, she's my eternal rock. I can always count on her. I can't betray her—no matter how strong the temptation."

"How noble," Ruby said icily. The two were now conspicuously motionless amid a bedlam of swaying bodies. A few gypsies stared. "Life is short. Why not enjoy it while we can?"

"Yes, life is short," Dark Sun sighed. "Especially if Dark Moon finds out about this. And yes, we should enjoy life. But my relationship with Dark Moon is worth more than anything else the world can offer. It's my home, no matter how lost I am. It's my anchor to something permanent, no matter what else is torn from me. It's bigger than the sum of two people. It animates my personal universe. A lifetime of companionship with her is infinitely more valuable than a few moments of pleasure."

Tears formed in Ruby's eyes. She looked like she was going to slap him. Instead, she twirled away into a pulsating group of dancers nearby. Her carefree movements suggested that she had already forgotten his rejection.

But he knew she hadn't. He had just shunned her during a terribly vulnerable moment, and shunning is second only to banishment in karmic ferocity. He reminded himself, with some foreboding, that she had once been a treacherous double agent.

The awkward dalliance with Ruby squelched the carnival spirit out of Dark Sun. He retrieved his father's journal and sidled off to a secluded spot to read by lantern light.

February 15, 2055

Mary and I had a fight today. She wants me to go to Washington to convince Kieran to come home. She thinks he can be "cured" of his fascination with the autocrats. I think it's an incurable disease. I told her the journey to Washington would be so dangerous that I probably wouldn't survive it. Now she's not talking to me. My family is unraveling. The world is unraveling.

As everything unravels, I'm discovering what I call a grand paradox. It's difficult for humans to survive as isolated individuals, and yet at the other extreme, it's dehumanizing being packed in like peas in a pod. We aren't hermits, and we aren't ants. We are independent individuals, yet we thrive in groups. We all want to be free, yet we all yearn to belong. The Taoist dualities in this paradox have led us into a confounding mess.

We're communal beings, deep to our evolutionary roots. Our nature as social animals evolved from millions of years of adaptation in small groups, where collaboration was necessary for survival. We learned that to help each other is to help oneself. Because this instinct for reciprocal generosity is so beneficial on the tribal scale, people mistakenly believe that it must also be beneficial on the grander scale of an entire society. It's not.

The difference is the level of emotional attachment. I freely choose to collaborate with my family, friends, and neighbors without force or compulsion. I want to enrich these personal relationships. They're woven into the tapestry of my life, so I help these people and share with them. The mutual synergy reverberates back to me with profound personal benefits.

This interdependence is voluntary. It only happens in real relationships, where there's an emotional attachment that moves the heart. No laws are required. No guns are required. All that's needed are the love, trust, respect, and generosity that naturally result from intimate bonds. This is true everywhere in the world. It's been true throughout history. It's our genetic disposition.

Harmony comes naturally when intimate groups pursue common interests. We all yearn to please our companions, and we're all averse to offending them. On the other hand, fear comes naturally when dealing with strangers who may be potential adversaries or threats to our intimate group. People aren't naturally disposed to love and trust millions of strangers. Whether commanded by kings, gods, or legislatures, forced collaboration erodes the heart and soul of humanity and destroys the backbones of entire societies. It requires intrusive laws to prescribe behaviors, and armed agents to ensure compliance.

This corrupts the true communal spirit that animates humanity. It transforms beneficiaries into thieves, providers into slaves, and administrators into tyrants. It breeds avarice, deceit, laziness, and cheating. It transforms citizens into both policemen and suspects. Families get replaced by the state. Personal relationships get replaced by sterile transactions with faceless bureaucrats.

There's a massive psychological divide between "inside group" relationships and "outside group" relationships. It all comes down to trust. In an intimate group, trust grows from shared concerns, reciprocal generosity, and reliable respect for each other. Something else must act in the place of such trust in order for relationships between strangers to proceed. Shared concerns, reciprocal generosity, and reliable respect don't come naturally in very large groups.

What's the resolution for this grand paradox? How can humans organize into broad social entities like cities, states, and countries without destroying atomistic social entities like individuals, families, and local communities?

Kieran thinks the solution is the autocracy of the Elites. As I watch the world unravel, I'm convinced he's wrong. Forced collectivism breeds social disintegration. Rational individualism breeds social cooperation.

But how does society facilitate that? I don't have the answer. Neither does James. As he lazes through life, I wonder what's fermenting inside his head. He seems strangely divorced from the great problems of existence.

Dark Sun chuckled at the irony. The great problems of existence had found him, despite his youthful attempts to avoid them.

While he was reading, Dark Moon had quietly sat down beside him. When he finished, he studied the moonlit festival that was still rollicking. Its free-spirited exuberance resurrected a bit of carnival in his heart. He impulsively put his arms around Dark Moon and kissed her.

"What was that about?" she asked.

"Everything, Moonbeam. I'm thrilled that you're my wife. I admire your passion for helping others. By the way, how is Teema?"

"She's still in pain. Kozlowski stopped by and gave her something to ease her discomfort, but she looked even more uncomfortable while he was there. I could tell she wanted to join the party, despite her pain and exhaustion. Who doesn't like a celebration?"

"I know our kids love them. Remember a few years ago when we visited the traveling carnival that some gypsies set up near Independence?"

Dark Moon smiled, her face suddenly aglow. "Yes, it was a magical! The sounds and laughter were infectious. The games were so much fun. The animals were so exotic. The food was so delicious. Clowns did silly tricks. Dancers, musicians, and mimes flitted about.

"The kids' eyes were as big as saucers, and their smiles were as wide as forever. It was impossible for them to fully absorb the wonder of it all. They ran from booth to booth, stall to stall. It was as if life had to be lived in one ephemeral day, and they were going to exhaust themselves in the attempt.

"When they joined in a square dance, they didn't know what their feet should do, but they didn't care. It was priceless. I love how kids aren't weighed down by the problems in the world. They're absorbed in the uninhibited joy of the moment. Sometimes I wish I were a kid again."

Dark Sun listened to her while studying the adult gypsies, who were celebrating just like Curious and Cammy at the traveling carnival. "Don't surrender your childhood innocence so easily," he said. "There's a bit of carnival in every day, no matter what happens. I expected the gypsies to be in mourning when we got here. I was confused when we arrived at a celebration. But now, I fully understand why Osiris led them down that path. No matter what this existence throws at us, we should choose happiness. If we're going to endure the struggle of being alive, let's *live*."

He took her hand and pulled her up. He wrapped his arms around her waist. She nestled her head against his shoulder. They danced all by themselves, enjoying a moment of private bliss, even though in the darkest corners of their hearts they feared more sorrow was to come.

THIRTY-ONE
CURIOSITY

The important thing is not to stop questioning. Curiosity has its own reason for existing.

— Albert Einstein

"Why do you want to go on living?" repeated Curious to the dumbfounded guard who brought breakfast to their cell.

The pimpled sentry stood with mouth agape. Either he didn't speak English, or he had no answer. He merely stared in mute horror at Curious. Then he turned and fled down the antiseptic hallway, as if the simple question was more awful than the unjust confinement of Curious and Cammy, or more awful than the suffocating Darkness.

Curious added this incident to his growing list of discordant ways that the various guards who visited their cell reacted to his questions. He was merely trying to learn the motives of the people who had chosen to imprison him and Cammy. But whenever he asked questions like "why do you wear that awful uniform?" or "would you trade places with me?" all he got in return was awkward silence.

Even when he and Cammy were escorted to the studio for the filming, no one would answer their questions about what was going on. "Why are we being filmed?" Silence. "Who are these two people with us?" Scolding glares. "Why were we kidnapped?" Flustered distraction. It was as if the simple act of asking questions was taboo. Maybe speaking itself was taboo. Or maybe saying something taboo was grounds for severe punishment. In any case, there was no real discussion about anything.

His attempts at conversation usually elicited alarmed looks over shoulders. Everyone he talked to seemed intellectually frozen, much like the Amish were technologically frozen. Perhaps the inclination to think had disappeared at roughly the same time as the permission to speak. Conformity seemed to have stifled all creativity, adventure, and openness.

This was alien to him. He had always felt the urge to explore and to discover. He loved the characters in *The Adventures of Huckleberry Finn*, one of the many mesmerizing books in his grandfather's trove. The youths in that story loved to explore. They saw magic and possibility in every encounter.

He recalled the time he was digging a hole on their farm with the outlandish notion to reach China. He found a bone and wondered what creature it was from. Digging deeper, he found fragments of a clay pot with strange markings. He wondered what exotic people had made it, and how long ago.

It dawned on him that many people had come and gone on this very spot, each with a wondrous story extending eons into the past. Energized by curiosity and imagination, he dug deeper until his shovel struck an arrowhead. He wrenched it out of the ground and studied it. His mind raced to images of desperate battles between ancient combatants.

He dug further until he was laboring in a pit deeper than he was tall. Dirt fell into his disheveled blond hair with each heave of the shovel. Sweat poured down his shirtless body as the sun blazed down on his burnished skin and wiry frame. The dig became a treasure hunt, a mystery adventure, a puzzle-solving challenge.

The dig was an allegory for his life, which was filled with a burning desire to explore, to understand, to question, to discover the nature and workings of everything. He had to find the truth. He couldn't imagine a life without this desire. But that's all he saw in Washington. People were mentally straitjacketed inside their massive beehives. They questioned nothing, which meant nothing would ever get better or more interesting. No kid would accept that kind of life, so why did adults? He was immensely puzzled. Happiness had to come from making things better or more interesting, didn't it?

He had a lot of time to think about such things. His pain was tolerable now that his leg had been operated on. The strange video that he and Cammy were forced to make actually brightened his spirits by giving him hope. It implied that there was a purpose to their captivity. They were valuable to someone, which meant they would be kept alive. At least for a little while.

Suddenly, the earth shook with a force that stunned him out of his reverie and frightened him to the core of his being. The sudden jolt was accompanied by an enormous explosion. Cammy screamed. They heard the agitated footsteps of guards scrambling in the hallway.

Another explosion. Chunks of plaster fell from the ceiling of their cell. He fought through his fright to understand the meaning of this onslaught. It dawned on him that the clues about the urgency of their situation were now coalescing into a horrifying reality. There was a reason that the beehive tenders were in a rush to get the video made. There was a reason that the captors who had driven them across the country were harassed by urgent phone calls to speed up.

Perhaps there were some things he didn't want to discover. Like maybe they weren't going to be around as long as he had just hoped.

THIRTY-TWO
DISINFORMATION

> Though blessed we are with eyes
> Reality hides in clever disguise
> While finding truth is our ambition
> Clarity seldom comes to fruition
>
> — *The Poems of Dark Sun*

The roar of engines and a staccato burst of gunshots startled Dark Moon from her sleep.

In her wakening confusion, the ruckus triggered a horrifying flashback to the night her children were kidnapped by shadowy assailants. She commingled reality with a dreamscape filled with black-clad bodies that were once again crashing through windows and attacking her family. She flailed her arms in the darkness, reaching for her kids. She tried to scream, but she was paralyzed.

She snapped fully awake when Dark Sun shook her. They scrambled out of their carriage to assess the threat. She saw quick bursts of condensation in the frigid morning air as her short breaths matched her rapidly beating heart. Snow would be coming soon.

In the thin light of dawn, they saw Hawkeye and Saul shooting at a retreating plane that had just buzzed them at low altitude. "What's going on?" Dark Moon asked Eve, who was staring skyward.

Eve shivered in her night clothes and pointed. "That plane circled overhead and then dove at us. It dropped something just outside our camp. Then our guys started shooting at it."

They spotted Osiris gesturing for others to join him. Gypsies quickly gathered behind him. He stood a few paces from a metallic canister that was partially imbedded in the soft soil.

"Careful," Saul cautioned. "The plane had the Elites' insignia. It could be a bomb that didn't detonate."

Osiris nodded. "Everybody step back!"

After everyone retreated, Osiris pumped several bullets into the canister. There was no explosion. Saul and Osiris crept up to the object as if approaching a sleeping bear. Saul flipped it over with the barrel of his rifle. It had a lid secured by two clasps.

Osiris inspected the object for triggers or switches. Seeing none, he shrugged and undid the clasps. He opened the lid, reflexively turning his shoulder to shield himself. Nothing happened. He peeked inside and spied a manila envelope riddled with bullet holes. He extracted a mangled document and began reading.

After a few moments, he looked up. His gaze found Dark Sun and Dark Moon. "It's for you two," he said gravely. He reluctantly handed it to them. Dark Moon snatched it and began reading. She was momentarily puzzled, then her hands trembled. Her face turned ashen.

Unnerved, Dark Sun took the document and scrutinized it. Anguish washed over his face. It was an officious Death Notice, issued by the Elites. Across the printed text was a handwritten message that read: "Audrey and James, we know who you are. Follow all future instructions precisely, or you'll receive a Death Notice for your kids too."

The notice documented the death of Dark Sun's father a long time ago. Its stark finality shocked him. "Part of me hoped my father was still alive," Dark Sun said, his lips trembling. "Reading the handwritten words in his journal made him seem so alive. But now—"

Dark Moon lifted his bearded chin with her finger. "Sunshine, there's a ray of hope in that awful note."

He looked at her dumbly, slowly shaking his head. "It implies that Cammy and Curious are still alive," she continued.

Dark Sun nodded, although his heart was still rent by grief. "But my Dad . . ."

Osiris put a gentle hand on Dark Sun's shoulder. "Your grief is understandable, my friend. The awfulness of death rips the mask off our delusions about life." He turned to Dark Moon. "Please, console him while we get this caravan moving again. We do indeed have reason for hope."

Osiris convened an emergency meeting. For the past two weeks, they had been mired in the same spot while they repaired their carriages, buried their dead, and waited for the return of their mates from Atlanta. Today's message from the Elites triggered renewed urgency to get moving again. However, the recent encounters with the Caliphate, the Outcasts, and the Elites left Osiris uncertain about what to do next.

He addressed his lieutenants. "We've lost many loved ones. We're surrounded by enemies. The Elites are up to something vile. How should we proceed?"

Saul, who was familiar with the territory controlled by the Elites, proposed a direct route toward Washington. It included taking Interstate 64 through Kentucky into West Virginia. There they would pass through Charleston and head into the George Washington National Forest. Then they would turn north on Interstate 81, which ran along the foothills of the Appalachians. From there, they would head to the capital.

This route ran through much wilderness, which would conceal them from warring factions and bands of renegades. The Elites could still contact them if they chose to, because the caravan was almost certainly a blinking red dot on one of their electronic screens. They assumed that the Elites would eventually make full contact with the tribe somewhere along the way. The trick was to avoid being accosted by rogue forces in the meantime.

The Council of Elders ratified the risky plan. The gypsies dispersed to prepare for the arduous journey. A heavy pall fell over them as they eyed for the last time the burial mounds of those killed by the Caliphate. Twenty-seven of their compatriots had been murdered, including eleven women and four children. The unfathomable loss would haunt the nearly two hundred survivors forever.

When the caravan got underway, Dark Sun retrieved his father's journal. He had been ruminating about the Death Notice all morning. He opened the book, braced for the sadness that would come, knowing now the words were from a man he'd never see again.

April 3, 2055
What is truth?

It's hard to tell anymore. The mindless slogans of the Elites are plastered on billboards. Their deceptive bilge is hurled at us by public radio broadcasts. Popular culture has devolved into a smug echo chamber of collectivist memes.

Schools no longer teach subjects; they teach kids to be subjects. Kids aren't challenged to think; they're programmed to groupthink. As Lenin said, four years of indoctrinating plants a seed that can never be uprooted. Kieran was infected, as were millions of others.

I learned my lesson. I stopped sending James to school. Now his education comes from my collection of banned books.

The Elite propaganda has inundated society for so long that it has become the prophesied Big Lie. Dissenting voices are shouted down by politically correct mobs of media and influencers. Contrarians are demeaned as extremists, deniers, flat-earthers, anti-science, racists, and hate-mongers. The most outspoken are ridiculed, doxed, or banished. As

Ralph Ellison put it, people are never more hated than when they try to be honest.

The only safe words are false or meaningless ones. Real communication has ceased because all real words are considered dangerous. Nietzsche said that a man's worth is measured by how much truth he can tolerate. By this measure, the acolytes of the Elites are worthless.

Fake news and Doublespeak assault us in a social media torrent that never rests. Facts have evaporated into the ether of official proclamations that are merely rumors, diversions, or lies.

Ironically, the Elites laud their "transparency." However, the few documents they make public are heavily redacted. Decisions are made in back rooms behind closed doors. The Deep State is shrouded from public scrutiny by an impenetrable fog. No one in the byzantine bureaucratic maze is ever held accountable for failure or deception.

The Internet used to be an antidote to the unholy alliance between the government, the media, and popular culture. But politicians eventually realized it was a threat because its "heretical content" was outside their control.

They fixed that problem the way they fix them all. They regulated and censored the Web. They conspired with Big Tech companies to manipulate the algorithms that arrange search results for viewing. Heretical content was suppressed, and content favorable to the narrative of the Elites was prioritized. The Internet is now the Deep State's version of Orwell's memory hole.

The Elites also colluded with the Big Tech companies to gather personal data from social websites. They use the information to bludgeon their adversaries. The tech companies were eager to collude, because the government protected them from liability and ensured their monopoly.

Truth is always the victim of mythology and power. Then life devolves into a contest over which god or tyrant the proles are obliged to submit to.

Mythology and power are the yin and yang of human subjugation. Power can't be sustained without mythology, and myths can't be sustained without force. The aristocracy uses power and mythology to skew the historical, social, moral, and cultural tide in its favor. Those in power write the history, which is then used to craft moral justification for their rise to power. Oceania's Ministry of Truth has always existed, in some form or another. Today it's called Google.

All tribes and creeds exalt their own traditional "truths." They also dismiss the "truths" of others. Why are we so mesmerized by the truth of our group, instead of accepting truth from any source? The Buddha exhorted us to believe nothing unless it agreed with our own reason. Reliance on facts and reason is the only sane path forward, even though it sometimes requires extraordinary courage. A is A. The universe is what it is. We dance to its laws, not to the beat of magical thinking. It doesn't matter what we wish or hope.

Life is hard enough in the cold light of truth. But when reality is blurred by errant dogma and muddled by power mongers, life becomes brutally challenging.

Can power ever become the victim of truth? Only if we peel back the layers of our accumulated conditioning to move closer to the kernel of objective truth. If we don't do that, one myth is as good as another.

Dark Sun marked his place in the journal and tucked it away. He was pretty sure he knew the answer to his father's rhetorical question about truth and power.

After a hard day of travel, the caravan made camp. They arranged their carriages in a defensive circle near a copse of trees. Fires were started, livestock were tended, food was prepared, and gentle music wafted in the chilly evening air.

As the dusk deepened, their routine was disrupted by a cacophony of engine noise arising from the east. The gypsies scrambled for cover. A hovercraft skimmed the treetops and levitated above their camp, kicking up a cyclone of dust and debris.

Torrents of wind spun dirt devils. Cautiously, gypsies emerged from cover with rifles at the ready. Saul caught Osiris's attention and pointed at the Elites' dreaded insignia on the underbelly of the craft.

Osiris nodded. As he raised his arm, signaling to be ready to fire, a brilliant beam of white light projected from the bottom of the hovercraft. It looked like a dazzlingly incandescent tether connecting the vehicle to the ground. An indistinct shape gradually materialized inside the column of light. At first, it was a shimmering mishmash of pixels, but then it slowly began organizing. As the pixilation added more and more detail to the evolving shape, it became recognizable as a human form.

"It's a hologram!" Ruby shouted above the roar of the hovercraft.

The hologram coalesced into a three-dimensional image of a young girl with platinum blond hair. As the pixels finished materializing, a startlingly lifelike figure stared out at them with stunning blue eyes.

"Cammy!" Dark Moon shouted in anguish.

THIRTY-THREE
GOLD

There is no more dangerous menace to civilization than a government of incompetent, corrupt, or vile men.

— Ludwig von Mises

A mighty quake shook the earth.

Regis glanced wide eyed at Cosimo. The centurion brushed away flecks of debris that had fallen from the ceiling onto his Armani jacket. He glared at Regis as if holding him accountable for the affront to his exquisite apparel.

The two men were in the Presidential Emergency Operations Center. The secure facility was located deep beneath the East Wing and the North Lawn of the White House. It was designed precisely for emergencies such as the ongoing aerial bombardment by the Outcasts. It served as a vital communications hub for the government to maintain continuity of leadership during extreme crises.

The ferocious explosions above ground, however, weren't foremast on Cosimo's mind. "My Influencers tell me there's a torrent of secure communications zipping between Atlanta and Outcast Island," he observed. "Something big is afoot."

"We're aware of the activity," Regis replied. His mood brightened. He expected a more dire conversation. "It doesn't matter. The war will be over in ten days. My plan is gaining momentum."

"At the rate these bombs are falling, it will be over much sooner than that." Cosimo nervously extinguished his cigarette. He lit another with a shaking hand.

Regis took perverse satisfaction in seeing this unusual crack in Cosimo's unflappable veneer. "We'll soon shock the world. Don't forget that I'm as eager to save my political legacy as you are to execute the Syndicate's plan—whatever it is."

"The Syndicate doesn't give a shit about your legacy," Cosimo replied. "Or your socialism. We don't give a shit about *any* politician or philosophy. However, your socialist policies can be useful tactics. They condition the proles to think less and to follow orders more. They erase all wealth but the Syndicate's. They destroy societies that we decide need to be destroyed."

Regis jumped to his feet, but the sharp stab of pain in his aging back erased nearly all of his bravado. "I give a shit about my legacy! I've championed progressive causes my whole career! The people wanted my socialism! I made America a better place!"

Another bomb fell nearby. Glasses and pens chattered on the conference table. "You've wasted your career," said Cosimo. "There are three classes of people in the world. None of them are described by your socialist philosophy. There are the rulers, who exist to run the world. There are the fools, who exist to be ruled. And there are the renegades, who are too smart to be fools and too independent to be rulers. They must be eliminated. Which class are you in?"

Regis didn't answer.

Cosimo smirked. "The truth hurts."

Another bomb rattled the furniture. Regis sat down. His shoulders slumped. If he were a turtle, he would have withdrawn into his shell.

"Face the facts," continued Cosimo. "Political power has nothing to do with your good intentions. It has everything to do with cunning, deception, and might. The Syndicate isn't interested in what is good and moral. We're interested in what is useful and necessary. We genuflect to a god called gold. We harvest it from the blood and tears of fools, no matter which creed or party they worship. He who has the gold rules the world. The rest is just illusion."

Regis shook his head slowly. "The proles may be fools, but there are millions of them. They'll always agitate for what they believe to be their rights. Listening to them made me a successful politician."

"Yes, the witless masses lay claim to rights, but even that's part of our illusion. Where do rights begin? Where do they end? Who enforces them? They're a hollow demand on an unheeding universe. To salve the bleeding hearts of the proles, we offer them the illusion that they're voting for their leaders, when in fact all of the candidates are merely puppets anointed by us. These Manchurian candidates amuse their constituents with theories, policies, and other such gibberish, but their pitiful charades are just pixie dust to dazzle the mob with. They claim to be helping the people, but they're merely helping themselves to whatever scraps we allow them. All politicians are beholden to us and always will be. The media, the educators, and the pop culture icons are beholden to us and always will be. We can establish any opinion we wish in the minds of the proles—if they desire to have any opinion at all. They're content with the show. They're oblivious to the misdirection of our elaborate shell game. The Syndicate uses these illusions to create and destroy nations at will."

"Toward what end? Or are you just narcissistic sociopaths?" Regis winced, wondering if he had overstepped his bounds.

Cosimo ignored the jab. "Our eternal goal is to accumulate wealth. It's not driven by narcissism or sociopathy. It's driven by the simple desire to be fabulously rich. It's the most sensible and rational goal in history. We intend to live gloriously and will do so by riding on the backs of the fools. We're certain our goal is rational, because the fools would trade places with us if they could. But they can't."

"How can the Syndicate pull this off? There are too many people—"

"The fools are easily misled," Cosimo interrupted. "Our Influencers manipulate politicians, bureaucrats, judges, and bankers to do what we ask. The proles are very gullible, and the politicians are very malleable. We started America toward its demise using some simple tactics. We influenced one political party to insist on expanding the social safety net without raising taxes, and the other party to insist on reducing taxes without diminishing the net. What happened? The nation became indebted to our shadowy network of banks. Then we influenced Americans to sacrifice their legendary productivity for the chimeras of climate control, equality of outcomes, and social justice. What happened? The Darkness! The final absurdity was that we influenced a country calling itself the United States to plunge into the abyss of class, gender, ideology, and race warfare. What happened? The Second Civil War! The Syndicate is fucking brilliant. We made revolt against freedom a popular movement!"

Regis was stunned. His career had been a duplicitous con in which he was also one of the marks. And it was too late to do anything about it. Another bomb concussed above them. Its impact didn't faze Regis, who was lost in his spiritual tailspin.

Cosimo continued, "When we decide it's time, the Permanent Revolution will occur. The proles will be so numbed that they'll accept the absoluteness of our rule. To placate them, we'll grant them food and other necessities. We'll allow them amusements like sports, pornography, drugs, alcohol, and prostitution. In return, they'll do whatever we tell them. People should never be allowed to act independently. Without the iron hand of absolute despots, civilization can't carry forward. The mob will always frenzy toward anarchy. The full manifestation of the Syndicate will emerge after the great powers of the earth have been laid low. America will be the last domino to fall. Then we'll crush every challenge to our authority."

Regis fought through blinding confusion. "How can you maintain such a tight noose around the entire planet?"

"Follow the yellow brick road. We control all of the money."

"How?" asked Regis incredulously.

"That's the whole point of the Syndicate. We're not capitalists who invest in industry and machines. Those investments can be gained or lost due to competition and other uncontrollable variables. We don't want to get our hands dirty in filthy factories and tawdry retail outlets. Instead, we invest in political finance. We control the creation and flow of money around the world. Every country is indebted to our cartel of central reserve banks. Those debts hang like swords of Damocles over political leaders. Since we control their national finances, we control *them*, no matter what their ideology is."

"But how does that make the Syndicate rich?"

"The best way to steal money is to own banks. Whenever governments need to print more money to cover their budget deficits, the funds magically appear out of thin air as deposits into our banking cartel. We leverage those deposits into vast returns on loans and investments. Our financial empire is a mysterious maze of bundled tranches, treasury notes, hedge funds, and various derivates thereof. Our wealth is created out of thin air, and we're the only ones who know where it came from, or where it went. With that ethereal wealth, we buy real assets like gold, silver, and real estate. While the world drowns in debt and in fiat money, we hoard property and precious metals. We use our hoard to lavishly compensate our influencers, who have infiltrated all of the world's institutions. The world's reserve banks are the Syndicate's golden geese."

"Won't the cryptocurrencies eventually put your banking cartel out of business?"

Cosimo unleashed a guttural laugh. "First of all, if we run into any kind of financial trouble, the governments around the world will bail us out with more printed money, because if we fail, the world fails. Cryptocurrencies are no threat to us. Bitcoin was created by a mysterious group that most people call Satoshi Nakamoto. That group was really the Syndicate. *All* of the cryptocurrencies were created by us. We named one of them Etherium as an inside joke, because all of the crypto wealth comes out of thin air, and it all belongs to us. Blockchain-based currency was our way of making certain that no government in the world could regain control of the financial system. We've always desired that the banking system be extranational, and the shadowy cryptocurrencies make it even harder for sovereign governments to monitor and control it. It's a beautiful thing."

"Beautiful to whom?"

"To us rulers, you fool. The ruling class will always find a way to rule the world. An honest study of history confirms that. The Syndicate was born in the fourteenth century when formal monetary and banking systems first emerged. We've been in control of history ever since. It doesn't matter what political or economic system a country chooses. It doesn't matter if the Right or the Left is in charge. It doesn't matter whether the workers, the capitalists, the bureaucrats, the nobility, or the bishops have power. It doesn't matter whether the Elites, the Jackals, the Blessed, or the Caliphate are ascendant because the hidden financiers are always the biggest winners. Money is the central nervous system of economies and political systems. Whoever controls the money rules the world. We can make markets and nations move in any direction at any time. We are the rulers of the world."

Cosimo paused. He was alarmed by the ghostly expression on Regis's pallid face. He sensed that his dupe was losing the will to carry forward.

"Bear in mind," Cosimo said, "There's only one way for you to exit this game that you chose to play. Let me know when you've lost the will to live."

Cosimo tossed his cigarette onto the floor and picked up his hat. He strutted toward the elevator door. He flinched when another bomb rattled the structure. Once again, Regis took pleasure in the centurion's slight loss of composure.

Perhaps not everything in the world went according to the Syndicate's plan.

THIRTY-FOUR
EXPEDITION

> Those nearest our hearts are so far away
> The future seems unreachable from today
> But nothing worthwhile is easy or free
> To achieve your goals, daring you must be
>
> — *The Poems of Dark Sun*

Cammy's dazzling apparition stared at them with eyes that glittered like blue diamonds.

She floated eerily inside her prison of light, wearing a blood-red tunic. Near her heart was the royal purple symbol of the Elites.

She began to speak. Her voice was projected through speakers on the bottom of the hovercraft's hull, making it seem like the recorded words were coming from her. "I'm okay, Mom and Dad," the illusion assured, though her lips quivered. "But Curious is badly hurt. I have to tell you something very important. They said if you don't come to the capital in ten days, they'll kill us. Please hurry! We're very afraid. There are two—"

She abruptly stopped speaking. Her image was frozen, as if someone had pushed pause. Dark Moon lunged toward the lifelike hologram out of desperate yearning. "I'll save you!" she screamed, plunging into the light with arms extended. She passed through the diaphanous pixels and tumbled brutally to the ground. She pounded the dirt with her fists and wailed. Dark Sun sprinted to her.

"James and Audrey," blared a grating voice. Dark Moon and Dark Sun swung their heads toward the light column. Cammy's apparition had been replaced by images of a middle-aged man and woman. They too wore red tunics bearing the globe logo. They preened like royalty poised to scold peasants. The man bore a haughty scowl as he spoke. "I'm sure you recognize us. We Elites know who you are. We also know *where* you are. Any attempt to outwit us will end in death for you and your children. As my beautiful niece just indicated, you have ten days to arrive here in Washington. This command comes directly from Regis, so your total obedience is required."

The dour couple dematerialized leaving just a blue light for a moment before the radiant column disappeared, seemingly retracted into the belly of the vehicle. The hovercraft revved its engines and thundered off toward the east, scattering debris around the caravan as it accelerated.

Dark Moon melted into the embrace of her kneeling husband, pale with shock. Dark Sun was rigid with anger and frustration but maintained his composure while he consoled Dark Moon.

"Do you know those two?" Osiris asked.

"That was my brother Kieran and Dark Moon's sister Katarina. They joined the Elites long ago. They're dead to us."

"How could they do this to you?" asked Fatima.

"They're true believers," said Dark Sun. "They worship Regis like a god."

"There's no shortage of such zealots," observed Osiris. "What do they want?"

"I have no idea," replied Dark Moon. "They may not know either. I'm sure they're not the masterminds in this. They're order followers."

"They mentioned Regis," interjected Saul. "If he's involved, this is a huge deal. The ten-day deadline implies urgency. Maybe it's because Richmond fell to the Outcasts a few days ago, putting their army within striking distance of Washington. Why is your family so important to the Elites?"

Dark Sun shook his head. "This makes no sense! We've never been important to anyone!"

"I know how you feel," said Saul. "But this makes sense to *them*. I guess we'll find out why in ten days—"

"That means we have a huge problem," said Osiris. "Our plodding caravan can't make it to the capital that fast."

"*You* don't have a problem," said Dark Sun. "Dark Moon and I do. This isn't your battle to fight. We'll go alone."

"My friend, you're one of us now. And going alone is impossible. You'll never find the way, and there are terrible dangers in the mountains. It would be suicidal."

"So what do we do?" Dark Moon asked.

"We'll recruit volunteers to escort you on horseback to Washington," Osiris said. "It's about six hundred miles from here. An experienced, determined team with good horses can ride sixty miles a day. So it's possible to get there in ten days—if nothing bad happens along the way."

Silence followed this suggestion. No one had a better idea. "Don't you need approval from the Council of Elders?" asked Dark Sun.

"No approval is needed for a voluntary mission."

Despite the late hour, Osiris summoned everyone for a tribal meeting. When the gypsies were settled around a roaring bonfire, Osiris explained the need for an expeditionary force. He described the mission and its dire risks. He outlined the skills required of the team members. "This mission is voluntary," he announced. "Given the grave dangers, parents of children are discouraged from going. Those selected will leave with Dark Sun and Dark Moon at dawn. If you wish to be considered, come to my carriage to discuss."

Osiris led Dark Moon and Dark Sun to his carriage, where they settled in to wait for volunteers. To kill time, the couple gazed at the menagerie of African totems, crafts, and knickknacks that Osiris had collected over the years. Osiris shared intriguing stories about his collection. As the clock ticked the minutes away, they began to fear that the life-threatening nature of the mission had scared everyone off. Dark Sun glanced at Dark Moon with a look of solemn disappointment.

There was a knock at the door of the carriage. Osiris opened it and was dumbstruck. "Teema!" he exclaimed.

"I want to go on the expedition," she said softly, as he helped her up into the carriage.

"My dearest Teema. You're still recovering from your wounds. The journey through the Appalachians will be brutal. The wilderness is full of dangers. You can't—"

"I'm going!" declared Fatima, louder this time. She winced in pain.

"I love you more than words can describe," Osiris said. "But I can't let—"

"Father, I love you too. I love you for everything you've done for me. I love you for your courage in leading this tribe through terrible times. I love you for your compassion for lost souls. I love those things so much that I want to *be* you. But the only way I can do that is to fight the same battles and confront the same dangers that you have all your life. Fate has given me this opportunity. You prepared me for this moment."

Osiris recognized the stubborn set of Fatima's jaw and the fire in her dark eyes. "I don't doubt your courage, my dear, but—"

"I was kidnapped as a child," Fatima interrupted. "I know full well the terror and hopelessness Curious and Cammy are experiencing now. I can't sit idle while they're suffering like I did. You wouldn't. My mother Ayaan wouldn't have."

Osiris's leathery cheeks were moist with tears. His shoulders slumped. "You're right," he said, more resigned than enthused.

"Thank you," said Fatima. "Also, I want to lead the expedition, just like you would."

"I can't just declare you the leader," Osiris sighed. "Those who will be most affected by your leadership should be the ones to judge if you're truly worthy."

Fatima nodded toward Dark Sun and Dark Moon. "They're the ones most affected. Ask them."

Osiris sighed again. He looked apologetically at Dark Sun and Dark Moon. "My friends, should Teema lead the mission to rescue your kids?"

"I can't think of anyone better," Dark Moon confirmed without hesitation.

"But she can barely walk," said Dark Sun, shaking his head at Dark Moon. "We have to be there in ten days, not ten weeks—"

"She'll be perfect!" said Dark Moon emphatically.

Dark Sun saw the firm resolve etched in his wife's face and realized that a decision had already been made, which was not unusual. He looked at Osiris sheepishly. Osiris smiled knowingly. "Yes," Dark Sun muttered.

"So be it," Osiris conceded. Dark Moon hugged Fatima and thanked her profusely.

There was another knock at the door. It was Kozlowski. Osiris beckoned him in.

"I saw you walking here," he said to Fatima, with grave concern etched on his face. "If you're going on the expedition, you'll need medical care. Curious will need medical care too, when we rescue him. I'm a trained soldier, and if we encounter any Warriors of Pathless Land, I can mediate. I want to go."

Fatima suddenly realized that leadership came with emotional ambivalence. "There's no doubt we can use you, Kerry. However, promise me something before I accept you on the team."

He raised an eyebrow. He wasn't expecting a challenge or a cool reception. "Okay, what?"

"If I'm mortally wounded, you'll leave me behind to die. The mission is to save Curious and Cammy not me. I'm volunteering knowing full well the risks and so are you. The children, on the other hand, are being held against their will."

He glanced at Osiris, who muttered, "You'll either love her or hate her by the time the mission is over." Kozlowski returned his attention to Fatima. "I promise to leave you to die, Teema."

"Great!" she exclaimed with mock enthusiasm. "Welcome to the team." An awkward silence ensued. The charged tension between Fatima and Kerry filled the tight quarters. Fortunately, voices rose outside the carriage. There was an insistent knock.

Osiris opened the door to find Ruby, Hawkeye, and Saul queued outside. "Well," he said, "Has my contingent of former Elites come to volunteer?"

"Is there room for us?" asked Ruby.

"Not in the carriage, but perhaps on the expeditionary force." Osiris waved Dark Moon, Dark Sun, Kozlowski, and Fatima outside. "Teema has been chosen leader. Kozlowski has already volunteered."

The three former Elites eyed the recently arrived Outcast coldly. The level of tension rose another notch.

Ruby addressed Fatima. "You'll need someone who's familiar with the political ways of the Elites, once we get to Washington," she said. "I know how to manipulate them." She flipped her red curls.

Fatima curled her lip in disdain. "A slutty dress and garish red lipstick won't cut it on this mission."

Ruby didn't flinch. "I'm tougher than you think. Hawkeye is my personal trainer. I can shoot almost as well as he can."

"You're not a good fit—"

"I can do anything you can. Is it because you don't trust me?"

"Yes, and that's because you haven't earned it." Fatima paused, realizing that volunteers were slow in coming. She shifted gears. "Okay, fair warning—if I let you on the team and you betray us, I'll shoot you on the spot."

"That won't be necessary," Ruby said tersely. "I'm volunteering for this mission because I'm tired of being doubted and shunned. I know my reputation. This is an opportunity to earn trust and respect. Give me a chance."

Fatima had an aversion to Ruby, but she was indeed a proficient shot and was familiar with the Elites. Fatima nodded her head stiffly, accepting Ruby onto the team. She expected a chill between them the entire mission.

Dark Sun cringed when Ruby bounded over and slid beside him. She winked almost imperceptibly. He didn't want her on the team, but he remained silent. He knew that voicing his concerns about the libidinous gypsy would just cause more tension. He ignored her, even though she was lightly brushing against him. He squeezed Dark Moon's hand.

Hawkeye spoke next. "Ruby knows the political ways of the Elites. I know their military ways. I was raised in the Appalachians, so I know the mountain passes like the back of my hand. And I can shoot," he said with a wry grin. He had recorded the highest score in the history of the Elites' marksmanship testing.

Fatima nodded. "You're perfect for our team. But who'll coordinate the caravan's defenses in your absence?"

Osiris nudged Fatima. "I'm old but not feeble. I can handle things here. Hawkeye should go with you. You're sure to run into trouble on your journey, and he's a great warrior."

"You're in," Fatima said to Hawkeye. "Saul?"

A cigarette dangled from Saul's lips. "Helping innocent victims of the Elites would be a good penance for me. Ruby knows their politicians. Hawkeye knows their fighters. I know their secret police. You'll need me, too."

Fatima silently calculated the pros and cons of Saul's involvement. Having three former Elites on her team was unnerving, but their familiarity with the enemy would be invaluable. She barely knew Saul, but she sympathized with his scarred youth, and he carried himself as a battle-tested fighter. Osiris trusted him, and her father had an uncanny knack for such things. "Welcome aboard," she said.

An uncomfortable stillness fell over the group. Fatima worried about the several layers of tension that entangled the team. They were a talented collection of resources, but cohesion was vital for success on this mission. As she fretted over this problem, she saw someone approaching in the dim light of the bonfire.

"I want to go," Eve announced meekly when she neared them. Everyone looked at her in astonishment.

Fatima tried to mask her derision, but it snuck through. "Do you realize what you'd be getting into?" She saw little sense in burdening the team with the deadweight of a frail person whose life had been immersed in victimhood.

"Perhaps it seems foolish," Eve conceded. "But I've wasted my life hiding behind a thousand petty excuses and blaming a thousand imaginary oppressors. I'll cook; I'll sew; I'll keep watch; I'll be a nurse. I've even learned to shoot a bit. And . . . " she hesitated, as if her next words were brutally uncomfortable. "You and Dark Moon are my only friends. Please, let me go with you."

Fatima wanted to be decisive in her role as leader but didn't know how to handle this awkward request. Eve seemed sincere in her desire to earn redemption, but she was sure to be a liability. Fatima sensed that everyone was staring at her and taking note of the elapsed time of her indecision. She subtly glanced at Osiris.

He smiled, because the proper answer was clear to him. He had learned much about Eve when she worked like a dynamo to help stabilize the traumatized tribe after the attack by the Caliphate. He nodded discretely to Fatima in the affirmative.

She returned her attention to Eve. "You're my friend too. There's great power in that, for both of us. You're in."

As midnight approached, the eight members of the expeditionary force prepared for their journey. Osiris allocated sixteen strong horses to them—eight for riding and eight for carrying supplies. The team packed weapons, clothing, camping gear, medicines, and other items necessary for survival in the wilderness. They stashed some food, but much of their sustenance would have to come from hunting and gathering along the way.

Dark Sun packed his father's gun, gold, and journal. Dark Moon packed the tracking device the Outcasts gave her in Atlanta. That was everything of value they had left. While the eight prepared, they discussed what to call their team. After some debate, they settled on "Eagles." They were on a soaring adventure to swoop in and snatch Curious and Cammy from the lair of the enemy. They would be fearless and noble birds of prey as they did so.

The Eagles bunked for a final night of rest in the security of the caravan. When dawn broke, the entire tribe arose to bid them farewell.

Osiris addressed the eight. "This mission will test your resolve and your courage. According to Saul, the Elites have ravaged the territories between here and Washington with a brutality rarely seen in human history. During their retreat in the face of Outcast victories and Caliphate aggression, they've left a trail of burnt towns, slaughtered villagers, and horrible abuses of women and children. Destitute people are eating corpses. Contagious diseases are sweeping the landscape. Wild animals are feasting on stray humans. Renegades rape, steal, and murder. Conscription gangs capture and sell people to the Elites as cannon fodder for their military. Organ harvesters kill stragglers to sell body parts to the Elites. No one controls the area between here and the Appalachians, so every faction has forces roaming about. Time is running out for the Elites as the Outcast armies march northward. That means time is also running out for Curious, Cammy, and the eight of you.

"Let me know if you want to withdraw from this dangerous mission. There'll be no shame in changing your mind this morning. However, once the team is underway, quitting won't be an option."

Osiris paused to let his invitation to renege sink in. None of the Eagles flinched. He saw nothing but grim, steely resolve on their faces. He nodded solemnly and continued.

"Very well. The caravan will follow behind you, although we won't be able to match your pace. Our best hope is to meet you on your return journey when you have Curious and Cammy safely in tow. Elude enemies when you can; fight like banshees when you must. Expect no mercy. Give no quarter. Your enemies certainly won't. There are no rules in the human jungle out there.

"With that, we bid you farewell. Godspeed, Eagles!"

The Eagles mounted their horses and waved to their somber tribemates. The crowd parted ranks to allow the eight to canter toward the east. Osiris said goodbye to each as they paraded by. When Dark Sun and Dark Moon passed, they thanked Osiris for everything the tribe had done for them, and for everything the Eagles were about to do. He nodded and said, "That's who we are."

When Fatima approached, Osiris grabbed the reins of her horse and called up to her, "Hey, Eagle."

"Yes, father?" She gazed down at him serenely, as if this moment was exactly as it should be.

"Fly brave and proud."

"I will."

"One other thing."

"Yes?" Fatima urged.

"Come back safely."

"Father, I'll make the best of whatever life places before me, just like you taught me." She knew, as he did, that she could make no promises about a safe return.

"Yes, I suppose so," he said softly. "It's just that, well, some things transcend my silly lessons. Please come back." His eyes were transfixed by her radiant face, like he was seeing her for the last time.

Fatima returned his imploring gaze for a moment. Then she blew a kiss down to him and smiled brightly. She spurred her horse into a cantor to catch up to the rest of the departing Eagles. She didn't look back.

Osiris stared at her receding figure through watery eyes. He blew a return kiss in her direction as her curly black hair danced wildly in the wind of a looming squall. He imprinted her image into the deep recesses of his brain that preserve sacred, never-to-be-forgotten memories. His beautiful young Eagle had flown her nest, a glorious but despairing moment all parents must endure.

"Fly true, dear Teema," he whispered. Her fate was out of his control now.

He glanced nervously at the storm that was gathering from the northwest.

THIRTY-FIVE
PERIL

> Love is the missing factor; there is a lack of affection, of warmth in relationship; and because we lack that love, that tenderness, that generosity, that mercy in relationship, we escape into mass action, which produces further confusion, further misery.
>
> — Jiddu Krishnamurti

Curious tugged at his hair with both hands. He had never known such fear.

The building shook again and again. Small chunks of plaster fell from the ceiling of their cell, sprinkling them with jagged pebbles like an indoor hailstorm. A succession of deafening explosions rocked the earth. Cammy put her hands to her ears. She yelled at Curious to do the same.

Another bomb fell. The concussion was so violent that Cammy lost her balance. She stumbled, then draped her body across Curious to protect him in his wheelchair. Plaster dust fell on them, as if a bag of flour had ruptured above their heads. Sulfurous smoke seeped in through the ventilation system. The single bulb in their cell flickered and then went out.

Air raid sirens had been blaring for what seemed like an eternity. The capital had been under siege for the last several days, but it was getting more intense. Cammy heard frantic shouts in the hallway outside their cell. She questioned their guards about what was going on. They ignored her, but their haughty arrogance had been replaced by a mien of fear and helplessness. That pleased her.

Yesterday, a frightened guard told Cammy that the bombings were her fault. That made no sense. When she asked why, the guard spat on her and cursed the Outcasts. She asked why he hated her. He said he resented having to feed an enemy when their own people were starving. He had no choice, though, because they were under orders to keep her and Curious alive, no matter what. He mentioned something about a person named Regis and then left abruptly. Cammy shook her head in dismay. There was no reason for the Elites to hate her. There was no reason for anyone to hate her. She felt as confused as Alice in Wonderland.

The air raids began shortly after she and Curious had been forced to record a message for their parents. She didn't understand why she was ordered to say what she did in front of the cameras. She drew great comfort from it however, because the message implied her parents were still alive somewhere. It also implied that her parents were being encouraged to come to the capital, which was also reassuring. She realized that the sinister forces arrayed against her parents were overwhelming, but at least she didn't feel so horribly alone now.

The message to her parents also conveyed urgency. Cammy now understood why. The bombings were increasing in duration and intensity each day. It was clear that the Elites' situation was getting worse. She feared she and Curious would be collateral damage because there was no escaping this rabbit hole. The very next bomb might land directly on them.

She recalled overhearing that the two people named Kieran and

Katarina, who were involved in recording the message to their parents, were related to her somehow, but she had never heard of them before. They were filled with hatred too, like the guards. She couldn't understand why they would want to hurt her and Curious. Maybe that's why her parents had never mentioned them. Katarina reminded her of the witch in *Hansel and Gretel*.

Another bomb exploded nearby. More tremors. More plaster falling from the ceiling. Cammy tightened her hold on Curious as she lay across him. She braced for the next explosion.

She did her best to hide her tears from him.

THIRTY-SIX
EAGLES

> Lonely those that choose to lead
> Doubt and fear in icy veins bleed
> But lo the fate of the aimless horde
> If to the fore no hero steps toward
>
> — *The Poems of Dark Sun*

P urple clouds threatened on the horizon.
    The Eagles covered ground rapidly after they trotted away from the caravan, but then the skies let loose a downpour. A cold, daunting wind swooped in from the northwest, driving the frigid rain sideways. Visibility plummeted. The washboard road melted into an obstacle course of rain-swollen rivulets and washouts. The wretched bite of early winter was upon them.
    Until the foul weather assaulted them, Fatima had a joyful sense of adventure. The pride of leadership and the exhilaration of a horseback jaunt all coalesced into a feeling of grand purpose and competence. But

when the torrents of freezing rain started, her exuberance dissipated as quickly as the heat from her body. She shivered and her teeth chattered uncontrollably. She began counting horse steps to endure one minute to the next. She was crestfallen at how quickly her sense of grand purpose had collapsed into leaden drudgery.

They crossed the Ohio River into Kentucky and looped around the forbidding Louisville reservation. They passed just north of Fort Knox, America's abandoned gold bullion repository, which had been pillaged during the chaos of war. It was rumored that the bullion ended up in the vaults of shadowy offshore banks.

They struggled up a steep incline on eastbound Highway 64, then paused to rest the horses on the hilltop. The weather had finally eased, and the setting sun broke through the clouds. They gazed out over the valley below, grateful for the warm rays to dry their clothes. It was a serene moment, until Hawkeye signaled for their attention. He had spotted something unusual in the valley, something that looked like telephone poles snaking over the gently rolling hills for as far as they could see.

"What do you suppose that is?" he asked.

Saul squinted, then scowled. "If it's what I've heard about, it'll darken your hearts."

"What have you heard?" asked Dark Moon.

Saul tossed his cigarette to the ground. "There was a mass crucifixion in this area. If this is the spot, those are thousands of wooden crosses lining the road down there. Each has a dead body nailed to it."

Dark Sun cringed. "Have the Romans invaded America too?"

"No, the Caliphate. They crucified everyone from a Blessed monastery near here. The monks tried to extend their domain into the Ohio River valley from the Mississippi. As self-anointed fishers of men, they foolishly tried to convert some Muslims to Christianity in territory that was already claimed by the Caliphate. The massacre was a warning from Caliph Timur."

"That's insane!" said Eve. She had witnessed much brutality on her reservation but nothing like this. The deaths from the gangland rampages in her old neighborhood were usually counted in the single digits.

"Yes," said Saul, "and this isn't the first time it's happened. Ottoman Muslims tortured, hung, and crucified hundreds of thousands of Armenian Christians. They don't mess around."

Fatima shook her head numbly. She had seen many horrors in her lifetime but was queasy at the thought of riding past dangling corpses. "Someone should demolish those hideous crosses down there and bury the bodies properly," she said.

"Some people tried," said Saul. "But the jihadists ambushed them. They apparently want this monument to Allah's vengeance around for a long time."

"Is it wise to stay on this road?" asked Fatima. "What if the Caliphate is still waiting in ambush?" She felt a sudden lance of pain from the wounds inflicted on her a few weeks ago by the jihadists.

"We don't have a choice," said Saul. "The only remaining bridge across the Kentucky River is on this highway. We won't be able to ford the river if we detour, especially after today's rain."

"I agree," said Kozlowski. "I'm sure the Caliphate is pre-occupied with the Pathless Land forces invading Indiana. They won't waste resources guarding dead infidels here. Let's stick to our route."

Fatima nodded. "Okay, let's go."

As the Eagles descended into the valley, they saw that there was indeed a long line of crosses. They were spaced about thirty feet apart, and each bore a carcass with crude spikes hammered through its appendages. Many of the bodies were clothed in the brown robes of the Blessed monks. All of those had been decapitated. Some of the corpses were women and children. They were naked. Their soft flesh had been devoured by scavenger birds. Their wind-blown hair was the only clue to their gender.

Fatima shivered as they trotted past the crucifixes. The chilling wind had resumed its fury, but a more insidious chill penetrated to her bones. She sensed a silent truth from the passing skeletons, a message that death ends all lies, deceptions, and pretenses. Death renders the harshest and most unforgiving judgments. It doesn't matter if your carcass is buried by wealthy attendants in a plush casket or if it's abandoned on a tree. Everyone meets the same end.

Did the Blessed faithful deserve to die like this? Fatima wondered. When she was growing up, she had heard the endless scorn heaped upon the Christians by sheikhs and clerics in her madrassa. Certainly, she disliked the Blessed's compulsive efforts to push their beliefs on people and to portray their God as supreme. She resented the Christian crusaders for invading her ancestral lands and colonizing and proselytizing all of the continents. She despised Christianity's unsavory history of inquisitions, censorship, patriarchy, slavery, internecine wars, and genocide.

But did that justify the jihadists terminating the lives of these monks and their families? That couldn't be the truth the carcasses were shouting down to her from the crosses. The Islamists were certainly guilty too. They were guilty of oppressing women, for the medieval harshness of their Sharia law, and for their zealous imposition of theocracy on unwilling people.

No belief could be judged so supreme that such crimes were warranted. Beliefs aren't irrefutable truths. Death, however, is an *irreversible* truth. How can fallible beliefs justify the irreversible act of murdering heretics? Fatima questioned. They can't, proclaimed the crucified victims, even though Jerusalem, the epicenter of three of the world's major religions, has been the site of more slaughters than any other city on Earth. Death, not truth, has always been the product of conflict between organized religions.

The rain turned to sleet. Fatima shuddered and spurred her horse on, as did the rest of the Eagles. After ten miles, the line of crucifixions abruptly ended. At the foot of the last cross, she noticed three mutilated bodies lying on the ground. She could smell their rotting corpses. The crucified carcass looming over them was dangling awkwardly by one skeletal arm from the wooden crossbeam. She deduced that the victims sprawled on the ground had tried to remove the corpse from the cross but were ambushed and killed.

One of the victims on the ground wore a dress. A crow pecked away at her corpse, scavenging her remaining flesh. Her hollowed eye sockets seemed to bore directly into Fatima's brain; perhaps accusing her or perhaps warning her. Fatima shivered again, this time from a morbid premonition of her own future.

The Eagles travelled hard the rest of the evening, braving the inclement weather. They needed to make good progress early in the expedition, in case worse hardships arose later. Exhaustion eventually set in when the sleet turned to a heavy snow. Fatima selected a grove of trees for their campsite.

They set up tents, hunted game, and lit a fire. The trees broke the wind, but it was still bitterly cold. After dinner, most of the Eagles climbed into sleeping bags. Hawkeye stoked the fire.

Dark Sun was too wired to sleep. The grim ride past the crucified corpses haunted him, and the holographic messages from Cammy, Kieran, and Katarina added more confusion about his family's mysterious predicament. He brushed snow off a log and sat down by the fire. "I can take the first watch if you want to get some sleep," he offered to Hawkeye. "I'm not tired and want to read more of my father's journal anyway." He opened his father's journal and began reading.

April 14, 2055

Regis is all we hear about now. Regis is our Savior. He'll save us from greed. He'll save us from the climate. He'll save us from hunger. He'll save us from injustice. He'll save us from world strife.

But he can't save us from greed because his government confiscates more money than all the thieves, con artists, and robber barons combined. He can't save us from the climate because his taxes and regulations are useless against powerful natural forces. He can't save us from hunger because his bureaucrats produce nothing. He can't save us from injustice because the ultimate injustice is his Elites claiming eminent domain over everyone. He can't save us from world strife because force is needed to implement his policies.

The real question is who's going to save us from Regis?

As crisis after crisis erupted, Regis responded with bigger government, which is his answer to every problem. When America implemented the Universal Declaration of Human Rights, he seized the opportunity to suspend elections and establish one-party rule. He declared that such a massive and historic initiative required continuity of leadership. It required removing obstacles like fickle democracy, individual rights, and inflexible constitutions.

Regis is a narcissist who's adored by media sycophants. His mythos fools many people who instinctually adulate those with power and fame, even when their actual behavior proves them unworthy. But underneath the endless delusions spun by Regis' mythology machinery lays the reality of a fractured society at war with itself.

This leads me to another grand paradox. The most beneficial leaders aren't the ones with the most power. The leaders who truly nurture us are our parents, our mentors, and the heads of our local volunteer groups. They care about us, and they know us as real human beings. They've earned trust and respect through demonstrated virtue. They usually include our interests when they make decisions.

These leaders have great potential to help us, but very little power to impose themselves on us. We could choose to ignore them, but we don't, as long as they continue to demonstrate their sincerity and worthiness.

Our relationships with distant political leaders are exactly the opposite. They don't know us personally. We're statistical abstractions to them. They naturally care more about their own interests than ours. It's hard for us to trust them and for them to be empathetic with us. There are too many ways for them to harm or swindle us without our knowledge. We can't shame them, because we'll never meet them.

And yet, we allow these distant leaders great power to tax our wealth, administer a police state, and wage war. That often makes us easy targets for the covetousness, superstitions, retributions, prejudices, dogmas, ideologies, and aggressions of people who lust for power.

These distant leaders consider their beliefs to be superior to everyone else's. Many of them are utopians who want to establish an earthly paradise no matter the cost to the rest of humanity. They believe their motives to be angelic, even if it means making everyone else pawns in their grand crusade.

They're also convinced that anyone who opposes them is of the devil. This angel-versus-devil conflict exists between the Blessed and the Caliphate, between the Left and the Right, and between the East and the West. The outcome is often a lot of dead people.

None us are born angels or devils. People become devils when they start thinking that they have special missions or special knowledge bequeathed by some god or ideologue that requires the absolute commitment of others.

Political leaders become devilish when they stop protecting citizens from thieves, rapists, and killers and instead insist on universal conformance to their dogmas. The Final Solution comes to mind. Religious leaders become devilish when they stop focusing on individual enlightenment and salvation and instead insist on universal conformance to their dogmas. The Inquisition, the Crusades, and radical Islam come to mind.

That's one of the reasons why the world is forever in a mess. Everyone believes they're right and everyone else is wrong. Everyone wants to be king and to create a world that fits their utopian vision. The problem is that there are seven billion other people who have the same desire, but with countless conflicting visions. When some people seek to acquire the power to implement their personal utopian vision, trouble begins.

In a large society, leaders and followers are abstractions to each other. Machinery of the state, like police, armies, and bureaucrats, are necessary to fill the void of personal relationships. Overbearing leaders sometimes feel so superior and have so little organized resistance they can't resist the temptation to use the tools of the state to impose their absolute wills.

The end always justifies the means for such leaders. Individual lives are nothing compared to their collective ambition. That's how jihadists justify training their youths to be suicide bombers. That's how the minions of tyrants like Stalin, Hitler, and Regis justify their abominations. History is littered with countless innocent casualties to the grand marches of secular and divine 'Isms'. Every attempt to force heaven on earth results in hell on earth instead.

We focus too much on who should rule, rather than how to stop any ruler from causing too much harm. We literally give strangers the power to use force against us to make us do things against our will. We might as well lock ourselves in chains and hand them the keys.

We yearn for our leaders to be honorable father figures who protect us from harm, advocate for our interests, and make decisions for our benefit. Yet the distant leaders we grant power to are more likely to harm us than help us. They're more likely to confiscate our wealth, spy on us, lie to us, and entangle us in pointless foreign wars than they are to protect our fundamental rights.

People make this mistake over and over and end up with tyrants. We embrace the cult of powerful "saviors," instead of the reality that each person is responsible for their own life. We delude ourselves into thinking that our instinctive personal trust in Father is scalable to a political trust in Dear Leader.

It can never be.

The campfire had collapsed into a heap of dying embers by the time Dark Sun finished reading. He listened to the babbling of a brook and the hoots of an owl as he contemplated his father's words. Then he heard the hiss and crackle of a radio.

He tracked the sound to Kozlowski's tent. He yanked open the door flap and saw Kerry lying on his sleeping bag with an electronic device pressed to his ear.

"What the hell are you listening to?" Dark Sun asked distrustfully. He was surprised that any radio broadcast could be received in the wilderness. The Elites transmitted propaganda everywhere by satellites, but Dark Sun was pretty sure Kozlowski wasn't listening to their bilge.

"Do you always barge in uninvited?" Kozlowski muttered. "It's a radio show called *Voice of America*. It's broadcast from Pathless Land."

Dark Sun snickered. "America is dead. Why would you Outcasts have a show called that?"

"The irony is delicious. A century ago, *Voice of America* was broadcast globally as a beacon of hope to destitute countries ruled by corrupt dictators. Now, America itself is in the same mess. And its ray of hope is getting broadcast by people it cast out. Our show has a large underground audience in the former Southern states. They've supported us ever since we invaded the continent."

"And just what ray of hope is *Voice of America* sharing tonight?" asked Dark Sun.

Kozlowski's demeanor suddenly brightened. "Important news! J is speaking tonight at a public meeting in Richmond. He does this whenever our forces liberate a city. He explains the vision of Pathless Land and reminds them what a free society is like. It's usually well received. People understand that we're not at war with them; we're at war with their masters. Now that we've taken Richmond, we're very close to Washington. The end may finally be near for those tyrants."

Dark Sun's heart sank to his toes. "That means the end may be near for my kids." He became more aware than ever that time was running out.

Kozlowski frowned. "All we can do is rendezvous with the Elites quickly and play out whatever hand they deal us. I know that you think you haven't chosen sides in this civil war, but you have. Everyone has, consciously or unconsciously. The conflict cuts right to the essence of what civilization ought to be. You'll eventually realize that we're not enemies. Get some sleep. We need to ride hard in the morning."

Dark Sun nodded, and then noticed a pen lying on the floor next to Kerry's sleeping bag. He hadn't seen a writing utensil more sophisticated than a crude pencil in many years. Kerry noticed his stare. "Take it," he said. "I've got plenty more."

"Thanks." Dark Sun picked up the pen and rolled it in his fingers, assessing its craftsmanship like it was a piece of fine art. He saw a phrase engraved on the casing: "Neither coerce nor be coerced." He looked quizzically at Kozlowski.

Kerry smiled. "That's the motto of Pathless Land."

Dark Sun returned to his own tent. He curled up beside Dark Moon, who was fast asleep. He laid in the darkness, alone with his thoughts. He thought about the race against time to save his children. He thought about how he had become intertwined, as if by fate, with unusual people and strange circumstances. He thought about his deceased father. He thought about his own end drawing near as entropy marched toward its inevitable victory.

His thoughts rampaged at such a torrid pace that he felt an urge to write them down. He wanted to slow them to an understandable crawl, to craft them into something clear and permanent. He thought about *Voice of America*. He thought about the musings in his father's journal. He thought about the courage and compassion of Fatima and Osiris. He thought about what inspired people to fight evil and to protect their loved ones.

He got up.

He retrieved his father's journal, went back outside, and sat by the fire. He flipped to an empty page near the end of the journal. He clicked the pen and began to write.

His pulse quickened. He wrote down everything that was swirling in his head: his fears and ideas, his hopes and torments, his nightmares and dreams, his past and future, life and death, love and hate. All the while, he sensed the spirit of his father guiding his hand. Powerful emotions surged through him. Ideas took over, bursting forth into existence from a hidden wellspring. He felt different. He felt purpose. He was now a creator.

And then, from his chaotic scrawl of notes and ideas, he composed his first poem.

THIRTY-SEVEN
DISEASE

> My life is barren as salted ground
> Nowhere to run; death all around
> Cruel Fate cut through me twice
> Disasters turned my heart to ice
>
> — *The Poems of Dark Sun*

The morning air was dank and cold. The snow crunched underfoot as the Eagles broke camp and mounted for another arduous ride. They ate hard biscuits as they rode. Frigid droplets of mist seeped into their clothing. The horses' breath was visible in the frosty morning.

It was Dark Sun's turn to lead the equine procession. Everywhere he looked, destructive forces had torn the landscape asunder. Village after village had been torched, leaving behind nothing but scorched foundations and blackened chimneys. Were they destroyed by the retreating Elites, the marauding Caliphate, or the invading Outcasts?

He didn't know, but he was certain that the dead didn't care which faction was the culprit. Maybe they should have cared more while they were still alive, he thought.

Abandoned farms lay fallow between the villages. They were choked by weeds and brambles and bordered by rotted, broken fences. Decomposing bodies dotted the terrain, testifying to the insanity of humanity's self-destruction.

Dark Sun was horrified by the various methods people had crafted for slaughtering each other. One carcass was missing an arm, likely hacked off by a sword or scimitar. The skull of another had been crushed by a blunt weapon. A crude wooden spear impaled a headless torso. The primitive savagery screamed that mankind was on a slippery slope toward oblivion. Dark Sun recalled a prophecy by Albert Einstein in one of his father's bootlegged books. The scientist posited that World War IV would be fought with sticks and stones. And swords, clubs, and spears, Dark Sun silently amended.

Given the widespread destruction, Dark Sun mulled the near certainty that the Eagles would be attacked by an enemy faction or a rogue gang. The anticipation of battle was daunting. Dark Sun was frightened down to his marrow. How did it feel to get shot by a bullet? How painful was the splintering of bones and the tearing of flesh? Would he faint at the sight of his blood spurting from a severed artery? What horrific final thoughts would torment him if he was thrust at death's door?

He had spent most of his life on their obscure Kansas farm, far removed from the roiling civil war. The isolation was fertile ground for contemplation, not violence. Deep down, he was a farmer and a budding writer, not a warrior. He feared his own cowardice in the coming tribulations on which icy-veined fighters who liked the caustic smell of gunpowder and the coppery taste of blood thrived. There would be no need for poets pondering the mysterious depths of the human condition. It saddened him to think about a world without poets and other intellectual and artistic aspirants. What would Curious grow up to be in such a world? Hopefully not a killer, but what was left for him? A century ago, young boys dreamed of becoming astronauts, sports legends, and famous musicians. Such potential was now lost in the Darkness, a wretched milieu in which dreams were nightmares and individual ambitions were subordinated to collective machinations. Dark Sun sighed heavily.

He was startled out of his dour reverie by a group of men who suddenly materialized from the mist up ahead. As the point person he signaled a halt to the Eagles, cursing himself for neglecting to keep a watchful eye. He also cursed this potential delay in their effort to save Curious and Cammy. Their tight schedule didn't allow for disruptions.

Fatima, Hawkeye, and Saul spurred their horses to join Dark Sun for a quick confab. They peered through the haze to assess the threat up ahead. The men opposite them did likewise. The two bands stared at each other across a translucent gap, waiting for a provocation that might trigger hostilities.

Saul took off his sunglasses and counted through the haze. "There's six of them. They're armed."

Fatima nodded. "There might be more in the woods. What faction do they belong to?"

"They're rogues. No uniforms. Guns don't match. Amateurish tactics. If there were more in the woods, we'd already be dead. They look as confused as we are."

"They're scavengers," said Hawkeye, squinting into the distance. "They're towing a wagon full of scrap metal. They're probably afraid we're going to kill them and steal their shit."

Many drifters had become scavengers, for lack of any other way to carve out a living in the disintegrating society. They trailed behind the civil war battles, plundering whatever wasn't destroyed. They swarmed the carnage like locusts, stripping everything bare as they passed through. They used the bits of gleaned treasure for bartering. They weren't killers; they merely recycled the leftovers of killers.

"We don't have time for this stalemate!" Fatima snarled. "If they're afraid, let's act like we're not!" She pulled a rifle from the scabbard of her saddle. She tucked it under her right armpit and grabbed the reins with her left hand. Hawkeye nodded and then did the same. The other Eagles mimicked her strategy too.

"Let's go!" Fatima shouted. She dug her heels into the flanks of her horse and exploded into a gallop toward the scavengers. She screeched an incoherent banshee cry. The others tore down the road behind her. They echoed Fatima's warbling with a cacophony of shouts and whistles. The thundering hooves of their mounts flung snow and mud in all directions.

The scavengers were paralyzed as the rampaging horses and screaming marauders bore down on them. Then, one by one, they dashed into the woods. The Eagles galloped past their position, then slowed to a trot and gaped backward. The scavengers had melted away.

"Cowards!" Saul bellowed into the distance.

"Thieves!" Ruby shouted.

"They're neither," Fatima admonished, breathless from their mad dash. "They're just trying to survive the shitty world your former faction created."

Saul stared at his leather boots, feigning concern about the slop splashed on them during their stampede. Ruby avoided eye contact with Fatima. "We're not Elites anymore," she mumbled.

"Sometimes it's hard to tell!" Fatima snapped.

Dark Sun smiled insincerely at Saul. "How's your epiphany coming along?" Then he nudged his horse beside Fatima's. "Great idea to charge those scavengers."

"They weren't really a threat," Fatima said quietly. "Like most people, they just want to be left alone."

They rode for another hour to put distance between themselves and the scavengers, and then Fatima called a halt to give the horses a break for food and water. Dark Sun hurriedly tended to his horse. Then he propped himself against a tree trunk to read another entry from his father's journal.

April 23, 2055

Mary came down with pneumonia again.

It's her third bout in the past two years. Her body has to heal itself each time, because there are no doctors around here anymore. This episode is quite virulent. How long before the disease finally kills her?

She's a strong woman, and we have the advantage of being farmers, which means we have fresh air, decent food, and get lots of exercise. But it would sure improve her chances if we had antibiotics and steroids. Those simple remedies are long gone. The whole medical industry is gone.

At least we live far away from most people. Travelers through here say that epidemics are sweeping the cities. Smallpox, typhoid fever, and tuberculosis are the main culprits. Millions are dying, if the hearsay is true.

The demise of the medical industry began when healthcare was made "free." That removed the cost of unhealthy lifestyles from everyone's personal calculus, so society had to bear the risk of individual carelessness. When the "free" healthcare became a crushing financial burden on taxpayers, the government cut doctors' fees and rationed services. This meant fewer competent doctors and less access to care.

Imperious boards were set up to do the rationing. Originally, it was based on a sterile algorithm involving each person's life expectancy and value to society. Over time, the rationing became a function of whom you knew or which faction you supported. Eventually, when the economy collapsed, the "free" services were impossible to get, unless you were a high-ranking Elite.

Euthanasia was the only medical procedure that was readily available for commoners. Killing the elderly freed up resources that were becoming dearer with each passing year. When people turned eighty, they were deemed too feeble to contribute their fair share to society. The Elites secretly exterminated them, unless they were party members. As the Darkness became darker and resources became scarcer, the termination threshold dropped to seventy years.

Many children were sent to similar rendering centers that were euphemistically called "orphanages." These were essentially postpartum abortion clinics. The parents of these "orphans" had violated the One Child policy, or their unwanted children had birth defects. Society could no longer afford to care for defective children who were unlikely to contribute their fair share.

Government control of healthcare also led to the mass collection of private information about every citizen. Since all activity somehow affects health, the Elites used that pretense to record everyone's "activity" in their meta-databases, allegedly for "research." They gathered employment, education, and travel histories. They compiled fingerprints, retina scans, financial transactions, purchases, e-mails, social media postings, smart device activity, DNA test results, gun licenses, internet searches, face recognition images, license plate scans, and phone records.

The most prolific tools for their snooping were the ubiquitous voice-controlled personal assistants like Alexa and Echo that were in millions of homes before the Darkness. These devices were surveillance goldmines, much like Big Brother's fictional telescreens.

The bureaucrats eventually knew everything about everyone every minute of every day. The SIN chips they implanted inside each person linked their physical movements with computerized dossiers via chip readers, drones, and GPS satellites.

This immense repository of information was stored in a secret facility in Utah. The Elites collaborated with Microsoft, Google, and Facebook to mine the data. The NSA, IRS, CIA, Department of Homeland Security, and Department of Justice eventually "borrowed" this metadata to harass domestic adversaries who were considered threats to the regime.

The healthcare system evaporated into oblivion, but the surveillance state it spawned sunk its teeth deeper and deeper into the private lives of everyone. When the civil war pitted citizens against their government, the SIN chips and the electronic dossiers became potent rebel-hunting weapons for the Elites.

Everything the Elites touch becomes diseased and turns to shit.

At least for us common people.

. . .

A wave of sadness washed over Dark Sun as he closed the journal. His mother's next bout with pneumonia claimed her life. His father had disappeared by then.

The Eagles resumed their journey. Kozlowski joined Dark Sun at the head of the procession. They chatted amiably as they rode along, sharing perspectives on life in their different worlds. Dark Sun felt a growing sense of kinship with the Outcast. He also appreciated the medic's efforts in Atlanta to save Fatima and the other gypsies. This made him wonder about the healthcare system in Pathless Land.

"Is healthcare free in your country, like it was in Old America?" he asked.

Kozlowski shook his head. "Forcing someone to hand their money over to a stranger doesn't count as 'free' in Pathless Land. It also doesn't count as 'caring.' People who think it does deserve the dysfunctional society they'll end up with. What a person does with someone else's money reflects shallow virtue signaling. What they do with their own money reflects true conviction. Caring is essential to humanity, but it's deeply personal and can't be compulsory. It's born out of compassion for family, friends, and neighbors. It's the exact opposite of the impersonal acts of theft administered by faceless bureaucrats."

"Who will care for the unfortunate if others aren't forced to?"

Kozlowski laughed. "Can 'care' and 'force' be properly linked in the same thought? Let me ask you something. Do you know that Teema's liver and spleen aren't her own?" He paused. "Probably not, because she doesn't even know it."

"What do you mean?"

"In Atlanta, the only way to save her was to replace her damaged organs. I transplanted an artificial liver and spleen."

Dark Sun was taken aback. "But . . . I thought Pathless Land doesn't do charity work."

"Pathless Land doesn't. But our *people* do. Charity is as natural as seeing, hearing, and feeling. It's part of our shared instinct for society.

It's a pleasurable act that brings joy to both the giver and the recipient. There was a wave of compassion in the hospital for the injured gypsies. We routinely set up funds for innocents who get wounded during our battles to liberate America. The Elites, the Jackals, and the Caliphate continually found ways to harm Teema. Our libertarian society saved her life."

After they rode together in silence for a while, Kozlowski broke the tedium. "We should be extra cautious. Some of the dead along the road were freshly killed."

Dark Sun blanched. "I look the other way when I see cadavers."

"They were disemboweled. That means organ harvesters aren't far away."

The two men rode together in silence again. Dark Sun was more attentive to his surroundings after Kozlowski's heads up. Near the top of a hill, he saw two more corpses with fresh blood oozing from their exposed entrails. The bodies were swarmed by flies and crows. One was a woman, the other a child. Dark Sun gaped at them, mesmerized by the macabre that had become commonplace.

When they crested the hill, Dark Sun's heart skipped a beat. People were in the valley below, less than half of a mile away. He was surprised to see a motorized vehicle blocking a horse-drawn cart on the road. He raised an arm to signal a halt to their march.

The Eagles gathered around him on the top of the hill. They studied the scenario below. There were six people standing on the road.

Saul removed his sunglasses to get a better look. "Shit," he muttered.

"Bastards," said Kozlowski. "I was afraid of this."

"Afraid of what?" Dark Moon asked. "It looks like a truck and a handyman's wagon."

Saul spat on the ground. "Organ harvesters."

"How can you tell from this distance?" Eve asked.

"The ice cream truck is a dead giveaway. Organ harvesters refurbish them using junkyard parts. The ghouls need them to freeze their bounty until it can be sold."

Four of the six people had guns. The other two, a man and a woman, were unarmed. They appeared to be pleading with the armed men. Suddenly, the woman dropped to her knees, her hands folded in supplication. One of the four aimed a rifle at her head. The unarmed man lunged at him, only to be struck to the ground by another assailant.

Fatima's head whipped back and forth between the drama in the valley and her fellow Eagles. Her eyes were wide with panic. She froze.

"Let me shoot!" begged Hawkeye, as he leveled his rifle and aimed.

A shot rang out below. The woman's head exploded backward in a shower of crimson gore. It recoiled grotesquely from the smoking rifle barrel of her attacker. Her lifeless body fell to the ground, like a sack of grain.

"Goddamn it!" shouted Hawkeye. He triggered his rifle without waiting for an order from Fatima. The man who murdered the woman collapsed to the ground as if his legs had suddenly turned to rubber.

The surviving organ harvesters spun toward the source of the mysterious shot. They spotted the Eagles on the hilltop and opened fire. Fatima's horse took a bullet in the chest. The animal buckled and fell sideways, spilling her in a vicious tumble. The other Eagles dismounted and plunged to the ground as bullets whizzed by.

Saul, Hawkeye, and Dark Sun returned fire from their prone positions. Another harvester crumpled to the ground in the valley. More bullets kicked up snow and dirt around the Eagles.

A woman screamed horrifically behind Dark Sun. He fought through the terror of wondering who it was and continued shooting at the attackers. His fear that the scream might have come from Dark Moon tore at his sanity, but he forced himself to confront the mortal threat coming from the valley below.

After a fierce exchange of gunfire, they killed the last two organ harvesters. The battle stopped abruptly, leaving an eerie, almost suffocating silence. The lone survivor in the valley was the unarmed man. He crawled frantically to the slain woman and laid across her lifeless body.

Dark Sun rolled over, looking for casualties among the Eagles.

Hawkeye and Saul were unhurt. They kept their rifles trained on the valley below, in case any of the fallen attackers moved. Kozlowski was helping Fatima to her feet. She held her shoulder in obvious pain, but she wasn't bleeding. To his heart-stopping relief, Dark Sun saw Dark Moon helping Ruby to her feet. They were both well enough to run toward Eve, who was sprawled on the ground.

Eve didn't move, except for a couple of involuntary twitches. The snow-covered ground around her turned pink as her blood oozed in a widening circle.

Two vultures circled overhead.

THIRTY-EIGHT
LOVE

> Do not go gentle into that good night
> Rage, rage against the dying of the light
>
> — Dylan Thomas

"This is the last time I'll see you."

The doctor's words were so unexpected that Curious had to think twice about their implication. The elderly Virginian had ministered his shattered leg several times since he and Cammy had arrived in Washington. The medic was cranky sometimes, but he was the only person in Washington that Curious had grown attached to, perhaps as a surrogate for the grandfathers he had never met. "Does that mean my leg is all better?" Curious asked anxiously.

The doctor furrowed his graying eyebrows. "No. There's much work to be done yet. I'm quite concerned about the bone grafts."

Curious' heart dropped to his toes. Pain was one thing. Permanent damage was another. "Then why won't I see you? Will I see another doctor?"

"That's not for me to decide," said the old doctor softly. "I'm heading north with my wife tomorrow."

Curious shook his head in confusion. "Why?"

The doctor avoided his eyes. "The Outcasts captured Richmond. That's only a hundred miles from here. Regis has ordered all skilled comrades to evacuate Washington. Surely you've felt the bombs dropping on us lately."

Curious nodded, and then shivered. He felt like he was losing his last remaining friend besides Cammy. "What'll happen to me?"

The doctor didn't answer. He pretended to study the medical chart in his hand. Curious knew the old man was pretending, because his eyes were closed. He thought he saw a tear forming in the corner of one eye.

"What will happen to me?" Curious persisted, despite a growing sense he didn't want to know.

The doctor opened his eyes, now red and moist. "I wish I knew."

"Somebody must know something! Why did they kidnap us? Why did they bring us here?"

The doctor's shoulder's slumped. He stared at the floor. "I have no idea. In some way, we're all captives."

"No, they keep me in a cage. You're able to run away."

The doctor turned a shade of red. "I can run from the bombs, but I can't run from the Darkness. It's not like in the old days. Before Regis. Before the Elites."

Curious often wondered whether Washington was always a sterile, cold, hostile place. "What was different then?"

"Back then we believed in 'love your neighbor.' Now we're told to 'love everyone.' It ruined the meaning of love, and in some way ruined the meaning of life. Now love is confused with obligation. Love is dead, except the love I have for my wife. I'm sorry you never got to experience the old ways. This . . . this just isn't worth it anymore."

Curious felt tears forming in his own eyes. He suddenly recalled asking the young guard who had brought him food why he wanted to go on living. Now he was haunted by the same question. He was at the end of his rope. His leg was ruined. He was being held captive by alien people for an unknown purpose and escape seemed impossible. Bombs were falling around them every day now. The next one may have his name on it. The thought of such a violent end shook him to his core. And now the friendly old doctor was leaving him.

If he was a horse, someone would shoot him to put him out of his misery. He found himself envying horses. Maybe the doctor could do something humane. "Can you inject a poison to kill me?" he asked.

The doctor dropped his chart to the floor. It rattled sharply against the tiles.

He eyed the shelves of vials lining his office, where he knew lethal chemistry lurked. He shook his head, astonished that he briefly considered Curious' horrific request as an act of mercy in the face of inevitable tragedy. The tears that had been welling up in his eyes ran down his wrinkled face. "My boy, I'm so sorry. Is that what we've come to?"

Curious' mind reeled. He was confronted with the stark reality that everyone lives behind a fragile pane of glass that separates existence from nothingness. For some, the glass is transparent through which they see only the nothingness. For others, the glass is a mirror in which they see in its panoramic reflection every joy that makes life worth living. It was likely he was going to die very soon, so the thought of a peaceful transition to death by lethal injection had some appeal. On the other hand, there was still the thin hope that his parents were alive and coming to rescue him. The jarring realization that death was so near, and yet rescue was still possible, had a profound impact on him. His pane of glass, which had always been a mirror to joy, was under ferocious assault by powerful forces. It seemed about to shatter any second, plunging him into a despair of nothingness.

In the dire urgency of the moment, he experienced a wrenching hunger for reunion with everyone and everything in his life that had ever brought him joy. He wished with all his might that these joys would magically reappear. He wished that they would last forever, much like he wished that the stories in his favorite books would never end. Powerful images flashed in his head. It was like he was seeing a rapid slideshow of the highlights of his life. Suddenly, he was romping with Sparty and Brutus. Then he was exploring the meadows and marshes with Cammy, looking for frogs and snakes. Then he was eating homemade maple syrup on hot buttery pancakes. Then he was playing catch with his dad on a warm summer day.

The fact that he might suddenly evaporate into oblivion meant that each of those joys would evaporate too. He would never see his father smile again when he caught the ball, never hear the haunting calls of whip-or-wills as he drifted off to sleep, never touch the soft fur of his pet rabbits, never taste homemade strawberry jam, or never smell the lavender scent of his mother again. Those were just a few of the priceless treasures in his life. As he squirmed in the daunting shadow of the Grim Reaper, he desperately wanted those joyful images to keep scrolling in his mind. He wanted those divine moments with his loved ones to go on forever. He wasn't ready for his own story to end.

He suddenly realized that love and joy give meaning to life. And he could never willfully surrender them. He looked up at the doctor. "No, we haven't come to that," he said with grim resolve.

Relief washed over the doctor's face. He had been watching with apprehension the clouds of emotion scud across the boy's face. "I envy you," he said. "You have two things I don't. Youth and hope."

The doctor opened a drawer. He pulled out an envelope and wrote something on it. He handed it to Curious. "I have no use for this now. It's yours, for better or worse. May your journey be blessed." He smiled forlornly. He ran a hand through the boy's unkempt hair and then headed for the door.

After the door shut, Curious looked down at the envelop. In hastily scrawled cursive, the message from the doctor read, "I lied about evacuating to the North. My wife and I are heading South, to Richmond, to the Outcasts. I owe you that one bit of truth. I couldn't say so out loud because people are always listening. Please put this envelop in the shredder by my desk when you're done with it."

Curious smiled, then tore open the envelop. He extracted a laminated white rose. He stared at it in surprise and wonder. Was it the calling card of Hope or a summons from the Grim Reaper? He put the envelop in the shredder.

The sirens began wailing as bombs fell again. An orderly charged into the office to wheel him back to his cell. A tremendous explosion shook the building.

The lights went out. There were screams all around him.

THIRTY-NINE
FORGIVENESS

> To break the imaginary spell
> Aspire to Heaven, not Hell
> Forgive sins, large and small
> Forgive yourself, most of all
>
> — *The Poems of Dark Sun*

Dark Moon stood over Eve's body in disbelief.

Osiris had warned the Eagles about the mortal dangers awaiting them on this journey. But the stark reality of a dead friend lying at her feet was altogether different from his hypotheticals. It was shocking in a way that humans are never prepared for. In one minute a person is a living being with an ego, a personality, and a history and then in the next it is a wasting composition of inanimate minerals. It's impossible to understand death because death is the end of knowing.

The Eagles gathered around Eve's body. Ruby's scalp had been grazed by a bullet, but she was oblivious to the blood streaking down her neck. Fatima's shoulder hung limp and askew. She was withdrawn into an emotional shell, staring at Eve's dead body like it was the talisman of an evil spirit. Kozlowski's hands were bloodied from checking Eve for a pulse.

A gunshot shattered the heavy silence. Heads spun toward the sound. Saul had euthanized Fatima's wounded horse. Since she was in shock, he took command of the feckless group. He instructed Dark Moon and Hawkeye to begin digging two holes to bury Eve and the woman who was shot. He directed Kozlowski to dress Ruby's head wound and to sling Fatima's shoulder so she could ride. Then he led Dark Sun on horseback toward the bloody scene in the valley below.

They halted amid five bodies strewn on the snowy ground. The sole survivor, a hulking bear of a man, was weeping over the murdered woman. Saul told Dark Sun to tend to him, then dismounted and checked each fallen body for a pulse. One villain still had a heartbeat. Saul finished him the same way he had Fatima's horse, but it wasn't an act of mercy. He cringed, not out of concern for the dead man but for himself. He had a gruesome flashback to his violent life as a young hoodlum.

Dark Sun laid a hand awkwardly on the shoulder of the bearlike man sprawled over the deceased woman. They remained that way for a while as the stranger sobbed. Then the man looked up at Dark Sun. "They killed my wife." His tortured face belied the stoicism in his voice.

Saul joined them. The two Eagles helped the distraught man to his feet. "I'm sorry," Saul said, putting a gentle hand on his massive arm. "For what it's worth, I just killed the last of those bastards."

"Alicia is still dead," the man intoned flatly.

Saul removed his sunglasses. "That's true."

"Truth is all I have left," he replied.

The three men fell silent, transfixed by the dead woman on the ground. In the terrible presence of death, what is there to say between strangers? All words ring hollow in the face of such suffering.

Dark Sun assessed the hulking man who was mourning the loss of

Alicia. He was of average height but built like a blacksmith. He had powerful shoulders, a barrel chest, and forearms muscled by a lifetime of toil. He looked brutish, but Dark Sun detected a quiet intelligence. His clothes were homemade and ill-fitting. His untamed mane of graying hair was crudely clipped to shoulder length. He had a straggly beard, bushy eyebrows, and two streams of tears zigzagging down his leathered face.

The man looked at Saul with a vacant expression. Saul squeezed his shoulder. It was like squeezing a tree trunk. "My name's Saul," he offered.

The stranger shook his head slowly. "The only person I trusted in this world is lying dead at my feet."

"Trust is indeed hard to come by. My real name isn't Saul, and his real name isn't Dark Sun, but that's what we call ourselves. What shall we call you?"

"It doesn't matter," he muttered.

Saul scanned the desolate panorama around them. He eyed the five dead bodies splayed on the ground. He thought about Eve up on the hill. "That's probably true."

Dark Sun shook his head. "Things matter, if you decide they do." He looked at the distraught man and continued, "Since truth is all you have left, we'll call you Verax."

The stranger raised an eyebrow and looked more intently at Dark Sun. "That's Latin for 'Truthful One'."

Dark Sun smiled. "Where did you learn Latin?"

"My father," replied Verax, cracking his stoic veneer. "He was a brilliant teacher, not that it was of any use. Schools disappeared when the Darkness came, so he fulfilled his passion by drilling information into my brain. It was a wasted effort. Conjugations, syllogisms, and theorems don't put food on the table in this dysfunctional world. Now I'm just a damn good handyman. I make things, but I try not to think about things."

"My dad schooled me too," said Dark Sun. "His effort was also wasted. What will you do now?"

Verax looked down at Alicia. He glanced at the four dead men who paid the price for murdering his wife. He scanned the ravaged landscape of a world spinning out of control. "It doesn't matter," he concluded again.

"It could," suggested Dark Sun once again. "Join us. We need a handyman, and you could use some friends right now."

"Who is 'us'?" Verax realized he knew nothing about the strangers who had materialized to render justice to his assailants.

"There are eight . . . seven of us." Dark Sun felt a sharp pang of grief. "We don't belong to any faction. We're heading to Washington to rescue my two children who've been kidnapped by the Elites. We may get killed in the attempt. One of our friends is already lying dead up on that hill."

Verax absorbed the insane description of the Eagles' adventure. "That's the craziest thing I've ever heard," he muttered. "But at least there's purpose in the madness. I'm sure you love your children, and now I hate the Elites. Paybacks are hell. I'm in. *Dum spiro, spero*."

"While I breathe, I hope," Dark Sun echoed in translation. He looked at Verax with growing admiration. "Finally, someone I can talk to. You're going to be a great addition to our team."

Saul gave Dark Sun a look from hell, and then put his sunglasses back on. The three men loaded Alicia's body onto the back of Saul's horse and Verax rode behind Dark Sun back to where the rest of the Eagles were dealing with their tragedy. Verax's sorrowful tale was explained to them. They offered condolences for his loss of Alicia, as did he for their loss of Eve.

They began arranging burials. They would leave the dead organ harvesters on open ground for scavengers to devour. Verax, Hawkeye, and Dark Sun chiseled the shallow holes in the frosty ground. When they finished, the Eagles gathered around the makeshift graves. Verax hefted Alicia's corpse. He kissed her icy lips and then knelt and lowered her into one of the holes. Kozlowski, Saul, and Hawkeye set Eve into the other grave.

Fatima, her wounded shoulder in a sling, sobbed bitterly and shivered violently. Kozlowski wrapped a blanket around her, but it didn't help. He was growing increasingly concerned that she was withdrawing into herself and disengaging from the team.

They hovered awkwardly over the graves, braced against a biting northwest wind. Each knew that something should be said to commemorate the solemn interments, but they remained silent with heads bowed. Finally, Dark Moon nudged Dark Sun and whispered, "Hey poet, some lofty words would help right now."

Dark Sun blushed, coughed nervously, and then began a eulogy:

"Dear friends, the passing of Eve and Alicia draws the essence called God hauntingly near. In his shadow, we seek comfort, understanding, and deeper perspective about our unexpected losses. We discover how temporary we are, compared to the infinite. We discover how imperfect we are, compared to the ideal. We discover the depth of our grief, compared to perfect joy. We discover how little we know, compared to perfect wisdom. Most of all, we discover how precious life is, compared to death.

"So, we huddle together in the embrace of God's essence. We're desperate for the immortality it promises. We aspire to the perfection it proclaims. We hope for the blaze of joy it portends. We yearn for the answers it may reveal. However, the simple but powerful lesson is always the same. God is love.

"To live is to love, and to love is to live. Love offers the immortality of a timeless bond with another human. Love teaches us that even though we're imperfect, we can be forgiven and therefore healed. Love conquers pain with the joy of companionship. And love frames the greatest wisdom, which is to appreciate each precious moment of our existence with those we hold dear.

"As we bury Eve and Alicia, we bury some of our love with them. But great love remains among us. It's a renewable resource that shall carry us through. We know that someday we'll meet the same fate as the departed. But for now, we cling to the hope of immortality with a desperate and wild embrace of the blessings called love and life.

"Rest in peace."

The others nodded silently. Dark Moon rubbed his arm in appreciation.

The Eagles shoveled dirt over the graves. Verax placed upon Alicia's mound an intricate metallic butterfly made from scrap materials for a birthday that was now never to be. His artwork wasn't beautiful in an ordinary sense, but the craftsmanship was remarkable, and the simple gesture in such a dismal realm was starkly poignant.

After the funeral, the Eagles set up camp in the valley. Snow fell heavily, making a misery of lighting a fire, cooking food, and pitching tents. Verax, Hawkeye, and Saul scavenged everything useful from the ice cream truck. They discussed the possibility of driving it to Washington, but there wasn't much gas in it, and the balding tires would never get it through the snowy mountain passes. Hawkeye set it on fire so that no other organ harvesters could use it. A gust of hot air washed over them from the massive fireball. Snow melted in a wide swath around the burning hulk.

The night was tortuous for the Eagles. The wind whipped, the snow drifted, and awful images of death haunted their sleeplessness. They shivered from the cold, from emotional exhaustion, and from skin-crawling noises of the wild that seemed much too close to their flimsy tents.

The weather eased when dawn broke. They gathered tools, materials, and food from Verax's cart and stashed them in leather saddlebags borne by the spare horses. They hid the cart in a copse of trees so that Verax could reclaim it on their return journey.

Dark Moon rode point when the Eagles resumed their eastward trek. The day was as tortuous as the night. She felt a burgeoning sense of doom about her children. The Eagles were running into so many delays that their ten-day deadline seemed impossible to meet.

She was also haunted by disturbing images of Eve's murdered body. It didn't help that the Eagles were drawing nearer to the main battlegrounds of the civil war. Bodies were strewn everywhere. Most of them were civilians slaughtered by the retreating Elites. The flesh of many of the dead had been devoured by maggots or scavenging vermin, leaving behind bleached skeletons being scoured by voracious insects for the last bits of bone marrow. Other cadavers were bloated like roadkill, the gases of internal decomposition bursting their clothes. Their filthy, swollen faces were stretched into hard, shining masses of unrecognizable putridity. Many of them were shoeless, their blackened feet testifying to the desperation that preceded their demise.

Stalin observed that one death is a tragedy, but a million deaths are just a statistic. The countless corpses tormenting Dark Moon were more than statistics to her. She saw each one as someone's son or daughter, mother or father, sister or brother, friend or lover.

There were so many bodies littering the ground that they were like natural vestiges of the landscape, but to her they were still individual lives that had been squandered pointlessly. She felt the pain of each as a mother would, and it was unbearable. The horrors ground her soul to powder like a spiritual grist mill. This senseless carnage couldn't be real, she thought. But there it was.

How was such evil possible by a species that laid claim to morality? What mesmerizing power hypnotized people into hurling themselves against each other, each knowing the outcome was likely to be their demise? What psychopathy perverted rational people to mangle each other on such a brutal scale? She shuddered. There were no sensible answers to these questions.

The next three days were uneventful. The Eagles rode hard, taking advantage of clear weather. They pushed eastward along the vestige of Highway 64 toward Charleston, West Virginia. The horses began to struggle as they ascended the Appalachian foothills.

At dusk following a grueling ride, they stopped and made camp. After dinner, Dark Sun grabbed a lantern and sauntered to a small hill to read another entry from his father's journal. He paged to where he had inserted the laminated white rose.

He was instantly surprised. The date on the journal entry was two years later than the previous one. It was dated just three months before his father disappeared.

August 17, 2057

Mary suggested that I begin writing again. I think she's tired of that faraway look in my eyes. I'm tired of it too.

I haven't written since April of 2055. The ill wind of my own son's treachery caused my hiatus.

Like many young adults, Kieran and his girlfriend, Katarina, were smugly self-righteous. They were sure they knew what was best for everyone else. Their preachy idealism was benign at first. Then they began lusting for the power to satisfy their utopian urges to save the environment, the poor, the children, and the oppressed.

They sought to reengineer everyone else's lives to suit their own ideals. But the hardest lesson for a person to learn is that they are only themselves. It's wrong to impose one's own desires and ambitions onto others. It's wrong to impose the personal burden of dealing with entropy from some onto others.

Kieran and Katarina were enraptured by the teachers, the pop culture idols, and the media sycophants. They were convinced that achieving their utopian dreams was as simple as forcing everyone to put the common good above individual desires. They were inspired to be among the Elites.

I was ashamed that they couldn't see through the flimsy veneer. Their teachers weren't teaching; they were indoctrinating. The bureaucrats weren't serving the people; they were serving a political machine. The cultural icons weren't enlightened; they were using their faddish elitism to expound on weighty matters beyond their comprehension. The media weren't keeping the Elites honest; they were part of the grand illusion.

Kieran and Katarina couldn't see that the dark side of giving leaders so much power to "do good" is that it gave them equal power to impose their self-serving ambitions on everyone. Power tends to corrupt, and absolute power corrupts absolutely, as Lord Acton warned. The corruption infected Kieran and Katarina. Like many true believers, they succumbed to the "ends justify the means" mind-set. They joined the security apparatus of the Elites.

In April of 2055, they led a contingent of secret service thugs to our area for an "inspection." It was actually a forensic search for evidence of insurrection. They didn't have warrants—such things don't matter anymore. My home was searched more thoroughly than most. They were hoping to find evidence of my involvement in the rebellion.

Their search wasn't thorough enough. I hid this journal, my weapons, and my books in the foundation of my home. But the close call spooked me into laying low for a while.

My instinct was vindicated. The thugs made repeated visits to ransack my house. My disgust with Kieran grew with each violation. I believe his motive was to prove his devotion to the Elites by blowing the whistle on his own father. Such a supreme act of loyalty would earn him power and prestige. That's the nirvana of everyone in their cult.

Despite the risk, I've resumed writing down my thoughts here, thanks to Mary's prodding. But my role needs to be more active than just ruminating in a journal.

I'm beginning to see the world differently now.

Dark Sun snapped the journal shut. He felt a glimmer of understanding. When he was an obscure farmer in Kansas, the Elites had been a mere abstraction. However, recent events helped him realize that the Elites had always been integral to his life. His brother and Dark Moon's sister joined their secret service. They tormented his father for years, and perhaps had a hand in his disappearance. The Elites kidnapped his children. Now he and Dark Moon were heading directly into the gaping mouth of the beast, and yet he still didn't know why this was happening. Were they being summoned to Washington because they had an illegal second child? Was this how Kieran and Katarina had chosen to torment him and Dark Moon, just as they had found reasons to torment his father? What horrors were going to happen at the end of this journey? Would one of their children be killed right before their eyes as punishment?

Just when Dark Sun felt like his head was going to explode, he heard someone crying. The whimpering came from the hillock next to him. He momentarily forgot his own travails and went to assist the anguished soul.

After stumbling through thistles and vines in the dim lantern light, Dark Sun came upon Fatima, who was prostrate on the snowy ground. Her body convulsed as she cried.

Dark Sun knelt beside her and put his arm across her frail back. She trembled like a wounded bird.

"Teema?"

She ignored him.

"Teema, what's wrong?"

She slowly sat up. She stared up at him blankly, trying to reconcile his unexpected presence with the darkness of her inner turmoil. Her brown face was mottled by a concoction of snow, mud, and tears. Her dark hair was an awful tangle. She had purple bags under her eyes. "Alicia and Eve are dead," she moaned through lips that were blue from the cold.

"I know. There's nothing we can do about it. We have to move on."

"I can't," Fatima whimpered. "It was my fault that they were killed."

"What are you talking about?"

"I froze when I saw the organ harvester put a gun to Alicia's head. Hawkeye waited for my order, and then had to decide on his own to shoot. But it was too late. I failed as a leader. Now she's dead. My life has sucked in so many ways, but I've never been responsible for such a horror. I can never forgive myself!"

"Teema, please—"

"I've ruined everything! I can't lead this team now. I can't suffer the humiliation of going back to my father. I can't even live with myself. I hope a wild animal tears my flesh apart on this hill."

"Stop it!"

His shout stunned her like a slap to the face. Her dark eyes were wild and frightened.

"Teema," Dark Sun said gently. "You're missing something important."

"I'm not missing anything. My failure is very clear."

"Teema!" Dark Sun shouted again. "You have to remember the extraordinary message that Jesus gave us."

She looked up at him in surprise. "What do you mean?"

"He forgave everyone. Likewise, your loved ones will forgive you. And you should forgive yourself."

"Why would anyone forgive me?"

"Why wouldn't we? Which of us has never responded poorly to fear, exhaustion, or temptation? If held to a strict accounting, we'd all be judged badly. And if those judgments were final and indelible, life would be horrific. Each affront would forever be a wound, each insult forever a scar, each agitation forever a conflict. Forgiveness is the only antidote to our inherent frailties as humans. Without it, relationships are impossible. Without relationships, we're just wild animals embroiled in tit-for-tat vengeance."

"Forgiveness won't bring Alicia and Eve back to life."

Dark Sun sighed. "That's the awful truth of our existence. The law of causality only works in one direction. What's done is done. That's why forgiveness is so vital. If someone who has erred is contrite and has made amends, then forgiveness is necessary to maintain a relationship with that person. Forgiveness can't erase a transgression or the pain that resulted from it. However, it enables us to let go of bitterness and vengeance. It gives people an opportunity to learn from their mistakes and move on. Without forgiveness, we'd be stuck in anger and hatred, punishing ourselves spiritually by taking on the mistakes of others. But there's more to forgiveness than forgiving others. The most powerful forgiveness is to absolve yourself, which was Christ's transcendent lesson. Just as we can't live in peace with others unless we forgive them, we can't live in peace with ourselves unless we forgive ourselves. It's the only way life can be tolerable for us fallible humans in this harsh and imperfect world. We're flawed, but not condemned to eternal hell because of it. Forgive yourself. For everything."

Fatima stared up from the frozen ground at Dark Sun, who was kneeling beside her on one knee. She stared beyond him at the stars that were emerging in the night sky. She stared beyond the stars into eternity, and then beyond eternity into the depths of her soul. "You sound like one of those Blessed zealots," she murmured.

"Hardly. I see religion as a source of wisdom and inspiration, not as a means for controlling others."

"Same here," she said. "But I want to be left alone now."

Dark Sun hesitated. She was clearly at a crisis point, a moment of piercing self-doubt that perhaps threatened her very existence. A part of his brain insisted that he stay by her side and nurse her through the crisis, despite her dismissal. The rest of his brain conceded that the crisis was hers to resolve alone.

He headed for camp, but not without heavy foreboding. He stopped to look back at her several times, second-guessing his decision to leave. As he stumbled through the underbrush, he thought about his own need to forgive. After reading the latest entry in his father's journal, he was consumed by hatred for Kieran and Katarina. He hated that they tormented his dad. He hated that they were involved in the kidnapping of his children. He hated that they had coerced him and Dark Moon into this deadly journey.

He thought about what he had just told Fatima about forgiveness. His arguments were sound. He knew that the only way to clear his mind of hatred was to forgive Kieran and Katarina, despite their heinous acts. But he also knew that forgiving them was impossible. Fatima had made an inadvertent mistake, but the vile actions of Kieran and Katarina were malicious, intentional, and self-serving.

Despite the lesson from Jesus, he concluded that there are times when complete rejection of relationship is the only sane path. He knew he would suffer from the burden of his unresolved anger, but sometimes turning the other cheek is itself a sin, especially when innocents are in jeopardy. Gandhi was wrong when he said that the Jews should have offered themselves to their German butchers. Forgiveness is a mistake if it emboldens evil.

He was going to save his innocent children, and he was going to make Kieran and Katarina pay.

FORTY
CAGES

Life is like a game of cards. The hand you are dealt is determinism; the way you play it is free will.

— Jawaharlal Nehru

Cammy glared at the steel bars caging one wall of their cell. They weren't benign adornments. They embodied a malevolent intent to quarantine her and Curious to an eight-foot cube. She hated being cooped up like an animal. She was experiencing acute claustrophobia; not just constriction by a tight space, but also constriction by unremitting captivity.

Prior to this, her life had been blessed with so much freedom that she had almost no awareness of it, like a fish fully accustomed to its watery world. Sure, her parents set rules, most of which she followed, although not as often as they believed. She lived by Twain's adage that rules were made for the guidance of wise people and the obedience of fools. She and Curious had free run of the Kansas prairie around their ranch. Every day offered adventures. Some of them ended badly, but most led to joy.

Now she was trapped in a terrestrial purgatory where she was breathing but unable to live. The grimness of captivity left Cammy remorseful for every creature that she and Curious had ever stuck in a box for their amusement. She imagined the walls of her cell closing in on her inch by inch. The ceiling sank steadily lower. The lights grew dimmer. Sometime soon, the walls and the ceiling would wrap around her captive body like a coffin. The lights would fade to the darkness of six feet underground. In her darkest moments, she even considered taking her own life.

She felt the same wrenching heartache of every dissident exiled to a gulag, of every slave laboring under a scorching sun, of every prisoner pulling an oar in the fetid cistern of a war galley, of every genocide victim queuing in a concentration camp. The surest way to learn the value of personal freedom is to lose it. She was on the wrong side of the bars and was learning that there was no right side.

She experienced the stark reality of free will. She had read in her grandfather's books that some philosophers denied the concept. They argued that all actions were determined by external causes that merely teased with the illusion of choice. It was clear to her that none of those philosophers had ever been confined in a cell like this. If they had, their frustrated wills would have shredded their delusions of a completely mechanical universe. The rage resulting from the loss of freedom is free will screaming to be unchained.

She recalled a time when she was lazing by the bay window of their ranch on a sunny afternoon. She was sitting in a chair beside their German shepherd Brutus and a potted peace lily. She had fallen asleep basking in the sunlight pouring through the window. She remembered when she awoke, the sun had moved in the sky, so she was no longer bathed by its soothing rays. Brutus, however, had roused himself from his snooze long enough to move from the shadow that had crept over him to a spot on the oaken floor still warmed by the sun.

It had dawned on her that Brutus had chosen to do exactly what she wanted to. In many ways, he was a creature just like her, with desires, senses, and mobility, along with a brain capable of choosing better rather than worse. For Brutus, "better" was the warmth of the sun rather than the chill of a shadow, just as it was for her. He could sense where the warmth was, he had legs to move him there, and he rationally chose to do so.

Then she had noticed the peace lily. The plant was leaning toward the window. Its leaves were arched, and its stalk was curved, to maximize the sunlight it could absorb. She remembered she had turned the plant around earlier in the spring, only to observe in amazement a few days later that its stalk and leaves had repositioned themselves for optimal sun exposure.

The plant could somehow sense the position of the sun. It "desired" more sun rather than less. Even though it had no legs, it had enough biological mobility to arch toward the life-giving orb.

She remembered thinking in this sense that the lily was like her and Brutus, except that its possible actions were more limited. Brutus had legs, but the rooted plant didn't. She could make a crude chair for her comfort, but the peace lily and the dog couldn't. They each had different levels of evolved abilities to fulfill their desires, but their preferences for better rather than worse were similar. The main difference, however, was she had greater capabilities and a greater capacity to choose from a wider range of activities. She could run through the forest, shoot a slingshot, climb a tree, read a book, understand language and humor, and appreciate art and literature. Her possible choices were nearly limitless.

This left her no doubt that she possessed the wild and wonderful characteristic of free will.

Sitting in front of the bay window that summer day, she concluded three simple things. All living creatures desire "better" rather than "worse." Given the chance, they will choose "better." The higher up the evolutionary ladder, the more sophisticated were the possible choices, but the choice was always for the better when all things were considered.

It struck her that the natural inclination of all living things to pursue better over worse had to be one of the most powerful forces in the universe. It motivated all effort, achievement, and invention. Everyone prefers love over hate, ease over burden, collaboration over conflict, and life over death. Every sane person wants to change their circumstances for the better.

As Cammy struggled with the claustrophobia of the prison cell, another conclusion dawned on her. If all living things prefer better over worse, then constraining their ability to choose is a horrifically immoral act, unless their actions are intended to physically harm someone else. And since humans have the most sophisticated array of possible choices, the suffering that results from limiting a person's ability to choose is profound. Perhaps the simplest definition of hell is being prevented from choosing better rather than worse.

Cammy stared at the bars blocking her escape from the cell. She was suffering in a way that no person should ever have to. She wanted to be anywhere else—preferably with her mom, dad, and Curious back in Kansas—than on this hellish side of the bars. Someone was preventing this. She hated whoever that unseen, evil person was. She fumed at the bars of her cell again. She despised all of the physical and psychological cages described in her grandfather's history books, especially the myths, dogmas, superstitions, prejudices, ideologies, propaganda, and political correctness. She noted the irony. Man has free will, yet too often is trapped in social cages, like animals in a perverse kind of zoo. She had learned in a very personal way that nothing is viler than one person caging another. If a person can no longer choose, what is left of their personhood?

An overwhelming anger welled up inside her. She shook the bars of her cage with all of her might. She screamed, whipping her tangled blond hair around like a mad person. Her radiant blue eyes seethed with fury.

Curious looked on in trepidation. He wondered if he had to add his sister to the growing list of people he feared.

FORTY-ONE
KARMA

> The universe keeps perpetual score
> Its candid ledger our peril to ignore
> Every act echoes through eternity
> Earning us either hell or felicity
>
> — *The Poems of Dark Sun*

Surreal nightmares about death and perverse cruelty tormented Dark Sun.

Whenever the nightmares shocked him awake, he fretted about Fatima. Once, he got up and trudged in the darkness and heavy snowfall toward the hillock where he had left her. Halfway there, he decided once again to respect her wishes to be alone. He returned to his tent.

At dawn, he and Dark Moon were awakened by frantic shouts. They scrambled out of the tent to investigate.

"Teema's gone!" Kerry shouted as they emerged into the chill of morning. Normally, Fatima was the first to rise. She would stoke the fire, cook breakfast, and roust the others. Kerry, noticing that none of that had been done when he awoke, checked her tent.

By now, the whole team was alerted to the crisis. The heavy snowfall had covered all traces of the path Fatima had taken in her mysterious disappearance. Kerry was ashen faced. Fearing the worst, he split the Eagles into two search parties. He instructed them to head in opposite directions into the brambles. He led one group, and Hawkeye led the other.

Dark Sun ignored Kerry's instructions and sprinted toward the hill where he had left Fatima. Fear gripped his heart, and his conscience berated him for his folly. He realized now how foolish it was to have left the tormented girl alone in the wilderness.

Everyone quickly deduced from his frantic dash that he had some insight into Fatima's whereabouts. They abandoned their searches and sprinted behind him.

Dark Sun abruptly stopped running. Fatima emerged from the thick brush. She was filthy and sodden from head to toe. Her clothes were torn by brambles, and her exposed skin was scratched. Her black hair was a tangled mess. Her eyes were bloodshot and sunken.

She approached Dark Sun and took his hands into hers. "Thank you," she said softly. His heart still raced from fear and self-admonition, but he knew instantly that she had vanquished her inner demons.

"I forgave myself," she continued. "I made a tragic mistake, but I'm a good person. I refuse to waste my life hating myself, just as I refused to consider myself a second-class citizen when my family was in the Caliphate. I'm not going to live in the past. Your words helped me find peace." She walked away from the group as though nothing unusual happened.

The Eagles stood there puzzled. Suddenly Fatima started barking out orders to prepare for the day's journey. Her businesslike commands made it clear no questions were to be asked about her strange disappearance. Kerry approached her with deep concern etched on his face, but she breezed past him as if he were invisible.

Fatima rode point when they commenced their journey. Her position at the head of the column reestablished her leadership. The horses labored as they ascended the wooded foothills of the Appalachians. The wind picked up as the ridges and dales grew higher and deeper. The road snaked through striated cliffs. Yellow birch, mountain maples, and pines covered rocky outcroppings. Rusting train trestles arched majestically over gaping canyons.

The Eagles headed into the decayed suburbs of Charleston, West Virginia. They crossed the Kanawha River over a corroded bridge that creaked ominously in the wind. In the hilly distance they could see the massive gold dome of the defunct state capital. It was illuminated by a stray glint of sunlight, providing a momentary flash of rapturous beauty.

The homes were dilapidated. Their terraced yards were tangled jungles. A few haggard vagrants picked among the ruins. Fatima looked sadly upon them as the mounted Eagles trotted along the winding river. She guessed that many of them had once enjoyed comfortable lives but were now fugitives eking out whatever existence they could. Fate was unkind to them, although she knew they couldn't be fully absolved of complicity in their own demise.

Some of the wanderers had been abused or tortured. A filthy young girl was chained to a brutish man who dragged her in tow like a perverse trophy. A young man was missing a hand. An older woman had been scourged with a bull whip; her exposed shoulders and arms bore the telltale mishmash of welts.

Crude forms of justice had replaced the collapsed legal system. Due process, fairness, and burden of proof were obsolete. Now, justice was barbaric and self-serving, meted out by gangsters, cult leaders, and tin-pot dictators. Punishments included amputation, flogging, and stoning. Indentured servitude was common; wretched souls sold themselves or their children into slavery to pay off debts or to recompense for crimes.

The Eagles cantered past walking skeletons wearing threadbare clothes and blank expressions. Evidence of malnutrition was palpable—

thinning hair, missing teeth, pallid skin, and distended bellies. Some had fever blisters and oozing pustules on their exposed skin.

The forlorn wanderers gave the passing Eagles wide berth, fearing the armed strangers mounted on rare and valuable horses. They eyed the loaded pack animals covetously but took careful note of the rifles cradled by the riders. Some paused and looked dolefully at the Eagles, their eyes pleading for food, silently praying for mercy from mounted nobles who looked like gods to them. The plaintive wretches were nudged along by their cohorts. To the dispossessed, everyone is an enemy.

Fatima's cumulative impression from the wretched milieu was that hell is a very real thing here on Earth. It's created every day by the ill effects of flawed decisions and moral depravity. The evidence around her was immutable. The destitute people they passed didn't have to die to go to hell; they had to die to escape it.

She wondered if there was a heaven somewhere. Was the grand cotillion of human history headed toward a glorious utopia or toward ultimate disaster? She feared the answer. It seemed to her that the economic, political, and sociological arrows of humanity had always been aimed toward the Darkness. It was a horrific cesspool fed by poor choices and destructive acquiescence by billions of people over the centuries.

At the end of a long day's ride, the Eagles bivouacked on a rocky cliff overlooking a canyon. A frigid mountain stream cascaded over the ledge into a dark void below.

Ruby and Dark Moon were by the water's edge, filling canteens for the Eagles and water bags for their horses. After a spate of small talk, Ruby asked bluntly, "Why do you stay with Dark Sun?"

Dark Moon looked up slowly from the canteen she was filling. "What do you mean?"

"What do you see in him? He's not much of a warrior. And when it's time to chop wood and pitch tents, he disappears to read his silly book. He's quite handsome, though."

Dark Moon's eyes shot lightning bolts at her. "That's no concern of yours."

Ruby returned Dark Moon's bellicose stare with a catty smile. "Don't worry. He rejected my advances at the carnival—eventually. But he's a good kisser."

Dark Moon slapped Ruby's face with every bit of her farm girl strength, sending Ruby's canteen tumbling along the rocks. Ruby stumbled backward and plunged into the icy stream. She screamed at the surprise of the fall and the shock of the frigid water. She flailed against the strong current and grappled with slimy rocks in the near darkness. Dark Moon hovered on the bank like a blond Valkyrie, offering no help even though the waterfall was just downstream.

The Eagles heard Ruby's frantic cries and sprinted to the scene. They paused for a heartbeat to discern why Ruby was flailing in the water and Dark Moon was hovering menacingly above her, then Hawkeye and Saul plunged into the stream. Dark Sun went to Dark Moon's side. He could tell by her combative posture that a conflict had occurred. She ignored him.

"What the hell happened?" demanded Saul, after he and Hawkeye emerged from the water with a shivering Ruby in tow.

"The bitch pushed me in!" Ruby yelped through chattering teeth.

"The whore made a pass at my husband!" Dark Moon's clenched fists and belligerent glare made it clear she was ready to resume fighting as soon as the peacekeepers disappeared.

"It was just drunken flirtation at the carnival," Ruby offered in defense.

Dark Sun now understood why Dark Moon was ignoring him. "Moonbeam, I didn't do anything—"

"Shut up! I thought I could trust you!"

"He's telling the truth," Ruby interjected sullenly, in a half-hearted attempt at conciliation. "He enjoyed my kiss, but then he brushed me off and went on a sappy spiel about how much he loved you. You'd have been proud of him, except that he's lazy and can't even protect your children."

Dark Moon lunged at Ruby again. She was restrained by Dark Sun, Saul, and Kerry. Hawkeye stepped in front of Ruby, partly to shield her from Dark Moon, and partly to stunt her inflammatory behavior.

Ruby pushed futilely on Hawkeye. "Out of my way! I can fight my own battles!"

"Maybe," he said gruffly. "But I've had enough. You flaunt your beauty and openly seduce other men. It pisses me off! Either we're a couple or not. Decide!"

"The rest of us have something to decide too!" Fatima said. "You made a pass at Dark Sun? You taunted Dark Moon about it? There's too much at stake for such destructive behavior. We need complete unity and trust on this mission. Convince me not to abandon you here and now!"

Ruby fell silent. She shivered from the onset of hypothermia and from a deep foreboding that she had alienated her only companions amidst perilous mountains with winter looming. Her behavior was irresponsible, as it had been all of her life. This intense confrontation set her adrift in an existential crisis that was beyond her capacity to fathom. Even though her natural instinct was to dismiss the concerns of others, it was clear that their store of tolerance had just run dry at the worst possible time.

"Let me help you," Fatima said, since Ruby was standing mute. "You can't separate an act from its consequences. If your fun harms you or someone else, what have you gained? Certainly not a better life. Certainly not better relationships. Certainly not the trust needed for collaboration in this godforsaken world. If everyone acted as if their hedonism had no harmful consequences, we would all be savages. I refuse to lead a band of savages. Plead your case now or be gone! I warned you it might come to this when you joined the Eagles."

Ruby cowered wide-eyed before the dour faces glaring at her. Her teeth chattered. Her entire body was tortured by the bitter cold and the chill of her soggy clothes. She wrapped her arms around herself. A profound loneliness washed over her. She realized in that moment that her life and relationships had yielded nothing but sadness and disappointment, despite her lust for joy. Her emotional harvest was barren, and the demons of kismet were exacting their toll.

She had sown discord and mistrust for far too long. Years ago, she fled the Elites when they discovered she was a double agent. Now she was on the verge of running for her life again, this time because she had alienated her only remaining friends. Her brain fogged over. She became lightheaded. She dropped to her knees, and then lowered her forehead to the ground. Something in her broke.

No one moved. After a long moment of dreadful silence, Ruby tremulously raised her head. Tears streamed down her cheeks. The dark specter of abandonment had laid bare her soul. She rose to her knees in supplication. She looked up at Hawkeye with moist, reddened eyes. "I'm sorry," she said in a throaty whisper. "I do love you. I choose you alone. I'll earn your forgiveness, if you'll let me." She looked up at Dark Sun. "I'm sorry. You're an honorable man who didn't deserve being seduced. Forgive me." She looked up at Dark Moon. "I'm sorry. I'm jealous of the love you share with your husband. I wanted to hurt you out of spite. Please, forgive me." She looked up at Fatima. "I'm sorry. You're trying to lead us under terrible circumstances. I'm just fucking things up. Forgive me." She looked up at the rest. "I'm sorry to you all. If you'll give me another chance, I'll earn your trust."

The Eagles glanced back and forth between Ruby, who was kneeling and shivering, and Fatima, who was lost in stony contemplation. Suddenly, Hawkeye sprinted toward camp. He returned a moment later with a blanket. He knelt beside Ruby and draped it over her trembling shoulders. The icy-veined sniper and hardened Appalachian backwoodsman curled his body around hers. "I'll go with you if you're banished. We'll survive somehow."

"That won't be necessary," said Fatima. "Her apologies seem genuine, but time will tell. I'm the last person who should withhold forgiveness. I encourage each of you to forgive her too. Let's move on. We have a lot to do and very little time."

The Eagles returned to the routine of making camp. One by one, they chatted with Ruby and made peace. Dark Moon, however, went directly to her tent. She ignored everyone, including her husband.

Dark Sun paced the darkened camp listlessly, nursing the sharp sting of her cold shoulder. When he passed Kerry's tent, he heard a radio once again. He poked his head inside. "Can I join you? My tent is rather frigid right now."

"I'm sure it is. Make yourself comfortable."

He crawled into the cramped quarters and folded his lanky frame into an awkward position. He gestured toward the radio. "*Voice of America?*"

"Yup. Tara is buzzing with excitement."

"Tara?"

"The capital city of Pathless Land." Kerry had forgotten that mainlanders knew little about the mysterious place they disdainfully called Outcast Island.

"So why is Tara buzzing?"

Kerry grinned. "Our armies liberated Manassas, Fredericksburg, and Bull Run."

"That's good news for you, but it scares the shit out of me. What'll happen to Curious and Cammy if the Elites collapse?"

Kerry frowned. "I hadn't considered that. I'll alert Teema that we should move even faster. I need to check on her wounded shoulder anyway."

He rushed from his tent. Dark Sun exited and settled beside the campfire. He reckoned Dark Moon needed more time to find forgiveness. He extracted his father's journal and opened it to his mark.

September 24, 2057

I had a revelation today that changed how I think about everything.

The long ideological conflict between the collectivism of Marxism and the individualism of Capitalism lies at the root of many of the world's conflicts. But both philosophies ignore the most important piece of the social puzzle.

The Marxism of the Elites is a witch's brew of collectivized relationships that inevitably yield servile, childlike dependency on an overbearing state. It doesn't value the uniqueness and sovereignty of each person. It ignores the reality that individual brains are the filters through which all experiences, emotions, and concepts are processed. Instead, it asserts that each person is subordinate to a hypothetical social brain of "we."

"We" is a ghostly figment of imagination. Everything that happens is the result of a specific individual choosing a specific action. As Ludwig von Mises put it, "It is always the individual that thinks. Society can no more think than it can eat or drink."

And yet the imaginary we is the Marxian justification for subordinating the dreams and desires of millions of real I's to a deified state.

This fiction leads to absurd conclusions like "Freedom is only possible through subservience" and "Progress is only possible through sacrifice." The most absurd of all is that equality is only possible if the Elites are more equal than everyone else.

Since Capitalism is the antithesis of Marxism, it's tempting to assume that it's necessarily the answer. But that syllogism isn't true. Capitalism is also flawed, although in a much different way.

Capitalism recognizes the sovereignty of each person, but it defines each in terms of an abstraction called Economic Man, *a purely rational actor seeking maximum utility defined by supply and demand curves.* Economic Man *is a rugged Darwinian, competing with everyone else over scarce resources.*

Whereas Marxism presumes an imaginary we seeking to optimize society regardless of individual interests, Capitalism presumes an imaginary utilitarian seeking to optimize himself regardless of social interests.

Marxism and Capitalism have wildly divergent visions for society. Marxists believe that if the state had a powerful enough computer to calculate a perfect five-year plan enforced by a big enough bureaucracy, human felicity would result. Capitalists believe that if purely rational individuals were set entirely free in a market economy, human felicity would result.

Both philosophies are oblivious to the real fount of human felicity.

Both are utterly irrelevant for nearly all human interactions and for the fulfillment of deep-rooted desires. Very few of the countless decisions people make each day are functions of Marxist or Capitalist theory. There's nothing in the concepts of the Marxian Species Being or the Capitalist Economic Man that enriches our souls, fuels the passion in our hearts, seeds our dreams, or inspires the generosity of family and friends. There's nothing in them that moves people to smile, to shake hands, or perhaps even to die for others.

Neither philosophy is a source of meaning, purpose, or values. A motive more powerful than force or utilitarian gain must be at work in human relationships. How does Marxism or Capitalism explain the selfless love of a mother for a child? Marxism fails, because it regards mother and child as cogs in a social machine, to the point where it proposes to substitute state for mother. Capitalism fails, because it regards the decisions of the mother as selfish utilitarianism, to the point where it suggests that child is a synonym for an additional consumer or worker in the markets.

Neither philosophy can explain why a parent takes two jobs so that their child can live a better life than they did. They can't explain why a friend helps a companion in need. They can't explain why neighbors collaborate. They can't explain why a soldier voluntarily risks his life.

A more fundamental impulse called Karma can explain. Karma is the aspect of reality that accounts for the effects of our actions on others. I don't mean the mystical Karma of bardos and reincarnations speculated by Eastern religions, but rather the law of cause and effect in all human relationships.

The consequences of every human action are etched into the omniscient ledger of reality. This is necessarily true, because existence is altered by every action. The present state of the universe is the product of its past. It's constructed by every mechanical and volitional act that's ever happened. This scorekeeping happens even when there isn't a priest, a magistrate, or a king watching. You can't avoid it or fool it.

Karma is a mirror reflecting to you the effects of your behavior on *people around you, for better or for worse. Every action of yours, no matter how trivial, has some impact on those people.*

Each of your actions also affects you. As you act, so you become. You are the sum of all your decisions. Every choice etches a permanent mark on your soul. Your future you is constantly being constructed by present you, who was constructed by past you.

Karma is a form of immortality. As our actions ripple through eternity, they leave permanent imprints on the universe. Every act alters the configuration of reality somehow, somewhere, and with some magnitude. And since everything in the universe is synchronously connected to everything else, all of existence is affected by each act. It's this polyhedral complexity of life that gives rise to Lorenz's butterfly effect.

Everyone prefers being treated better rather than worse. Everyone also prefers positive feedback rather than negative feedback. These preferences distinguish good behavior from bad behavior. Everyone participates in this karmic synchrony. We are continuously judging and being judged.

Without this karmic feedback, entropy would have devoured our ancient ancestors long ago. Emotions like guilt and shame, concepts like fairness and conciliation, and strategies like shunning and banishment, are all evolutionary artifacts of Karma that help maintain group harmony. Harmonious groups survive. Conflicted groups don't.

As humans evolved, moral precepts emerged to formalize our maturing notions of karmic right and wrong. They were gradually codified into various religions and systems of ethics. These spawned rules for good behavior that were easily teachable and transmittable from generation to generation.

Moral laws like "One good turn deserves another" and "Do unto others as you would have them do unto you" emerged as simple karmic guides for making good decisions in relationships. Every culture in history has evolved such guides. Confucius, Lao-tse, the Buddha, and Jesus Christ all pointed to them. They are as old as humanity itself. All formal systems of ethics and morality are derived from ancient karmic guidelines.

The hormonal biochemistry of our bodies evolved to prefer the positive karmic feedback of smiles and laughter, and to abhor the negative karmic feedback of shaming and shunning. Thus, our social inclinations to love our families, to be generous, and to value trust and fairness are as heritable as our drive for self-preservation.

People don't think like Marxists or Capitalists in their daily lives. They think like human beings who simply want to be loved, respected, trusted, and included. Karma motivates how a parent relates to a child, a spouse relates to a spouse, a friend relates to a friend, and a neighbor relates to a neighbor.

In order to thrive, people must understand how their actions affect those around them, and then adjust their behavior accordingly. Our actions trigger emotional counterreactions from others, which we're hardwired to care about. While the center of each person's universe is a selfish one (because individual brains are the source of all perceptions, emotions, and desires), our actions are constantly influenced by empathy and consideration for others. Individual survival, which is the most selfish interest, ironically depends on successful collaboration. Humans thrive in groups, not in isolation.

Another implication of Karma is that heaven and hell exist here on earth. We create our own hell through unwise acts that engender guilt, remorse, distrust, misery, retribution, and hatred. We create our own heaven through wise acts that engender self-esteem, generosity, achievement, and good standing in our community. Positive Karma yields happiness, and negative Karma yields suffering. It's all Karma.

Ignoring Karma has an eventual cost. A hedonist may have reckless fun today, but destructive consequences will eventually torment him. A thief may enjoy his illicit booty today, but the police or an irate victim will eventually catch up with him. A liar may revel in his deception today, but damaged relationships will eventually haunt him. An idler may thrive on his freeloading today, but those he suckles from will eventually shun him or seek vengeance.

Karma doesn't determine everything *that happens to us, because some of our fate is due to chance or to events beyond our control. We experience unfairness and injustice living in an entropic world among seven billion other people, most of whom are strangers to us. The only sane path forward is to recognize what's in our control and to avoid the debilitating belief that we're the victims of everything.*

I refuse to be a victim from now on. I'm feeling an irresistible call to write a different script for my life. As the world collapses further into this awful Darkness, as more people kill each other over errant ideologies, as more of my friends disappear, it's become painfully clear that I can't just write arcane words in a journal.

I need to act. Karma compels me to.

Dark Sun was so engrossed in reading that he didn't notice everyone else had settled in for the night. He sensed the stillness around him when he looked up from the journal. The embers of the fire were cooling to ash, and the night sky was ablaze with stars. He trudged toward his tent, uncertain of the reception he would get from Dark Moon. He hoped she was asleep.

She wasn't.

"I'm glad you're here, Sunshine," she whispered. Encouraged, he slid next to her in their conjoined sleeping bags.

"Are you mad at me?" he asked tentatively.

"I was, but after I calmed down, I chatted with Ruby. It was tense, but she was gracious. She told me that when she propositioned you, you responded with the most beautiful expression of love for me she had ever heard. She cried later that night when she realized no one would ever say anything like that about her. Her jealousy triggered our fight today."

"I suppose that makes sense," said Dark Sun, who was often mystified by the sudden emotional pivots of women.

Dark Moon snuggled closer to him. "Do you remember what you said to her that night?"

"I remember a lot of it because it was all true. I told her that you make me feel special. You understand my deepest thoughts. You overlook my frailties and forgive my failures. You inspire me to do what's right and good. You're beautiful, kind, trustworthy, patient, and wise. In this brutal world, you're my eternal rock, the one thing I can count on no matter what. With you by my side, I'm never lonely. The warm glow of our relationship is worth more than anything else the world can offer me. It connects me to something permanent, no matter what else is torn from me. Our love is bigger than just the sum of two people. It fills my universe with meaning."

"Thank you." Dark Moon shivered under the blankets and wrapped her arms around him. He slipped his hand under her night shirt and gently stroked her back.

"I'll always love you, Moonbeam."

"I'll always love you too." She caressed his forehead. "It's a cruel world, but you've protected me and cared for our family every step of the way. Despite the hardships, our years together in Kansas were the best of my life. You brought joy to me and our kids. You loved me for who I am. I would be lost and lonely without you."

Dark Sun smiled and then kissed her passionately. They made love, momentarily ignoring the concerns of the world. They melted into the immense joy of their private universe, oblivious to the coldness of the night, the dangers of their journey, the despair of the Darkness, and the fear for their children. For a brief twinkling, they were outside the reach of the grand marches of philosophies and isms, none of which could ever rise to the ecstatic power they were sharing now. It was just the two of them, celebrating the rapture called love.

Dawn would come soon enough, with its pantheon of demons pouring forth through the gates of hell. But for now, a glimpse of heaven.

FORTY-TWO
SUBMISSION

The strength and power of despotism consists wholly in the fear of resistance.

— Thomas Paine

Cammy smiled for the first time in a long time.
A guard appeared at their cell with a tray of food. She and Curious hadn't eaten for two days. The gnawing emptiness in their stomachs had driven them to a silent ill-temper that was interspersed with frenzied fantasies about food. Cammy surmised that the disruption in food delivery was due to the unremitting air raids that had become a psychological torture. Or perhaps the Elites had simply run out of food. Or maybe they saw no point in feeding the two of them anymore.

Nothing ever smelled so good as the food brought by the guard, even though it was pedestrian fare. Cammy hurried a plate to Curious and then grabbed a plate for herself. They savored the grub like it was their last meal. The constant air raids made that a distinct possibility.

Cammy was so absorbed in devouring her food that it took her a while to notice that the guard had quietly remained in the cell after delivering the tray. Cammy looked up in surprise. The guard was an older woman she had never seen before. Her blood-red uniform was standard issue, but it looked like it had been fitted before the onset of a famine. Her shoulders were hunched and her back had an unnatural curve. Her haggard face was almost as gray as her straggly hair. Her eyes were lost in dark sockets. There was a sadness about her. She looked beaten, not from actual blows but like someone who had been convinced by a lifetime of abuse and misfortune that existence was a futile endeavor.

"My name is Sophie," said the guard in a scratchy voice, breaking the spell of their awkward stares. "What's yours?"

Cammy hesitated. She didn't trust any of the guards assigned to their cell. She wanted to be free from them all. However, this woman looked docile and harmless. Despite her desperate appearance, there was something genuinely human about her, which was rare in Washington.

She decided to take a chance. "Everyone calls me Cammy. My formal name is Chameleon."

"Chameleon! What a perfect name for this awful world."

"I hate it. For the same reason."

Another awkward silence ensued. Sophie cleared her throat a couple of times, struggling to find words. She approach Cammy and brushed a crumb of plaster from her hair that had fallen from the ceiling. Cammy flinched at this unexpected show of intimacy.

Finally, the woman said, "I'm sorry."

"For what?"

The hag waved her emaciated arms at the cell confining them. "For this. For what they're doing to you."

"If you're sorry, why are you helping them?"

Sophie cast her eyes to the floor. "What choice do I have?"

"Everyone has a choice. You could blindly follow orders. Or you could do what's right."

The old woman shook her head. "If we don't follow orders, they don't feed us. Or they punish us. Or sometimes people just disappear after the blackshirts come for them."

"So then you choose to obey them, even when you know it's wrong?"

Sophie's sad eyes drifted to a faraway time and place. "When we were kids, they made us join the Social Justice Youth Brigade. They taught us to obey the Elites in all things and to disobey our parents if they interfered. Their books taught us to conform. Their songs taught us to conform. It was like a cult, except everyone was in it. As teens, we all had to do national service, which wasn't really service as much as it was more songs, more books, and more devotion to our leaders. The marches, the demonstrations, the banners, the chants, the slogans, and the pumping fists became a mysterious power that swept us along. There was a rapturous sense of fellowship and purpose. When we became adults and started to outgrow the rapture, the civil war started. We were told it was treason to disobey, that total war required total commitment. We were told to hate the rebels, to hate the Outcasts, to hate the Caliphate, to hate all enemies of the Elites. There was always someone to hate. We were told Regis would save us, but only if we gave him our complete obedience. We were conditioned to obey from birth, so it came naturally. Besides, the Elites fed us, housed us, and gave us medicines, at least for a while. In that sense, they loved us, and we loved them, because we just wanted to be taken care of. How could we go against their wishes? Especially when everything became a crisis. We needed a strong authority. We submitted to that authority. And now we always submit."

Cammy gestured toward Curious, who was sitting wide-eyed in his wheelchair, terrified that his sister was interacting so freely with one of their tormentors. "Look at my brother's ruined leg! Was it right for the Elites to do that to him?"

Sophie shook her head again from the violent confusion of her inner turmoil. "It's not for me to decide what's right. That's up to Regis and his ministers. They say he's doing everything that Lincoln did to save the country from civil war long ago. So it must be right. It is right, isn't it? Please tell me it's right."

Cammy's started to feel the rage burn inside of her again. She balled her fists. "But it's not! It wasn't right for the Elites to take my grandpa away! It wasn't right for them to kidnap us! It wasn't right for them to cripple my brother! It's not right to keep us in this prison! We're going to die here! And yet, you wear their uniform and follow their orders—"

"What else can I do?" Sophie interrupted, burying her head in her hands and sobbing. "I'm terrified of starvation, of their secret trials, their tortures, their executions. Maybe our leaders do bad things, but I'm not responsible. I'm innocent, aren't I?"

"You're not innocent if you know but do nothing to stop them!"

"But that's just it. I don't *want* to know what they do or why they do it. I just want to survive, to live another day."

Cammy shot an accusatory glare at her. "My family was blind to this, and now everything is ruined for us. Maybe my parents could have done something if they had known. Maybe *you* should do something now. You can't unknow what you know."

Tears pooled in Sophie's dark eyes. "My conscience gets too heavy when I think about such things. It forces me to choose submission or risk death. The choice is too awful! How can one person fight such a powerful machine?"

Compassion for the haggard woman lessened Cammy's anger. "Life is always on the edge of death. Our lives may end with the next air raid. Shouldn't you fight for what's right while you still have a chance?"

Sophie shook her head numbly. "You don't understand. Even though you're the one behind bars, I'm as trapped as you are."

"No! These bars are real—I can't escape them, no matter how hard I try. You're caged by something in your own mind."

Sophie paused. She peeked furtively over her shoulder to see if anyone was in the corridor outside the cell. It was empty. She looked back at Cammy, her moist eyes suddenly alive. "That's why I stayed to chat with you. There's no one else to talk to. I can't trust any of them. But you're not one of them."

"How can talking to me help?"

"I need courage." She glanced again at the empty corridor and then reached into her uniform. "A stranger handed me this leaflet today." She passed it to Cammy.

Cammy quickly scanned the crinkled two-page document. It was titled *Resistance*, and it was authored by someone named J from a group called the White Rose League. "What does it mean?" she asked.

Sophie became strangely energized, as if awakened from a trance. She pointed to a paragraph on the first page. "Read this!"

Cammy focused where Sophie pointed:

"We are your conscience speaking. Isn't it true that every honest person is ashamed of his government these days? Imagine the dimensions of shame that will befall you and your children when one day the veil is lifted from your eyes and the horrible crimes of oppression reach the light of day! You slumber in dull, stupid sleep, which just encourages the fascist criminals. Each of you wants to be exonerated of guilt. But you can't be! Many of you voted for the Elites, when there used to be elections. Your silence now is deafening. Your inaction is a deadly act. Why did you allow these thugs to rob you step by step, of one right after another, so that today nothing is left but an oppressive state presided over by villains, keeping everyone in fetters? Is your spirit so crushed by abuse that you won't raise a hand? Their power comes only from your passivity. There are many millions more of you than of them. Have you forgotten it is your right—or rather, your moral duty—to challenge them? To tolerate this fascism is to be complicit. To tolerate this evil is to take on the same infinite burden of guilt as the perpetrators. If you refuse to exercise your free will, if you refuse to act, if you refuse to put your own hand on the wheel of history, then you cowards deserve your destruction.

No one will care about your screams then. Arise from your stupor! Every person has the capacity to change the path that humanity is on. Every person can jolt the hypnotized masses from their stupors. Every person can be Jefferson, Gandhi, or Rosa Parks. Find that courage! Your allegiance should be to moral principles, not to corrupt leaders and their vile orders."

Cammy looked up from the leaflet. "So do something!"

"Do what?"

"Every revolution begins with a single spark," said Cammy. "Pass this leaflet on to someone else. Join the White Rose League, whatever that is."

Suddenly, a door clanged in the corridor. Staccato footsteps sounded, getting louder by the second. Two soldiers appeared in the doorway of the cell. The emotionless men were clad in black. Their pistols were drawn.

"Sophie Magdalena," one of the soldiers began in a stentorian voice. "You were ordered to deliver food to the prisoners. Instead, you chose to consort with the enemy. Come with us."

Sophie froze. She locked eyes with Cammy, seeming to pass a telepathic message to her. Then she glanced down at the leaflet. Sophie's body blocked Cammy's hands from being seen by the soldiers. Cammy slipped the leaflet into her own waistband.

The soldiers grabbed Sophie's arms with their iron claws and yanked her out of the cell. She resisted but said nothing. She stared at Cammy, wide-eyed and unblinking, until one of the soldiers smashed the stock of his pistol against her temple. She crumpled into the arms of the other soldier, unconscious. They dragged her helpless body away.

When they were gone, Cammy stared into the haunting emptiness of the silent corridor. "Goodbye, Sophie," she said softly. "You waited too long to wake up." She sat down on the cold floor, imagining the horrific fate the haggard woman was about to endure. She pulled out the leaflet written by the White Rose League and read the whole thing. A tear dripped from her cheek and mottled the austere paper.

Something swept over her that she couldn't explain, like an otherworldly draft blowing through the bars of the cell. It seemed like a ghostly message of some kind, sent by an unseen guardian angel. She began to wonder if she hallucinated Sophie's visitation.

Real or not, it changed her. She vowed not to make the same mistake as Sophie. She would wake the people of the world from their dull slumber—if she survived long enough to make a difference.

The air raid siren sounded again.

FORTY-THREE
TRADERS

> When the best within you
> Is traded for the best within me
> One for one yields more than two
> Such is the golden math of "we"
>
> — *The Poems of Dark Sun*

The thunderous roar of a hovercraft awoke the Eagles.

The vehicle zoomed in from the east and levitated directly above them in the gray dawn. The backdraft from its rotors and thrusters whipped up the snow and frenzied the tethered horses. The Eagles scrambled from their tents.

A brilliant shaft of bluish-white light lanced from the bottom of the craft. The mesmerizing light reflected off millions of swirling snowflakes, making the camp seem like the inside of a large snow globe illuminated by the flashlight of a giant.

A hologram inside the light beam slowly materialized into a three-dimensional image of a young boy. He had long sandy blond hair and large brown eyes. He was alarmingly pale and thin. Tears ran down his cheeks as he sat rigid in a wheelchair. His left leg was in a cast from his ankle to his upper thigh.

"Curious!" screamed Dark Moon. She instinctively rushed toward the illusion, just as she had with Cammy's hologram, but Dark Sun restrained her. She struggled against him, repeatedly screaming her son's name. He was amazed by her strength.

"Mom, Dad," Curious croaked. His voice was weak, despite the amplification of the hovercraft's sound system. "You have to come now. There's no time left. They told us the war is going badly. Bombs fall on us every day. We'll be killed if the enemy gets here before you do. Cammy figured out—" The audio recording ended abruptly. His image faded back into the blue light.

"Damn it!" Dark Moon screamed. Was he being tortured? Was he being fed? How badly hurt was he? How close were the bombs falling? Like any mother, she bore Curious' pain and suffering as if it were her own. In that moment, it was too much for her to bear.

Suddenly, a holographic image of Katarina pixilated into view inside the light shaft. "Listen carefully," the ghostly image said. "You have two days. There's not enough time to get to Washington. Come to Lynchburg, Virginia instead. Meet us at the old courthouse for further instructions. Any delay will be fatal . . . to everyone."

A deafening roar drowned out Katarina's voice. The crescendo originated from the mountain ridge to the south. Two brilliant flashes of orange erupted near the invisible thunder in the sky. Then two luminous streaks with vapor trails rocketed toward the Eagles, piercing the twilight at incredible speed.

The streaks intersected with the hovercraft. An explosion erupted above the camp with the brilliance of many suns. The shock wave knocked everyone to the ground. Hot shrapnel rained down. In the next instant, two fighter jets thundered past, cutting through the black smoke billowing from the explosion.

Kerry jumped to his feet and gestured toward the sky. "Those were our planes!" Then he heard Dark Moon wailing.

"My son is going to die!" she yelled into the blowing snow. Tears of frustrated rage streamed down her face. "They're dropping bombs on him! Did you see his leg?" She fell to her knees in the snow and clutched her head in her hands. "He'll never run again," she moaned. "You should have seen him run in Kansas. He was such a joy! His flying hair, his beautiful smile. And now his leg is ruined!" She sobbed bitterly. "Everything is ruined! I want my Curious back!"

Dark Sun consoled her, gently massaging her shoulders and whispering into her ear. He wondered what Cammy had figured out.

The rest of the Eagles, seeing Dark Moon's desperation and realizing the near impossibility of their dilemma, gathered to strategize. "Is it even possible to get to Lynchburg in two days?" Ruby asked.

"It's winter, and there are many mountains between here and Lynchburg," Hawkeye replied. "Two days would take a miracle—"

"Then we'll make a miracle happen," declared Fatima.

Saul nodded. "What's left of Highway 64 still cuts a path through the mountains. Let's hope the bridges are intact. We've got eight riders and sixteen horses. We'll ride them harder than we should. If any falter, we'll leave them behind. We'll shed some supplies to lighten our loads. We'll ride twenty hours a day, and sleep for four."

"I'll ride point the whole way," Hawkeye volunteered. "I grew up in these mountains—I know what to watch out for. We'll be riding in the dark much of the time."

"No more talk," said Fatima sharply. "We've got a plan. Let's go!"

The Eagles broke camp. Within minutes, the pack horses were cinched, and the Eagles mounted for the arduous ride.

Hawkeye deftly navigated around rockslides and washed-out sections of road. Most of the guard rails had rusted completely away, which exposed the Eagles to a precipitous plummet into the canyons below if their mounts stumbled. They were now so high up in the mountains that clouds wafted below them in ethereal wisps.

The snow continued to fall. The temperature plummeted. The

wind howled through the passes. At times it seemed like they were completely hemmed in by towering rock walls.

The horses wearied as the air thinned and the snow deepened. When they were navigating a particularly harrowing precipice, an exhausted pack horse faltered and plummeted into the depths below. Its last wailing neigh was suffocated by the howling wind.

The group stopped and stared in horror into the chasm that had swallowed one of their animals in the blink of an eye. The same thought haunted each of them—it was mere chance that the deceased horse was without a mount. Their miracle was slipping out of reach, and their trek was getting more treacherous.

Near dusk, they rounded a hairpin switchback and came upon an unexpected sight. A motorized all-terrain vehicle had skidded off the snowy road and was wedged into a shallow culvert. A man, a woman, and a child stood shivering beside the damaged machine, looking very much like cruel fate just had the last laugh. The mother appeared to be praying. The young girl leaned against her father. She was bleeding from wounds in both of her hands and a gash to her forehead.

The marooned strangers were startled by the sudden emergence of the mounted Eagles from the blinding snow. The two groups eyed each other nervously, silently considering the implications of this unusual encounter in the desolate mountains. Hawkeye concluded that the family posed no threat to them. "Hello!" he shouted through the driving snow. "Do you need help?"

The father eyed Hawkeye as if the Grim Reaper had finally materialized. The mounted Eagles had guns and were headed toward the territory of the Elites, so he assumed they were somehow associated with the tyrants. He shouted back, "We don't want your kind of help. We're defenseless, so take what you want. The wolves will devour us soon enough anyway." The young girl looked up at him in horror. Her face was streaked with rivulets of blood.

Fatima dismounted and approached him, crossing the snowy footprints of a bear that had recently ambled through. The father was gray-haired and haggard. His snow-dusted shoulders drooped. He looked like he had endured a hard life that had just gotten impossible.

"We're not takers," Fatima offered gently.

He looked at her with cynicism. He was numb to his bleeding daughter, their wrecked vehicle, and the brutal weather. "Bullshit! You Elites took everything from everyone. My family is fleeing to the Northwest Territories to get far away from the likes of you. Unfortunately, it looks like our exodus has ended at this culvert."

"We're not with the Elites," Fatima replied calmly. "We're gypsies."

"Then why are you headed *toward* the Elites? Common sense says to run the other way."

"They're extorting us," she sighed. "We're not a threat to your family. Let's camp here for the night. We have food, tents, and a doctor—it looks like your little girl could use some help. Our handyman can look at your damaged vehicle. My name is Teema."

The man glanced at the rest of the armed Eagles, then at the imposing mountains, and finally at the endless snow billowing through the pass. "We're at your mercy," he conceded. "I'm Joe. This is my wife, Miriam. And my daughter, Kristen."

Saul, who had dismounted and sidled beside Fatima, nudged her. "We've only ridden sixteen hours so far today. We need to ride twenty. There's no time to be Good Samaritans. Lynchburg is still a long way off."

Fatima glared at Saul. "Tell this injured girl there's no hope. Tell her family we're in a hurry, and they should just wait here until the carnivores begin hunting tonight. We have to help them!"

"Tell Dark Moon and Dark Sun that Curious and Cammy are going to die because we're dawdling here!" Saul shot back. "It's not a fair world. We have a mission. I feel bad for these folks, but they're not our problem."

"Damn it!" shouted Fatima. "This world sucks, but let's figure out how to make it suck a little less. What if Osiris thought I wasn't his problem when he found me years ago?"

"You can't save everyone," replied Saul. "Even Osiris learned that lesson long ago. We've passed by hundreds of lost souls already. These are just a few more."

"I know I can't save everyone. It would be too exhausting to try, and too soul crushing to even think about. My dad taught me to focus on my own little world and to choose missions wisely. This family has stumbled into my world, and I think it would be wise to save them."

Saul threw his arms up in dismay. "What's your plan?"

There was a tense silence. The stranded family looked wide-eyed at Fatima, wondering if some sort of salvation was really at hand for them. Dark Sun and Dark Moon stared at her with alarm, wondering if she was about to jeopardize their children by playing Good Samaritan for strangers.

"I have a sketchy plan," said Fatima, finally. "It involves some trading. And we'll need a little luck."

Dark Moon's face blanched. "Teema, there's no time—"

"Please, trust me for a few more minutes." She abruptly barked out a string of orders. "Verax, see if the ATV can be repaired. Kerry, tend to Kristen's injuries. Saul and Dark Sun, tether the horses, set up camp, and make a fire. Ruby and Dark Moon, prepare food for everyone. Hawkeye, pick spots for our night watch. Move!"

Everyone scrambled to their assigned tasks. Fatima joined Kerry to serve as his nurse while he tended to Kristen. He worked silently and efficiently by lantern light. He gently removed her bloody hat and mittens. The girl whimpered in fear and agony while Fatima cradled her. Kerry stroked her trembling shoulder and soothed her with warm words of solace. He injected her with a twilight anesthetic. Then he picked out bits of jagged glass from her wounds and stitched them closed. He applied antibiotics and bandaged her hands and head. By the time he finished, the young girl had fallen asleep in Fatima's arms, exhausted by the trauma.

Kerry silently observed the two of them huddled together. Snow gently wafted from the dark sky, settling upon their hair and coats, glittering in the lantern light. They appeared angelic to him. He thought about Fatima's wondrous compassion today. It would have been easy for her to forsake the stranded family, but she chose the more difficult yet more merciful path. Her firm resolve to do the right thing was exactly what the world needed. "I love you," he blurted out, almost unconsciously.

Fatima looked up at him, startled. Their eyes met. They held each other's gaze for a long moment. Then she looked down at the innocent sleeping girl. Bitter tears welled in her eyes. "Kerry, I can't . . . not yet. Maybe never." She paused. "We might not see each other again after tonight."

It was Kerry's turn to be startled. "What do you mean?"

"When we finish with Kristen, I'll explain to everyone the trade I have in mind. Then you'll understand better." There was an unspoken reason she and Kerry might never be together. She wasn't sure she could ever trust a man enough to become intimate, not even someone like him. It was impossible for her to forget how the men of the Caliphate, the Elites, and the Jackals had all found ways to mistreat her as a young girl.

She avoided Kerry's imploring gaze and wriggled out from under Kristen. She covered the sleeping girl with a blanket. "Carry Kristen to the campfire and summon the others. I need to chat with Verax."

Kerry hefted Kristen and carried her to a comfortable spot, nodding as Miriam and Joe thanked him profusely. He summoned the Eagles, who gathered around the raging campfire. Fatima and Verax joined them after their chat. Ruby and Dark Moon served warm food.

When everyone was settled, Fatima broached her proposal. "We have a dilemma," she began. "My team has to get to Lynchburg quickly, and we can't strand Joe's family here. Both situations are matters of life and death. I have a way to save everyone."

She paused. All eyes were upon her, like when a conductor raises his baton to commence a concert. She swallowed nervously, then continued. "Verax thinks he can repair the all-terrain vehicle. It's useless to Joe's family, but it's of great value to my team—"

"Why is it useless to us?" Joe interrupted angrily. "That ATV is all we have left!" Miriam's jaw dropped, like her family had just been betrayed. Kristen awoke from the sound of her father's distressed voice.

"There's no gas where you're headed," Fatima explained softly. "That's why we're all riding horses. When you run out of gas, you'll be stranded like you are now."

"You're going to take the ATV because you need it and think we don't?" Joe blustered. "You're no different than the Elites!"

Fatima folded her hands in supplication. "Please, hear me out. I'm not going to take anything, because that's not the world I want to live in. I'm asking you to trade the repaired vehicle to us, in exchange for more useful things."

"Like what?" Joe asked.

"Horses, guns, and ammunition. And you'll need food to tide you over until you find a community where you can work and trade for more."

Joe's haggard face turned ashen. "You're going to leave us in these mountains with horses we don't know how to ride, guns we don't know how to shoot, and just enough food to keep us alive until we're out of your sight?"

"I understand your distrust', replied Fatima gently. "You're fleeing a society where it comes naturally. Please, let me finish. Since the ATV can only carry four people, half of my team will use it to speed to our destination, and the other half will stay behind to train your family and get you safely on your way. If you keep heading west on Highway 64, you'll run into a gypsy caravan led by a tall black man named Osiris. When you tell him that I sent you, he'll protect you like his own."

"Why would you do this for us?"

"The trade makes us all better off," said Fatima. "You were headed for disaster with the ATV. Now, you'll be prepared for the lifestyle you're adopting. And the ATV can get my team to Lynchburg faster than our horses can carry us through the snow and mountains."

Joe gaped at her in confusion. "The Elites would just take the ATV. There's no one here to stop you from doing that."

"Theft is force, and initiating force is the root of all social evil.

Everyone chooses the kind of world they live in, at least to some degree. I'm choosing a world where people trade rather than steal."

"I don't see how your vision is possible in the Darkness."

"I don't see how life is worth living if such a world *isn't* possible. Traders gain without harming others—trades wouldn't happen unless those involved believed they were each better off for it. Trading is a holy union of self-interest *and* collaboration. To satisfy yourself, you have to satisfy others. It's how a peaceful society miraculously multiplies fishes and loaves."

"You are so right!" exclaimed Kristen.

Joe looked at his precocious daughter in surprise. "I'm a Doubting Thomas," he said. "All I know is that we were misfits in the faction we're fleeing."

"Nobody belongs there. It's a world of conflict not collaboration. I know you're skeptical, but we can make a small difference here. It's a start. You'll be less skeptical after you spend time with Osiris and his tribe."

Joe pondered Fatima's proposal as the fire crackled and hissed. "Your trade is fair," he concluded. "But I have another problem." He flashed a thin fold of government currency. "This is our life savings. Is it worth anything beyond these mountains?"

Fatima frowned. "Worthless societies print worthless money. I suggest using it as toilet paper. Things like guns, food, and horses are the currency of your new world. They have real value."

Joe's shoulders assumed their customary sag. "I hate the Elites. I tried turning the other cheek for years, but they had more fists to hit me with than I had cheeks."

"Hatred is an expensive waste of energy," Fatima said. "Forgiveness is free."

"Forgiveness? Our lives are ruined! I often wanted to barge into their bureaucratic temples, kick their desks over, and throw shit around. But they would have crucified me."

"Good news," said Kerry. "Pathless Land's air force is knocking their temples down as we speak."

"Pathless Land?"

"It's where we Outcasts call home. You're an Outcast now, by choice. There's a better world coming for everyone."

"I'm still stuck with this wad of useless money. My life's effort is apparently worth the same as toilet paper."

"Wait!" Dark Sun blurted. He jumped up and ducked into his tent. He emerged a moment later grasping something in his fist. He extended his hand to Joe and opened his palm. Firelight reflected off a small bar of gold, like a genie effervescing out of a bottle. "Take this."

Joe was stunned. "But . . . that's gold! I have nothing to give you in return."

"It's a gift. There's more to human interaction than trades. It doesn't profit a man to gain the whole world and lose his soul. Consider it thanks, because your ATV gives me hope that we can save my kids. Consider it sympathy for your plight—I'm sure Kristen is as precious to you as my children are to me. Consider it an invitation to support Teema's vision."

Joe threw the wad of currency into the fire. He accepted the gold bar from Dark Sun as if it was a sacred object. They shook hands, and then spontaneously hugged. Miriam arose and hugged Dark Sun. "Bless you," she said. "Meeting your team was a miracle. You gave us hope and something to believe in."

Dark Sun nodded. "Spread the word about Teema's vision. Just don't spoil it by turning it into a theocracy. There's enough violence in the world already."

Joe and Miriam gave him a quizzical look. Kristen nodded her head.

Joe looked around at the congenial faces of the Eagles and shook his head. "I'm still struggling to understand why you're helping us like this."

Fatima smiled. "Dark Sun and I have already shared our reasons." She turned toward Saul and looked at him pointedly.

Saul sighed, knowing that his spotty metamorphosis was being called to account. He took off his sunglasses. "Joe, when you accused us of being with the Elites, you were partially right," he confessed. "I defected from them, so I'm indirectly one of the thieves who took everything from you. Old habits die hard, but I'm trying to cleanse my soul. I'm sorry I wasn't eager to help at first. Now it feels right."

Joe nodded. "I appreciate your honesty. I'm not perfect either, so I won't cast any stones."

Ruby laughed. "I'm glad you're not a stone thrower. In some religions, I would have been stoned to death by now. I'm a former Elite with some soul cleansing to do too. I behaved badly, often with other men. I thought only of myself and the fun I could have. Helping your family is a chance for me to clean up a mess rather than make one."

Miriam smiled. "Your humility is admirable."

"My turn for confession," Hawkeye said. "I was a sniper for the Elites, long ago. I killed some people who didn't deserve to die, which haunts me every day. Now I've committed my life to protecting innocents."

"My God!" exclaimed Kristen. "I have a thief, an adulterer, and a killer sitting next to me. And yet I feel safe for the first time in a long time. You saved yourselves earlier and then saved my family today. That seems like the right order of things. Bless you all."

Fatima suddenly stood up. "We've got a lot to do yet tonight." She organized another flurry of activity. Dark Sun and Saul were assigned to harness horses to the ATV and drag it from the culvert so that Verax could repair it. Hawkeye, Ruby, and Dark Moon were assigned to divvy up the Eagles' supplies into three caches. One cache would be for the destitute family, another for the four Eagles proceeding ahead in the ATV, and the last for the four Eagles staying behind to train Joe's family. Kozlowski was assigned to pack medical supplies for Kristen and to train Miriam on how to clean and dress her wounds. Fatima quizzed Joe about the dangers lurking on the road to Lynchburg, where his family had recently passed through.

When everyone finished, Fatima convened a quick meeting of the Eagles. "We need to split up," she reminded everyone. "Dark Moon and Dark Sun will go in the ATV, because they need to meet with

Katarina and Kieran in Lynchburg. Verax will go, because the ATV may need repair again. Kerry will go, because Curious will need medical care when he's rescued. Kerry, you'll be the leader."

Fatima glanced at Kerry. He met her gaze and nodded—he now understood the separation she referred to earlier. When she looked away, he hung his head. He knew there was a good chance he would never see the beautiful Arab girl again. He knew she had warned him at the start of this adventure that he might have to leave her behind at some point. He also knew he would have to honor his word to do so. He just hadn't realized how painful it would be.

Fatima continued. "I'll stay behind with the rest to prepare Joe's family for their new lives. Then we'll head to Lynchburg on horseback as quickly as we can. Let's get some sleep. The ATV leaves at dawn. Who wants first watch?"

"I'll take it," said Dark Sun. His mind was too unsettled for sleep anyway. This delay in the mountains heightened his anxiety about reaching Lynchburg in time. The impending split of the Eagles would make them even less safe than they were. The ATV team would be without the martial expertise of Hawkeye, the leadership of Fatima, and Saul's knowledge of the Elites. Ruby would not be missed.

Everyone else drifted off to their tents. Dark Sun tucked Dark Moon into her sleeping bag and kissed her forehead. "I love you, Moonbeam," he whispered. He headed out to stand watch.

The fire was waning. Dark Sun was mesmerized by the falling snow and the eerie whistling of the wind sluicing through the passes. As he put another log on the embers, he heard an unnatural sound. It was Kerry's radio. He listened intently but couldn't discern anything from the broadcast. He assumed it to be another edition of *Voice of America* . . . until he heard Kerry speak.

He leapt from the rock and hopped through the snow to Kerry's tent. He lurked outside, eavesdropping on a muffled conversation that he couldn't quite hear. He poked his head in and loomed menacing in the doorway. "Who are you talking to?"

Kerry jerked his head up. He pushed a button on his radio. "I was making a report to my superiors."

"Have you been reporting to them all along?"

Kerry looked at Dark Sun with earnest. "I beg you to trust me like . . . like a brother. I swear on my love for Teema that my actions are honorable. I'm trying to save your children . . . and many others. You must keep this to yourself for a while longer. Much will be revealed soon."

The flickering light from the campfire chased shadows across Kerry's face. Dark Sun studied it intently for signs of deception or betrayal. Instead, he saw profound tranquility. He also saw something oddly familiar that he had never noticed before. There was something recognizable in his eyes and in his manner. He felt a connection that he couldn't explain. Almost against his will, he said, "I'll trust you . . . until you prove unworthy."

"Thank you. Please, sit down."

"I'm keeping watch."

"So am I, in my own way," Kerry said. "Everything will be okay for a few minutes."

Dark Sun sat cross-legged at the foot of Kerry's sleeping bag. "Anything new on *Voice of America*?"

"Our leaders announced a temporary cease fire all along the battlefront in Virginia."

Dark Sun did a doubletake. "Why? Just yesterday they had the Elites on the run—"

"I'm sure J has a sound strategy, which he's not going to reveal on a radio broadcast. The good news is that the lull in hostilities may buy us enough time to get to Lynchburg before it's overrun."

"Are you revealing our location in your reports?"

"My superiors have always known our location—Dark Moon was given a tracking device in Atlanta. That's how our fighter jets knew to destroy the hovercraft this morning."

Dark Sun shook his head in confusion. "Why did they destroy it?

What if they'd blown it up before we heard the message from Kieran and Katarina?"

"Maybe our generals were afraid it was about to attack. Maybe they were afraid the Elites were no longer interested in you and your kids now that their world is collapsing. Maybe they're looking out for us."

Dark Sun's head was spinning now. Every bit of information from Kerry made things even less coherent. They were being tracked by both the Elites and the Outcasts. He had an eerie feeling that his family was somehow akin to the ark of the covenant in the eyes of some very powerful people. "What did Katarina mean when she said that everyone will die if we don't make it to Lynchburg in time?" he asked.

Kerry shrugged. "I can't speak for her. But by now it should be apparent that your family is very important to both sides in this war. If things go badly in the next few days, the results could be tragic."

"Does this have anything to do with the fabled treasure of the Outcasts?"

Kerry looked up in surprise. "Possibly. But our treasure isn't a *thing* like the Hope Diamond or a trove of gold."

"What is it?"

"J describes it as a path to a pathless land."

Dark Sun shook his head violently. Every sentence Kerry uttered was more confusing than the last. "What sense is there in a path to a pathless land?" Dark Sun asked.

Kerry sat up straighter. "It's the only path to peace on Earth. Wouldn't it be great to find a place where people could freely collaborate? A place where they could believe and think what they wanted to? A place where dreamers could write the script for their futures in a world of infinite possibilities? A place where each person was free to rise above the conditioning of society, the tension between sectarian religions, and the compulsion of bureaucrats? A place utterly opposed to coercion, where differences were resolved by facts and debate rather than by force or mob rule? A place where the tribal attachments to race and creed no longer divided us? A place where secular, religious, and criminal tyranny were consigned to the dustbins of history? A land where the only path that mattered was the one you blazed yourself? Wouldn't a path to such a place be priceless?"

"I suppose," replied Dark Sun with little enthusiasm. He couldn't see beyond the immediate dilemma of rescuing Curious and Cammy. Liberating the rest of humanity was a task for another day—or another life.

"It's your birthright," said Kerry, as the campfire twinkled in his eyes. "It's everyone's birthright."

"If that's so, why were Curious and Cammy kidnapped? Why is there an endless civil war? Why are we wallowing in the Darkness? It seems to me our birthrights are violence, despair, and death."

"That's certainly the path that most of humanity has been on. But another path can be chosen."

"I don't see that choice on my life's menu right now."

Kerry smiled and put a consoling hand on Dark Sun's shoulder. "My brother, life is about to become even more complex for you and your family. Your menu options will get very dire. Brace yourself."

FORTY-FOUR
POWER

> In a universe where energy abounds,
> The lust for power knows no bounds.
> Hence a problem that we must solve:
> How does society end coercion of all?
>
> *— The Poems of Dark Sun*

Lantern light danced in the pre-dawn gloom.

The four Eagles who were going to sprint ahead in the ATV were prepped for their journey. The vehicle was laden with food, guns, ammunition, medical supplies, and tools. Two full cans of gasoline remained from the stash that Joe's family had hoarded before they fled the Elites.

Dark Moon and Dark Sun clambered into the rear seat. Verax jumped into the front passenger seat. Kerry took the keys from Joe and shook his hand, and everyone said their farewells.

Before Kerry could slip into the driver's seat, Fatima approached and tugged his arm. She led him away from the others. She gazed into his eyes and said softly, "Kerry, I couldn't sleep last night. When you said you loved me, I should've listened to my heart instead of my fears. I don't want you to leave without knowing how I feel. When you took care of Kristen last night, I saw sympathy in every stitch and bandage. You saved my life in Atlanta. You stayed by my bedside reading, chatting, and monitoring my recovery. You left your family and friends to be with me without any promise of a relationship between us. And now you're risking your life to finish the mission I chose to lead. I never thought a man would treat me like you have." She took his hands into hers. "This is so hard for me to say. I love you, Kerry."

Kerry said nothing but felt everything. He kissed her in that spellbinding way meant to last forever. Fatima returned his kiss with passion, though it was salted with bittersweet tears. She couldn't shake her fear about what the future held.

An enormous frustration welled up inside her. She abruptly released from their embrace and pushed him toward the ATV with surprising fury. Kerry saw the tears on her tormented face. He wanted desperately to hold her one more time, but he knew the moment had passed.

He hesitated, imprinting the scene into his memory. Then he climbed into the ATV and started it up. The engine roared to life, breaking what remained of the spell. He steered onto the road toward Lynchburg.

He glanced in the rearview mirror. In the eerie red glow of the taillights, he saw Fatima's receding figure. Eventually, her image slipped from sight, fading from the red halo into the gray dawn. A part of his soul evaporated into the twilight too.

He forced himself to focus and pressed hard on the accelerator. There was only one day left to get to Lynchburg. They rumbled along snow-covered I-64, heading east through the undulating mountains. Dark Sun stroked Dark Moon's hair as she rested her head on his shoulder. She softly called out for Curious. He couldn't tell if she was sleeping or not. She subconsciously called out the kids' names more and more.

The ATV handled the hairpin turns and the snow well. Dark Sun marveled at its power to plow through deep snowdrifts and climb the steep grades. Before the Darkness, powered machines were ubiquitous in America. Now, they were a rare luxury. It saddened him that humanity had squandered the technology to ease its burdens and to satisfy its yearnings. He'd have given anything for a tractor on their farm. Planes, cars, and countless other contraptions once enhanced the lives of billions of people. Now, horses, hand tools, and candles were meager substitutes. It wasn't because the universe had run out of energy. As Einstein postulated, the supply was nearly infinite.

But usable energy was hard to come by now. Nuclear power was outlawed for fear of weapons proliferation and contamination from spent fuel. Fossil fuels were taxed out of practical use for fear of climate change and environmental damage. Hydroelectric power was abandoned to protect endangered species and wetlands. Solar and wind energy were unreliable and costly to harness.

To make matters worse, radical Islam destabilized many oil-rich countries, preventing access to their enormous deposits. A nuclear exchange in the Middle East destroyed Israel, crippled Iran, and made vast stretches of oil-producing land untouchable. The economic collapse that came hand in hand with the Darkness was the last straw that turned the lights of the planet off. Humanity was returned to the edge of barbarism by irrational conflict, environmental paranoia, and collectivist dysfunction.

Dark Sun decided to read another entry from his father's journal. He opened it to the white rose.

October 1, 2057

I've been so busy preparing for the next phase of my life that I haven't finished writing down all my thoughts on Karma. I'll leave the next few pages blank to remind myself that I have unfinished business here.

The next few pages were indeed blank, starkly so. A sharp pain stabbed Dark Sun's heart. The barren pages were a palpable reminder that his father was gone. The unfinished entry was permanently suspended in time, like a movie production left in limbo because the star died.

Suddenly, he had an idea. He would finish the journal entry himself, in honor of his father. He had read enough of his dad's musings to be confident he could continue the train of thought. His father had unintentionally handed an intellectual baton to him across a gulf of twenty-seven years. A chill went up his spine. He fumbled for the pen Kerry had given him and began writing.

December 12, 2084

Hello father. Thanks for this opportunity to write in your stead. If you could read this, I'm sure your critique would be scathing.

Your thoughts on Karma resonated with me. We're motivated by love and concern for ourselves and for those who are dear to us. We protect the ones we love. We're generous and compassionate with them. We trust each other. We're collaborative beings, deep to the core.

However, not all relationships are borne of affection. We're surrounded by countless strangers. We can't avoid interacting with them, often in complex networks. So what moderates these impersonal interactions? This is the most important social question facing humanity. The answer can't be Karma, because its power is too diffuse when there's no real relationship between people. There is often temptation to be mean, cruel, or deceptive with someone who is a stranger to us and who is unlikely to ever be encountered again.

Yesterday, I learned a profound lesson when our friend Fatima arranged a trade with some strangers. We had the power to simply take from the stranded family whatever we wanted. We will likely never see them again. No one else was around to witness the event. There would have been no external repercussions if we had acted like knaves.

But if we had stolen rather than traded, there would have been terrible consequences. Initiating aggression against others may be the very definition of evil, because the most basic moral rule is not to harm others. Abusing innocents adrift in a brutal world would have stained our consciences. It would have left the stranded family even more cynical of the human spirit and even more likely to approach their next interaction with strangers prepared for violence rather than peace.

Who knows, the next group of strangers we encounter may have more guns and less compassion than us. They may be deluded by an "ism" into believing that harming others is okay, if their cause is "just." What then? Who will protect us? Who will protect anyone? Is that a world worth inhabiting? Is that a world that can survive? Perhaps the Darkness has already answered these questions.

Transient interactions between strangers lack the karmic suasion inherent in family, friendship, and local community. They also lack a foundation of trust. It's impossible for each person to know and care about millions of others, beyond the shallow level of abstraction.

There's no naturally repellent force for bad behavior among strangers in a broad society. There's no collective guilt, no collective remorse, no collective shame, no collective responsibility, no collective forgiveness. We're just anonymous ciphers in a huge spiritless algorithm.

This alienation is fertile ground for the seeds of evil that lurk inside everyone.

Karma tempers evil in close relationships because people get nudged toward good behavior by positive and negative feedback. But what tempers evil when the lust for gain and self-preservation gets unleashed in a world of nameless victims? What restrains dark-hearted villains from raping, pillaging, and killing strangers? Since the dawn of history, people have leveraged superior attributes, numbers, organizational strategies, knowledge, guile, and weapons to take advantage of "others."

I learned from your history books that when evil behavior goes unchecked, societies breed abominations like Capone's organized crime,

El Chapo's gang warfare, Stalin's collectivist massacres, Mao's cultural purges, Hitler's ethnic cleansing, and Timur's theocratic terrorism. Governments should protect us from such horrors, but history demonstrates that they're often the worst offenders.

Anarchy isn't the answer. It lacks laws and enforcement mechanisms to protect family, friends, or neighborhoods from criminals, gangs, and invaders. It's a war of all against all as people contend for limited resources on a crowded planet. Anarchy is a path to endless submission, fear, and conflict.

Totalitarianism isn't the answer either. The more a government tries to exert control, the less control it ultimately achieves. Rigid dictates violate our innate preferences to live without such constraints. They breed anger, contempt, and distrust. They expose the naked truth that governments are policemen, soldiers, tax collectors, prison guards, and executioners.

As anger and distrust accumulate, revolutionary sentiment is spawned. Totalitarian leaders respond with even more force to affirm the illusion of their control, which only triggers more rebellion. When enough people decide that the cost of submission exceeds the cost of rebellion, mutineers kill their rulers.

Totalitarians try to replace voluntary private relationships with involuntary bureaucratic ones. They want to become your parent, your doctor, your priest, your employer, your babysitter, your chauffeur, your landlord, your source of information, and even your conscience. They proclaim, "It takes a village," but they're the mayor, the judge, the sheriff, the banker, and the tax collector of the village. They abhor independent, non-conforming people.

When the state takes control, the scorekeeping of Karma becomes irrelevant. There's no reason to tally the merits or demerits of someone's behavior if it isn't of their own volition. The consequences of involuntary actions are disowned by the actor.

Without this karmic accountability, everyone is tempted to behave badly under the cover of social anonymity and bureaucratic enabling.

There's no payoff for good behavior, yet plenty of rewards for bad behavior. Shame disappears from society. Capable people go on the dole. Honest people resort to lying. Motives become debased. Mindless duty replaces voluntarism. Political allegiances trump principles. Good people learn to look the other way. Then society collapses, and the Darkness follows.

So total freedom without order is bad, and total order without freedom is bad too. In societies with no laws and in societies with oppressive laws, the strong will tyrannize the weak. Both types of societies will end in chaos, one from the violence of anarchy and the other from the violence of revolution.

So how can interactions between strangers happen freely and peacefully? This is where I'm lost. This is where the world is lost. Can we create a society without the warfare, gang violence, oppression, and brutal disregard for individual rights that has characterized life throughout most of history?

Father, I've filled the pages you left blank. I've also run out of wisdom. What's the solution for this dilemma? I wish you could answer these questions for me.

Dark Sun returned the journal to his satchel. He watched the rugged mountain scenery scroll by his window, trying to distract himself from disturbing thoughts about the plights of his children. He wondered if they had given up hope about their father coming to save them. They had good reason to, he concluded.

Dark Moon was gazing at the passing scenery. Kerry and Verax were monitoring the road ahead. The midday sun poked through a rare gap in the clouds, casting jagged shadows across their path.

After rounding a sharp bend, Kerry jammed the brakes, skidding the ATV to a sudden stop. The occupants lurched forward and snapped to attention. Up ahead, three military vehicles and a squadron of ten soldiers were guarding a barricaded bridge that spanned a river. Sunlight glinted off their weapons.

"Damn it!" snapped Kerry. "An Elite checkpoint! I didn't expect one this far from Washington."

"Are we in trouble?" asked Dark Moon, snapping out of her daze.

"We have illegal weapons. None of us have SIN chips in our ribs. I'd say we're in trouble."

The soldiers waved them forward, guns leveled. "Should we make a run for it?" asked Dark Sun.

Kerry shook his head. "Where would we run to? If we go back to where we came from, we'll fail at our mission. The only way to Lynchburg is across this bridge."

"I could offer them one of my bars of gold to let us through."

"These thugs will take your gold, and everything else too."

"Then we'll have to fight," concluded Dark Sun somberly.

"We're outgunned . . . badly." As Kerry spoke, soldiers scrambled into the assault vehicles because the ATV wasn't advancing as directed.

Kerry spun around to face Dark Moon. "In Atlanta, you were given a tracking device with an emergency signal. Trigger it. Now!"

Dark Moon's hands shook as she fumbled in her bag. She pulled out the strange device and pushed its only button. A red light flashed. It beeped once.

"Okay, hide it," Kerry said. He shifted the ATV into gear and inched up to the barricade. Soldiers immediately surrounded them. He opened his window.

A sneering, pug-faced soldier peered in and looked around. "You're undocumented!" he barked. "Our scanner isn't detecting any SIN chips!"

Kerry feigned indignation. "How dare you detain us? We've been summoned to Lynchburg by Regis. What's your name, soldier?"

Kerry's statement was true, but even if it had been a lie, the mere invocation of Regis's name would have upended the soldier's equilibrium. The pug retreated from the window and summoned his superior. After a brief exchange, the officer approached the ATV.

"Regis doesn't invite vermin like you!" the officer barked. "This is a conscription checkpoint. Even though you're undocumented, if one of you volunteers to join our military, we'll allow the rest to go back where you came from. If no one volunteers, the consequences will be severe."

"That's a peculiar offer," Kerry replied, stalling for time. "The war must be going badly for your side. Or nobody cares enough about your shitty society to fight for it. Or you Elites are no better than the Jackals and the Caliphate. We politely decline."

The officer jabbed his gun barrel into Kerry's shoulder. "The only thing stopping me from killing all of you is that I need to fill my volunteer quota."

Kerry smirked. "You're not looking for volunteers. You're looking for slaves. That's all you Elites ever want. And the worst form of slavery is to force someone to risk their life fighting for an unjust society. The only time you allow your citizens to have guns is when you want them to kill people your regime opposes. Let's make this really simple. I shouldn't tell you how to live your life and you shouldn't tell me how to live mine. Everything falls neatly into place after that."

The officer kicked the door of the ATV with his jackboot. He noticed that his troops were staring at him awkwardly. He glared at Kerry but muted his anger. "Let's be reasonable," he offered. "I'll sweeten the pot. If one of you volunteers, I'll let the rest go across this bridge, no questions asked. I help my quota and three of you can go wherever you want."

"That's a terrible deal! We *all* want to go to Lynchburg, and *none* of us want to die fighting for your side. What gives you the right to abduct one of us?" Kerry glanced furtively toward the southern mountains. He frowned, then returned his attention to the officer. He still needed more time.

The officer fumed. "You must do as I say!" Spittle flew from his quivering lips. "I'm a commissioned officer of the Elites! You're just . . . nobody! Accept my offer or die!"

Kerry chuckled. "The harder you try to establish order by brute force, the less order you'll get. Eventually, everyone becomes a law breaker or a rebel. Your days are numbered." Kerry glanced again toward the south. He smiled. "Actually, your *seconds* are numbered."

"Selfish bastard!" screamed the officer. As he turned to bark a command to his soldiers, a thunderous roar rent the air. Everyone except Kerry spun toward the unexpected din coming from the south. He jammed the gears of the ATV into reverse and punched the accelerator to the floor. The vehicle lurched backward, slinging snow and mud from all four tires. Two soldiers standing behind the vehicle were crushed as it ran over their bodies.

Four fighter jets screamed loudly as they approached the bridge. Their cannons strafed the landscape ahead of them. The soldiers were frozen, their eyes wide and their mouths agape in horror. The armor-piercing rounds ravaged everything in their path, including the terrified soldiers arrayed around the assault vehicles. A crimson mist wafted to the ground and settled on their shredded bodies.

Kerry's sudden maneuver pulled the ATV just outside the strafing pattern. On his command, the Eagles leapt from the vehicle, guns at the ready. They riddled the few surviving soldiers who were fleeing in terror.

The jets banked toward the south, then dipped their wings in unison as they flew their return leg over the skirmish site. Kerry raised his rifle to acknowledge their salute.

The rest of the Eagles were soaked in a cold sweat despite the chill of winter. They quickly scavenged guns from the dead soldiers and supplies from their outpost. Then they leapt back into the ATV. Kozlowski accelerated toward the bridge. They crashed through the barricade and sped across the river.

Dark Sun exhaled a heavy sigh of relief. "How did you know those jets were coming?"

"I didn't know for sure. But we control this air space, and our jets are always on patrol. Dark Moon's distress signal alerted our field commanders that we needed immediate intervention. I reported to them last night that we were heavily armed and had an ATV, so I figured they'd realize that if we were in trouble, it was big trouble. Jets can move quickly, and they can handle big trouble."

"You report to your commanders?" Dark Moon asked.

"Yeah, Dark Sun knows all about my radio." He winked at Dark Sun in the rearview mirror.

Dark Moon elbowed her husband. "Why didn't you tell me?"

"He made me swear to secrecy! Apparently, the only purpose was to get me in trouble with you." Dark Sun scowled at the back of Kerry's head.

"Everything will become much clearer when you meet J," Kerry said.

"You mean *if* we meet him," corrected Dark Sun.

"No, until. I have a hunch that your paths will cross soon."

Dark Sun suddenly felt insecure, like a child figuring out that the adults around him had been hiding an uncomfortable secret from him for a long time. An unnerving tingle ran up his spine.

Tomorrow was unfolding as a day of great portent. They would arrive in Lynchburg and meet with Kieran and Katarina. There, they would learn more about the fates of Curious and Cammy.

After weeks of harrowing uncertainty, tomorrow would determine his family's future.

FORTY-FIVE
KLEPTOCRACY

There are two ways to conquer and enslave a nation. One is by sword. The other is by debt.

— President John Adams

"You should be pleased," Regis said. "The Outcasts ordered a cease fire all across Virginia. The tide is turning."

Cosimo frowned. "Then why are we in this bunker?"

Regis and Cosimo were meeting in the Raven Rock Mountain Complex, an underground facility in Pennsylvania. It was protected by long tunnels with massive blast doors. It housed all the functions of a small city, including dining halls, infirmaries, giant fuel tanks, communication networks, utilities, filtration systems, and dormitories.

Five thousand people worked in the impregnable complex. In extreme emergencies, it was the temporary headquarters for the president, his cabinet, the Supreme Court, congressional leaders, and their families. Its existence was clear evidence that the aristocracy start wars and survive them. The proles fight wars and die in them.

"We're here as a precaution," Regis replied. "The Outcasts can't be trusted. They might suddenly start bombing again. Their last bombardment blew a giant crater in the North Lawn of the White House, right above our heads in the PEOC. I recall that the detonation made you flinch. Until then, I didn't believe you were capable of fear."

"I wasn't afraid," said Cosimo. "I was startled. There's a difference."

Regis was certain that Cosimo wasn't as dauntless as his customary bravado suggested. There were unmistakable signs of concern in their last meeting. He probed for other cracks in the Centurion's veneer. "Maybe you're not afraid of bombs, but aren't you afraid the world will uncover your treachery? Aren't you afraid the proles will revolt, take back your precious gold, and kill you?"

Cosimo shrugged. "If the proles rise up, they'll assassinate you, not me. They don't even know the Syndicate exists. That's one of the differences between your role and mine."

"Surely you fear something," Regis persisted. "Maybe your fellow centurions are conspiring to steal your share of the Syndicate's spoils."

Cosimo shook his head. "That's impossible. We each have so much wealth that there's no jealousy between us."

"You're not immune to fear. No one is."

"True." Cosimo inhaled his cigarette and stared off into space. "I fear two things. Entropy and renegades."

Regis warmed at his small victory. "How do you deal with those two threats?"

"That's precisely why the Syndicate exists. We fight entropy with wealth, which buys us everything we need to optimize our lives. We fight renegades by stepping on the throats of the world's leaders, so we can suppress any attempt to overthrow us and take our wealth."

"Who could possibly threaten the Syndicate?" asked Regis. "According to you, its centurions and influencers control everything."

Cosimo sighed. "We can only control those who *submit* to our control. Fortunately, most people do."

Regis warmed a bit more. It seemed like the centurion was taking him deeper into his confidence. "Why are people so willing?"

"You should know better than anyone," Cosimo smirked. "Greed. Lust for whatever crumbs of power we leave them. Desire for security. Belief in the myths we spread. Unwillingness to take responsibility for their personal affairs. The few incorrigible individuals who are immune to these weaknesses are the ones we fear. They're potential sparks of revolution. The Syndicate hates revolutions it didn't orchestrate. That's why the Outcasts must lose this war."

"How do you keep unwanted revolutions from happening?"

"Usually we prop up autocratic regimes: theocracies, monarchies, and dictatorships. Unfortunately, that tactic has failed with you Elites. I hope you didn't think we propped up your regime because we believe in your socialist theories. Capitalism has many advantages over socialism, including its incredible capacity to generate wealth. We gladly siphon that wealth when we allow capitalism to briefly flourish. But Capitalism has one awful, intolerable flaw."

Confusion washed over Regis's face. "Given the Syndicate's lust for money, I assumed it preferred to conspire with capitalists."

"Capitalists have to work too hard for their money. They have to take too many risks. They have to pander to proles in free markets. Their businesses often fail. The Syndicate prefers a rigged game where we can reliably siphon money from everyone without their consent. But business risk isn't the biggest issue with Capitalism."

"What is?"

"Capitalism breeds people who accumulate their own wealth and who think independently. That makes it a mortal threat to the Syndicate. Socialism, on the other hand, breeds people who follow orders and who allow their meager wealth to be confiscated."

Regis bristled. "Socialism protects the weak from the strong."

Cosimo laughed. "How naïve! Socialism is just another form of slavery. Workers of the world submit to the dictatorship of the proletariat! The truth about the human condition is that the ignorant must always submit to the wise. The weak must always submit to the strong. That's why the Syndicate prefers autocracies and theocracies. We leverage our power through the mindless loyalty of proles to absolutist creeds and elitist parties. Our power is only threatened when there are millions of independent thinkers."

"Then why did the Syndicate allow a country such as old America to rise up in the first place?"

Cosimo scowled. "We didn't. Those rebels were the type of uncontrolled demons that the Deka fears. They thumbed their noses at the British Empire. They thumbed their noses at the historical alliance between church and state. They thumbed their noses at *us* by granting sovereignty to individuals rather than to our captive kings and bishops. They turned the world upside down. Those non-conforming renegades were the most severe challenge to the Syndicate ever."

"So what did the Syndicate do?"

"It took a couple of centuries, but we trampled the rebellious American spirit. Our influencers gradually coerced the American proles to bite the candied apples that we offered. We destroyed the American culture of individual accountability by rewarding sloth and punishing ambition. We pitted the races, creeds, classes, and genders against each other by inflaming their grievances. We stirred the anger of the have-nots and emboldened those who wallowed in victimhood. It's easier for the proles to embrace a messiah like you who promises to take care of them and to punish their tormentors than it is for them to take care of themselves. In the end, the proles always surrender their freedom, and the Syndicate always wins."

"Do they *surrender* their freedom, or do you take it?" Regis asked.

"They surrender it. Liberty contains the seed of its own destruction. It gives people the latitude to *abandon* their freedom in exchange for security and submission. Freedom always becomes an envious mob, an envious mob always becomes class warfare, and class warfare always reduces a society to ashes. If that doesn't happen, we simply abolish private property—for everyone but the Syndicate. Freedom in the deepest sense means the ability to convert your efforts into your property, and to dispose of it as you see fit. If you can't do that, every other aspect of freedom is hollow."

"Aren't the Outcasts just as dangerous as the old American rebels?" asked Regis.

"Ah, you're finally beginning to understand why the Syndicate needs the Elites to defeat the Outcasts! Contrary to popular belief, the wars that we orchestrate aren't fought for territorial gain, because our dominion covers the entire world anyway. They're fought to rearrange power structures according to our long-term needs. Unfortunately, Outcast Island has always been outside our control, partly because it was disconnected from our cartel of banks and partly because it seemed pointless to risk sending our influencers there to manipulate that anarchic hellhole. We miscalculated. Their anarchy spawned the kind of renegades that we've always feared. They've broken out of their island prison and are overrunning your dominion in North America. Your fate is tied to defeating them. So is mine."

Regis brightened. "I have good news in that regard."

"I could use some."

"J is about to fall into my trap," Regis said. "It's just a matter of days now."

Cosimo raised an eyebrow. "If true, that would indeed be good news."

Regis puffed out his chest. "I'll personally bring him to his knees. In a very public way, I'll show the world that the White Rose pamphlets his planes drop from the skies are just empty platitudes."

"Don't be so cocksure," replied Cosimo. "Lightning bolts come from the sky too, sometimes in the form of words that incite the proles. Rebellion can spread like wildfire from a single spark. The Outcasts have already overrun half of your continent in just a few months."

Regis fell silent. Clearly, Cosimo wasn't impressed with his bravado. But he knew that the centurion would be ecstatic when J's head was delivered on a golden platter. Soon enough, he consoled himself. Then an uncomfortable thought pierced the balloon of his optimism.

"Why have you revealed so much about the Syndicate in our last few meetings?" he asked Cosimo. "For years, you insisted I would never learn any details."

Cosimo flashed that unholy smile that Regis always dreaded. "Because it won't matter soon." He grabbed his hat. "Besides, at this point, who would you tell? And who would believe you?"

"Are you suggesting that no one would believe the leader of the Elites?"

"I don't suggest. I'm telling you that the Syndicate can propagate a bigger lie than any truth you or anyone else reveal."

FORTY-SIX
EPIPHANY

> I won't grieve the past; I will learn from it
> I won't bow to the present; I will change it
> I won't fear the future; I will create it
> I have free will; I will use it
>
> — *The Poems of Dark Sun*

They reached the outskirts of Lynchburg that evening. The snow had stopped. The clouds were low and shone reddish-purple from the setting sun.

The city was near the front lines of the war. Oily smoke wafted from smoldering tanks that were now just tangled metal. The trees were shorn of their foliage by napalm and bombs. Their charred, naked trunks stood like stony sentinels pointlessly guarding a realm that had already been obliterated. Mortar fire had churned the ground into rolling swales of muddy snow. Dead bodies punctuated the landscape.

There was no active combat, however. It was eerily still, like the windless eye of a hurricane. It was as if every surviving soldier and war machine had suddenly withdrawn into hiding, like prairie dogs scurrying into their burrows. Dark Sun recalled that Kerry had mentioned a cease fire, which was now palpable in the form of an unnatural calm. He felt a disturbing sense of being watched.

They set up for the night inside an abandoned building and parked the ATV out of sight from the road. They worked without chatting. The anticipation of tomorrow's rendezvous hung in the air like an impending jury verdict. Minutes seemed like hours. Their journey thus far had been arduous and dangerous, but the most perilous stage lay just ahead.

After a solemn dinner, Verax retired for the night. Kerry worked on writing a letter to Fatima that might never get delivered. Dark Moon calmed her jangled nerves by obsessively re-organizing their meager supplies. Dark Sun grabbed his father's journal and opened it to the bookmark.

November 26, 2057

This will be my last entry. My world is about to be turned upside down.

Kieran and Katarina returned to our area today, accompanied by the usual cadre of jackbooted soldiers. They're searching for rebels again. If they've done their spying properly, they'll bust my door down.

My sedition is out in the open now. I started my own rebel cell. I made anti-government speeches in the public square in Independence. I set up a courier system to coordinate activities with rebel cells in the Old South. I've given the Elites many reasons to apprehend me.

If Kieran is smart, he'll jump on this opportunity. Surely his superiors will laud him if he arrests his own father for the good of the collective. But my desire isn't to advance my son's career. I despise the path he and his ilk have chosen. Let the miscreant have his thirty pieces of silver. I have bigger ambitions.

I've become acutely aware that my life is ebbing away. When I was young, life seemed like an endless summer. I gave no thought to each passing day. The future seemed like an ocean of time that extended far beyond the horizon.

But the ocean shrank to a lake and the lake to a pond. As each passing day drains the pond a bit more, I judge myself harshly, not for what I've done but for what I haven't done.

I hid here for years, lurking on the fringes of the conflict, rationalizing that I was protecting myself so that I could protect my family. But I was delusional. The conflict has to be faced head-on because the Darkness will swallow everyone if the battle is lost. To not fight back is to lose by forfeit. It's not a question of if but when.

The best way to protect my family and future generations is to create a world in which the proper conditions for living can endure forever. I can't do that by cowering like a feckless mouse in my little hermitage. The problems of our common existence confront us at every turn. Everything is political.

It takes more to protect our loved ones than a shoulder to the door when the wolves come knocking. No barricade is strong enough when their bloodlust boils over. We can cover our eyes and ignore the raptors of the world, but they won't ignore us. The Jackals, the Elites, the Caliphate, and the other purveyors of social entropy will devour us. Bureaucrats will try to take money and liberty from us. Theocrats will try to prescribe our thoughts and behaviors. Jihadists will try to behead us. Criminals will try to rob or kill us. They all want something from us.

Another lesson I've learned is that reputation is everything. A personal history of good works is the only foundation upon which relationships can be built. It's the basis for trust, the belief that we're going to respect and protect the interests of each other. Without trust, relationships are unstable vessels that will capsize in the slightest storm.

I'm ashamed of the dismal reputation I've earned thus far. I dread the condemning stares of widows and orphans who've lost their husbands and fathers in the civil war. They see me as a coward who was hiding in a rat hole like vermin. I even see it in the eyes of my wife, though she tries mightily to disguise it. I know Mary needs me as a *protector, but she needs me more as a champion, like the other men in the village who chose to fight. The world always needs more warriors and fewer cowards.*

Overcoming fear is the toughest battle a person will fight. As C. S. Lewis put it, "Courage is not simply one of the virtues but the form of every virtue at the testing point."

I'm going to become a fearless warrior who channels energy toward life rather than death, toward good rather than evil. Bringing positive energy to the world is a personal responsibility. No human action ever occurred unless performed by a specific individual. If everyone abdicated personal responsibility in favor of "collective action," it would give entropy a free pass to victory. Everyone would wait for everyone else to accomplish something while entropy stealthily sucked the life out of us all.

The paths to heaven, Valhalla, self-actualization, or any other state of psychological perfection are navigated by individual works. Karma and the Ten Commandments are individual mandates.

I won't achieve moral perfection because my neighbor was noble. I won't inherit glory because my neighbor fought the good fight. No surrogates are possible in the calculus of self-worth. Moral perfection can't be absorbed by osmosis from my social class, race, creed, or any other external source. I can't be a hero through someone else.

As da Vinci noted, people who make a real difference don't wait for things to happen to them, they go out and happen to things. This involves great risk, but there's a price to pay for every decision, because every decision has consequences. Doing nothing is the costliest decision with the worst consequences, because entropy never rests. It's a relentless killer of individuals and societies. So I must act.

Unfortunately, the fight is over in America—for now. The fascists, the gangsters, and the theocrats have won—so they think. In truth, we've all lost, and the Darkness is our well-deserved fate.

America has met its demise, like so many other foolish civilizations. The Jackals are sowing an anarchic killing field in the Southwest. The Caliphate is sowing a theocratic killing field in the Midwest. The Elites are retreating eastward, but the inhumanity of their dwindling regime rages on.

The true warriors for life and liberty have been deported to Outcast Island. I've decided to join them. No matter how diverse their races, creeds, or nationalities are, they all have something in common—they've been rejected by the diseased societies of the world.

This is my opportunity to build the reputation of a hero. Totalitarianism must be destroyed, so I'll light the fuse for its demolition. The Outcasts will become a phoenix, rising from the ashes of the Darkness.

Mary and I are reconciled with what's about to happen. I love her completely. She's always been my shining light in the Darkness. We're both willing to embrace our difficult futures. She'll surely struggle to raise James without me, but she knows it must be done. In her wisdom, she's been expecting my metamorphosis. She saw it coming before I did.

I think she's finally proud of me. I'm finally proud of myself.

We've decided not to divulge my chosen fate to James. Mary will explain that I was captured, like so many others. Hopefully, he'll resign himself to the belief that I was killed. That will be better than ruminating about my circumstances his entire life.

Perhaps in some distant future, fate will reunite us. In that unlikely event, I hope he'll understand why I had to abandon him and Mary. Maybe he'll even forgive me.

There's the pounding on my door I've been expecting. My time is at hand. This chapter of my life is over. The old me no longer exists. The past is just memories; the future is an unlimited field of pure potential.

As I sign off this journal for the last time, it will be my first opportunity to sign as my new identity.

Dark Sun turned the page, then stared in astonishment at the bold initial hastily scribbled at the end of the journal entry:

J

"Holy Shit!" he exclaimed to the unheeding night. Startling realization exploded like a firecracker in his brain at the sight of the single letter J. One solitary character of the alphabet explained everything.

His father is J, and he's leading the rebellion pouring out of Pathless Land!

All the obtuse journal entries and all the strange events leading to this point now made perfect sense to him. The Rosetta stone for deciphering everything had been in his hands all along, but he had been blind to it. The kidnapping of Curious and Cammy wasn't a random act. It was a vile stratagem done with great purpose by conniving cutthroats. His children were being used as pawns to coerce his father out into the open, likely to his death. It was a last-ditch effort by the Elites to stall the onrushing Warriors of Pathless Land.

The horror of his family's predicament hit him like an emotional freight train. He would be forced to choose between sacrificing his children and betraying his father. He would have to pick between killing his own priceless treasures and destroying the priceless treasure of an entire nation.

The implications of his epiphany crashed down upon him. The sheer impossibility of his predicament pummeled his consciousness. There was no good answer to this dilemma. And yet, he knew he would be forced by Kieran and Katarina to choose a path tomorrow morning.

There would be no sleep for him on this wintry night. He wondered if he would ever sleep again. "Father, what should I do?" he beseeched the dark, vast universe.

The heavens responded with nothing but silence. He was now the script writer.

FORTY-SEVEN
BETRAYAL

> Love can be a mortal weakness
> And the cause of great distress
> It can be extorted by evil
> And hatred's sly betrayal
>
> — *The Poems of Dark Sun*

Dark Sun paced around the campfire for hours.
He probed every corner of his mind for a resolution to his grim dilemma but found none. Either his children or his father were imperiled. He considered offering himself up instead, but he knew that the gamemasters in this extortion weren't interested in his noble sacrifice. His only role was to connect J to his kidnapped grandchildren, and there was no opting out.

He considered shielding Dark Moon from this awful dilemma, but she would encounter the horrific truth at the courthouse anyway. He awakened her just before dawn and explained his epiphany and its implications. She was rocked by the revelation. Like him, she feared that all their options led to tragedy. She trembled at the horror of their situation.

Dark Moon looked at Dark Sun sorrowfully. Tears streamed down her resolute face. "There's only one solution. I know that you love your father, but you haven't seen him for twenty-seven years. He's old now. Our obligation is to our children. Their whole lives are ahead of them."

Dark Sun scowled. "That means I have to betray my father."

"Yes!" said Dark Moon more forcefully than she intended. She softened after seeing the impact of her stark reply on Dark Sun's face. "I loved him too. I thought of him as my own father after my parents were killed. But Cammy and Curious are our kids! I can't sacrifice them! Please tell me you can't either!"

"How can I decide that my father must die? How can we decide for Pathless Land that their leader's life is worth less than the lives of our children?"

Dark Moon sobbed, "There's no way to compare the value of one life to another. It's a hellish choice, but we'll have to make one. I'm choosing our kids, and so are you!"

Dark Sun scowled again. "I need more time to digest this. There has to be another solution."

They debated whether to inform Kerry but concluded it would be unwise. They feared he would be motivated to protect his leader at the expense of their children, who were of little personal concern to him. He had been honorable thus far, but they didn't know him well enough to trust him with this pivotal information.

At sunrise, the four piled into the ATV. They were pensive as they traveled along the James River toward the center of Lynchburg with the Blue Ridge Mountains at their backs.

Heavy thoughts weighed on each of them. Verax longed for his murdered wife. Kerry fretted about Fatima's safety back in the mountains. Dark Sun contemplated the staggering implications of his father still being alive. Dark Moon fumed over her husband's indecision about the fate of their kids.

The anticipation of being reunited with her children was almost more than Dark Moon could bear. Minutes seemed like hours. She poked Kerry and begged him to drive faster. She was desperate to tousle Curious' long blond hair and to gaze into Cammy's beautiful blue eyes. She wrestled with a terrible fear that some tragic twist of fate would dash their reunion.

Kerry navigated toward the old historic Court House, their appointed meeting place with Kieran and Katarina. Horrific evidence of the civil war was everywhere. Many buildings had been flattened by artillery or were burned-out carcasses. Bullet holes peppered the facades of others.

The scene reminded Dark Sun of a picture of Hiroshima he saw in one of his father's books. The devastation from the atomic bomb attack was beyond comprehension. The city of Hiroshima eventually recovered, but he wondered if humanity would ever recover from the philosophical detonation that caused the Darkness. The question reminded him of Victor Frankl's admonition: "Since Auschwitz we know what man is capable of. And since Hiroshima we know what is at stake."

Despite the copious evidence of recent battle in Lynchburg, the hilly streets were eerily deserted, as if the extras on a movie set had suddenly scurried into hiding. The Eagles were silent as Kerry steered onto Court Street. Their much-anticipated meeting was about to become a momentous reality.

When the tarnished dome of the courthouse loomed ahead, they saw that the town wasn't completely deserted. Tanks were tucked on both sides of the ancient building, which had long ago been converted into a museum. Armed guards flanked the entry, standing as rigid as the salmon-colored columns that framed the portico. Snipers aimed their weapons from the parapet of the adjacent First Unitarian Church. A contingent of soldiers lurked across the street behind the Lynchburg Confederate Monument.

A detachment of military police materialized from the shadow of the courthouse and flagged the ATV to a stop. The MPs ordered the Eagles out and removed their weapons. They were escorted up the courthouse steps and through a set of doors into a large atrium. The museum display cases had been haphazardly shoved from the center of the atrium to make room for this encounter.

Soldiers stood at attention along the walls and on the elevated stage at the rear of the atrium. An officer advanced from their ranks. He eyed the Eagles warily. He ordered a body search that was administered with intrusive efficiency. Then he stepped back and bellowed that all was ready.

An officious group burst through a large oak door that flanked the stage. A man and a woman led a coterie of ministers and armed guards. Everyone except the soldiers wore the standard blood red uniforms of the Elites.

"It's been a long time, brother," greeted the tall man leading the entourage.

Dark Sun did a doubletake. He barely recognized Kieran. He had recently seen his likeness in a hologram, but it must have been computer-enhanced to make him look younger and warmer. The perfunctory man greeting him now was gray and balding. His face was harsh and unyielding. His dark, manic eyes jittered nervously. His skin was pallid, like he had been cooped up indoors too long. He exuded a staleness of spirit more suited to a robot than a person.

Dark Sun shuddered at the sight of his tormentor. He kept his composure despite the urge to punch him in the face. "You're not my brother anymore. You're a satanic monster who's holding my two children hostage. You're using them to extort J, their grandfather."

The doting ministers behind Kieran murmured in surprise. Verax's jaw dropped. Kerry nodded his head and smiled. The icy woman beside Kieran maintained her stoic glare, but Dark Sun knew she was shaken. He deduced she was Katarina, Dark Moon's sister, although she too was barely recognizable. Her hair was dyed raven-black and was cropped short. She had a chalky complexion. Her piercing amber eyes were like those of a wolf. Her haughty, angular appearance sharply contradicted the softer and more human image portrayed in the recent hologram.

"So you figured it out," Katarina snipped.

Dark Sun silently wished eternal damnation on her. "How can you do this to us?"

Kieran smiled wanly. "We're serving the common good. That's the only measure of morality now."

"Extorting your father is a moral act? Kidnapping your brother's children serves the common good?"

"I'm proud of what we're doing," said Kieran. "In order to fulfill the needs of the collective, our leader Regis requires that you surrender your children or your father."

Dark Sun shook his head. "I beg you to return our kids! Do you really want this blood on your hands? Human lives don't belong to Regis."

"Ah, but they do!" smirked Kieran. "Everything belongs to Regis because everything belongs to the society he leads. The universe cares nothing about the fate of any one individual and neither do we Elites."

"Bullshit!" interjected Kerry. "Your society may not care about me and those that I love, but I do. The role of society should be to protect our rights, not to trample them!"

Kieran arched an eyebrow. "Well now! You must be one of those looney White Rose extremists. If governments allowed people to exercise their individual wills, society couldn't solve its collective ills, like climate change, inequality, and social injustice."

Kerry sneered. "We must necessarily have rights and free will outside of government, because we *create* governments."

"You're a sniveling idealist. To stop some people from exploiting others, the state must control everyone. It's simple pragmatism."

Kerry pointed his finger at Kieran. "The state should *prevent* people from being divided into rulers and the ruled, not *create* that division. Its primary mission should be to ensure freedom for the free. The state is merely a collection of people like you. You're just power brokers who want to use the guise of the common good to force others to serve your own agenda!"

Kieran gestured smugly toward the soldiers surrounding them. "We don't care what you think. History is written by the victors. And the Elites are going to win."

"Don't be so sure," Kerry shot back. "Your goons who tried to conscript us in the mountains suffered from the same delusion, and now they're riddled with bullets."

Kieran smirked at the four unarmed Eagles. "How amusing. Even if you could kill Katarina and me, it would resolve nothing. The children would still be hostages, and the price for their release would still be my father's head. The supreme advantage of our collectivist society is that we consider individuals disposable—except our leaders. You, on the other hand, believe that the fates of your family members are more important than social progress. Your foolish attachment to your loved ones is your ultimate weakness, whereas our rational detachment is our ultimate strength."

Dark Sun's jaw dropped. "Your strength is that you've conned people into thinking their lives are disposable? My weakness is that I love my children and my father and will do anything for them?"

"Here's the reality of your situation," Kieran replied. "Your father will be sacrificed, or your children will be. You must choose."

"He's your father too," Dark Sun reasoned, desperately trying to crack Kieran's callous veneer. "Curious and Cammy are your family. They're real people—*your* people."

Kieran snickered. "To hell with your maudlin argument! We won't let a few insignificant individuals obstruct our pursuit of justice, equality, and fairness. Blood relations are nothing compared to our forward march toward a utopian society."

"If the Elites prevail, why should us peons bother living at all?"

"You peons may not have a choice. Our father's insurrection has caused millions to be slaughtered in this civil war," replied Kieran. "You called me satanic, but J is evil incarnate. He's exposing everyone to the chaos of selfish individualism. We Elites are fighting to establish order and to eliminate exploitation."

"If you don't call this extortion off," Dark Sun snarled, "I swear by everything I hold dear that I'll hunt you down and kill you."

"Ha! You nonconformists will always be the hunted," Kieran replied. "Let's conclude this. We'll release your children when J is delivered to Regis. You and Audrey must arrange this personally, in order to positively identify our father's grandchildren for him. And if he considers not surrendering, we want him to witness the agony and terror etched on your faces. This is the only reason you two are still alive. As always, your role is to serve the collective."

Dark Sun glared at Kieran with a burning rage. He wanted to strangle the last smug breath out of him, but he knew it would ruin everything. "You're *forcing* us to do this. The only reason your extortion has any effect is because we love our family."

Kieran's face stiffened. "You have exactly two days to deliver J to the McLean House at Appomattox. Regis will be amused by the symbolism—another rebel leader surrendering to us at that hallowed spot. Hail to Regis!" The ministers and soldiers snapped to attention and saluted, right arms outstretched in front of them in perfect Pavlovian ritual.

Kieran turned toward the oak door.

"Wait!" shouted Dark Sun.

Kieran spun sharply. "Were my orders not clear?"

"Perfectly. But give me the courtesy of answering two questions."

"Fine," snipped Kieran.

"Why didn't you take me and Dark Moon when you kidnapped our kids in Kansas? Why did you make us trek across the country to meet with you?"

"Not even we Elites are perfect," replied Kieran. "We intended to abduct all of you, but our special forces botched the job. They didn't expect your violent resistance. When you killed some of them, the spineless survivors panicked and fled with just the kids. By the time we heard the mission had been botched, we learned that you had already joined that caravan of armed gypsies. The Outcasts control the air space west of here, so it wasn't possible to send a large enough contingent to overwhelm the gypsies and snatch you. We had to bide our time and lure you here, where we still have military control."

"How do we know our children are still alive?" asked Dark Moon.

"We transmitted holographic images of them along the way."

"Those images were recorded. Curious and Cammy could be dead now."

Kieran feigned offense. "Are you calling us liars?"

"That would be an insult to liars," interjected Dark Sun.

"I knew you wouldn't trust us; you're a selfish renegade like our father. I have a surprise for you." Kieran waved his arm with an exaggerated flourish toward the oak door.

His soldiers and ministerial sycophants stepped aside, leaving a clear view of the slowly opening door. The widening breech revealed Cammy standing behind Curious, who was sitting in a wheelchair.

"My God!" screeched Dark Moon. Her heart leapt in her chest, and her diaphragm spasmed. She bulled her way toward the doorway, oblivious to every soldier in her way. The two kids shouted "Mom! Dad!". Dark Sun yelled "They're alive!" His body was supercharged with adrenaline as he rushed headlong toward his children.

Dark Moon and Dark Sun fought the soldiers who intercepted them with desperate frenzy. They frothed with hatred and bitter frustration, punching and kicking like dervishes as they tried to slip past the thugs. The soldiers clubbed them with their weapons, but the two parents had no regard for their own safety. They had trekked a thousand miles and braved many dangers for this moment.

Dark Moon clawed through the mayhem to within a few feet of Cammy. She reached out desperately for her terrified daughter, who stretched her thin arms toward her mother. Their fingers touched for one electrifying moment, like God giving life to Adam on the ceiling of the Sistine Chapel. Then both were ripped savagely away from each other.

The mayhem was over as suddenly as it began. Curious and Cammy screamed in horror as their overmatched parents were beaten and wrestled to the ground. Guards shoved the wide-eyed children back into the inner sanctum. The oak door slammed shut with a resounding thud.

Dark Sun and Dark Moon were dragged to the courthouse entrance and pushed down the front steps. They bounced brutally to the flagstones below. After a brief skirmish, Kerry and Verax were subdued and then pushed down the steps behind them.

"You have two days!" Kieran shouted from the top of the courthouse steps. He observed the brutal handiwork of his minions on the bloodied Eagles with perverse satisfaction.

Kerry scrambled to his feet and quickly assessed the injuries to his companions. Soldiers hovered nearby, rifles at the ready. Fortunately, none of his teammates were severely wounded. They hobbled to the ATV and sped away from the courthouse.

Kerry drove like a maniac while dodging potholes and mortar craters. Dark Moon trembled with fury. Dark Sun was outwardly calm, but abhorrence for his brother boiled in his soul. Verax held his bloodied arm and stared coldly into the distance.

"How do we find my father?" Dark Sun asked.

"I'll take you to him," Kerry said. "A tougher question is how do we let Teema and the rest of the Eagles know where we're going?"

"Leave that to me," said Verax. "As soon as we find J, I'll backtrack with the ATV to rendezvous with the Eagles. Then I'll backtrack further and meet up with Osiris and the gypsy caravan."

"Alone?" asked Dark Sun. "It's dangerous as hell out there."

"I'll have my hatred for the Elites to keep me company."

"Kerry?" asked Dark Moon.

"Yeah?"

"How do we know you're really taking us to meet J? You admire and respect your leader. You could double-cross us to save him. I'm sure he means more to you than my children do."

Kerry drove in silence for a moment. "Your concern is logical," he said finally. "I do admire and respect J, even more than I've let on. I owe him the opportunity to decide his own fate. He has a right to know about the vile attempt to extort his grandchildren. He should choose his own path. It's a horrible, ungodly choice, but it's his to make."

"That *sounds* honorable," said Dark Sun, who was shaken by Dark

Moon's question. Kerry did indeed have the power to betray them at this decisive juncture. "But those are just words. Either my children are going to die, or your leader is going to die. Why should we believe that your loyalty to J won't trump giving our children a fair chance?"

Kerry stopped the vehicle. He turned to face Dark Sun. "The reason is very simple. J is my father too. He would never forgive me if I betrayed you."

FORTY-EIGHT
REUNION

>Life rages, lonely and impermanent
>A brief lightning flash in the firmament
>Love is life's sublime animating force
>Uniting two souls into a single course
>
>— *The Poems of Dark Sun*

"You're my brother?" Dark Sun stared in astonishment at Kerry. His heart pounded. "How old are you?"

Kerry turned to face Dark Sun. "I'm twenty-five."

"My father disappeared twenty-seven years ago—"

"*Our* father. He was exiled to Outcast Island in late 2057."

Dark Sun shook his head numbly. "Then what happened?"

"He met Olga Kozlowski, an exile from Poland. My mother is an agitator just like her great-grandfather, a legendary revolutionary who challenged Soviet fascists long ago. She shares our father's intellectual curiosity. They worked closely together to help found Pathless Land. They fell in love and then I came along."

"He didn't wait very long."

"Don't judge," Kerry said softly. "He knew he never would see your mother again. Giving up such hope was one of many brutal sacrifices he made over the years. Don't begrudge the happiness he found with my mom."

Dark Sun eyed him coldly. "Why do you go by your mother's last name? Are you ashamed of ours?"

"You don't use ours either," Kerry reminded him. "When we decided to liberate old America, I volunteered to serve as a medic. I changed my surname to Kozlowski in case I was captured. Father thought it best to sever the obvious connection with him, for his sake and for mine. Given how the Elites abused your family, it was a wise decision."

"When did you learn we were half-brothers?"

"The possibility first emerged when you and Dark Moon were in Atlanta. When our agents read your journal, it was evident you were connected to my father. As we studied your strange circumstances—the kidnapping of your children, the drones spying on you, and your unusual trek toward the capital—our suspicions grew. It appeared that you were being lured into a trap that would entangle Dad. We decided to keep tabs on you, so I was assigned to join the gypsy caravan. If the Elites were investing precious resources to monitor your obscure tribe, we needed to also."

"I thought you joined us because you were infatuated with Teema," said Dark Moon.

Kerry blushed. "Okay, maybe I volunteered. Dad was opposed at first, but I convinced him that I should tackle dangerous missions, just like him. Right now he's here in Virginia, leading our troops."

Dark Sun's heart skipped a beat when he heard that his father was so near. "Why didn't you tell us about being my brother earlier?"

"We weren't sure how you two would react. You might have disrupted our plans."

"So why tell us now?"

"Because you need a reason to trust me. Otherwise, the three of you might overwhelm me right now, and that would ruin everything, including the rescue of your children."

"Suppose we trust you," Dark Sun said warily. "How does that improve things? Either my . . . our . . . father is going to die, or my kids are going to die. And I'm still not sure which option you're in favor of."

Kerry smiled in a way that reminded Dark Sun of Curious. "Dad says he has a plan, although he hasn't shared the details with me. I trust his judgment. We need to let this play out, just as he's allowed it to play out ever since the scheme of the Elites became clear in Atlanta." He paused. "Dad loves you. Abandoning his family decades ago took a terrible toll on him. Seeing you again will be a great joy for him."

Dark Sun fell silent. He needed more time and mental clarity to fully absorb the implications of this sudden revelation. He didn't know what to think about his father marrying another woman so soon after being separated from his first family. However, these misgivings were overshadowed by a burning desire to see him again, and by desperation to rescue Curious and Cammy. He put a hand on Kerry's arm as a gesture of peace, knowing that they could sort things out in a better time and place. "Let's get moving. It seems we have the fate of the country in our hands."

Kerry nodded. He resumed driving down Highway 29 toward Danville, where the army of Pathless Land had set up temporary field headquarters. He radioed ahead to announce that they were coming. He requested an escort of soldiers to meet them halfway with extra fuel and food.

When they met the escorts, Dark Sun and Dark Moon were transferred into an armored personnel carrier (APC). Kerry handed the keys of the ATV to Verax. The extra fuel and food were loaded into it. He instructed a squadron of soldiers to follow Verax in another vehicle as he backtracked to rendezvous with the trailing gypsies.

"Lead Teema and Osiris to Appomattox," Kerry told Verax. "Waste no time."

Verax nodded and climbed into the ATV. Kerry lingered for a moment and then pulled an envelope out of his jacket. He handed it to Verax and said, "Please give this to Teema." The bearlike man nodded again and then sped off.

Kerry watched the ATV drive away, wondering how Fatima would react to his bared soul. He felt a pang in his heart as the ATV disappeared over a hill, knowing that Verax was more likely to see her again than he was. He feared that he might never know her reaction to his letter.

The rest of them proceeded toward Danville. Dark Sun gazed out his window and noticed the insignia painted on the tank flanking their APC. It depicted a ferocious eagle clutching a lightning bolt in one talon and an olive branch in the other. The raptor seemed to be challenging adversaries to pick one or the other. It also had a stemmed white rose clenched in its beak. Under the insignia was a three-letter acronym. "What does PLA stand for?" he asked Kerry.

"Pathless Land of America. It's the formal name of our nation."

"But you Outcasts were kicked *out* of America."

"We were kicked out of a geographical location with the hollow legacy of that name, but we brought the spirit of America with us into exile. The original *ideal* of America was created three centuries ago by a bunch of rebel heroes. Now a bunch of rebels from Pathless Land are finishing what they started."

"But you're flying a different flag."

Kerry nodded. "We embrace the principles of old America, not its corrupted symbols. We did keep the old national anthem, however. My favorite line is 'the land of the free and the home of the brave'."

"Why?'

"Because freedom and bravery are inseparable. Those who want freedom must be brave enough to defend it against others who are determined to take it away. And one needs courage in order to take responsibility for oneself in a free society."

Dark Sun studied the small PLA flags fluttering on the escort vehicles. They had a background of very faint red, blue, and purple stripes, almost like watermarks on a legal document. Hundreds of brightly colored stars were randomly superimposed over the stripes. "Your flag is unusual," he said. "It's just faded stripes and a jumbled rainbow of stars."

Kerry laughed. "We're a society of free individuals—they're represented by the wildly diverse stars on the flag. Our creative chaos is organized by moral and political principles that weave us together. They're represented by the subtle stripes underlying the stars."

"Not much structure in that."

"I think you've got it!" Kerry said impishly. "There's a reason we call our nation Pathless Land. We each create our own unique paths through life. The only function of our nation as a formal entity is to ensure that we all can live safely and freely. Our government is in the background, like the faded stripes. It doesn't prescribe our paths for us. It simply protects our basic rights."

Dark Sun fell silent as they drove through a pine grove and crossed over the Dan River. He questioned how brilliantly his own star shone. The reunion with his dad was suddenly clouded by a sense of dread. His father was a great man. Dark Sun was afraid of being judged unfavorably by comparison, and there's no judgment more unnerving than that of a parent.

How would his father see him? He didn't like his own answer. All he'd done so far was hide out in Kansas with Dark Moon and their children. Even that had turned to shit. His house was a pile of rubble, and his kids had been kidnapped. He had nothing to show for his life but poverty and tragedy, which seemed to be natural states in this entropic world.

Great unseen forces had been steadily eroding the foundations of his existence. He now knew that this was an unavoidable aspect of Karma. All events affect everyone—somehow, someway, no matter how indirectly. Ignoring these external forces doesn't make them go away, because the law of causality *can't* go away. To be alive is to be intertwined with existence in all directions—right, left, up, down, near, far, past, present, future. The only question is to what extent each person has a positive or negative influence on the vast Karmic matrix. It was in this regard that Dark Sun dreaded the impending judgment by his father.

He also dreaded the catastrophic decision that lay before them. It tormented him to the edge of madness. He pictured his children being shot in the head, with gore and bone exploding in crimson mists from their skulls. He imagined his father hanging from the gallows, his head at an unnatural angle, his legs kicking wildly in his death throes. It was to be one ghoulish nightmare or the other.

As these morbid thoughts haunted him, time stood still and yet flew by in an instant. He was startled out of his introspection when the vehicle halted at a military checkpoint. They had arrived in Danville, which had been the brief headquarters of Jefferson Davis of the Confederate States of America at the end of the first Civil War.

Kerry placed his hand on a biometric scanner, and they were whisked through the barricades. They pulled into the makeshift camp past a faded entrance sign that read "Dan Daniel Memorial Park." The army had set up its mobile headquarters along the Dan River in a secluded clearing that had once been a public park.

They stopped near an orderly complex of large army tents shrouded by camouflage canopies. Snow-dusted military vehicles were everywhere. A crowd of soldiers were assembled in the center of the complex. They converged on the arriving vehicles. Dark Sun, Dark Moon, and Kerry disembarked into the midst of a boisterous reception. The ebullient greeting suggested that a momentous event was unfolding. Dark Sun and Dark Moon looked around, bewildered by the smiling, welcoming faces. It was all very unmilitary-like, except for the honor guard that seemed poised to lead them somewhere.

The honor guard pivoted and then parted the ranks of the crowd. On command, a twenty-one-gun salute rent the air. Dark Sun looked down a corridor of onlookers. His heart skipped a beat when he saw his father standing there waiting at the other end. He had aged dramatically from what Dark Sun remembered, but there was no mistaking his unforgettable smile. Dark Sun was frozen in place until Kerry nudged him forward. He walked slowly toward his dad, suddenly unaware of the crowd, the dire circumstances of his life, and even time itself. He felt like he was passing through a hazy membrane into the bright glow of an alternate reality where everything was as he had always hoped it would be. By the time he reached his father, he had slipped completely through the looking glass into a long-suppressed place in his heart called home.

The two men hugged. A powerful wave of wholeness and comfort washed over them and warmed their souls. They cried shamelessly, bridging a twenty-seven-year void with tears of joy.

Eventually, they released their embrace. They grasped shoulders, studying one another with watery eyes. Dark Sun was alarmed by his father's deteriorated condition. His hair was gray and thinning. His skin was wrinkled and splotched with liver spots. His eye sockets were dark and hollowed. His emaciated body looked exhausted, making his field uniform seem a couple of sizes too big. But a fire still blazed in his emerald eyes, belying the terrible toll that exile, nation-building, and war had taken on him.

"Audrey and I are unofficially married!" Dark Sun blurted. "We have two beautiful children."

"I was delighted to learn that," his father rasped. "She's a wonderful woman, and you're a lucky man. So am I. This moment nearly completes my life. My final act will be to rescue my grandchildren."

"I have so much to tell you," Dark Sun said. "I read your journal. I even filled in some of the pages you left blank. I'd like to return it to you." He extracted the dog-eared book from his coat.

"Keep it, James. Remember me by it." J reached into his own coat and pulled out a different book. "We don't have time for me to recount the past twenty-seven years, but I wrote most of it down. Here's my second journal. Kerry alerted me that you were on the way, and this is the best gift I could think of for our reunion. I'm entrusting it to you."

Dark Sun's hands shook as he accepted the sacred gift. "This is priceless, but I'd love to hear your story in your own voice, rather than read it in a journal."

"The journal will have to tell the tale. The world is about to be turned upside down. We have little time left, so we have to focus on a few important things. Let me greet Audrey properly and then you and I will retreat to my tent for a private chat."

J turned toward Dark Moon, who had followed behind Dark Sun. She nestled into his embrace. "Thank you," he whispered into her ear. "It was my fondest dream that you and James would be together. I've always loved your passion, your sense of life, your kindness. I'm sure that Curious and Cammy are the most wonderful children with you as their mother."

Dark Moon wept. She squeezed J harder. "After my parents were killed, you and Mary became their surrogates. One of my favorite memories is reading your books with James by the fireplace in your living room. Your house became my school, and the only place I felt safe and loved. I couldn't have made it through those terrible years without you. There's one word I always wanted to say to you, but you disappeared before I was bold enough to."

J raised an eyebrow. "What word is that, my dear?"

"Dad," she whimpered.

Tears streamed down his sallow cheeks. "You've helped complete my life today. Now you and your family must carry on with courage and love. Build a world where your precious stars can shine—freely, safely, and brightly. There's nothing more important. And now, I must go. Your inner beauty will grace my thoughts until the very end."

Dark Moon's demeanor suddenly changed. She looked at him with sorrowful eyes. Her body shook. "Dad?"

"You have no idea how wonderful that sounds. Yes, my dear?"

"I don't want Cammy and Curious to die!" She felt horribly conflicted as she blurted this out because the only alternative was brutally obvious.

J sighed heavily. "I don't either. Please trust that all will be as it should." He kissed her on both cheeks and then released her with a sad, lingering gaze. He turned and disappeared into his private tent with Dark Sun.

Their eyes adjusted to the relative darkness as they shuffled past an array of computers and telecom equipment to a corner of the stuffy tent that appeared to be J's mobile office. It was surprisingly austere for the leader of a nation. A handful of bare light bulbs were strung along the ceiling, casting distorted shadows on the walls. It smelled of canvas and mold.

"Before we begin, I need to know something." J's voice was barely audible as he struggled through a sudden riptide of emotion. "Please tell me what happened to your mother."

Dark Sun looked down at the canvas floor. He was unable to hold his father's gaze, which was heavy with dread. "Mom died long ago from pneumonia." He lifted his head and looked his father in the eye, almost accusingly. "She struggled on the farm. She worked until her fingers bled, but it was too much for her. She never saw her grandchildren. She never remarried. She loved you until the very end. Your name was the last thing she moaned before she died."

J stared blankly and slumped in his chair. Dark Sun wrapped his arms around his father's shoulders and felt his skeletal body shaking. He suddenly realized that there was another reason his father had warned there was little time left.

"I tried to find you," J said quietly. "Once we gained control of the airspace west of the Appalachians, I sent a search party to our old home in Kansas. All they found was charred rubble and some dead bodies. They noticed the tracks of a military vehicle. Our agents interrogated the factions in the area. We became aware of the gypsy caravan making its way east. We watched it from a distance and rescued it when it was attacked by the Caliphate. When you and Audrey came to Atlanta with the injured gypsies, the puzzle pieces began fitting together. The puzzle was solved after we took a DNA sample from your hand."

"Why didn't you bring us here then?" Dark Sun asked. He realized with a start that this was essentially the same question he had asked

Kieran and Katarina. Once again, he felt like a pawn in a complex chess match.

"I intervened by inserting Kerry into your caravan. Bringing you and Dark Moon here wouldn't have helped Curious and Cammy, and it would have prevented us from leveraging the vile strategy of the Elites. My plan requires them to believe they're in control of events. Your painful journey had to play out as it did, with you and Audrey none the wiser. I'm sorry, but there was no other way."

"Kerry told me you had a plan," Dark Sun said hopefully.

"I'll explain shortly," J said as he put a skeletal hand on his son's shoulder. "But first, we're going to have the father and son chat I never thought we'd have. You have much to learn, and it's all vital to what's about to unfold."

Dark Sun wondered how his life could get any more tortured and twisted than it already was, but apparently there were more surprises in store. He wondered if he would suddenly awaken to the realization that his father wasn't really standing beside him, or that his kids hadn't survived the attack in Kansas, or that none of it had ever happened. He was no longer sure what was reality and what was nightmare.

He desperately hoped this moment was real, and that his father's plan would end his family's suffering.

FORTY-NINE
CREDO

> We're born into a callous universe
> With unyielding laws as our curse
> Live true, work hard, love well
> Rage until the dreaded final bell
>
> *— The Poems of Dark Sun*

Dark Sun rolled his eyes at his father, much like he did as a teenager decades ago. "A father and son chat? This hardly seems the time—"

"It's the perfect time," J said brusquely, "Because it's our last private time together. I'm going to orient you to Pathless Land. I've given this lecture hundreds of times, but this will be my most satisfying delivery. My thoughts will come at you like a tsunami. Sit down and listen carefully."

Dark Sun nodded in bewildered submission. Their last private time together? They had just been reunited! He sat on a canvas army chair as though he were still the obedient child back in Kansas. This wasn't a chat; he was getting another lesson. He felt thirty years younger. He smiled.

"Entropy is the starting point," J began, pacing the tent in a painful shuffle. "Because it frames the endpoint. No order lasts forever, including the order called life. I'm going to die soon, and no one can stop that. You're going to die too. Everyone will. Even the planets and stars will disintegrate someday.

"Life is a temporary counterpoint to entropy. It can organize existence for its own purpose and create localized order in an otherwise mechanical universe.

"Every form of life channels energy from its environment so that it can survive as long as possible. As life evolved, this ability became more sophisticated, yielding ever more elaborate order.

"We all yearn to live forever, even though it's the one thing we *can't* do. Our aversion to death makes us instinctively defensive, acquisitive, and competitive. It drives us to continually improve our circumstances in order to prolong our lives."

J circled Dark Sun, focused like a maestro conducting a symphony of syllogisms. "Entropy is why life is filled with toil and hardship. It imposes a burden of perpetual self-renewal in an existence biased toward chaos. Living things must constantly eat, breathe, and protect themselves in order to maintain their essential order. Life is a Sisyphean task, an exercise in constantly pushing a rock up a hill, with the daunting knowledge that it will ultimately be futile. This burden isn't a curse from the heavens or an unfair abuse by other people. It's simply the tribute that living things must pay to *be* alive.

"Sustaining life is an individual responsibility, because death is an individual outcome. Despite this, humans evolved a powerful instinct for companionship. The people most likely to survive and prosper are those who collaborate, not those who are always conflicting with others. Collaboration is fueled by self-interest. It's the most effective long-term strategy for helping oneself. It's a rational recognition that our common enemy is entropy, not people of other races, creeds, and tribes.

"This is why our ancestors formed small groups. Early humans survived because they cooperated in tribes. Tribes with tighter social bonds and more effective cooperation strategies were more likely to survive. If a tribe thrived, its individual members also thrived. If a tribe was dysfunctional, its members perished.

"Thus, successful collaboration traits were passed on to future generations, while unsuccessful traits weren't. Cooperation was so fundamental to our evolving species that our ancient ancestors didn't require priests or kings to instill it. The instinct *predates* organized religions and formal political structures, which are a *product* of that instinct.

"Humans don't have the biggest fangs, the swiftest legs, the strongest arms, or the toughest armor. Instead, we communicate, trade, and work effectively in groups to use our talents and our available resources for mutual advantage.

"Successful collaboration requires trust, reciprocity, honesty, dependability, kindness, fairness, tolerance, gratitude, justice, and forgiveness. Our genetic bias toward these traits evolved during millions of years of natural selection. Nearly all of us are born with their latent seeds. When the seeds flower, we call it good. When the seeds get corrupted, we call it evil. For example, growing your own food is good. Stealing food is bad. Sharing or trading food is beautiful.

"As our language and reasoning skills evolved, we codified these positive traits into religious and cultural norms. These formal systems helped encourage, teach, and enforce collaborative behavior.

"But these survival tools are only part of our story. What's the purpose of mere survival? Fighting entropy is exhausting and ultimately futile. Why expend the effort?"

Dark Sun interrupted. "I've been wondering that a lot lately."

J smiled. "Everyone wrestles with that question. Philosophers claim to know the abstract meaning of life, but they're all wrong. There's nothing to know. There's no axiomatic purpose hard wired into the mechanical universe, nor written in a majestic script across the insentient heavens.

"And yet, we choose to go on living. We're *desperate* to. Why?

"Because we *create* our meaning. Meaning doesn't arise from the lifeless cosmos; it germinates in our individual hearts and minds. It's not dictated to us by ancient books or graying wizards; it's forged in the hot furnace of our unique hopes and dreams. We're the creators of purpose every minute of every day.

"Every sane person prefers better rather than worse. We prefer success rather than failure, joy rather than sadness, love rather than hate, ease rather than burden, collaboration rather than conflict, and life rather than death. We *care* what happens to us. What we choose to care about is our meaning. If we didn't prefer better over worse, if we didn't care about anything, we would choose to do nothing. Then entropy would kill us, and the further evolution of life would cease.

"We choose to go on living in order to inhale the exuberance of nature, revel in our achievements, bask in the radiance of love with others, and laugh in the face of entropy as long as we can. The preciousness of life is entirely due to its brevity and fragility. The looming specter of death magnifies the urgency of our short lives. It fans the torrid flames of joy and love that crackle as our individual experiences.

"We're not seeking utopia, which is impossible in an entropic world. We're simply trying to improve our circumstances. The present offers challenges, and the future offers hope that we will rise above them. So we act on that hope. If we succeed in our efforts, we experience happiness. If we fail, we experience sadness.

"As we act, life offers an endless series of choices. But which actions are truly right or wrong? What frames the concept we call morality?

"Right actions don't originate from mystical tomes, nor from the grand pronouncements of sages. They originate from the need to establish a rational hierarchy of values to combat the rigors of entropy, and from the need to make good decisions as we act. Right actions move us toward sustainable joy. Wrong actions don't.

"Sustainable joy emerges when present self can regularly congratulate past self for having made good decisions. It results when present self sacrifices some gratification today to gain greater satisfaction for future self later. Sustainable joy comes from a balanced life that includes positive relationships, a healthy mind and body, enough wealth for leisure, security against entropy and villainy, and deep self-esteem.

"Sustainable joy is the opposite of hedonism. A hedonist pursues pleasure today even if it causes suffering tomorrow. A person committed to sustainable joy invests a piece of each day toward tomorrow's success, security, or pleasure.

"It's not easy for present self to know the full consequences of its actions on future self. We each have imperfect senses, imperfect memory, imperfect knowledge, and imperfect judgment. Free will is a glorious blessing, but it's fraught with error. This is true for every person who has ever lived. Be wary of any claim to absolute knowledge, especially about right and wrong.

"All knowledge is provisional, subject to further discoveries, interpretation, and refinement. Almost every conclusion of the past has been somehow modified or disproved. True wisdom lies in recognizing errors, not in perpetuating them.

"Because of this uncertainty, life compels us to constantly exercise our reasoned judgment. If we don't, we submit ourselves to the judgment of others who might be more fallible than us, or who might be less interested in our well-being. All people, and thus all human doctrines, can lead us down the wrong path if we're not careful.

"There are countless creeds and isms, most of which contradict each other. Many of them have useful insights into truth, but none are infallible. Truth always gets muddled in translation by people who profess to interpret it for us. The only way to directly validate truth is to step outside historical conditioning and fallible ideology into the Pathless Land of detached, open-minded observation. As Roger Bacon said, 'Cease to be ruled by dogmas and authorities; look at the world!'

"We must courageously exercise our rationality to avoid becoming intellectual captives of our cultures, our histories, our churches, our leaders, our nations, and our fears. They squeeze us into tight boxes that imprison our minds and isolate us from direct contact with reality."

J's voice caught in his throat with the rasping sound of death. Dark Sun heard his own heart beating like a clock, counting down what little remained of his father's life. He wanted to abandon the lecture, but he knew that his father was expressing his love by sharing his wisdom.

J recovered his voice. "Does this mean we should ignore the wisdom of others? No! Humankind's ability to accumulate knowledge and to learn from the discoveries and experiences of others is a powerful evolutionary advantage. It led to the development of language, economics, common law, tools, property rights, and technology. They enable everyone to stand on the shoulders of giants and improve upon earlier developments.

"Even though we benefit from humankind's cumulative wisdom, we shouldn't be spellbound by it or chained to it. It's vital to understand this paradox. The wisdom of others is helpful in our *search* for truth, but if we suspend reason in favor of blind acceptance of dogma, we can't be sure that we've *found* truth."

J grabbed a canvas chair and sat directly in front of Dark Sun. "The thousands of choices we make each day decide our futures. We're the sum of all our decisions. Either we're improving our lives and adding to our happiness or we're causing ourselves pain and adding to our misery. Heaven and hell are psychological states created by each person right here on Earth.

"As an adult, there's no better person to decide what's right for you than *you*. If others decide what's right for *you*, it will usually be through the filter of what's right for *them*. When others substitute their meaning for yours, it's often to control you or to diminish you for their own personal gain. If you abdicate the rational exercise of your natural free will, you'll be the plaything of others.

"We experience life through our own brains and hearts. No one can think for us, feel emotions for us, or dream for us. These are all inherently personal acts. We perceive reality through our own filters, memories, and biases.

"Since life is an individual experience, and since survival is an individual outcome, the sanctity of each human life must be the foundation of morality. Every life is an irreplaceable lightning flash in eternity. We each possess equal moral legitimacy to freely pursue our personal meanings. The value of our life isn't determined by others; we are each the center of our personal universes.

"Even though we collaborate for mutual survival and satisfaction, we aren't slaves to each other. It's immoral to obstruct people from improving their own lot. And the most pernicious evil is to force another sovereign person to bear the burden of entropy on your behalf.

"How can we freely and sanely coexist when there are billions of sovereign people desiring the same scarce resources and fighting the same entropic conditions? How can people be protected from forced submission when societies have so often enslaved people to satisfy the whims of certain elites or to mollify certain classes?

"The answer revolves around Karma. Since you've read my journal, you're familiar with the concept. Karma is a powerful closed loop phenomenon. Your peers care about your actions, and you care that they care. When this karmic feedback loop is allowed to hold people accountable for their actions, a key foundation is laid for a free and peaceful society.

"When force and coercion replace the moderation of Karma, the casualties are always free will and morality. This is necessarily true, because force is the opposite of free will, which can't be exercised without liberty; and coercion is the opposite of morality, which is meaningless if a person isn't free to choose.

"Thus, when a group gets too big for the power of Karma to moderate relationships, formal political structures are necessary to mitigate coercion. These structures include laws and constitutions. They also include enforcement methods to protect individuals from harming each other. The larger a society becomes, the more imperative this becomes.

"Unfortunately, most formal political structures devolved into perverse engines for *encouraging* coercion and aggression. They got manipulated and hijacked by people lusting for power, control, and wealth. They became extortion machines for enriching a select few and abusing the rest. They protected the power of the powerful. They spawned tyrants, warlords, slave masters, and genocidal dictators. They became the Elites, the Caliphate, and the Jackals. Then humanity gets divided into two classes—the ruling elites and those who must comply and conform to their dictates."

Someone outside the tent asked for permission to enter. J paused to beckon the visitor. An adjutant entered and saluted. "Sir, you requested my presence at this hour?"

J nodded, then looked around the tent like an absent-minded professor. He spied three envelopes and shuffled to retrieve them. Dark Sun noticed that there was a white rose embossed on each. J handed them to the adjutant and said, "Major Rodriguez, please deliver these orders to Generals Jackson, Zayed, and Perez. Make it clear that they're not to be opened until 10:00 AM tomorrow. There must be no mistake about that."

Rodriguez snapped to attention and saluted. "Yes sir! Will that be all?"

J hesitated. "One more thing. It's been an honor fighting alongside you."

The major looked at him quizzically. "The honor is all mine, sir."

J nodded. "You're dismissed. Godspeed."

Major Rodriguez saluted again and slipped through the tent flap. J stared wistfully at the drab canvas door for a moment and then returned his attention to Dark Sun.

"Where was I? Oh yes . . . Karma was sufficiently cohesive when early humans lived in small, isolated tribes. But in the last ten thousand years, we transitioned from hunting and gathering to agriculture, trading, and specialization, which gave rise to towns and cities. Our population exploded and our technologies blossomed. In just ten millennia, we morphed from small, isolated tribes to an interconnected world of seven billion people, most of whom are strangers to each other.

"Our primitive social, political, and economic systems were inadequate for this logarithmic transformation. The resulting disequilibrium overwhelmed the power of Karma to maintain social cohesion. Our chronic conflicts are an artifact of this chaotic transition from tribalism to globalism. In antiquity, tribal success came from effective in-group cooperation. Today's crowded world includes countless overlapping religious sects, political factions, social circles, races, and ethnicities. It's no longer possible to cloister in tight-knit tribes. We have to interact daily with "others."

"During this upheaval from sparse tribalism to populous pluralism, most of our attempts to structure a new order went badly. Almost all of them were grounded in secular or theocratic despotism. The results were often war, subjugation, slaughter, slavery, colonialism, terror, destitution, starvation, and now the Darkness.

"It wasn't until the last millennium that humankind began to understand that individual rights, the rule of law, and of the separation of church and state were all vitally important. Rallying around powerful visions like the *Magna Carta* and the *Declaration of American Independence*, we began to see the possibility for the peaceful and orderly coexistence of billions of people. We began to realize that the only way to unite all of the creeds, races, and factions is to paradoxically guarantee the freedom of each individual.

"For a large, diverse society to successfully collaborate, its social compact must include shared values that can compensate for the absence of karmic suasion. These values must be fundamental to humanity, not just to certain factions, classes, genders, races, or creeds. They must be derived from a common understanding of how a pluralistic society should properly integrate all of its sovereign individuals.

"There are three universal values that we've adopted as the keystones of Pathless Land. They're represented by the red, blue, and purple stripes watermarked on our flag:

"First, we value human life as sacred. As Christ taught, each life is important. The lives of the lowliest and the grandest have the same intrinsic value. The life of a serf is as legitimate as the life of a monarch, and all distinctions between the two evaporate at death. The concept of freedom means nothing if there isn't something precious about every human being. The right to live has no practical meaning if it's conditioned on the approval of others, if politicians and judges can abrogate it, if majorities can deny it to minorities, or if thugs can forcibly abuse it.

"Second, we each value our *own* lives, which means we value the freedom to protect and fulfill them.

"Third, we value family, friends, and neighbors as collaborative partners in our pursuit of sustainable joy.

"There are countless other values held by the billions of people sharing the planet, derived from countless political, religious, and philosophical perspectives. Given this exponential diversity, the only framework for a peaceful and effective society is one that protects the rights to life and liberty of each person. This will free them to live and believe as they choose, so long as they don't violate the similar rights of others. Any other path will lead to the violence and despair of the Darkness.

"Humans have a yin and yang duality. We're not naturally rugged individualists, but we're all individuals. We're not naturally cogs in a giant societal machine, but we all have an instinct to collaborate. Everyone yearns to be free, and yet everyone yearns to belong. We all have the urge to control others, yet we resist being controlled by others. A debate has long raged about whether we're individualists or social beings. We're both. A successful society will recognize that truth. Unfortunately, most societies have ignored our dual nature, resulting in slavery rather than freedom and alienation rather than belonging.

J glanced at the clock on the wall and sighed. "One last point, which will be the basis for the difficult decision our family must now make. Of all the motives for collaboration, the most powerful is love.

"We are each distinct beings, but we need others as the context for our joy. Love is a burning desire to adore another person and to be adored in return. Loving relationships yield a sense of permanence, belonging, and acceptance. They're the only antidote to the profound loneliness that comes from scraping out a harsh existence in an entropic world. That's why love is the subject of so many of our poems, songs, books, and artworks.

"Love is the great treasure of mankind, a gleaming jewel nestled deep inside each of us. We struggle for those we love. We share our joy with them. We collaborate with them. Love is that effervescent explosion of pure delight that animates our brief lives. It's the candle burning in the window when we stagger home after a hard journey. Love inspires our most unselfish acts and our most heroic deeds. Our loved ones are the touchstones in our personal stories. They're the golden threads in the rich tapestries of our lives. Our memories would be barren without them.

"Creating a fertile environment for love to flourish is the greatest gift anyone can give. As I mark my last breaths, my concern isn't for myself. It's for you and all the others I love who will remain after I die. You make the unwinnable struggle against entropy somehow worth fighting."

Dark Sun's head spun. It was full of morbid thoughts that were entangled with the urgency of their situation. "Father, why this abstract talk now? We've got horrendous decisions to make!"

"The things we need most *are* abstractions." J's voice was a hoarse whisper now. "Without love, collaboration, and purpose, we have no reason for existing. We have no guide for meaningful living. My words are integral to everything going on in the world. They're also integral to the plea I'm about to make to you. They explain what Pathless Land is about."

Dark Sun stood and locked eyes with his father, wrestling with a maelstrom of sadness, confusion, and doom. "What plea are you talking about? What does it have to do with Pathless Land?"

The glow in J's eyes was dimming. "Before I make my plea, let me express my love for you in this way. I'm going to surrender myself to Regis at Appomattox tomorrow morning, in exchange for the safe release of Curious and Cammy."

"That's your plan? They'll kill you!"

"They'll *want* to kill me."

"You can't do this!"

"I can do with my life as I please," J replied. "I've lived long, and

I've achieved most of my hopes and dreams. I'm very ill, so it's time for me to bid farewell. My only sadness is that I had to abandon you and Mary long ago to accomplish what I did. This is my chance to make amends . . . at least with you."

"But what about Pathless Land?"

"It'll carry on without me," J said calmly. "The spirit of Pathless Land is not a cult of leadership but a passion for its principles. The movement I started will continue. This leads to my plea. I want you and Audrey to join Kerry to help Pathless Land liberate America. That's the most important thing you can do for me, for your family, and for their posterity."

Dark Sun was stunned. Just a few months ago, he was an isolated farmer in Kansas. Since then, shock after shock had destabilized his world. Now he was being asked to join a revolution, unite with a half-brother he just recently found out he had, and leave behind his old life. The wheels in his head churned his thoughts into a muddle. "Who else knows your plan?"

"Olga does. She's at peace with it. She agrees that it's a magnificent way for me to exit this world. We've said our goodbyes, and she'll settle my personal affairs. A few trusted generals will know when they open the letters Major Rodriguez is now delivering. They will inform our cabinet and congress in Tara after tomorrow's events. Our constitution has a clear succession protocol. No one else can know my plan right now. I can't risk any interference."

"My God!"

"I'm paying the ultimate price to save your children. I'm asking you to pay a price to help save everyone. Are you willing?"

"I . . . I . . ."

J checked the clock again and frowned. "Life never presents options that are perfectly good. But you still must choose. Great people make the toughest decisions and see them through to successful conclusions."

"I can't choose between your life and the lives of my children!"

"I've already made that choice. I'm going to sacrifice myself no matter which path you choose for the future. I'm asking you to choose between helping to create a world fit for your children or hiding from wolves that will eventually devour you anyway."

"You fought the wolves, and now they're going to kill you."

"My final act tomorrow will complete my life. I've loved well and often. Creating Pathless Land was a great joy. Although death is at my door, the vision I fought for all these years is finally coming to fruition. There's no victory in that for the wolves. They're about to experience the fierce bite of Karma."

"How can you choose death so calmly?"

"I'm not choosing death. I'm choosing your life and the lives of your children. Life is an unbroken river of vitality and wisdom passed from generation to generation. I'm passing the baton to you as a supreme act of love. I'm just asking one thing in return. Help finish the dream of Pathless Land. It's time for your light to shine upon the world, James."

Dark Sun's eyes widened with trepidation. "And if I can't?" He felt like a soldier witnessing the demise of his hero in battle, knowing that in the next instant he would have to decide whether to flee in panic or to pick up the champion's sword and step into the breach. He had always yearned to do something more spectacular than farming and raising a family. Now that the moment was upon him, his knees wobbled, his bowels churned, and he broke into a cold sweat.

J smiled serenely. "You'll eventually face the daunting moment of your last few breaths, clenching nothing in your desperate fists but the legacy you're leaving behind. When you die, the universe tallies your karmic scorecard—who you were or who you were not; what you constructed or what you destroyed; what joy you spread or what sorrow you caused; whom you helped or whom you ruined. Death is the end of our individual existences, but our lives echo in karmic ripples for eons, perpetuating the effects of our choices. These ripples make the world better or worse, affecting everyone you loved and everyone they will love and so on. Choose wisely, son. Tell me tomorrow morning which path you're going to follow. I wish to know before I'm gone."

"I could just lie about my intentions to make you happy before you die."

J sighed. "You're not a teenager anymore. It's true that I won't know if you've kept your word. Maybe you'll be able to hide your duplicity from me and everyone else, but you can't hide it from yourself. Are you proud of who you are right now?"

Dark Sun turned white. This was the moment he feared most, the impending judgment by his father. "Ask me anything but that."

"My judgment means nothing. What will you think about yourself if you renege on our deal? How will the lives of you and your family be any better? Think hard. Lying accomplishes nothing of lasting value."

J paused, struggling for breath. He looked at the clock again. "We're out of time. As Buddha observed, existence is as transient as autumn clouds. A lifetime is like a flash of lightning in the sky, rushing by like a torrent down a steep mountain. My own flash is nearly spent. All that's left is for me to share with you the details of my plan. You can't reveal them to anyone, no matter what."

He put his arm around his son's shoulder, partly as a hug, and partly to hold himself upright. He explained the details of his plan. Dark Sun listened in astonishment. Just when he thought he couldn't be shocked any further, he was.

Tomorrow would be terrifying, spectacular, and tragic.

FIFTY
DEPREDATION

> Nearly all men can stand adversity, but if you really want to test a man's character, give him power.
>
> — Abraham Lincoln

The bombings stopped for a couple of days, and the air-raid sirens fell silent.

During the calm interlude, Cammy and Curious achieved something approaching normalcy, if such is possible for hostages in a sterile jail cell in an alien land. Food deliveries were regular again, and the guards, who seemed fewer in number with each passing day, left them otherwise alone.

The two occupied their time talking about their parents, their home, and their pets. They tried mightily to keep the belief alive that they were going to be rescued, although the thin veneer of hope was getting thinner by the day.

Heavy footsteps echoed in the hallway. It was time for their breakfast to be delivered. A tall uniformed man carrying a tray appeared. Cammy was about to wake Curious when the man lifted his head, revealing his face. It was Scarface.

Scarface waved a hand over the biometric scanner. The barred door opened with a harsh metallic scraping. Cammy instinctively retreated to the far wall of the cell where Curious still slumbered in his wheelchair. She shook him violently.

Curious struggled through the mental haze of the abrupt awakening. In a nightmare, he had been running from a menacing drifter he discovered rummaging for food in their barn in Kansas. When he saw Scarface ogling Cammy, he was uncertain if this scene was a surreal twist in the plot of his dream or something very real.

Scarface tossed the food tray aside, spilling its contents across the floor. He stalked Cammy with an unholy grin on his disfigured face. "I've waited a long time for this, pretty girl. Rumor is that you'll be gone tomorrow. I could be gone too if the bombs start falling again. If this is the end, I'm going to enjoy every second of it." He lunged at Cammy and grabbed her shirt. He yanked her toward him.

Cammy's piercing scream snapped Curious fully awake. He gaped in horror as Scarface ripped Cammy's flimsy shirt. She writhed and kicked and clawed, but she was overpowered by the much larger assailant. She screamed again, begging Curious for help.

Curious lurched from his wheelchair toward Scarface, forgetting in the horror of the moment that his leg was shattered. It buckled grotesquely under his weight. He crashed to the concrete floor, hitting his head. The pain was excruciating, but he thought only of the need to save Cammy.

He saw blurred images of Cammy scratching Scarface's neck and biting his hand as the lecher mounted her prone body. Scarface howled in pain and then punched her chin, knocking her head against the floor with a sickening thud. She was momentarily stunned, making it easier for him to wrestle her clothes off.

Curious ignored the throbbing in his head and the searing pain shooting through his useless leg. He crawled on his elbows across the rough concrete, dragging his crippled body toward his sister inch by inch. He screamed, not from pain, but from mortal frustration as he watched Scarface assault his helpless sister with animal obsession.

After what seemed like an eternity, Curious shimmied close enough to grab one of Scarface's legs. It was a pitiful effort. Scarface kicked him in the face, barely interrupting his assault on Cammy. Curious grabbed the leg again, only to endure another vicious boot to his forehead.

Cammy snapped out of her semi-consciousness. The full horror of her situation washed over her. She tried to punch Scarface, but her awkward attempts were futile against his grotesque body lying on her. She bit his ear, then gagged from the chunk of cartilage in her mouth and the coppery taste of his blood. He growled in pain, but his blind obsession was so powerful that he redoubled his effort.

Cammy screamed for help again. She heard only the echoes of her voice in the empty hallway. Most of the guards had fled north from the recent onslaught of Outcast bombings. The terror of her helplessness was more agonizing than the pain and humiliation from the brute assaulting her. She felt abandoned by everyone.

Where were her protectors? The horror of this moment would never dull for Cammy. When society's guardians are the abusers, who will save the rest?

A shrill alarm rang. It was louder and more insistent than the usual air-raid siren. The ear-piercing sound rattled Scarface. A look of horror washed over his face. He scrambled to his feet, pulled up his pants, and sprinted for the cell door, stepping on Curious as he did so. He disappeared into a crowd running down the corridor. He left the door open in his panic.

"Attention all comrades," a loudspeaker blared. "This is not a drill. This is a DEFCON-1 alert. Evacuate the city to your assigned emergency stations. Further instructions will be issued there."

There were shouts and screams as people scrambled down the corridor. Cammy was utterly disoriented. Were they all about to die? Escape was maddeningly near, but Curious was writhing on the floor in pain and unable to run away with her. Despite the adrenaline coursing through her terrified heart, she froze.

Tears poured down her face as she lay where Scarface had pinned her. Coarse images flashed through her mind in rapid succession. She thought of Curious and his shattered leg. She thought of the gun butt to Sophie's head. She thought of the vicious attack on their family in Kansas. She thought of the vile stench of Scarface's breath. She thought of the crowd of panicked strangers who ran by her cell with no intention of helping.

Her head filled with an indescribable hatred. It was a blurry montage of the crazed look in Scarface's eyes, the last hypnotic look in Sophie's eyes, and the terror in Curious' eyes as he looked upon her with a dreadful shock. Something snapped, and young Cammy died. In that same moment, a new Cammy was born.

Two guards loomed in the doorway. They looked around in confusion at the evidence of the violence that Scarface had done to the two kids. They lifted Curious and manhandled him into his wheelchair, ignoring his gut-wrenching screams of pain. They yanked Cammy up from the floor, ignoring her tears, her nakedness, and the blood on the floor.

"You're coming with us," one of them said, throwing a blanket around her. "A shit storm is about to happen."

FIFTY-ONE
RESISTANCE

> Staggering knight in rusted armor
> Weak from battles fought with ardor
> Wanting only to rest his weary head
> And sleep in peace like the holy dead
>
> — *The Poems of Dark Sun*

The day of reckoning finally arrived.

They departed from the PLA field headquarters in Danville in the morning, heading north toward Appomattox. Heavy snow fell, blanketing the pines and obscuring the hilly countryside. Dark Sun, Dark Moon, J, and Kerry rode together in a military convoy that crept along like a funeral procession.

Bells tolled a snow-muffled salute to the departing entourage when they passed a church tower along Highway 29. No one spoke. J kept his head down like a boxer preparing to enter the ring.

Dark Sun and Dark Moon had endured a miserable night filled

with apprehension. In the gloom of their tent, she had pressed him for details of his private conversation with J. He shared his philosophies with her, but not the essential element he had promised to keep secret. He assured her that his father had a plan that would end well for their children. She wasn't assuaged. Every scenario she imagined pointed to catastrophe.

Dark Sun wrestled with a maelstrom of emotions during the ride. He felt the morbid weight of his father's impending demise. He regretted not sharing all of J's plan with Dark Moon. He struggled with the problem of evil. It seemed that no matter how hard people tried, things went to shit anyway. Tyrants, drug lords, theocrats, and jihadists had taken over the world.

He also felt the crushing burden of the request his father had made of him. He doubted his courage or ability to fight in a revolt against the Elites. It was even more unlikely that he could convince Dark Moon to join him. He knew she just wanted to be a mother and ignore the rest of the world. Her vision was to return to Kansas after rescuing Curious and Cammy, rebuild their home, and farm in peace.

After a short while, J emerged from his contemplation. He lifted his head and saw the somber faces of his companions. Sensing that they were in desperate need of hope, he began describing the military capabilities of Pathless Land. He wanted to assure them that their contingent was safe and that a successful outcome to this venture was likely.

He explained that a vast array of armaments had been transported to the mainland from Pathless Land. The PLA Air Force controlled the skies over much of the country. The PLA Navy patrolled the Eastern seaboard. He said that they had even launched a few ballistic missiles capable of delivering nuclear warheads through the skies over Washington yesterday, just to put the Elites on their heels.

Ironically, Pathless Land's state-of-the-art military technology was designed and built by thousands of nautical and aerospace engineers and craftsmen who had been exiled to Outcast Island over the decades. The totalitarian regimes around the world considered them incorrigible because they clung tenaciously to facts and logic. This migration of technical skill was similar to the flight of Einstein and other German "misfits" from the national socialist regime to America, where they assisted in developing weapons that ultimately destroyed the fascists. When Pathless Land prepared for its invasion of America, it drew in human and natural resources from the Caribbean, Central America, South America, and Mexico in order to rapidly build its military capabilities.

As Dark Sun listened to his father, he pondered the phenomenon of war on American soil. The notion seemed unthinkable a generation ago, but from his father's history books, he knew that armed conflict in America was a frequent occurrence. Centuries ago, European colonial powers fought with each other, and with the indigenous Indians, for control of territory on the undeveloped American continent. The American colonists fought a revolutionary war against the British Empire in 1776, and then another war in 1812. In the nineteenth century, America fought Mexico over the Southwestern territories. Then the first American civil war erupted between the North and South, a brutal affair in which a half million Americans were slaughtered. And now, another civil war raged that had already claimed the lives of many millions.

Such conflict was to be expected. Despite heroic ambitions to be a Great Melting Pot, America was a tossed salad of cultures, religions, ethnicities, languages, and political philosophies brought by emigres from every nation. The miraculous social alchemy that briefly fused the diverse cultures together collapsed in the face of political divisiveness. Influencers, academics, and agitators who focused on identity politics worked feverishly for decades to inflame the toxic tensions between groups. As the factions jostled against each other, people rallied around differences rather than commonalities.

Two antagonistic cultures emerged from the waves of immigration to America—a northern and eastern culture that was collectivist, elitist, bureaucratic, and urban, and a southern and plains culture that was independent, rebellious, agrarian, and rural. The bitter antagonism between the two cultures caused a constant rift. The country was always two Americas on the verge of spewing scalding steam, even during the grudging collaboration that yielded the Constitution in 1787.

Dark Sun mused that the divide between these two cultures was still an unbridgeable chasm after all these centuries. He feared that the tribal differences would never be resolved. The collectivists and the individualists were destined to fight for all eternity, in some form or other. The conflict started in ancient Greece, and it had raged unabated ever since.

His contemplations were interrupted by their arrival at the small village of Appomattox Court House, a sparse collection of ancient clapboard buildings near the Appomattox River. They drove past an abandoned parking lot once used by tourists, and headed to the reconstructed home of Wilmer McLean, where the prisoner exchange would occur. General Robert E. Lee surrendered to General Ulysses S. Grant at this historic landmark to effectively end the first Civil War.

Their convoy turned off a dirt road through a narrow gate toward the two-story McLean House. The red brick building had two chimneys and a portico with white columns and railings. Two large bushes entwined in white trellises straddled the wide steps leading up to the front door. The estate was bordered by a white picket fence. Regis' military forces surrounded the building.

J's armored personnel carrier pulled up to the house and halted near a squat shed that was an icehouse long ago. Kerry and Dark Moon exited the vehicle. Before Dark Sun could follow, J pulled the door shut and said, "You're out of time. Are you going help Pathless Land with our revolution?"

Dark Sun's heart sank to his toes, even though he knew this moment was coming. He suddenly realized that it had been coming his whole life. Everyone eventually reaches this fork in the road. Some charge into the maelstrom with heroic ambition. Most, however, take the other fork and wither into obscurity. Pathless Land and adventure beckoned him in one direction. Kansas and solitude beckoned him in the other. He was paralyzed. It was far easier to dream of bold adventures than to embark on them.

He stared out the window at the Elite sentinels picketed around the McLean estate. Then he stared at the PLA forces queuing up behind J's APC. The opposing factions eyed each other coldly across the snow-covered yard.

Dark Sun imagined a similar scene two centuries ago on this very site, with grey Confederate soldiers and blue Union soldiers staring each other down after years of savage conflict. He felt the same irreconcilable tension that must have hung in the air like a dark pall on that historic day. He felt the hatred, distrust, and bloodlust. He felt the immense momentum of centuries of philosophical and political divide that led to today's watershed event.

He also sensed the haunting presence of his two kidnapped children, victims of that unbridgeable divide, presumably tucked somewhere on the compound. By osmosis, he felt the profound courage and conviction of his father, who was about to make the ultimate sacrifice for those he loved.

"I *want* to help," Dark Sun said. "But fighting in a civil war scares the shit out of me."

"So you're indifferent to the struggle?"

Dark Sun shrugged his shoulders. "What difference can one person make?"

"I made a difference."

"But you left your home and family behind."

"I've returned home, and I'm saving your family—along with millions of others." J put his hand on his son's shoulder.

Dark Sun had accomplished little in his life thus far. He could never measure up to his accomplished father. He was certain his father's assessment matched his. He put all his cards on the table. "I'm not a hero like you."

"You don't need to be. You just need the courage to stand up to evil and refuse to back down. Do you have my first journal with you?"

Dark Sun was puzzled. "Yes, but I don't want another lecture now."

J scowled. "Do you still have the laminated white rose you used as your bookmark?"

Dark Sun looked up in surprise. He pulled the journal from his coat and extracted the laminated white rose. He showed it to J. "It's not the original one that you stashed in the foundation of our home. Someone swapped it for a fresh one in Atlanta."

"I know. I instructed our officers to do that after we figured out who you were."

Dark Sun stared at him blankly.

"I'm the old rose," J explained. "You're the fresh one."

Dark Sun shook his head dumbly. "I still don't get it. Why a white rose?"

"It's the national symbol of Pathless Land. It represents purity in the face of evil."

"How does purity help against evil?"

"The white rose is our reminder that the only way to remain pure is to *resist* evil. Not to resist is to be complicit. In National Socialist Germany, five college students exposed to the world the horrors of a government run amok. While the adults around them acquiesced to the tyrants, these teenagers bravely distributed pamphlets calling the fascists to account for their atrocities. They risked death for their dissent against repression and genocide. They called themselves the White Rose Society."

"What happened?"

"They were caught and executed."

"Just like you will be. Today."

J nodded grimly. "But their unconquerable spirit lived on. The Allies captured some of the White Rose pamphlets. They later dropped millions of copies from airplanes all over Germany. The resistance of a handful of brave students became one of the daggers in the hearts of the tyrants. We've been spreading modernized versions of the pamphlets throughout the domain of the Elites. When we liberate towns in old America, people tell us the words in the pamphlets gave them hope and the courage to join us."

"All it takes is some words and a symbol?"

"It's not as simplistic as it sounds. The motto of Pathless Land is 'Neither coerce nor be coerced.' The first part is easy because the decision not to coerce others is within the control of each person. The second part is more difficult. It's not easy standing up to those who have the power to coerce because it usually means they have the power to abuse or kill you. As Einstein warned us, the world won't be destroyed by those who do evil; it will be destroyed by those who watch them do it. Resistance takes courage, the kind that can only come from an unyielding belief in the purity of your conviction. That was the lesson of the White Rose Society."

Dark Sun fingered the laminated white rose. He thought about the bravery of five unknown students from a century ago. He thought about the sacrifice his father was about to make. He thought about the suffering his kids had already endured. He thought about the mortal dangers he might have to face in his own future.

He handed the rose to his father. "I want you to carry this with you when you confront Regis today."

J took the white rose. He stuck it in the front pocket of his uniform so that the petals protruded above his military decorations. "I have something for you," he said. He extracted from his uniform a scrolled parchment sealed with ceremonial blue, red, and purple ribbons. He handed it to his son.

Dark Sun looked at it curiously. "What's this?"

"The treasure of Pathless Land. Open it when you return to Danville."

Dark Sun's hands shook when he accepted it. "I have something for you too." He reached into his jacket and unfolded a crumpled piece of paper. He handed it to his father. "I wrote this poem in your honor last night."

J read the handwritten words. He stared at the wrinkled sheet for several moments after he finished, unable to tear his eyes from it.

Finally, he looked at his son as if seeing him for the first time, even though it would be the last. "Thank you. We've traded our best creations with each other. Such is the proper way of men."

Dark Sun nodded.

"One more thing, James."

Dark Sun cringed. He sensed that the dreaded judgment of his father was about to rear its ugly head.

"I'm proud of you."

Dark Sun did a doubletake. "Why?"

"You were smart enough to pick Audrey as your mate. You carved out a living in this shitty world with no help from anyone. You defied the Elites to bring my two grandchildren into this world. You journeyed a thousand miles through the Darkness to get here. You've begun fulfilling your ambition to write. You have more courage, resourcefulness, and wisdom than you know. I think you're ready for anything. You just have to realize that the whole meaning of your life exists in that gap between who you are and who you wish to be."

A tear trickled down Dark Sun's cheek. "You have no idea how much that means to me."

Someone pounded on the door of their APC. J looked at his watch. "What's your decision?"

Dark Sun glanced at the unblemished white rose beckoning from his father's pocket. Suddenly, everything was clear to him. "I'm in." His heart skipped a beat as he spoke the words.

J smiled wearily. "Thank you. Pathless Land is the only hope for lasting joy and peace, for your generation and the generations to follow. I love you, James."

J abruptly exited the vehicle with Dark Sun in tow, slipping past Kozlowski and Dark Moon, who stared at them quizzically. J trudged toward the house, hunched with age, illness, and weariness. He struggled up the steps of the portico, acutely aware of the hundreds of eyes riveted upon him. The fate of millions would be altered today.

He had survived starvation, injury, and violent conflict while transforming the chaos of Outcast Island into the glory of Pathless Land.

The accumulated travail had enfeebled his body. Now that his end was approaching, an odd sense of relief accompanied his leaden steps. He wore his finest PLA uniform. This was how he wanted to go.

Dark Sun, Kerry, and Dark Moon linked arms as they followed in J's footsteps. A diverse contingent of PLA guards trailed behind. They entered into the cramped foyer of the McLean House. Their small entourage was herded single-file through a narrow doorway into a room already occupied by Regis and his black-shirted bodyguards.

The opposing leaders eyed each other menacingly as J hobbled across the room. Neither spoke. The atmosphere in the stuffy room was eerily still, like the ominous calm that precedes a tornado. Momentous history was being crafted in real time, and in mortal flesh and blood.

Dark Sun studied Regis. The leader of the Elites looked less imposing than he imagined. He wore the standard blood-red tunic, although it was adorned with a gaudy patch of medals, pins, and badges that seemed out of place on his aging body. He was bald, with a narrow gray face, prominent nose, and hawkish features. His dark eyes were buried deep in hollow sockets. Until now, Dark Sun's mental image of Regis had been of a powerful leader with a commanding presence. Instead, he saw that Regis had the condescending, elitist air of a smug professor endowed with irrevocable tenure.

Regis smiled like a crocodile at him. Dark Sun glanced away quickly. Given what the cretin had done to his family, he considered him nothing more than a hemorrhoid on the asshole of humanity whom he was now committed to eradicating.

Dark Sun scanned the room. It was decorated in its original nineteenth-century style, as if frozen in time. It had been well preserved as a national monument by the government. Red drapes shrouded the windows, and formal gold-framed pictures adorned the walls. The woven carpet had an intricate red, blue, and brown pattern. A simple fireplace, framed in black wood with a small hearth, protruded from the wall opposite the entrance.

There were two tables in the center of the room, among other antiques. Regis stood behind the simple wooden table on the right. J positioned himself behind the ornate marble-topped table on the left. He was unaware that it was the very table upon which General Robert E. Lee had signed the documents surrendering his Army of Northern Virginia two centuries earlier.

"Where are my grandchildren?" J's weak voice barely carried the short distance between their tables.

"In the old slave bunkhouse out back," Regis replied.

"How appropriate," said J. "The good news is that they're about to be freed, along with everyone else in old America. Bring them here, so I can see them."

"Let's not be hasty. They'll appear when it's time for the exchange. I've waited a long time for this meeting. It should make for legendary theatre, and my historians will take prolific notes. You and I are noble combatants. Let's do this formally and honorably."

"Only one of us is worthy of honor," J replied. "The other takes children as hostages, terrorizes millions of innocent people, and is a leech sucking the lifeblood out of America."

"I'm graciously allowing you to share your last words with all assembled here. However, this must be a civil discussion, or I'll end it quickly. Will you be surrendering your entire army, like General Lee?"

"The people of Pathless Land are each responsible for their own lives. I'm trading myself, in exchange for my two grandchildren."

Regis smirked. "Such a noble sacrifice."

"Perhaps not," replied J. "I won't make the same mistake as General Lee. He deeply regretted surrendering to Lincoln's powerful government. He said that if he had foreseen the results of subjugation, he would have preferred to die at Appomattox with his brave men."

Regis waved his hand dismissively. "Bold words for a man who's surrendering! When you're gone, your renegade nation will collapse and then the war will be over. My retribution against Pathless Land will be as brutal as Lincoln's was against the vanquished Southerners two centuries ago. We'll surround your armies and cut off their supplies. They'll learn that starvation is an awful way to die, just like the Confederates did."

"The Warriors of Pathless Land will spill their last drops of blood rather than surrender. You exiled us from our families and homes. You called us misfits, radicals, and extremists. And now you expect submission? Never! Instead, you're going to meet *your* demise today. The unholy reign of the Elites is nearly over. Pathless land is going to end the distinction between masters and slaves forever."

"Such hollow threats," Regis replied smugly.

"You won't live to see the sun come up tomorrow, unless you and your thugs lay down your arms right now. I'm offering you safe asylum in Pathless Land if my grandchildren are released and you unconditionally surrender. You will save the lives of millions if you do."

Regis stared in disbelief at the audacity of his opponent. He wasn't sure what the rebel had up his sleeve, but he now felt vindicated issuing a **DEFCON**-1 alert yesterday as a precautionary measure after ballistic missiles had arced over the capital. "You're confused about who has the upper hand here."

J touched the white rose protruding from his pocket. "I've never felt more in control. I'm about to change the world with one simple act."

FIFTY-TWO
SURRENDER

> The power of evil always grows
> Till you resist with the White Rose
> Hasten toward your holy goal
> Before entropy takes its final toll
>
> *— The Poems of Dark Sun*

Regis suddenly felt insecure. A small spark of terror flickered in his brain.

This was to be his triumphant moment. It was to be his opportunity to deliver J's head on a silver platter to Cosimo and put an end to the centurion's brazen threats. But something was amiss. He expected submission from J, not bravado. The color washed out of his face. His throat tightened.

He scanned the room. He eyed his own black-shirted guards with some assurance. Then his gaze wandered to J's Warriors of Pathless Land. He glared at J and said, "If your goons kill me, you and your family will die too. Nothing useful will come from our mutual slaughter."

"I expect something far better today," J replied. "I hope this is the last time the forces of tyranny and liberty are in mortal conflict."

Regis snickered. Some color returned to his face. "People are stirred into mortal rebellion by your pious rants about untamed liberty. Deep down, they fear living in a chaotic state of savage freedom. It always leads to wretchedness. People want a different kind of freedom—freedom from risk, consequences, and poverty. I've spent my whole life pursuing that for them."

"Yes, many people want to shed the burden of personal responsibility," J replied. "They want to be free from worry, accountability, and even entropy itself. They want to escape the consequences of their poor choices. They want others to take care of them and to clean up after them. However, that kind of freedom requires forcing other people to serve them. True freedom, which is freedom from coercion, does indeed expose everyone to the personal burden of entropy. All attempts to evade the personal burdens of entropy threaten others with coercion."

"People simply can't handle the harshness of your kind of freedom," said Regis. "They'll starve. They'll be homeless. They'll get abused. They'll be victims. They need us Elites to protect them!"

J coughed several times to clear phlegm from his throat. "The irony of your words is staggering as we stand on the very site where the Union conquest was sealed two centuries ago. The Confederates' flawed argument against freeing the slaves was identical to your modern argument for not allowing *everyone* to be free. You believe that all people are just children who must be protected by benevolent elitists. You treat them as inferior creatures unfit to manage their own lives. Overprotective masters don't prepare people to be competent adults, they train them to be perpetual children."

"It's a dangerous world," replied Regis, as thoughts of Cosimo crept back into his brain. "Pure freedom leads only to an anarchic state of nature ruled by the barbarism of rape, murder, and pillaging."

J nodded. "Then we agree that anarchy can't work. But anarchy isn't Pathless Land's philosophy. True liberty means to be free from attack or coercion by others. That's impossible if people are at the mercy of criminals, conquerors, slave masters, and tyrants. Our national government exists primarily to ensure individual rights, protect property, prevent foreign attacks, and provide a reliable judiciary to settle disputes."

"But people want our equality and security more than they want your freedom," Regis replied. "So we feed, clothe, and shelter them equally. In exchange, we ask only that they comply with our laws and contribute their fair share."

"Is the purpose of life to be fed and housed at the price of submission to exalted Elites?" J asked. "A society can have liberty, or it can have equal outcomes, but it can't have both. Free people with differing skills and ambitions will naturally achieve different outcomes. Enforcing equal outcomes requires massive state intervention. It also discourages ambitious people. That means *all* outcomes will be worse—except those of the overlords."

"But unregulated competition just leads to poverty for most and enrichment of a few," replied Regis. "It's unfair to allow successful people more rewards than others, because society is responsible for all success. People need to cooperate and share, not fight over scraps or preen like peacocks if they think they deserve more."

J shook his head. "Free markets are the most powerful cooperation strategy ever devised. Capitalism yielded the greatest fishes and loaves miracle in history, even though it yields unequal outcomes. Before it, the *entire world* lived in abject poverty for thousands of years. With capitalism, common people achieved lifestyles that only royalty could in the past. Everyone involved is trading away something less valuable than what they're trading for—a trade wouldn't happen unless both parties saw benefit. Free markets incentivize producers to use the fewest resources to yield the greatest output for consumers. Everyone is motivated to work hard, generate ideas, take risks, and innovate. Free markets create bounty, not scraps."

Regis smirked. "We don't care about heartless efficiency. We're not interested in your dog-eat-dog social cannibalism."

J gripped the stand in front of him to steady himself. "Free markets aren't the survival-of-the-fittest Darwinism you mistake them to be. All economic systems involve difficult choices because people have unlimited wants in a world of limited resources. Elitist leaders could make all the choices, or sovereign people could make their own decisions in free markets. Free markets are better, because choices are made without shots being fired or bureaucrats imposing their will."

"The government has to intervene on behalf of the people, or corporations will rule the world," Regis replied. Inwardly, he cringed at his own hypocrisy. The Syndicate appeared to be ruling the world *and* its governments. "You worship economic efficiency as if it's a golden calf. We Elites believe in equality, fairness, and social justice. A strong government is needed to protect people from exploitation."

J sighed. "In a truly free society, businesses can only succeed if they satisfy people with their goods and services. If economic decisions aren't based on efficiency and merit, then they'll be based on bureaucratic coercion, political allegiance, secret intrigues, and government corruption. That's the worst kind of exploitation, because there's no escaping the power of whoever is pulling those strings."

Regis rolled his eyes. "It's better to have a centralized power shepherding society than to let feral corporate dogs run amok, tearing into the throats of the sheep. There's no fairness or justice in free markets! The strong take what they want, and the weak never get what they deserve!" Regis cringed again at his own hypocrisy. The Syndicate was the epitome of the strong taking whatever they wanted.

J's words came haltingly now. "It's impossible for you smug aristocrats to make the right decisions for everyone because you have no objective way to judge what 'better' or 'worse' means to each person, especially when your own interests cloud your motives. The clearest definition of fair and just is what results from a free trade, because it wouldn't happen if either party considered it unfair or unjust. Relying on the state to define fairness and justice is to submit to the arbitrary whims of bureaucrats, tyrants, and schemers. That may be helpful one day, but disastrous the next."

"Would you rather have a wise and powerful leader establish justice or millions of anonymous strangers in unregulated markets?" Regis asked.

"I prefer justice from a jury of my peers," J rasped. "A free market is a karmic feedback system on a wide stage. If you satisfy the needs of others, your peers in the market will reward you. If you provide poor products and services, your peers in the market will shun you. Just as Karma dissuades you from lying, cheating, and stealing in personal relationships, it dissuades you from laziness, poor performance, and bad decisions in market relationships. How well you serve your fellow man determines how well you get served in return, because every person is a producer and consumer. Those who fear the fairness and justice of karmic verdicts are simply admitting they are deficient in what they bring to relationships or to markets."

"How can there be democracy if unregulated markets decide everything?" Regis asked. "Democracy and socialism go hand in hand because they both empower people to collectively decide things."

"True democracy isn't possible *without* free markets," countered J. "The mere act of voting for candidates who've been pre-selected by unseen forces is just a cruel illusion that doesn't constitute democracy. What does the vote of one person cast once every four years mean if the elected leaders and the unelected Deep State rule with unlimited power every hour of every day? It's like trying to bend an oak tree by leveraging a single twig. The most meaningful 'vote' is choosing how to earn and spend your income in a free market by making hundreds of real decisions. Under socialism, people aren't free to make the basic decisions integral to their daily lives. A democracy can choose to become socialistic, but socialism is never a democracy."

Regis chuckled. "People are the sources of their own problems. Leaving them free to make their own decisions is a recipe for disaster."

J grimaced from the pain that was assailing his whole body. "It's true that the world is populated with fallible people, some of whom want to harm others. Our primary challenge is to establish a society where people can freely make their own decisions, safe from ill-intentioned people. Pathless Land is devoted to protecting all citizens from all forms of coercion and violence, whether committed by individuals, groups, or tyrants. Even though people are often the source of their own problems, the worst thing they can do is forfeit their freedom to equally fallible elites who have no real interest in them. Individual ignorance is a problem, but a far bigger problem is the illusion that the Elites are blessed with perfect knowledge and saintly intentions."

Regis' face became rigid. "You keep blathering that people should have the freedom to choose, but guess what? They chose *me*! I was *elected* into this office long ago—before we suspended elections. I promised voters to redistribute from the rich, to support their struggle for social justice, and to protect them from evil corporations. It struck an emotional chord with them."

"Democracy is indeed one of the many paths to fascism," J replied. "The founders of old America feared that a big enough mob of voters would form in a pure democracy to overwhelm individual rights. Franklin said that democracy is two wolves and a lamb voting on what to have for lunch. Without the guaranteed protection of life, liberty, and property, democracy is merely an open invitation for politicians to offer gingerbread houses to voters, in exchange for the authority to control their lives. Fascism grows from the destructive belief that 'right' is whatever the majority say it is, even if it means stealing from an envied class, enslaving another race, or killing a hated faction. Pure democracies will always die violently."

Regis shrugged his shoulders. "If the majority want free things from the government, who's to say that's bad?"

J stared at Regis in disbelief. It was almost as if the president's brain had been taken over by some nefarious force. "Nothing is free in an entropic world. What the government gives with one hand, it must first take with the other. Freedom isn't the democratic privilege to vote for leaders who will then steal from some people and give to others. Freedom is a complete polity in which each sovereign person can choose where they live, where they work, where they shop, where their children go to school, where they worship, who they interact with, and how their earnings get spent."

"The voters gave us Elites a mandate to implement government programs to help the victims," said Regis. "Who are you to oppose the wishes of the people? Who are you to impede the progressive society that's helping them? I'm a hero, not a villain!"

"Dividing society into heroes, villains, and victims will end in disaster. Every faction thinks they're the victims of a villain. No one wants the other side to be in power. The Christians don't want the Jews who don't want the Muslims who don't want the Christians. The conservatives don't want the liberals who don't want the Marxists who don't want the conservatives. There's never agreement about who the villain is, who is being victimized, who the savior should be, or how much power to give that savior. One side's victim is the other side's oppressor. One side's savior is the other side's villain. If we keep fighting over which group should have power and which group should be condemned as villains, there will always be violence. Here's the heart of Pathless Land's philosophy: Coercion is the only villainy. Victimhood is the result of coercion. Saviors should do nothing but eliminate coercion."

"People voted for me and my programs. That's why I'm in power!" Regis cringed once again. There were others who were more powerful than him, but he had to maintain the pretense of his own power in public forums.

"Yes, some people voted for you, long ago," J replied. "But it doesn't matter how tyrants like you gain power. Fascists have gained power through the populism of the ballot box, the spiritual coercion of theocracy, the ancestral blood lines of monarchism, the class warfare of collectivism, and the brute force of gangs. Those are all just conduits for elites to lord over the rest. And it's not always clear who those elites are."

Regis' dark eyes grew large with hate. "You're a fool! To achieve the greatest good for the greatest number, individual desires must be sacrificed to society's needs in a sea of equality. We Elites must have the power and authority to decide what those needs are, and who must make the sacrifices. By definition, we must be more equal than the rest."

"The equal application of laws is the only form of equality that's compatible with liberty," J replied. "It's the only form of equality that can work in a pluralistic society with countless people pursuing their own paths. Christianity taught us that each person is born with intrinsic worth. Judaism taught us that everyone is equal before the law. America's founders taught us that the only moral purpose of government is to safeguard these principles. If the laws of a society treat some people as superior and others as subordinate, there will never be peace."

Regis glanced at his watch in agitation. He now regretted that there were so many witnesses to this event, which wasn't nearly as triumphant as he had hoped. It was also alarming that many of his blackshirts were listening attentively to J's words. But it would be humiliating to retreat now. He returned his attention to J. "Isn't capitalism just a synthesis of corporation and state where rich people abuse workers and the underclass? Aren't big corporations just as power hungry and oppressive as you claim big governments are?"

J cracked a weak smiled at Regis' distress. "Capitalism versus collectivism is a false dichotomy. The real issue is fascism versus freedom."

Regis shook his head in disdain. "The simple truth is that if people are given too much freedom, some will abuse others. That can only be resolved by collectivism, not capitalism."

J's breathing was very shallow now. "In a free society, the markets of capitalism and the communitarianism of collectivism will both emerge naturally. Communitarianism will emerge in the form of families, friends, neighbors, churches, and civic organizations. Markets will form as strangers transact with each other. Both philosophies agree that man is a social animal who thrives when collaborating. In combination, the two philosophies reflect our dual nature—we all yearn to be free as individuals, yet we all yearn to bond in groups. The two philosophies only become 'wrong' when people use them as justification for coercing others to do their bidding. Individuals or businesspeople who coopt the power of government are as wrong as collectivists who coopt the government. The challenge for humanity isn't to demonize freedom *or* communitarianism. The challenge is to constrain governments to their proper role of protecting individual rights so that voluntary social collaboration of all kinds can happen naturally and safely. Our constant conflicts aren't due to capitalism or collectivism per se, they're due to people hijacking the power of government to do their own bidding."

"But we need to prevent rich people from taking advantage of everyone else," Regis said. "Corporations can become powerful enough to force the lower classes into complete subjugation. They can also collude with politicians, bureaucrats, and regulators to corrupt the normal functioning of markets. We have to strip their power and redistribute their wealth." Even as he said these things, Regis understood that he was arguing against the tactics of his own boss.

J's throat was dry and constricted. "A corporation can only become too powerful if government leaders collude with it and sell the rest of us out. Rich people can only become too powerful if government leaders allow themselves to be bought by them. The philosophy of Pathless Land is very simple. People have the right to do as they please with their lives and property. They don't have the right to do as they please with the lives and property of others. Owning the property that you've earned is fundamental to freedom. If you don't, you're at everyone else's mercy, even for the basest needs. All mammals have a clear sense of this. Squirrels hoard nuts for the winter. Dogs protect their territory. Birds defend their nests. All attempts to override this instinct will end badly."

Regis pounded a fist on his desk. "Those vestiges of animal behavior are exactly what we must rise above in an enlightened society! People can't do whatever the hell they want! No one should have more advantage, privilege, or wealth than anyone else, because they come at the expense of others. There must be equality, even if it makes some people worse off! There must be fairness, even if it's unfair to some! There must be justice, even if it's unjust to some!"

"Pathless Land concentrates power at the lowest level of society, allowing people to voluntarily interact with families, friends, communities, and markets according to their deepest desires," replied J. "The karmic suasion inherent in those relationships draws free people together, whereas the fascistic state rips people apart, metastasizing like cancer in castles, courts, and ministries."

"Karma, shmarma. How can governments protect people without using force? Only powerful leaders willing to make difficult decisions can hold society together."

"It's true that people must cede a bit of individual freedom to protect their liberty in the broader sense. Government can be a useful tool in that regard, but the proper path for humanity is to choose political freedom over political force whenever possible. Government should *enable* freedom by protecting civil people from coercive people."

"Society can't allow such freedom, because it leads to division and chaos." Regis protested. "As Lincoln said, 'A house divided against itself cannot stand.' Society must have a rigid structure to enforce the conformity that's necessary for social progress."

"Force blows nations apart, because it's violence of some against others," J declared. "It takes cohesion to hold people together, not force. A nation should be held together by universal principals. If force is needed, its principles are flawed. Small groups should be held together by a common purpose uniting its members. If force is needed, they don't have a common purpose. Individuals should be held together by personal relationship. If force is needed, they don't have a real relationship. Marriages, families, and friendships don't need police, bureaucrats, and armies to function, even though they yield a social order more powerful and durable than all the legislative dictates combined."

Regis raised his arms in exasperation. "How else can a government make people do good if not by force?"

"Your question cuts to the heart of morality," J replied. "A vital essence of morality is to not initiate harm against others. Thou shalt not kill. Thou shalt not lie. Thou shalt not steal. Once these basic building blocks of morality are in place, higher levels of moral behavior become possible, such as generosity, compassion, and forgiveness. This view of morality opposes an overreaching government, which uses force to achieve its ends and harms some people to benefit others."

"You're a hypocrite" said Regis. "Your armies are using force to achieve your ends. Despite all your blather about collaboration, you're a warmonger. You're no better than me. Every freedom fighter who ever overthrew a tyrant has in turn become a tyrant. The proles just exchange yokes. You want to replace my dictatorship with yours!"

"You couldn't be more wrong." replied J. "I'm not going to replace you; I'm going to kill you. My armies will indeed overrun yours, but only to liberate Americans, not to conquer them. There's one path to peace on earth. It runs like a stake through the heart of every secular and theistic tyrant."

Regis smacked his palm on the table. "Your outdated delusions of liberty will be ignored, because my academicians will write the history after you're dead. The past and the future will be as I desire, because I control the present through the schools, the media, and popular culture. You're like Don Quixote, all alone tilting at windmills, thinking you're slaying giants."

"I'm hardly alone," said J. "As our soldiers sweep northward toward Washington, we're freeing millions of people who've been oppressed by the jackbooted thugs of your dwindling empire for far too long. We will avenge your chronic abuses with the last drops of our blood. We're going to start the world anew today by stepping over your dead carcass."

"You're delusional!" Regis fumed. "The believers of your outdated philosophy are dying off. We've filled the pliable minds of today's youth with our ideology. There's no resistance, because they don't know to resist. They share our values, not yours. They believe that justice, fairness, equality, and ecology can only be achieved by an activist government. They associate your unbridled freedom with abuse of women, minorities, the poor, and the environment. They've been immunized against those seditious pamphlets that the damnable White Rose League dumps all over my country."

"I authored those pamphlets," J said proudly, straightening his back as best he could. "You can't quarantine people from the truth forever. Like the Pied Piper of Hamelin, you've led the children into a modern Darkness. But the light is about to shine as the Warriors of Pathless Land end your tyranny."

Regis glared at J. His patience was exhausted. "Enough of your anti-social rants! There are bigger forces at work in the world than you'll ever know."

"And there are bigger surprises in store for you than you can imagine," J shot back.

Regis turned and signaled to an aide. "Let's get on with our prisoner exchange," he announced. "The two children will be here briefly."

A heavy silence filled the crowded room. Dark Moon looked at Dark Sun as she shook with anticipation. Tears filled her reddened eyes. She grabbed his hands and squeezed them tightly. Her heart skipped a few beats.

A door burst open. Three guards entered brusquely, followed by the two children, followed by three more guards.

Cammy's platinum blond hair was perfectly coiffed. She wore the blood-red uniform of the Elites, but every fiber of her being screamed that it didn't belong on her thin frame. She had bruises on her face, a blackened eye, and her jaw was swollen.

She looked about the room wildly, searching for her parents amid the jumble of strangers. Dark Sun's heart stopped when their eyes met. He knew immediately that she was a different person than he had last known in Kansas. He shivered, wondering what horrors she had experienced.

Curious was pushed along in a wheelchair by a guard. He also wore the uniform of the Elites. He looked weak, frightened, and in great pain. He had a swollen forehead. His eyes never strayed from his sister —until he heard his mother scream his name.

Dark Moon's scream triggered pandemonium. Guards swooped in to keep the parties separated. There were shouts from all directions, and intense scuffling as everyone jostled for position. Regis yelled above the din, "Enough! This is not how good socialists behave! The prisoner exchange must be made in an orderly manner. I'm in control here!"

The chaos subsided as the guards from both contingents restored order. J stepped forward and said to Regis, "Take me prisoner and free my grandchildren. Then let history proceed as it will."

"As you wish." Regis signaled to his guards. Two burly henchmen approached J, wrenched his arms behind his back, and applied handcuffs. Regis nodded toward the soldiers restraining Curious and Cammy. "Release them."

The soldiers stepped aside. Suddenly, after months of heartrending tribulations, nothing separated Dark Sun and Dark Moon from their children. Dark Moon flew first to her injured son. She kissed his face again and again, tasting the salty tears on his cheeks. She sobbed uncontrollably.

Curious wrapped his frail arms around her as best he could, oblivious to the onlookers, the drama, and the rest of existence. Life was pared to its core in that moment, and in that core was only love.

Cammy threw her arms around Dark Moon, hugging her tightly. Dark Sun threw his arms around his whole family. They became a ball of humanity, four people desperately caring for each other.

Regis squirmed uncomfortably seeing the tidal wave of sympathy for the reunited family, even from his own hardened Praetorian Guard. He thought it rather disloyal of them to acknowledge the outmoded emotions of stray individuals.

"Do you have any last wishes?" he asked J, interrupting the maudlin scene.

J carried himself with a strange serenity that belied the tension in the room. "I wish to hug my son goodbye."

"Do it quickly!" Regis barked.

Dark Sun rushed to his father and hugged him as if the embrace could somehow negate his rueful fate. "Thank you," he whispered to his father, nodding toward Cammy and Curious. "Your gift is priceless. We can never repay you."

"I'm paid in full," J said. "Your family's love for each other affirms my entire life. This is my grandest moment. Carry the torch of Pathless Land proudly."

Before Dark Sun could reply, Regis's thugs grabbed J by the arms and dragged him violently toward the door. J struggled against them just enough to turn and glare at Regis. "Sic Semper Tyrannis!" he shouted.

And then he was gone.

FIFTY-THREE
TREACHERY

> With the howl of a thousand wolves
> Treachery rode on thunderous hooves
> Just when glorious victory was at hand
> It slipped through my fingers like sand
>
> — *The Poems of Dark Sun*

A mad scramble erupted in the McLean House.
Regis, fearing an assassination attempt, charged toward the door, sandwiched by his Praetorian guard.

J's soldiers were under orders to stand down from any conflict with the Elites, unless to protect J's family from direct attack. They shielded the huddled family while Regis's minions bulled their way out of the tight quarters.

After the Elites fled, J's guards escorted Dark Sun's family outside. They saw the last of Regis's entourage pile into a convoy of military vehicles that had started to snake northward toward Washington. The family and their guards clambered into PLA vehicles that were idling nearby. Their convoy headed west toward Lynchburg. They could see the low silhouette of the purple Appalachians in the distance beyond the pine-covered hills.

The ride was bittersweet for Dark Sun. He was thrilled beyond words to be reunited with his children. His heart sang as Dark Moon babbled motherly words of love and comfort to Cammy and Curious between spasm-filled sobs. But the joy of their reunion was tempered by the fate of his father. He also worried about the injuries to Curious, which included a battered face and a broken leg. He worried even more that something awful had transformed Cammy. A profound sorrow haunted her eyes. Her tears were borne of mourning rather than joy, as if something unspeakable had happened during captivity.

Dark Sun had learned in the past few months that such bittersweet thoughts were quite normal. Life hangs in a tenuous balance in an entropic world. Joy and sadness are inextricably linked. There can't be one without the other, much like the Taoist yin and yang represented by two serpents eating each other's tails. To live is to toil and encounter misfortune. The motivation to endure such hardship is the joy that results from achievements and relationships.

In such an existence, stealing joy from someone by coercion or oppression is the most unholy evil imaginable. It would be like the dark Taoist snake completely swallowing the light one. It would erase the positive side of life's spiritual ledger and leave only the negative. There would be no comedy to counter tragedy or no blessing to offset disaster. Someone had stolen Cammy's joy, collapsing her into a cold, dark shell. Dark Sun silently vowed to kill the thief.

The line of PLA vehicles turned south when it reached Lynchburg, near the courthouse where they had confronted Kieran and Katarina earlier. As soon as the convoy changed direction, Dark Moon abruptly stopped fussing over Curious and Cammy and looked apprehensively out the window. Disoriented and alarmed, she spun toward Dark Sun. "Where are we going?!"

"To the PLA field headquarters in Danville."

"Why? It's out of our way! We need to head west to meet up with the Eagles."

"Moonbeam, there's no going back," said Dark Sun calmly, although he knew a furious storm was about to blow his way. "Our future is with Pathless Land. I promised my Father."

"You what?!" Dark Moon's face turned purple with rage.

"I'm sorry . . . I . . . I was sworn to secrecy."

"Stop this vehicle now!" Dark Moon pounded on the door separating their compartment from the driver, Sergeant Hernandez.

The vehicle skidded to an abrupt stop, bringing the entire convoy to a halt. Dark Moon opened the rear door and jumped to the ground. "Everybody out!" she barked, oblivious in her anger to the fact that Curious was crippled.

"Moonbeam—" Dark Sun pleaded with open arms in the doorway.

"How dare you?!" she screamed as he sheepishly disembarked from the vehicle.

Before Dark Sun could reply, a wave of fighter jets screamed overhead from the south, skimming the treetops and raking the landscape with hot exhaust. Dark Moon and Dark Sun instinctively ducked. Another wave of fighter jets flew over and then another. Seven more waves of warplanes thundered overhead in rapid succession.

"What's happening?" Dark Moon shouted above the din.

Dark Sun stared morosely in the direction of the receding planes. Tears poured down his cheeks. He shouted "Sic semper tyrannis!" into the wind, spewing defiance against some unseen foe in the distance.

Dark Moon momentarily forgot her anger about the convoy's change in destination, sensing that something even more apocalyptic was afoot. "What's going on?!"

Dark Sun looked at her with reddened eyes as a series of sharp explosions shook the ground like aftershocks from an earthquake. "Dad's plan is unfolding," he said in a quivering voice. "Those PLA jets are bombing the Elites' convoy. They're killing Regis and his entourage."

"But . . . Regis and your dad are in the same convoy." The color washed out of Dark Moon's face.

"That's true," said Dark Sun with infinite sadness. More explosions rocked the earth like a Fourth of July fireworks finale. The northern skyline glowed a furious orange. "He's probably already dead."

Dark Moon looked at him in horror. "My God! What have you done?"

Dark Sun stared with macabre fascination at the pyrotechnics raging beyond the hills. "This is the culmination of Dad's plan. He wanted our children returned to us. He wanted Regis dead. He's sacrificing his life to make both happen. In return, he wants us to join Pathless Land and help destroy the Elites. That's why we're heading to Danville rather than Kansas."

Dark Moon shook her head slowly, her eyes wide and her mouth agape. Dark Sun continued. "My father lured the Elites into a trap. Regis would assume he was safe during the prisoner exchange, because he had our children as hostages going into Appomattox and my father as a hostage on the way out. He also would assume that the PLA forces wouldn't attack him while father was captive in his convoy, because Pathless Land treats the life of each citizen as a sacred trust. They would never kill their own leader. Father figured Regis would be so certain of these advantages that he wouldn't expect the PLA forces to act just like the treacherous mercenaries of the Elites, who hold no concern for the individual lives of their people. In effect, my father killed Regis with the Elites' own corrupt philosophy, at the very moment when Regis felt protected by the presumed moral conviction of Pathless Land. Dad loved irony."

Dark Moon continued to shake her head in bewilderment. "You shouted 'Sic semper tyrannis.' Your father shouted that too when he was dragged from the Mclean House. What does it mean?"

"Thus always to tyrants. Brutus shouted it when he killed Caesar."

Dark Moon was dizzied by the swirl of cataclysmic events. She was desperate to latch onto something firm, safe, and familiar. "I don't care what you promised your father. We're going back to Kansas. We can rebuild our home. We can—"

"The Elites will just destroy it again! They'll want revenge for today. We have to fight them like my father did. And even if the Elites don't retaliate, the Caliphate and the Jackals are slowly moving toward Kansas."

More rumbles came from the north. These reverberations were markedly different from the earth-rending booms of the PLA bombs. The ominous sounds interrupted their conversation. They glanced nervously to the north. Sergeant Hernandez shouted that they needed to get moving. They ignored him.

"My home is a farm in Kansas," Dark Moon said firmly. "I want to raise our children there. That's my life. We'll be safe."

"Get back in the vehicle!" Hernandez shouted, this time with manic urgency.

Dark Sun waved him off, consumed by the pivotal debate with his wife. "Moonbeam! No place is safe in a world run by the Elites. The bastards kidnapped our children from Kansas! They blew up our home! They captured my father there and exiled him to Outcast Island! They're not going to forget his treachery today. When fascists are on the hunt, there's nowhere to hide."

Dark Moon shook her head vigorously and took a confused step toward the vehicle. "I'm a mother, not a fighter. I just want to protect my kids."

The rumbling from the north suddenly became more intense. They snapped their heads in that direction and saw a fleet of military vehicles cresting a nearby hill. They recognized the dreaded insignia of the Elites just as a hail of bullets tore into the snowy ground in front of them. Dark Sun hoisted Dark Moon into the armored personnel carrier. He leapt in behind her as bullets raked its plating.

"They're going to kill us!" shouted Dark Sun. "I knew those bastards would come after us!"

"They're avenging Regis' assassination," reasoned Dark Moon as gunfire erupted all around them. PLA soldiers maneuvered into position and launched rifle and rocket-propelled grenade salvos against the onrushing aggressors.

"That's impossible!" exclaimed Dark Sun. "The PLA jets just dropped their bombs. These attackers probably don't even know Regis is dead. They planned this ambush!"

"As did your father against Regis."

Before Dark Sun could defend his father's honor, a mortar shell slammed into their vehicle. The explosion lifted the APC into the air and spun it 180 degrees before it crashed to the ground. The occupants were tossed like bowling pins, ricocheting violently against the unyielding walls and ceiling. Dark Sun was dazed and bleeding from a blow to his head. His ears were temporarily deafened from the concussion of the blast. Smoke filled the vehicle. He smelled fire.

"Everyone out!" Hernandez shouted into the rear compartment. Dark Sun couldn't hear, but the sergeant's urgent gesticulations snapped him out of his fog. Both men groped in the smoke for survivors. Dark Sun's hands found Dark Moon's prone body. She writhed in pain, which meant she was alive. He carried her out the door and set her on the snowy ground away from the burning vehicle. Hernandez carried Cammy out and set her down beside Dark Moon. She screamed her brother's name in terror. Even though they were freed from their jail cell, they weren't free from their tormentors.

Dark Sun plunged back into the burning vehicle to rescue Curious. Flames licked at him from all directions. Oily smoke blinded his eyes and burned his throat. His heart skipped a beat when his hands found his son's wheelchair in the inky darkness, but the elation lasted for only a split second. The wheelchair was lying on its side. It was empty.

He shoved it aside and continued probing. Dread blackened his soul. He thrashed madly around the compartment. Scorching heat tortured every inch of his exposed skin. He shouted, "Curious! Curious!"

If there was a reply, he couldn't hear it. The nauseating smell of his blistering skin blended with the acrid smell of gunpowder and burning fuel. Starved for oxygen, he became disoriented. His rage to find

Curious was fading into unconsciousness. Then, as if in a slow-motion nightmare, two strong arms from some other dimension grabbed his feet and dragged his body from the sulfurous smoke to fresh air outside.

Hernandez set him near Dark Moon and Cammy. The sergeant headed back for another desperate attempt to rescue Curious, but the vehicle exploded into a giant ball of flames. The shock wave tumbled him onto the snowy ground. Shrapnel buzzed over their heads. "Curious!" Dark Sun screamed one last time, then his mind went black.

He regained consciousness moments later, but his surreal nightmare continued unabated. A pitched battle raged all around. PLA soldiers returned the gunfire of the ambushers from behind a defensive arc of disabled vehicles. Dark Sun spotted Kerry, who was spraying bullets into a hillside obscured by smoke and falling snow. Dark Moon was doing the same, a few yards further away. Cammy was also firing a rifle, even though its recoil shook her body violently.

Kerry noticed that Dark Sun was conscious. He paused his fusillade to retrieve a rifle from a dead PLA soldier. He threw it toward Dark Sun and shouted, "Use this, if you want to survive!"

Kerry's admonition triggered a burst of sanity into Dark Sun's delirium. His head was pounding, his ears were ringing, and his body was aflame with pain. His skin felt like it was melting off his hands and face. But he forced himself to ignore his afflictions. He grabbed the rifle and began shooting indiscriminately into the haze beyond their perimeter. With each pull of the trigger, he called out, "For my father!" or "For my son!" He was hypnotized by overwhelming anger.

A bullet whizzed by his head, stirring a light puff of heated air as it crackled past. The close brush with the projectile nudged him even closer to psychopathy. The caustic realization of Curious' gruesome death and the anguish of his father's massacre devoured his sanity. He regretted that the projectile missed, because it would have ended his nightmare. In the darkest hours, sometimes the only tolerable path seems to be extinction.

Then Cammy turned to look at him. Dark Moon glanced at him with grave concern. It was as if they both sensed his existential crisis.

He didn't know if Dark Moon knew that Curious was killed in the explosion. If she did, she remained remarkably focused on survival. Her resolve reminded him that their losses could be mourned later, but nothing would matter if they didn't survive this battle. In his daughter's tormented blue eyes, and in the telepathic love of his wife's worried glance, he realized that even the most sorrowful life can have purpose. The goblins of despair receded. He resumed firing at the enemy with renewed vigor.

The combatants were locked in a bloody impasse. Grenades and mortar shells had disabled the vehicles of both factions, rendering the smoldering hulks as nothing but shields protecting the soldiers from incoming bullets and frontal assaults. Both sides hunkered down, pinning each other with sniper fire and random fusillades. The sound of gunfire was deafening. Explosions rocked the earth. The sulfurous smell of gunpowder hung in the air. Bodies fell to the ground on both sides. The snow beneath them turned crimson.

The skirmish was a miniature version of the trench-warfare stalemates of WWI in Western Europe. Neither side could overrun the other because of the protective barricades. Neither side could afford to give ground because they would lose the protection of their barricades.

The intractability of the situation dawned on Kerry. He frantically surveyed the battlefield for an opening to end the stalemate. All he saw were fewer soldiers than they started with. He tried his radio several times, and then angrily threw it into the snow. No reinforcements were coming. All PLA units in the area were deployed in the attack on Regis' convoy. The platoon protecting Dark Sun and his family was running low on soldiers, ammunition, and hope.

A rogue gust of wind swooshed across the landscape, momentarily breaching the wall of oily smoke that otherwise shrouded the battlefield. In the breach, Dark Sun glimpsed something bizarre cresting the hill to the north behind the entrenched positions of the Elites. At first, he couldn't tell if he was hallucinating. But as the phantasm raced toward them through the cleft in the battlefield haze, it became more distinct and more real.

An ATV was towing a covered wagon painted with psychedelic colors. It was followed by an armored personnel carrier. The vehicles were barreling down a slope on Highway 29 toward the undefended rear of the Elites. The rest of the PLA forces must have spotted the unusual scene too, because they all stopped shooting and gawked.

Then it hit Dark Sun like a sledgehammer. The onrushing ATV was the one Verax had driven yesterday to track down Fatima and the rest of the Eagles. The covered wagon was from Osiris's gypsy caravan. The APC was the one that Kerry had assigned to accompany Verax. Verax and the soldiers must have driven through the night to meet up with Fatima and then with Osiris.

The vehicles stopped abruptly. People tumbled out to the snowy ground with guns levelled. Dark Sun recognized Ruby's red hair, Verax's hulking frame, and Osiris' wind-tossed dreadlocks. At least ten others poured from the vehicles and arrayed themselves in a firing line.

Once they saw the uniforms and the insignias of the Elites, the new arrivals knew which side was the enemy in this battle. They unleashed a torrent of bullets toward the unprotected rear of the Elites' barricaded position.

The ragtag cavalry had the element of surprise against an enemy that was completely exposed to them. It was human target practice for Hawkeye and the other deadly sharpshooters. The Elites screamed in terror, scattering pell-mell from their barricades. The battlefield became a cacophony of gunfire and shrieks of men scrambling for their lives in the crossfire. There was nowhere to run. When the last of them collapsed to the ground, the gunfire ceased. An eerie calm settled over the battlefield. No one moved.

The survivors pondered the hellish scene in a state of exhausted shock. The sudden calm unleashed a stark accounting in Dark Sun's brain. The past few hours had torn his world asunder. His father and Curious were dead. Cammy was rescued, but something horrible had happened to her. Dark Moon had refused to join him in Pathless Land. He had promised to fight in a revolution alongside a half-brother who was mostly a stranger to him. The leaders of the Elites and of

Pathless Land were both dead, leaving his unfamiliar new world in chaos.

His mind went completely numb. When someone is afflicted with a long series of tragedies, the impact of each new disaster becomes strangely muted. Without the counterbalance of occasional joy, there's nothing to distinguish tragedy from normalcy.

Dark Sun glanced over at Dark Moon. She was standing fifty yards away, covered in snow, soot, and blood. She looked at him in the same moment. They gazed at each other in stony silence. Through this window to her soul, he sensed several things immediately. She knew about Curious. Her world was torn asunder just like his. And she wasn't the same woman she had been an hour ago.

Dark Moon dropped her gun and slowly trudged toward him. Dark Sun dropped his gun and plodded toward her. Cammy staggered numbly behind Dark Moon, lost in her own traumatized mindscape.

The three came together in a corpse-strewn field near Lynchburg, in a country that had lost its moral compass, on a blue-green planet that was ravaged by totalitarianism and inhabited by people unable to live in peace.

For a brief moment, none of that mattered. They had each other. And somehow, as they embraced in the falling snow, commingling their blood and their tears, that was enough. It had to be.

They clung together in a way that the vilest demons could never tear apart.

FIFTY-FOUR
INTERDEPENDENCE

> Truth is plain for us to see
> We are one in our humanity
>
> — *The Poems of Dark Sun*

Dark Moon gingerly kissed Dark Sun's seared hands. He welcomed the soothing brush of her cold lips. The simple gesture broke their spell of despair. She inspected his body for other injuries. She wiped blood from his cheek and flecks of ashes from his singed beard. Her silent ministrations were the most human thing possible in the wake of their trauma.

"I'm sorry," Dark Sun murmured.

She continued fussing over him without responding.

"I'm sorry," he repeated, a bit louder this time.

She ignored him again.

"Can you hear me, Moonbeam?" With rising anxiety, he wondered if her hearing was damaged by the explosion of the APC. He looked into her eyes. He saw a haunting tapestry of sorrow and pain. And he saw another emotion he couldn't quite discern.

"I can hear you," she replied softly.

"I was wrong to insist that we join Pathless Land," he said. "There's nothing but violence here. We'll go back to Kansas. We'll rebuild our home. We'll farm again."

"No!" she snapped. She clenched her teeth, and her eyes were aflame. Cammy looked up at her with trepidation. Were her parents about to add to her turmoil? They were her last refuge in a fragile world.

Dark Sun was jolted a half step back. It was as if something had taken over Dark Moon's personality. She suddenly had a fiery determination not to be denied by anyone or anything. It was the same unyielding fortitude he had seen in his father's eyes when he was explaining his morbid plan.

"We're not going back to Kansas!" she exclaimed with blood-red fury. "They killed my little boy! They traumatized my beautiful Cammy! No child on this planet is safe from those monsters. Their savagery will never end until mothers wake from their slumber to destroy them! This is my war now! And I'll win this fucking war, because none of those bastards will ever hurt as bad as I do! They're going to pay for what they did to us!"

Dark Sun was stunned. "An hour ago, you wanted to get away from all of this—"

"I was blind to the deeper truth of this hellish world. Demons are fucking up innocent people. I'll find whoever they are. Every single one of them. Mothers can't protect their children by hiding. I'm going to fight evil head on!"

Cammy hugged her mother. The same fire burned in her own soul. It was how Sophie should have confronted her vile world when she had a chance. Waiting for the blackshirts to come was a futile strategy.

The gypsy cavalry slowly gathered around the devastated family. They stood mute, horrified by the carnage around them. After a few moments of silence, Osiris gently asked what happened. Kerry somberly chronicled the epic debate between J and Regis at the McLean House, J's suicidal strategy to kill Regis, and the ambush by the Elites that Osiris and the cavalry had fortuitously ended.

A fleet of PLA military vehicles approached from the north in tardy response to Kerry's earlier pleas for help. The troops were freed up after completing the annihilation of Regis and his key ministers. The rest of the PLA forces in Virginia were maneuvering toward Richmond to prepare for an assault on Washington.

The reinforcements combed the landscape for survivors. They stretchered the injured into vehicles for evacuation to the M.A.S.H. facility in Danville. Several APCs were commandeered as hearses for the many dead PLA soldiers.

During the search for survivors, the soldiers found the grisly remains of Curious inside the shell of the exploded APC. His savaged body lay tantalizingly close to the mangled wheelchair that Dark Sun had tossed aside during his failed rescue attempt. The soldiers solemnly summoned the family.

Dark Moon and Cammy chose not to come. Dark Sun followed the soldiers—he had failed to save his son and couldn't hide from his responsibility. The sight of his son's mutilated body ripped at his heart. His ten years living with his beautiful son had been vaporized in an instant. The stark horror of the scene transformed him. He saw with startling clarity why Dark Moon had changed her mind. He felt the same burning hot rage.

A part of him died. A part of them all had died. Their family would never be the same. The death of a child is so offensive to the natural order of life that there's no sane way to comprehend it. No parent should have to endure it. He rejoined Cammy and Dark Moon and hugged them. The three of them sobbed pitifully, lost in a world of seething pain that shouldn't exist. This awful moment would haunt them forever.

When the soldiers finished their battlefield triage, the convoy departed for Danville. There, the injured were hustled to the M.A.S.H. unit, and the dead were routed to a morgue. The Eagles and gypsies showered and changed into fresh clothing provided by their hosts. They were assigned tents in which to bunk. Most of them napped, succumbing to emotional and physical exhaustion.

Later that evening, they were treated to a private dinner by officers of Pathless Land. Dark Sun and his family, Fatima and the Eagles, and Osiris and his warriors gathered for food and drink in the mess tent.

The mood was very somber, so Osiris mingled among them with gentle reminders of how the gypsies had recovered from the trauma of the Caliphate attack in Indiana. He pointed out that choosing joy over sorrow was as important as choosing good over evil.

His persistent urgings awakened in them a profound need for emotional catharsis after the day's devastating events. His contagious spirit inspired them to embrace fullness and light rather than pain and darkness. In the tragicomedy of life, the only way to tip the scale toward sanity is to laugh, even in the face of disaster. A person can handle only so much grief.

As their moods lifted, they recounted the incredible events that transpired during their separations from each other. There were humorous tales, frightening tales, tales of bravery, and tales of sadness. Their bittersweet accounts wove fresh threads into the tapestry of their friendships. Their sorrow gradually receded into the background. Camaraderie and laughter moved to the fore as more and more wine flowed. Despite their many losses, important victories had been won. J was killed, but so was Regis. Curious was gone, but Cammy was saved. The gypsies were now reunited, and Pathless Land was emerging as a shining beacon of hope. They toasted their successes and the memories of those they had lost.

As the party enlivened, Dark Sun and Dark Moon wandered to an empty table in a corner of the large tent, alone with their sadness. Their losses were too overwhelming for celebration. Cammy followed them and cradled her head in her arms on the table, lost in a dark world all her own. Dark Moon rubbed her back and quietly shed tears.

Dark Sun drained another glass of wine and silently reminisced about the fleeting snippet of time he had spent with his father. With a start, he recalled that his dad had handed him something important outside Appomattox. He fumbled in his jacket and pulled out the parchments.

The scroll was scorched along its edges and stained with dried blood. He slapped it on the table, drawing the attention of Osiris and others chatting nearby. Intrigued, Osiris sat down next to the family. "What's that?" he asked.

"My father handed it to me before going into the McLean House. He said it was the treasure of Pathless Land. It just looks like sheets of paper to me."

Others crowded around the table, sensing that something interesting was developing. Kerry broke the hush that had suddenly fallen over the mess tent. "They're more than just sheets of paper, just like Jefferson's *Declaration* when copies were posted in colonial Philadelphia. That scroll is the Rosetta Stone of Pathless Land's philosophy."

Dark Sun's heart quickened. He unbound the red, blue, and purple ribbons binding the parchments and flattened the coiled sheets on the table.

"Read it to us!" pled Osiris, anxious to finally learn about the fabled Outcast treasure that was the subject of so many rumors.

Dark Sun picked up the first sheet. He began reading, his voice catching with emotion as he narrated words crafted by his father.

A Declaration of Free Interdependence
By
Pathless Land of America

On the 12th day of December in the year 2072, this *Declaration of Free Interdependence* was ratified by representatives of a new republic,

Pathless Land of America. It is our blueprint for peace, security, and prosperity.

Preamble

Human history is a soul-searing litany of tyranny, wretchedness, slavery, war, subjugation, and genocide. Contempt for the sanctity of human life has yielded unremitting barbarism and cruel oppression that infuriate the pure conscience. Innocent people have been continually assaulted by the covetousness, superstitions, prejudices, dogmas, aggressions, and ideologies of others.

Governments have not only failed to prevent these abuses, they have often abetted them. The multitudes of common people have been forever ravaged by secular and theocratic tyrants imposing themselves on everyone else. Our desperate yearnings for Justice and Peace cry out for a fresh and rational approach.

We are sovereign individuals who desire the benefits of society. We seek to ensure justice, provide for the common defense, and promote individual accountability. Our goal is to secure the blessings of free collaboration for ourselves and for our posterity.

Our new republic is conceived in liberty, committed to lasting peace on Earth, and dedicated to protecting the equal and unalienable rights of *all* people in our society.

We acknowledge that a perfect Utopia is impossible. We live in an entropic world where malevolent events naturally occur, where fallible people make mistakes, where villains torment others, and where everyone vies for scarce resources.

In light of this turmoil, a vital role of government is to protect the lives and rights of our citizens. We are consecrating a society in which people can freely choose their own paths, safe from others who may try to harm them or steal from them.

We endeavor to protect *all* citizens from *all* forms of coercion and violence, whether committed by individuals, by groups, or by governments. We believe that the only way to eliminate tribalism and the superficial divisiveness of skin color, creeds, and cultures is to unite around universal principles.

The motto of Pathless Land is our North Star: "Neither coerce nor be coerced."

Truths

We hold these Truths to be consistent with the nature of Humans and of Reality:

1. **WE LIVE IN AN ENTROPIC UNIVERSE.** Existence is ordered by transcendent laws. Among these, Entropy imposes on every individual the burden and responsibility to continually strive for survival and happiness.
2. **WE ARE COLLABORATIVE BEINGS.** To survive and thrive, we rationally engage in mutual trade, defense, customs, language, affection, and sharing of knowledge to further our self-interests.
3. **PEOPLE HAVE FREE WILL.** Every person has volitional consciousness, which gives rise to individual responsibility and moral agency. We are each the sum of our decisions and the consequences thereof.
4. **PEOPLE PREFER BETTER OVER WORSE.** People, acting according to their own judgment and values, will choose actions intended to yield better rather than worse outcomes. Protecting their freedom to do so is the keystone of morality in Pathless Land.
5. **WE ARE GUIDED BY KARMA.** Personal relationships are guided by social feedback that encourages trust, respect, honesty, generosity, and common sense. Transactional relationships are guided by market feedback that encourages efficiency, innovation, and proper resource valuation. Present Self is guided by the anticipated

judgment of Future Self, which encourages personal integrity and accountability.

6. **PEOPLE ARE UNIQUE.** People differ in their abilities, aspirations, and efforts. Thus, a free society will naturally yield unequal outcomes. It is impossible to have a free society and equal outcomes.

7. **EACH CITIZEN IS SOVEREIGN**. We endow *all* citizens with the rights to choose their actions, to enjoy the benefits thereof, and to think and believe as they wish, so long as they observe the similar rights of others. We consider all forms of coercion to be immoral.

8. **THERE IS AN OBJECTIVE REALITY.** Truth can only be validated by the free and continual exchange and testing of ideas, not by the immutable dictates of fallible leaders and institutions.

9. **PEOPLE ARE IMPERFECT.** Fallible people often choose to coerce others due to weak character or the influence of mysticism, collectivism, elitism, or bigotry. We are establishing this society and forming this government to achieve mutual protection from such aggression.

10. **GOVERNMENTS ARE CREATED BY PEOPLE.** Our government derives its limited powers from a Constitution ordained by citizens who have the unalienable rights of reformation and revolution. Laws established for practical governance should be few, simple, widely known, and equally applied. They should protect rather than harm our unalienable rights. They should ensure that political power remains uncorrupted by venal influence.

Dark Sun silently scanned the remaining parchments that included a detailed constitution. The last page was crowded with numerous signatures. A large capital J was scrawled in their midst, identical to the bold signature that ended his father's first journal.

Tears formed in Dark Sun's eyes. He sighed and glanced up at his tantalized audience. "It's a long document. I'll pass it around for you to read."

Osiris was the first to reach for it. When he finished a quick read, he realized with a start that he had always been much nearer to this treasure than he realized. His philosophy was like that of Pathless Land. All his gypsies lacked were a written constitution and a strong enough military to back it up.

"This is a vision worth fighting for!" he declared. He passed the parchments to Fatima, and then looked at Kerry. "Ever since I was in college, I've wanted a world where people of all races and religions could be treated with respect. I went about it the wrong way back then, but I've since learned many lessons. I fully embrace what you Outcasts are trying to do. I'd like to help spread your vision, but I might be too old now."

"We're the Warriors of Pathless Land," Kerry said stiffly. "And if anyone else is considering volunteering to help, it's time for full disclosure. Our quest is going to get more difficult. We eliminated Regis, but there are many tyrant-wannabes among the Elites eager to replace him. They'll be tempted to do anything to defend their dwindling domain, including using nuclear weapons. They've sent emissaries to other totalitarian leaders around the world to seek reinforcements. They've also sent emissaries to Timur of the Caliphate and El Chapo of the Jackals. They're trying to form an alliance of cutthroats, because we're an existential threat to them all."

"That's all?" asked Osiris with mock confidence.

"No," replied Kerry grimly. "There's some other evil afoot in the world. It's bigger than particular governments and tyrants. Our spies have been trying to penetrate it, but it's elusive as hell. My father wanted to ignore it because he preferred to fight obvious enemies like the Elites and the Caliphate. This vile entity is darker and more secretive. It's like a virus that can't be seen, but its effects are inescapable. We're not sure what this monster is or how to defeat it."

Osiris frowned. "How do you fight a ghost like that?"

Kerry shrugged. "We have powerful allies. Millions of people are eager to cast off their overlords after decades of submission. They're exhausted by the Darkness, the lies, the destitution, and the humiliation. They're giving us waves of support as we liberate town after town in old America. Like the first American Revolution, this is a war of the people, by the people, and for the people. And losing is not an option. Now that I've made my disclaimers, I'd be thrilled if any of you volunteered to help."

Osiris frowned again. "My mind is willing, but my heart is with my tribe. I'll have to sleep on it."

Kerry smiled. "Having seen the cohesive society you created with your diverse band of gypsies, I believe you'd fit perfectly in the culture of Pathless Land. It too was crafted by a band of misfits in a cauldron of chaos. My father would have admired you."

Osiris nodded, then looked off into the distance. Conversation bubbled about Kerry's dire warnings as the *Declaration* was circulated for everyone to read. He looked around the tent, pleased with the positive energy inspired by the keystone document of Pathless Land.

More wine was poured. The festive spirit gradually resumed for everyone except Dark Sun and his family. The celebration lasted deep into the night. The laughter, the music, and the glow of friendship were a cathartic bridge of hope from past to future.

Eventually, exhaustion set in. One by one, people meandered off to their assigned tents.

But there would be no sleep for many of them that night.

FIFTY-FIVE

APOCALYPSE

> We are opposed around the world by a monolithic and ruthless conspiracy. It relies on infiltration instead of invasion, subversion instead of elections, intimidation instead of free choice. Its preparations are concealed, not published. Its mistakes are buried, not headlined. Its dissenters are silenced, not praised.
>
> — President John F. Kennedy

The World Order building, which overlooked the East River from Manhattan, was locked down on a snowy December afternoon.

The international delegations that usually haunted the building had fled to safer havens because of Pathless Land's advancing armies. Or perhaps they had finally realized that their long history of feckless speeches and byzantine intrigues were useless in the face of surreptitious forces that were bolder and more cunning.

The lockdown was also a security measure for an emergency meeting of the World Order's Security Council scheduled for tomorrow. Two powerful titans were already in the Security Council chambers. The early arrivals sat in the semi-circular array of otherwise empty blue seats reserved for the fifteen member nations of the Council.

"I'm losing faith in you," said Six ominously in his Slavic accent. The room temperature seemed to drop with his utterance.

Cosimo shivered, then nervously toyed with the snake-encircled ring on his right hand. Six was his boss. He was one of the ten Hidden Hands in the Syndicate's secretive leadership circle called the Deka. Whenever Six met with someone, the room was darkened to preserve his anonymity. Cosimo could only see the man's looming silhouette. He had never gotten a good look at him.

Six had demanded this extraordinary meeting. The assassination of Regis, and the subsequent chaos among the surviving Elite leaders, spooked the Deka. They were worried that control of the world was slipping through their fingers. Pathless Land had proven to be a far more formidable threat than anticipated.

"Failure to obliterate Pathless Land will be terminal for you," continued Six without emotion. He rarely spoke to anyone outside of the Deka. He communicated almost everything with simple gestures or a few pointed words. Cosimo knew that it was a bad sign if he said a lot. He had already spoken more than usual, and their discussion had just begun. It was also a bad sign that Six had traveled all the way to America to meet with him. The secretive oligarch didn't like to be inconvenienced, and a price was usually paid by whoever caused it.

"Of course, your excellency," replied Cosimo as he nodded submissively. Despite the mortal pressure he was feeling, he was exhilarated to regain control of his fate after Regis's excruciating failures. He was spoiling for a fight.

While he waited for Six to make his intentions clear, Cosimo gave silent thanks to the deceased J. The Outcast leader had saved him the trouble of disposing of Regis. But the PLA assault on Washington was now more intense than ever, which belied Regis's naïve belief that J's death would end the rebellion. Cosimo knew that the rebel scourge was like a relentless beast from a B-grade movie. It wasn't enough to cut off its head. Every trace of its body and DNA had to be destroyed, or else the inspiration of a new Pericles, a new Cicero, a new Jefferson, or a new J would spread like contagion among the proles.

"What will the Security Council be told tomorrow?" Six asked from within the shadow that shrouded his face.

"What they already know," replied Cosimo. "They have no choice but to join the fight against the Outcasts. If Pathless Land conquers America, the twenty-first century will simply be a rerun of the twentieth century. America will topple global totalitarians like dominos, just like they did in the world wars and the Cold War. That would be bad for the Syndicate, and bad for every world leader we've propped up. Tomorrow we'll propose a formal Chapter VII resolution calling for an international assault on Pathless Land."

Six's silhouette shrugged. "Even if the other nations ratify it, it will take time for them to deploy their militaries. In the meantime, the Outcasts are massing in Richmond for a final assault on Washington."

Cosimo, sensing that Six had little patience left, quickly jumped to his fallback plan. "My influencers are already lining up support from the other factions here in America. A grand alliance with them will turn the tide against the rebels."

Six grunted disdainfully. "But the Elites are fighting a civil war against those factions—a war that you started."

Cosimo flushed. Six was clearly taking note of his missteps. "After today, the Elites will only be at war with one faction—the Outcasts."

"But the Elites have nothing in common with the other factions!" exclaimed Six with a rare burst of emotion. He regretted giving Cosimo so much free rein over the years. It dawned on him that he needed to quickly learn more about the quirks of American politics and culture, because his star centurion was making a mess of things. "Why would anarchists like the Jackals agree to an alliance with authoritarians?"

"They'll fall in line," said Cosimo with as much assurance as he could muster. "El Chapo became one of the richest men on Earth by peddling death in the form of cocaine, heroin, and meth. My Influencers explained to him this morning that if the Outcasts win, the plundering by his gangsters will come to a violent end. He understood immediately. Just like we in the Syndicate, what outlaws fear the most is an honest government that enforces simple laws protecting individuals and their property. The Jackals will be on our side—until Pathless Land is defeated."

"What about the American Caliphate?" asked Six. "Their theocracy is incompatible with the Elites' autocracy. They believe their religion *is* the government."

"They're a bit tougher," conceded Cosimo. "El Chapo is smart enough to realize his paradise will end if he's killed. Some of those Islamic jihadists think martyring themselves *leads* to paradise. However, their leader Timur is a reasonable man who knows that martyrdom is beneath him. My influencers are explaining to him how the Constitution of Pathless Land is like kryptonite to the Sharia law of his medieval theocracy. The Outcasts would squash his ambition to establish an Islamic State in America. He'll fall in line too."

"And the Blessed?" asked Six with increasing acrid.

Cosimo nervously toyed with his ring again. "My influencers are negotiating with them as we speak. It's hard to predict whose side they're going to be on. On the one hand, individual salvation and separation of church and state, which are both integral to Christ's teachings, are also key to Pathless Land's philosophy. The Syndicate couldn't survive in a world like that. Nor could the Elites. If the Christians decide to align with the Outcasts, that would be a disaster."

"On the other hand . . . ?" prodded Six.

"Most Christians don't understand their own religion," said Cosimo. "And few actually practice it. Many Christian sects are openly Marxist, and they've often abetted tyrants when self-preservation trumped their principles. Catholic popes turned blind eyes to the atrocities of the European National Socialists and the Chinese oligarchs. But when they have fires in their bellies, Christians aren't afraid of a good fight. The Bible is filled with tales of bloody conflict. Even Christ said he came to bring a sword, not peace. That aggression could come in handy."

"Only if they're on the right side," observed Six pointedly. "So will the Blessed ally with the Elites or not?"

Cosimo felt Six's legendary impatience. "We'll know very soon which side of history they choose to be on," he replied.

Six fell silent for a few moments, another bad sign. "The other factions don't seem like good allies for the Elites," Six eventually judged.

Cosimo waived a dismissive hand. "There are certainly hate-filled differences between all of their worldviews. But that's beside the point. Pathless Land is the ultimate evil that needs to be defeated by any means necessary. Their differences can be sorted out later, but there'll be nothing to sort out if Pathless Land wins. The Jackals, the Caliphate, and the Elites would be destroyed in that case—and maybe the Syndicate too."

Six signaled his frustration by changing the subject. "Who is going to replace Regis?"

"I have an unusual solution. I'm appointing two copresidents."

Six's ghostly silhouette leaned forward. "Interesting. Who are they, and why did you pick them?"

"I had two criteria," replied Cosimo. "They had to be unquestioningly obedient and psychopathically ruthless." Cosimo knew that the days were long gone when politicians could merely be patronizing virtue-signalers. Iron-fisted, unapologetic totalitarians were necessary for the current crisis. "The two I've selected have proven their icy-hearted willingness to do anything for their cause, including treachery and murder. They're blind followers who can be trusted to execute my orders. They're true believers in their secular religion. They have no consciences. They won't repeat Regis' mistakes."

"Their names?"

"Kieran and Katarina."

Six was silent for a moment. "They're the ones who orchestrated the plot to kill J?"

"Yes, your Excellency."

"Isn't Kieran the son of J?"

"Yes."

"Perfect. Any resistance to their selection?"

"No. My influencers are brutally effective." Cosimo's cohorts had orchestrated the emergency presidential appointments by swaying the secretive party committee responsible for making such decisions. Elections were no longer necessary in the one-party state of the Elites. When a Deep State becomes deep enough, elections are superfluous.

"Are you making any other changes?"

"Just one. We're changing the name of the party from the Elites to the Masters."

"Good," acknowledged Six. "It's time to pass the baton from politicians and aristocrats to dictators."

Cosimo nodded. Even though the batons kept getting passed from one generation of tyrants to the next, none of the tyrants ever really won. The Syndicate always won. The Deka and its centurions lurked in the background, pulling the strings and reaping the rewards, while others fought, bled, and died under opposing banners of futility.

"Yes, it's time," agreed Cosimo. "And when the Jackals, the Caliphate, and the Blessed align with the Masters, they'll be like the Four Horseman of the Apocalypse in the Book of Revelation: War, Conquest, Death, and Famine."

"What exquisite symbolism!" said Six with rare enthusiasm. "And are you the grand coordinator of these Four Horsemen?"

"Yes!" exclaimed Cosimo. "But only for the purpose of ensuring the Syndicate's prosperity."

Cosimo knew that his role as coordinator was the key to his eventual success. Nearly all of the organized violence in human history had been driven by the four nihilistic factions represented by the apocalyptic horsemen. They had all leveraged submission from the proles to fulfill their lust for power and wealth.

Cosimo didn't fear the Four Horsemen of the Apocalypse. The Syndicate could rearrange such chess pieces at will, all to obscure the real conflict in the world—the perpetual battle of a small cadre of wealthy elites versus everyone else. And Cosimo took great comfort knowing that the Syndicate had never lost a chess match. America had been a mortal threat for a couple of centuries, but the Syndicate was almost done destroying it.

Cosimo only feared independent thinkers who were driven by truth rather than by propaganda and by what was right rather than by what was expedient. Such people ignored the rules of his chess game. The American revolutionaries tipped over the chessboard once. The Outcasts seemed intent on trying it again.

He feared such renegades because they not only refused to be mastered by others, they refused to be the masters *of* others. They opted out of the Syndicate's chess game altogether, and thus were outside the Syndicate's masterful control. Their rebellious spark could ignite a broad revolt by the pawns. This would undo centuries of work the Syndicate had invested to disarm the proles, numb them with dogma, mollify them with handouts, and lie to them about everything.

He wondered who was going to step forward to lead Pathless Land, now that J was dead. Whoever did would automatically become the most hated and the most hunted person in the world.

From the shadows of the Security Council chamber, he sensed Six's dreadful stare bearing down on him. Then the oligarch arose and left without saying another word. Cosimo knew that he was down to one last chance to make things right.

FIFTY-SIX
HORIZONS

> Pilgrims on a fearsome path, all of us
> Seeking truth out of mystifying chaos
> Hoping darkness will be conquered by light
> So that the demons recede into the night
>
> *— The Poems of Dark Sun*

Sleeplessness haunted Kerry in his dimly lit tent. The shadows of moon-washed tree branches danced on the canvas roof. He studied the papers for a battlefield promotion left for him in an envelope by his father. It would thrust him into a military leadership role, making his muddled life even more confusing. His father and spiritual mentor was dead. He had gained a brother who, until recently, was just a name on a complicated family tree. He had found love in Fatima, but she hadn't responded to the letter Verax had delivered on his behalf, not even after her arrival today. Like most young men, he wanted to marry and start a family. But he also yearned to follow in his father's footsteps to help complete the vision of Pathless Land. Could he do both? Did he even have a choice? He sat for hours, sorting out his heart's desires.

Fatima lay in her bunk. Her heart was torn in two. In one half dwelt Kerry. She admired his integrity and courage, and knew he would fight for his principles to his last breath. When he first expressed his love, she couldn't reciprocate, partly because she was leery of male relationships and partly because of their uncertain circumstances. She regretted the lost opportunity, especially after Verax delivered the letter from Kerry pouring his heart out to her. She saw the potential to love him in a way she never thought possible.

In the other half of her heart dwelt Osiris, her adoptive father. She could never properly thank him for everything he had done for her. His actions were lifelong lessons in grace, generosity, and courage. He adopted her when it seemed he had no reason to. He embraced his diverse band of gypsies when it seemed he had no reason to. He embarked on a hazardous journey to save Cammy and Curious when it seemed he had no reason to. But she learned over time that there *was* a reason, and its name was compassion. He exemplified it in a way that she always treasured.

As she lay thinking about Kerry and Osiris, it dawned on her that her heart must really be portioned into thirds, because Cammy had burrowed her way into it too. Fatima had just met the beautiful young girl today, but in a way, she had known her for a long time. Memories of her own tortured childhood flooded her brain. In the dark solitude of her tent she became a frightened young girl again, a captive of the Jackals, orphaned from her family, lost in a world filled with equal measures of abuse and hopelessness. Such a world should never exist, certainly not for young girls. What unspeakable mental and physical harm had Cammy endured while in captivity? The horrifying possibilities brought back memories of cowering in an adobe hut, smelling the fetid breath of a brutish assailant. She felt the ravaged spirit of every young girl who had ever trembled in a living nightmare.

"Dear God, what should I do?" she begged the unheeding darkness.

She was paralyzed by indecision. She wanted to stand by Cammy's side to protect her from monsters. She wanted to trust Kerry enough to love him and to help him create a new world. She wanted to rejoin the gypsy caravan with her father, who had meant everything to her. She laid in her bunk for hours, mulling a decision that would be the denouement to many lives.

Osiris sat alone by a dying campfire. The flames had gone out, and the embers were turning ashen. He was old now, and the years had taken their toll. Countless struggles and endless toil had accumulated into an exhaustion that seemed impossible to rise above. The timing of his waning energy was unfortunate. He had always longed for a society like the one portended by Pathless Land's treasured *Declaration*. A decade ago, he would have volunteered his whole being to help the Warriors of Pathless Land create a world where diverse people could live as they ought to—freely, safely, and in peace.

He was tired of roving in the Darkness, never sure which faction was an enemy or a friend, never knowing when the color of his skin would color someone's opinion, never having a safe place to settle that could be called home, always evading rogues in a lawless nation at war with itself. But as Kerry warned, the upcoming battles would be difficult and more dangerous. War wasn't an old man's endeavor. He empathized with J's decision to exit as he did, expending his final burst of energy to help those nearest and dearest to him.

Osiris' life's work was embodied in his small society of gypsies that he had tended through a hardscrabble migratory existence. A persistent inner voice whispered that he could no more abandon his eclectic family than a mother could abandon her children. He felt a burning obligation to love and protect them until the very end.

He stared at the fading embers, wrestling as all old men do with elusive glories slipping from reach. Did he have one last blaze of energy left in his old bones for the final death match against fascism? Or was there nothing left but to fade away as the caretaker of an obscure band of gypsies while the young Eagles of the world soared? He stared into the embers for hours, even after their red glow had faded into oblivion. In the darkness, he wept.

Dark Sun and Dark Moon couldn't sleep either. They felt claustrophobic in their stuffy tent, so they decided to get some fresh air in the clear night. Dark Moon, filled with separation anxiety, wakened Cammy to bring her along. Cammy trudged behind her parents as they ascended a hill overlooking the silvery Dan River.

They huddled under a blanket against the cold of winter, mesmerized by the delicate glow of a million stars. Cammy snuggled alongside Dark Moon and began dozing again. Her parents were deep in thought when a shooting star arced majestically across the heavens like a celestial exclamation point for their silent reverie. After the meteor disappeared over the northern horizon, Dark Sun said softly, "Maybe that's an omen that 2085 will be better than 2084. I don't think I can survive another year like this one."

"2085 might be worse, if Kerry is right about what lies ahead."

Dark Sun pressed against Dark Moon's warm body under the blanket. "I should feel numb from what happened today," he murmured in the darkness. "Strangely, my head is clearer than ever. I'm learning that the best way to conquer suffering is to face it, measure it, and summon the courage to eliminate the causes."

Dark Moon sat up. "I feel the same!" She was still aflame with the passion that consumed her after the ambush on their family. "Your father's *Declaration* gave me some hope."

Dark Sun sat up beside her. "I'm hopeful too." After reading the *Declaration*, he was anxious to read his father's second journal. The first one had been a lantern light in the Darkness helping him to see the world through new eyes. He could hardly imagine the awful tribulations his father had experienced transforming the chaos of Outcast Island into the shining glory of Pathless Land.

"Sunshine?"

"Moonbeam?"

"Before we help the Warriors of Pathless Land transform the world, we should transform ourselves."

"How so?"

"We don't need to hide in the shadows from the Elites anymore. Now that we're joining Pathless Land, our aliases are unnecessary masks. Let's rip them off and reclaim our identities."

Dark Sun stared beyond the horizon toward Washington. He nodded his head, and then scooped up a handful of powdery snow. "World, I announce to you the triumphant return of Audrey. Dark Moon is no more!" He blew his handful of snow into her face like magic pixie dust to christen her rebirth.

Audrey scooped up a handful of snow. "World, I announce to you the triumphant return of James. Dark Sun is no more!" She packed the snow in her hand and pushed a snowball into his face. Dark Sun tickled her in retaliation. They laughed aloud. Life felt somehow different.

Cammy jolted upright, disturbed by the commotion. She looked about in the darkness, fearing that a new crisis was emerging. Audrey stroked her hair. "It's okay, sweetheart. We're just getting rid of our hiding names."

"Can I get rid of Chameleon? I hate it."

"Why do you hate such a clever name?" asked James.

"Because I'm not a reptile. And I'm not going to hide from any enemies."

James smiled ruefully. Cammy's mercurial personality had been abruptly altered. He detected something powerful blossoming in her. The seed of heroism, perhaps? He kissed her bruised cheek. "What name would you like?"

Cammy thought for a moment. "Sophie."

Audrey looked puzzled. "Sophie? Why?"

Cammy looked at her with sorrowful eyes. In those eyes, Audrey discovered a person she didn't know before. The child inside had been replaced by an adult who had a resolve so deep that the name Chameleon was indeed inappropriate now. "I'll tell you later," Cammy said. "Right now, I just want to sleep."

Audrey kissed her forehead, worrying with morbid concern what horrors had tormented her child. "You can pick any name you want, but you'll always be Cammy to me. Just know that we love you." Cammy closed her eyes and smiled. She shimmied back under the blanket. A thin pamphlet slipped out from a pocket of her white nightgown. James picked it up and did a doubletake. In the sparse starlight, he saw from the bold title that it was a publication by the White Rose League.

James wondered how she got it. Then he wondered why she kept it. As the starlight illuminated her iridescent platinum hair, it struck him that perhaps she was destined to become a White Rose warrior of a new generation.

"What's that?" Audrey asked.

"Cammy's future? My father wrote that pamphlet to awaken oppressed people. I don't know how she got a copy. He seems to have miraculously found a way to inspire her too."

Audrey took the pamphlet from James, but she couldn't read the small text in the dim light. She handed it back. "That reminds me. What did you write in the poem you showed your father?"

"Oh, it was the typical ode to a father who transformed a devil's island into a beacon of hope for the rest of the world and then sacrificed his own life to save his grandchildren and destroy a tyrant. I wrote that he was like a god to me and that I now understood why he left Mom and me behind in Kansas decades ago. You can read it when we get back to camp."

"I'd like to." Audrey kissed James again. "It's ironic that your father is godlike to you because he didn't mention God in his *Declaration*."

"Probably because enshrining a particular notion of God in such a document would introduce the possibility of a theocratic tyranny. A pious tyrant is still a tyrant."

Audrey nodded, then fell into deep reflection. From her interactions with the Caliphate and the Blessed, it was clear that separating religion from government was necessary for a peaceful society. A society's principles must be right and just for *all* people, regardless of their religious beliefs. Freedom isn't incompatible with religion, it's incompatible with theocracy, where espousing any belief other than the established orthodoxy can be fatal.

Audrey broke their silence. "Religions certainly have a history of disuniting rather than uniting. Did your father believe in God?"

"We discussed it yesterday. He had some rather heavy things on his mind."

"Well?"

"He defined God as everything about the universe we don't understand yet. Once we can explain something using facts and reason, it's no longer in the realm of God."

"What's *your* perspective on God, after everything fate has thrown at us?"

James rubbed his bearded chin. "God is another name for hope, the spirit inside us that blessedly contravenes pain and suffering. Why are there evil people in the world? Why did Curious die such a horrible death? Why did the Elites traumatize Cammy? Why did Eve take a bullet from organ harvesters? Why did my father have to commit suicide to save our kids? Why do we *all* have to die? The answers are too frightening to fathom, if there are answers at all. So, we mentally quarantine these questions, and then rely on hope as a counterpoint. That's the only way we can deal with life when it overwhelms us. We're desperate to believe that our struggles are vindicated by purpose, and that we'll be taken care of somehow. We yearn for something bigger than ourselves to protect us. Hope gives us some peace, despite our insurmountable odds."

"It's comforting to think of God as hope," said Audrey. "But I think people defer too much responsibility to whatever notion of God they have. We all want to be protected from harm, but rather than hope for God to do it, we should protect each other instead. We all want manna to flutter down from heaven, but rather than wait for God to feed us, we should multiply the fishes and loaves ourselves. We all want wisdom, but it shouldn't be confused with the opinions meted out by religious leaders who claim to speak for God."

James nodded. "Your observations would be just as true if you substituted government for god. There's great power inside each of us. Some people find strength and courage in believing that there's a god looking out for them, and sometimes that fuels the psychological stamina to fight colossal battles or endure overwhelming suffering. But it's not necessary to believe in a deity to find that inner strength. Oz didn't give the lion anything he didn't already have, except for belief in his own courage."

"Some say God helps those who help themselves," said Audrey. "Maybe that simply means finding the inner godliness inside each of us that allows us to bear any insult or struggle. We should unleash that divine potential to work our own miracles, rather than pray for a supernatural deity to work miracles for us."

"That seems right," said James. "Our innate godliness inspires compassion, goodness, and joy, whereas the institutional worship of cosmic deities too often leads people down tortured metaphysical paths that dead-end in hatred, violence, and death. Organized religions have used their platitudes and myths to play on the fears and insecurities of people who are desperately seeking meaning and help in the complex pilgrimage called life. These organized religions may or may not have elements of truth, but one thing is certain—tyrants find them useful. Tyrants understand that the perceived power of God can be hijacked to control others. The lesson to be learned is that all people are imperfect, so no person or group of people should ever be granted the power of God on Earth."

"We're not only imperfect, we're afraid," said Audrey. "We're drifting along on a giant rock in a dangerous universe, knowing that entropy will eventually kill us. It's natural to hope for the protection, the meaning, and the eternity that an omnipotent deity could offer. Maybe everything that we yearn to become is God, a reflection of ourselves in the most ideal state. Let's embrace that spark of God within us. Let's find meaning in loving others, and in being loved in return. Let's find happiness and peace in the here and now. Perhaps we'll each find God when we can look in the mirror of our soul and smile at what we see. For me, God is love, and my religion is wisdom and kindness."

"And those are exactly the things that Karma encourages," said James. "So maybe Karma is what we really mean when we refer to God. Karma sees and remembers everything, because reality is altered by every act. It keeps perpetual score, so it's the universe's ultimate judgment. It makes our existence eternal, because the effects of our actions ripple forever. It's a catalyst for justice and good behavior, because it leads everyone to either a personal heaven or a personal hell on Earth. It puts a premium on wisdom to help us follow our personal path to heaven."

"Maybe it's even simpler than that," said Audrey. "Perhaps the simplest definition of morality is the wisdom to behave sanely and collaboratively. Perhaps the simplest definition of sanity is preferring better over worse. Perhaps the simplest definition of collaboration is working with others to achieve better for them *and* for you."

James nodded and then noticed the first light of dawn breaking on the horizon. He stood up and looked all around. To the west was the past they had left behind in Kansas. It no longer existed. To the north and east were the entrenched forces of the Elites. The world needed to be saved from those raptors. To the south were the onrushing liberators from Pathless Land, with whom his future was now entwined. Beside him were Cammy and Audrey. His love for them would keep the fire burning in his soul.

He felt like he was standing precisely on the main fault line of humanity, that singular point in geography and time where all the accumulated tectonic forces that had been unresolved for millennia were about to grind together in a grand and final upheaval.

He was exhilarated. He now fully understood why his father allowed himself to be captured by the Elites twenty-seven years ago. He now fully understood why Audrey changed her mind to stay here and fight. He now fully understood why the Warriors of Pathless Land burst forth from their sheltered island to confront the great evils on the mainland.

He had been a pawn all his life, unaware of his subordinate role to unseen forces. Some pawns eventually awaken and are no longer willing to silently accept their fate. They suddenly realize that they don't have to passively bear their heavy grudges against the bishops, knights, and royalty who orchestrate their sacrificial movements. On that day, most likely when the royalty, the ecclesiastics, and the elites least expect, the chessboard gets wiped clean. That day had finally arrived for the former pawn known as Dark Sun.

He was still gripping Cammy's crumpled pamphlet from the White Rose League. It was a reminder that Pathless Land was the last and best opportunity for all the pawns to escape the darkness of war, mysticism, and submission. It was time for the pawns to confront the elites, the tyrants, the theocrats, the gangsters, and all of their other oppressors. It was time for the pawns to finally assert the sanctity of each human life.

It was time for the pawns to stop following the rules and to change the game altogether.

It was time for the pawns to eliminate the chess masters.

ACKNOWLEDGMENTS

Perhaps the only task more daunting than writing a novel is to properly acknowledge all of the wonderful people who assisted with the project. This book would not have been possible without the contributions and support of many talented and patient collaborators. This is my wholly inadequate attempt to recognize and thank them.

I am deeply indebted to my lovely wife, Audrey. Not only did she manage our household while I was immersed in this project, she invested countless hours helping to improve this book. She read, edited, and critiqued the manuscript at least ten times, which was a heroic feat of patience and endurance. She was my toughest critic and my greatest supporter, which is a hard combination to navigate. The novel in its final form was heavily influenced by her steady stream of ideas and suggestions.

I am indebted to Christian Carmody, who scoured every wayward phrase of my initial draft over the course of several months, and who offered up more words of help and suggestion than were perhaps in the novel itself. His guidance and feedback were immensely helpful.

I am indebted to Erin Schade, Christine Snyder, Patrick Keena, Fred Keena, Jimmy Keena, Colleen Hahn, Katie Keena, Niki Keena,

Maureen Carmody, Peggy Lothschutz, Terry Hughes, Andy Brandt, Terry Martin, Preston Whittington, Brian Tracey, Brian Andrew, and John Hyland for their assistance with proofreading, editing, and critiquing the early drafts of the novel. I thoroughly appreciate their willingness to bravely slog through my clumsy first attempts, and to offer ideas and suggestions that made the book much more vibrant and coherent.

I am indebted to Illumify Media Global for their tireless and often brilliant efforts to bring the final product to the marketplace. Mike Klassen, Geoff Stone, Karen Bouchard, and Illumify's network of support resources were consummate professionals in this endeavor. Their creativity, their hard work, and their dedication to this project polished the rough edges off the novel and made it glitter.

I am indebted to my network of friends and acquaintances who regularly engage with me in discussion and debate about political, economic, and philosophical issues pressing on our society. Their intellectual insights have honed and shaped my perspectives and have greatly influenced the concepts woven into the tapestry of this novel. I appreciate every thought and challenge put forth by Thayrone X, Angie and Patrick Colbeck, Sharon and Marco Lollio, Maribeth and Jim Schmidt, and Amy and Robert Nasir. I also appreciate the collective wisdom of the brilliant and sometimes contentious contributors to the political discussion board at NDNation.com.

Finally, and most importantly, I am indebted to all of the brave men and women who have ever served in the American armed forces. Without their courage and sacrifice over the centuries, our freedom would be nothing but a forlorn and distant memory. There are no words sufficient to thank them. While I cannot match their sacrifice, I can offer the power of my pen to complement the might of their swords in defense of our liberty.

ABOUT THE AUTHOR

James Keena is an author of critically acclaimed books and commentaries. A popular radio guest, he has also been a featured speaker at political and educational events throughout the Midwest. He is also the author of *Insurrection Resurrection*, a novel of political and religious satire, and a nonfiction work entitled *We've Been Had: How Obama and the Radicals Conned Middle Class America*. James has eight children and twenty grandchildren.

Visit him at: www.jameskeena.com

www.ingramcontent.com/pod-product-compliance
Lightning Source LLC
LaVergne TN
LVHW040035080526
838202LV00045B/3347